big
NATE
REVENGE OF THE
CREAM PUFFS

More

big NATE

adventures from

LINCOLN PEIRCE

Big Nate From the Top

Big Nate Out Loud

Big Nate and Friends

Big Nate Makes the Grade

Big Nate All Work and No Play

Big Nate: Game On!

Big Nate: I Can't Take It!

Big Nate: Great Minds Think Alike

Big Nate: The Crowd Goes Wild!

Big Nate's Greatest Hits

Big Nate: Say Good-bye to Dork City

Big Nate: Welcome to My World

Big Nate: Thunka, Thunka, Thunka

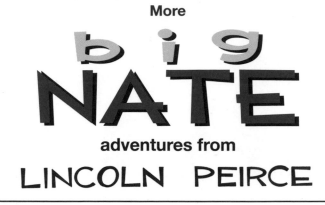

big NATE
REVENGE OF THE CREAM PUFFS

by LINCOLN PEIRCE

Andrews McMeel
Publishing®
a division of Andrews McMeel Universal

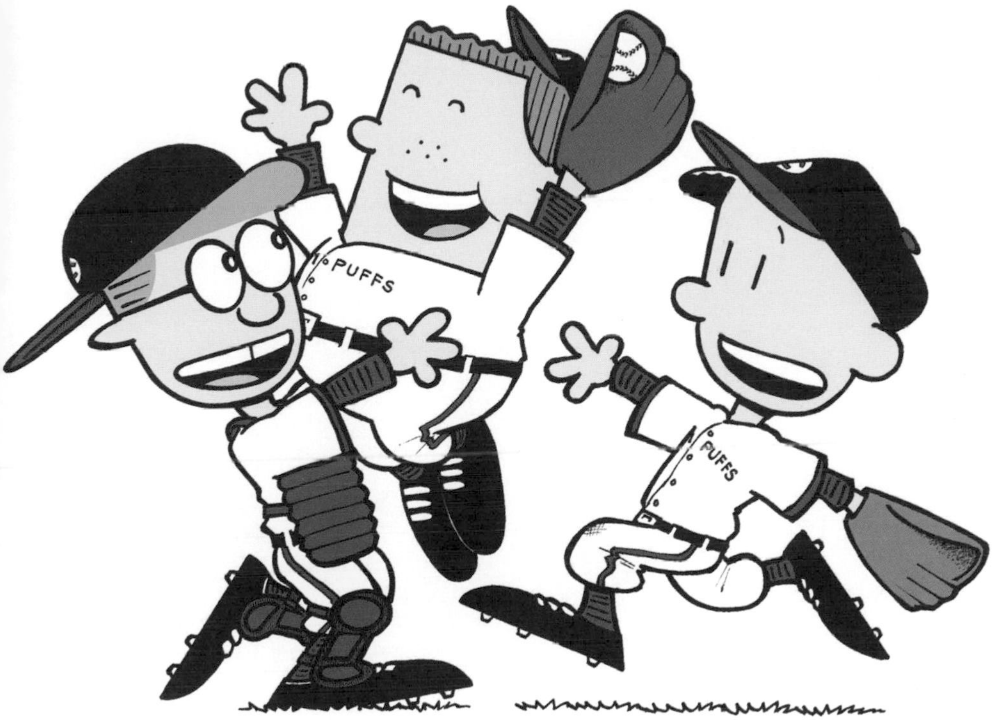
PUFFS
PUFFS

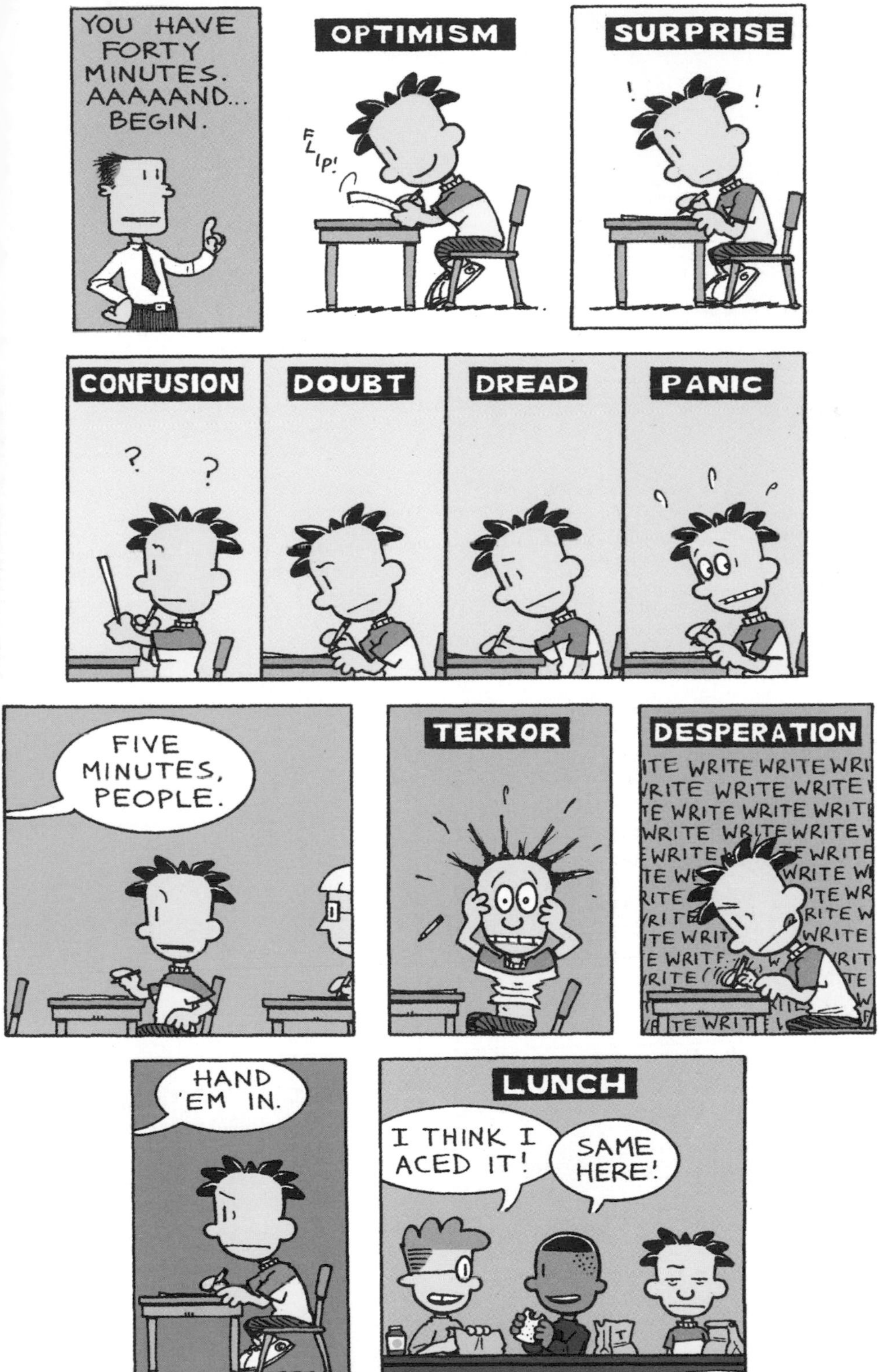
YOU HAVE FORTY MINUTES. AAAAAND... BEGIN.
OPTIMISM
FLIP!
SURPRISE
CONFUSION
DOUBT
DREAD
PANIC
FIVE MINUTES, PEOPLE.
TERROR
DESPERATION
HAND 'EM IN.
LUNCH
I THINK I ACED IT!
SAME HERE!
Peirce

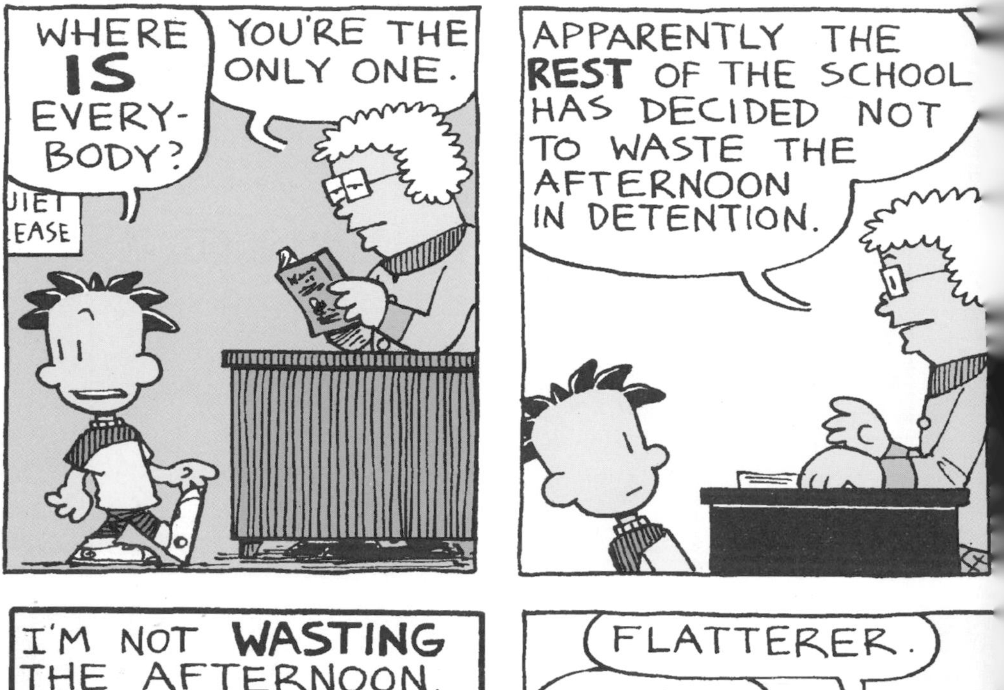
WHERE **IS** EVERYBODY?
YOU'RE THE ONLY ONE.
APPARENTLY THE **REST** OF THE SCHOOL HAS DECIDED NOT TO WASTE THE AFTERNOON IN DETENTION.
I'M NOT **WASTING** THE AFTERNOON, MRS. CZERWICKI! I'M SPENDING IT WITH **YOU!**
FLATTERER.
HOW'S ABOUT A GAME OF TABLE FOOTBALL?

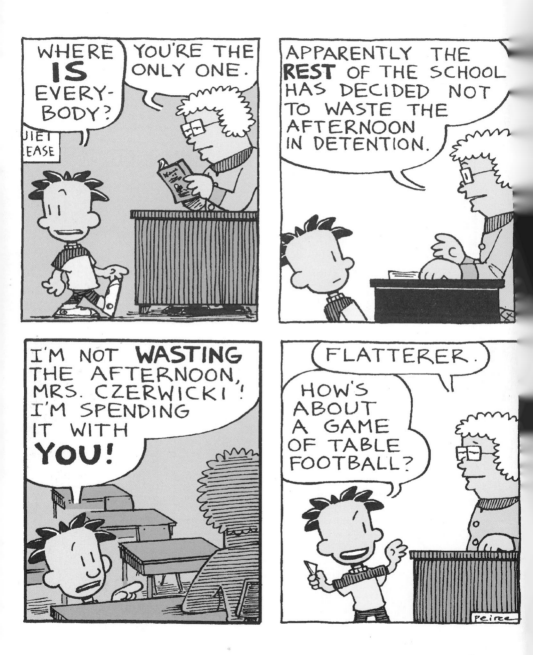

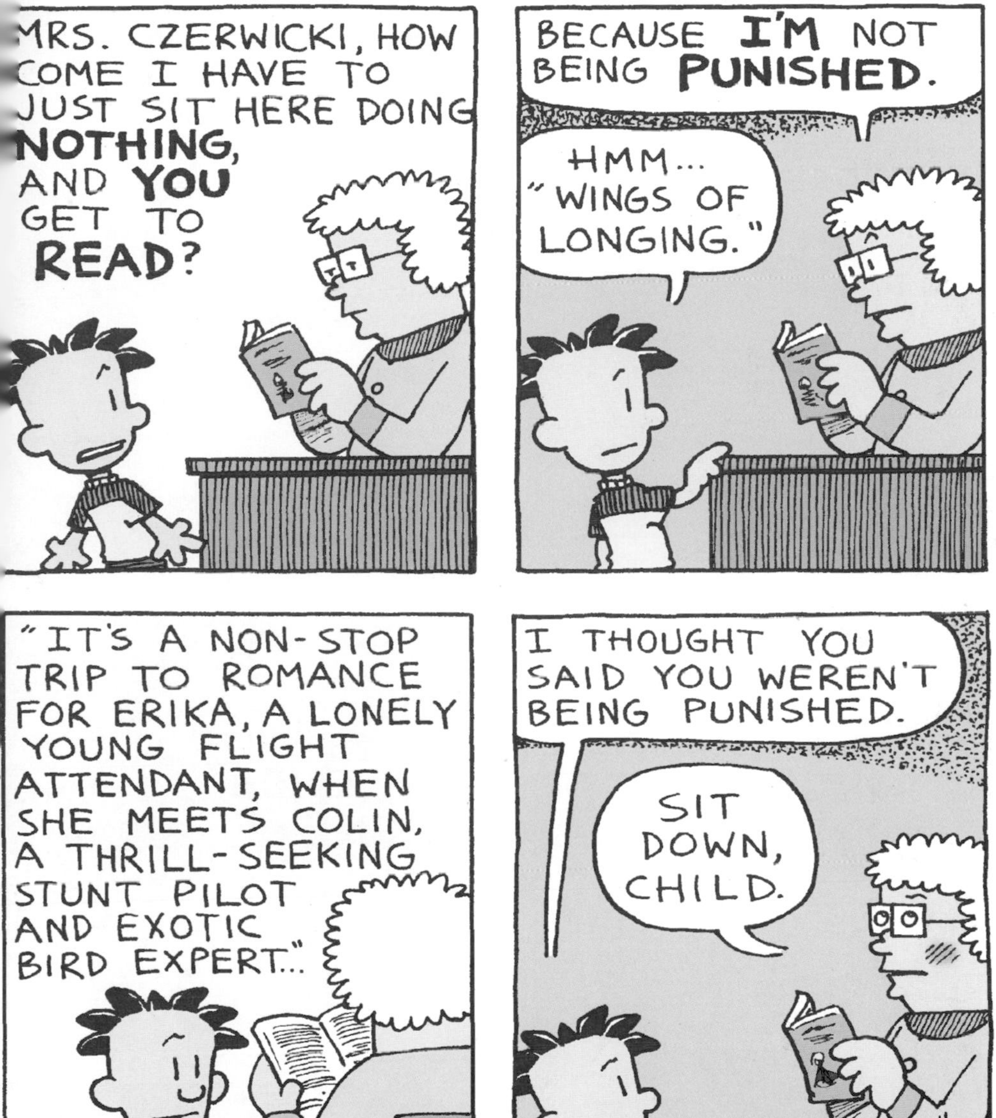
MRS. CZERWICKI, HOW COME I HAVE TO JUST SIT HERE DOING NOTHING, AND YOU GET TO READ?
BECAUSE I'M NOT BEING PUNISHED.
HMM... "WINGS OF LONGING."
"IT'S A NON-STOP TRIP TO ROMANCE FOR ERIKA, A LONELY YOUNG FLIGHT ATTENDANT, WHEN SHE MEETS COLIN, A THRILL-SEEKING STUNT PILOT AND EXOTIC BIRD EXPERT..."
I THOUGHT YOU SAID YOU WEREN'T BEING PUNISHED.
SIT DOWN, CHILD.
PEIRCE

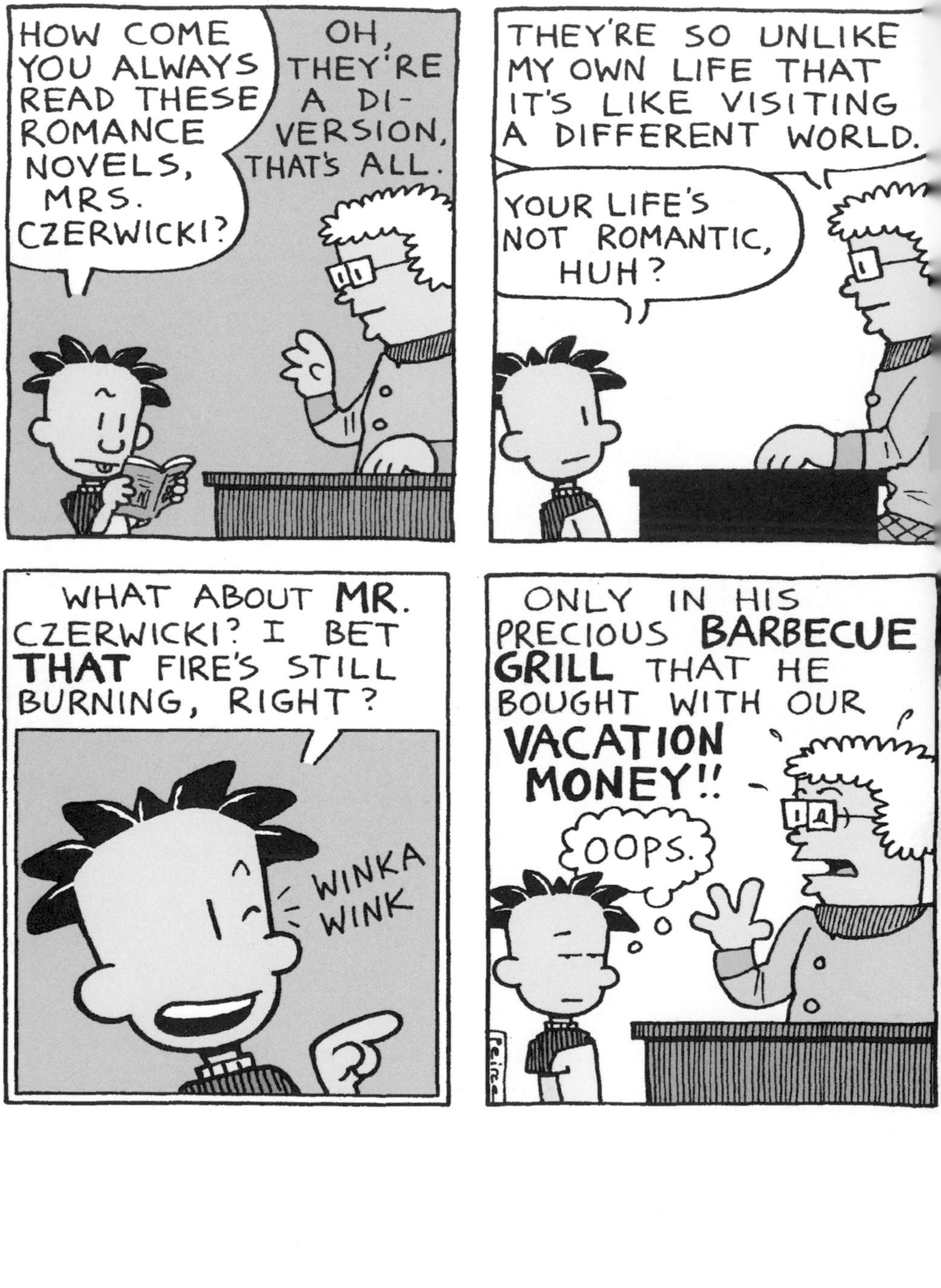
HOW COME YOU ALWAYS READ THESE ROMANCE NOVELS, MRS. CZERWICKI?
OH, THEY'RE A DI-VERSION, THAT'S ALL.
THEY'RE SO UNLIKE MY OWN LIFE THAT IT'S LIKE VISITING A DIFFERENT WORLD.
YOUR LIFE'S NOT ROMANTIC, HUH?
WHAT ABOUT **MR.** CZERWICKI? I BET **THAT** FIRE'S STILL BURNING, RIGHT?
WINKA WINK
ONLY IN HIS PRECIOUS **BARBECUE GRILL** THAT HE BOUGHT WITH OUR **VACATION MONEY!!**
OOPS.
Peirce

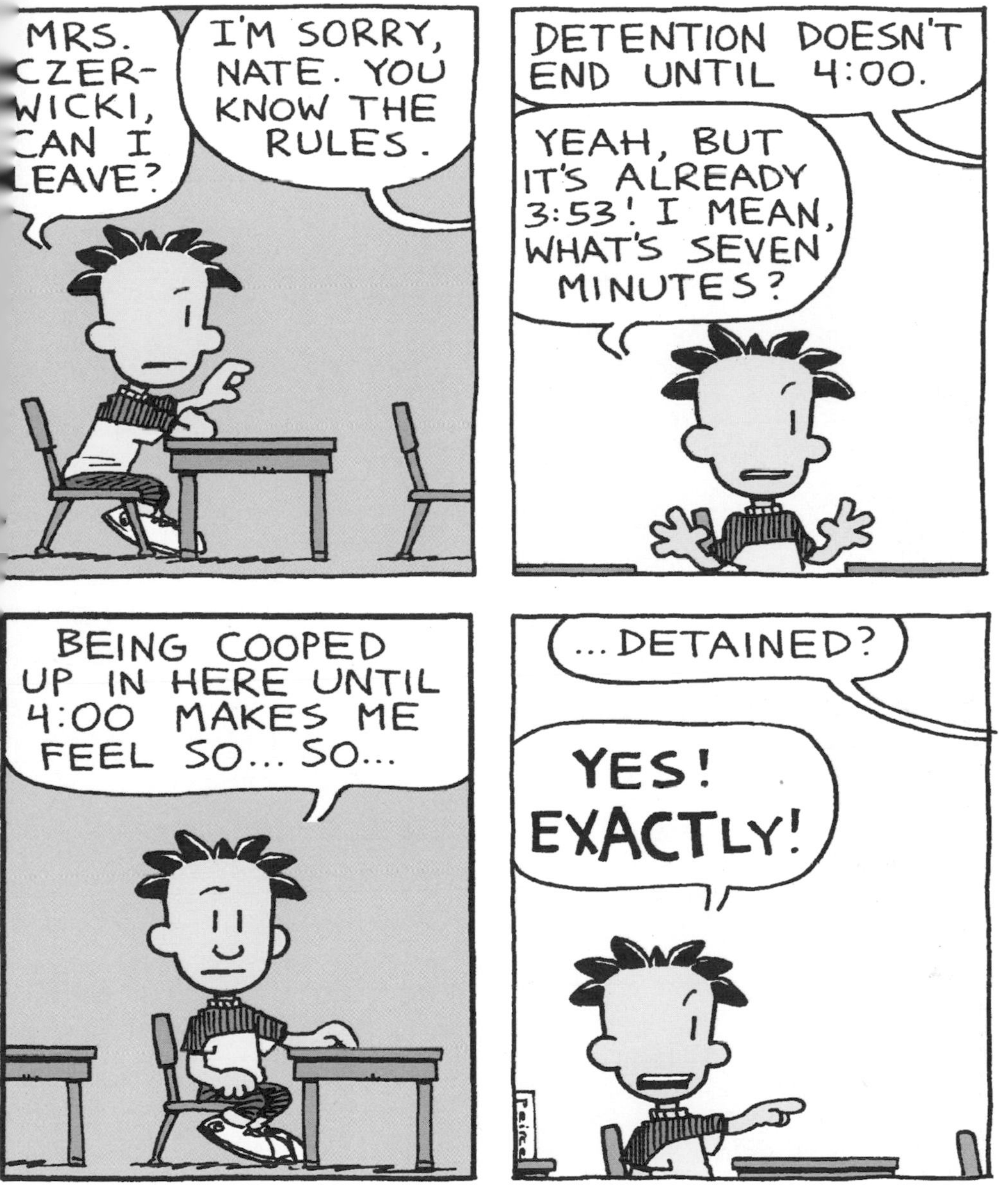
MRS. CZER-WICKI, CAN I LEAVE?
I'M SORRY, NATE. YOU KNOW THE RULES.
DETENTION DOESN'T END UNTIL 4:00.
YEAH, BUT IT'S ALREADY 3:53! I MEAN, WHAT'S SEVEN MINUTES?
BEING COOPED UP IN HERE UNTIL 4:00 MAKES ME FEEL SO... SO...
...DETAINED?
YES! EXACTLY!

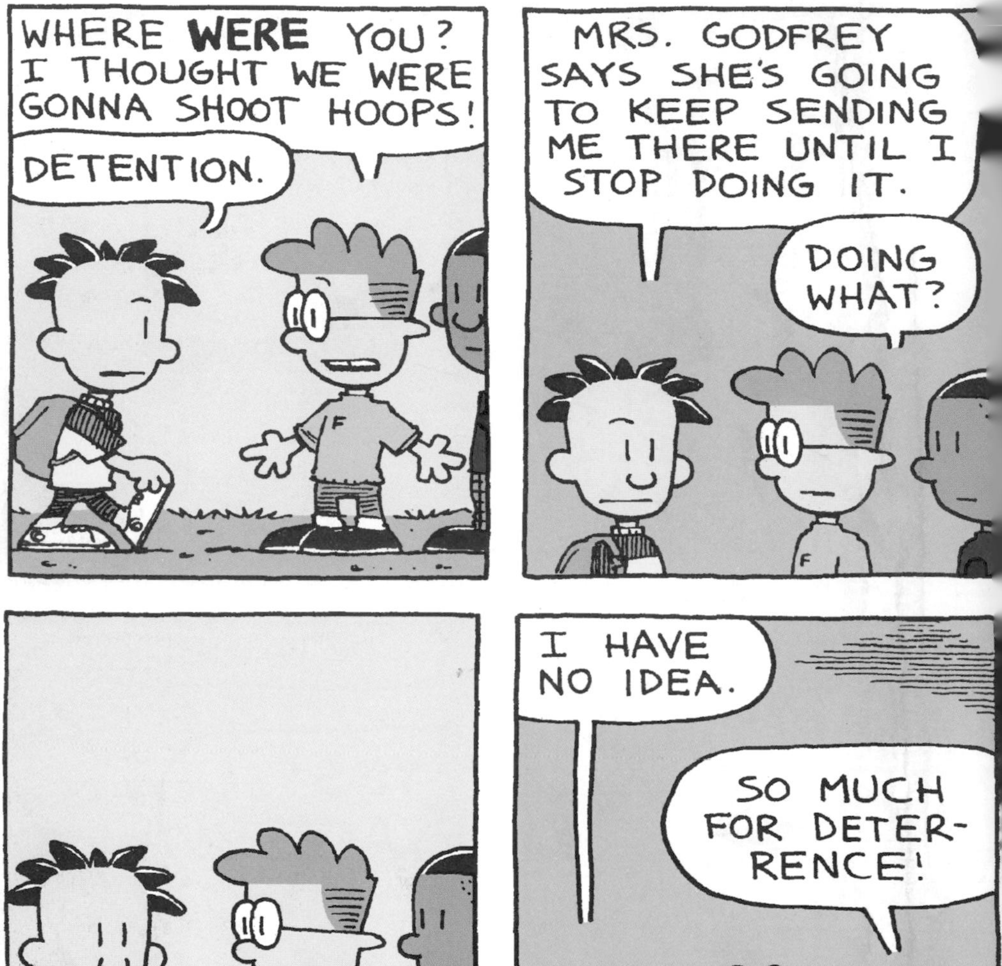
WHERE **WERE** YOU? I THOUGHT WE WERE GONNA SHOOT HOOPS!
DETENTION.
MRS. GODFREY SAYS SHE'S GOING TO KEEP SENDING ME THERE UNTIL I STOP DOING IT.
DOING WHAT?
I HAVE NO IDEA.
SO MUCH FOR DETER-RENCE!
peirce

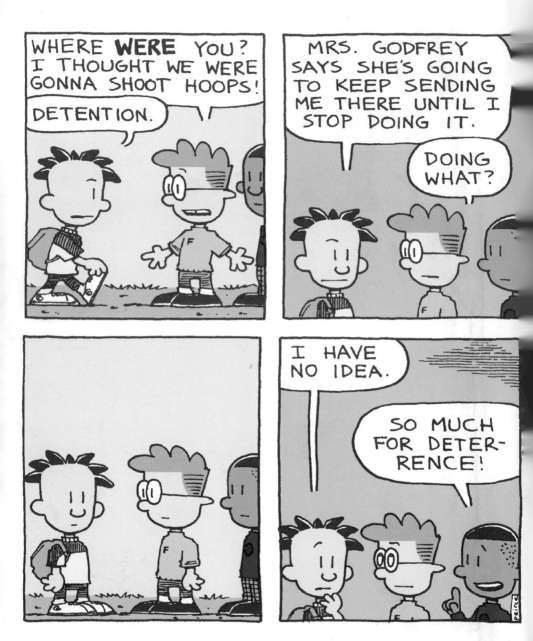

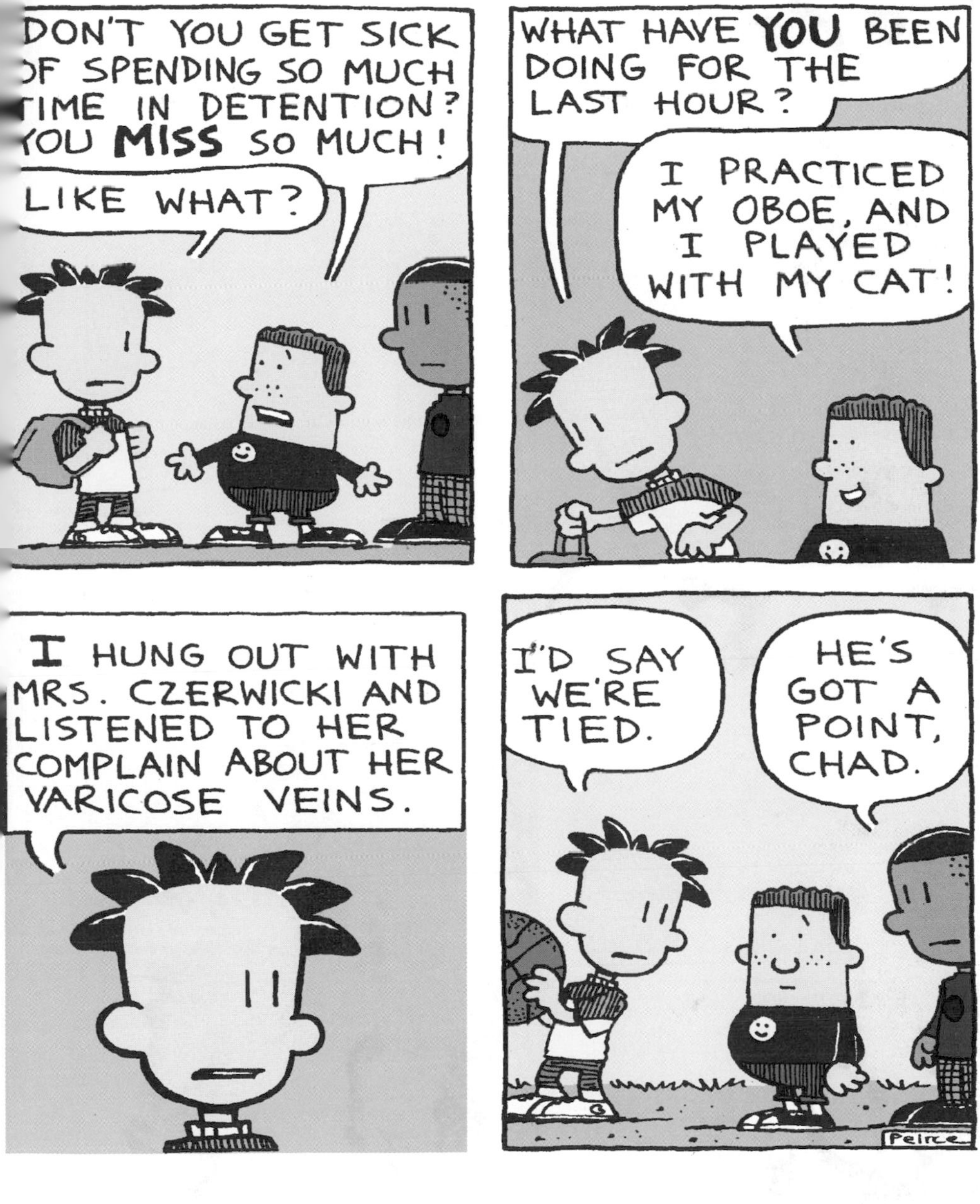
DON'T YOU GET SICK OF SPENDING SO MUCH TIME IN DETENTION? YOU **MISS** SO MUCH!
LIKE WHAT?
WHAT HAVE **YOU** BEEN DOING FOR THE LAST HOUR?
I PRACTICED MY OBOE, AND I PLAYED WITH MY CAT!
I HUNG OUT WITH MRS. CZERWICKI AND LISTENED TO HER COMPLAIN ABOUT HER VARICOSE VEINS.
I'D SAY WE'RE TIED.
HE'S GOT A POINT, CHAD.
Peirce

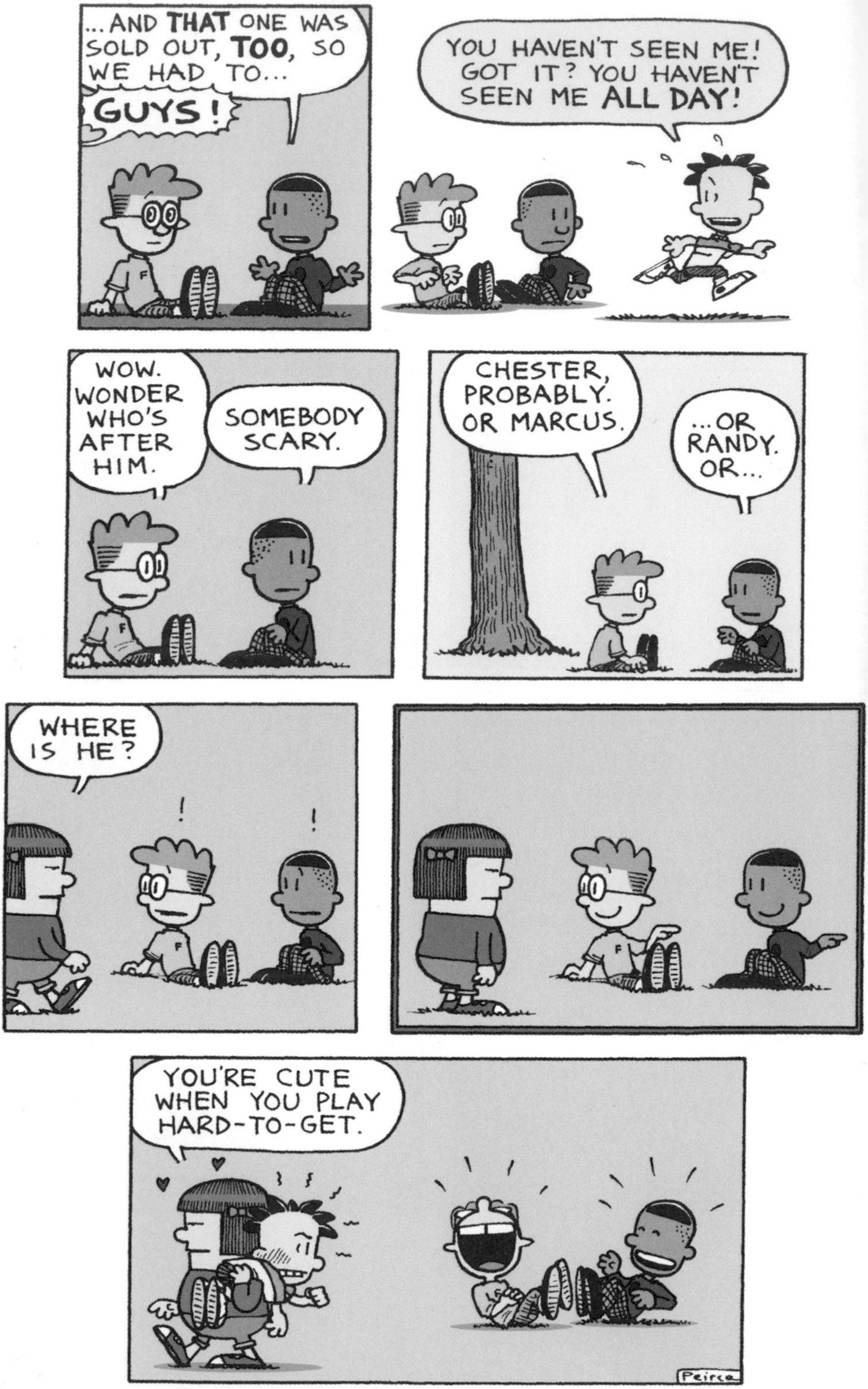
...AND **THAT** ONE WAS SOLD OUT, **TOO**, SO WE HAD TO...
GUYS!
YOU HAVEN'T SEEN ME! GOT IT? YOU HAVEN'T SEEN ME **ALL DAY**!
WOW. WONDER WHO'S AFTER HIM.
SOMEBODY SCARY.
CHESTER, PROBABLY. OR MARCUS.
...OR RANDY. OR...
WHERE IS HE?
!
!
YOU'RE CUTE WHEN YOU PLAY HARD-TO-GET.
Peirce

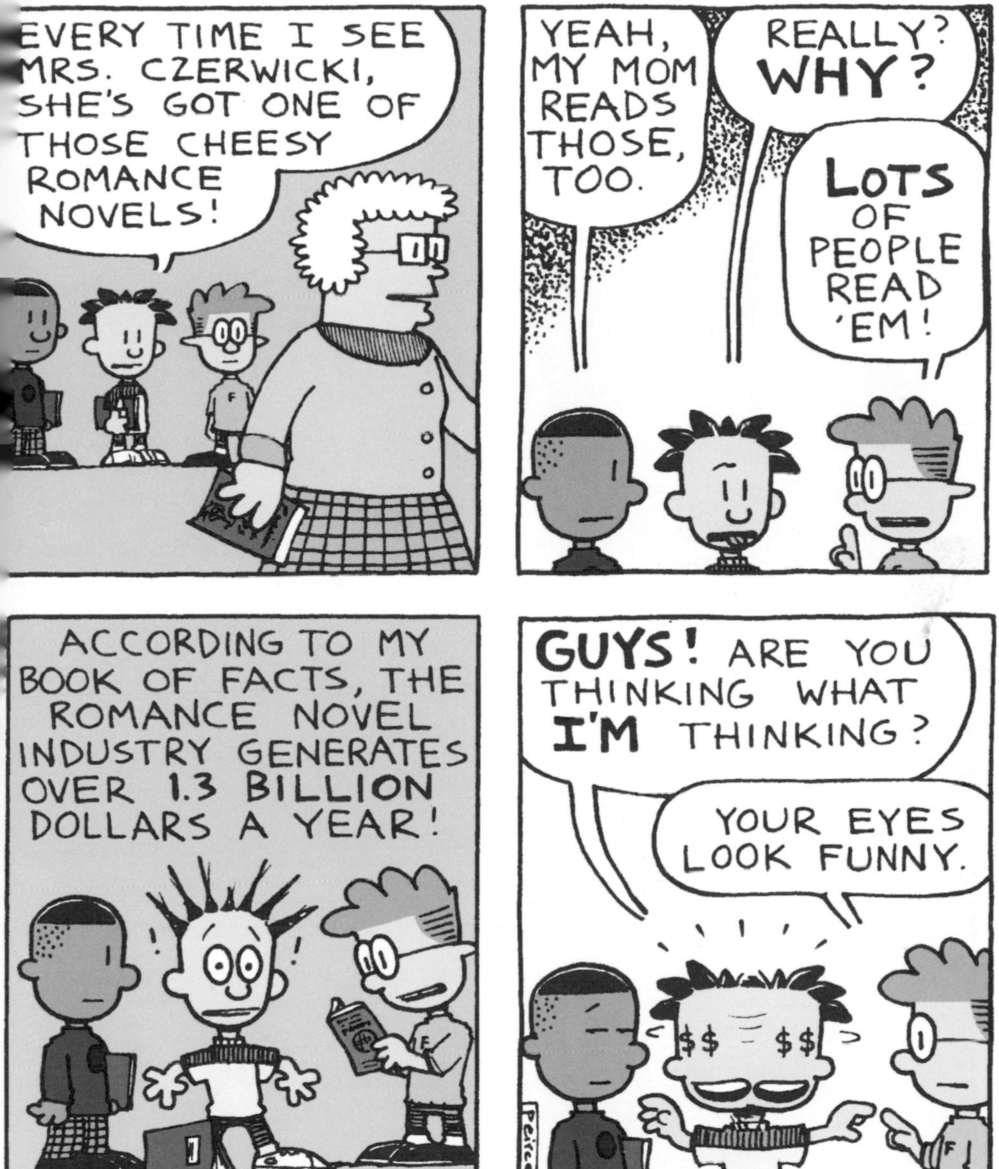
EVERY TIME I SEE MRS. CZERWICKI, SHE'S GOT ONE OF THOSE CHEESY ROMANCE NOVELS!
YEAH, MY MOM READS THOSE, TOO.
REALLY? WHY?
LOTS OF PEOPLE READ 'EM!
ACCORDING TO MY BOOK OF FACTS, THE ROMANCE NOVEL INDUSTRY GENERATES OVER 1.3 BILLION DOLLARS A YEAR!
GUYS! ARE YOU THINKING WHAT I'M THINKING?
YOUR EYES LOOK FUNNY.
PEIRCE

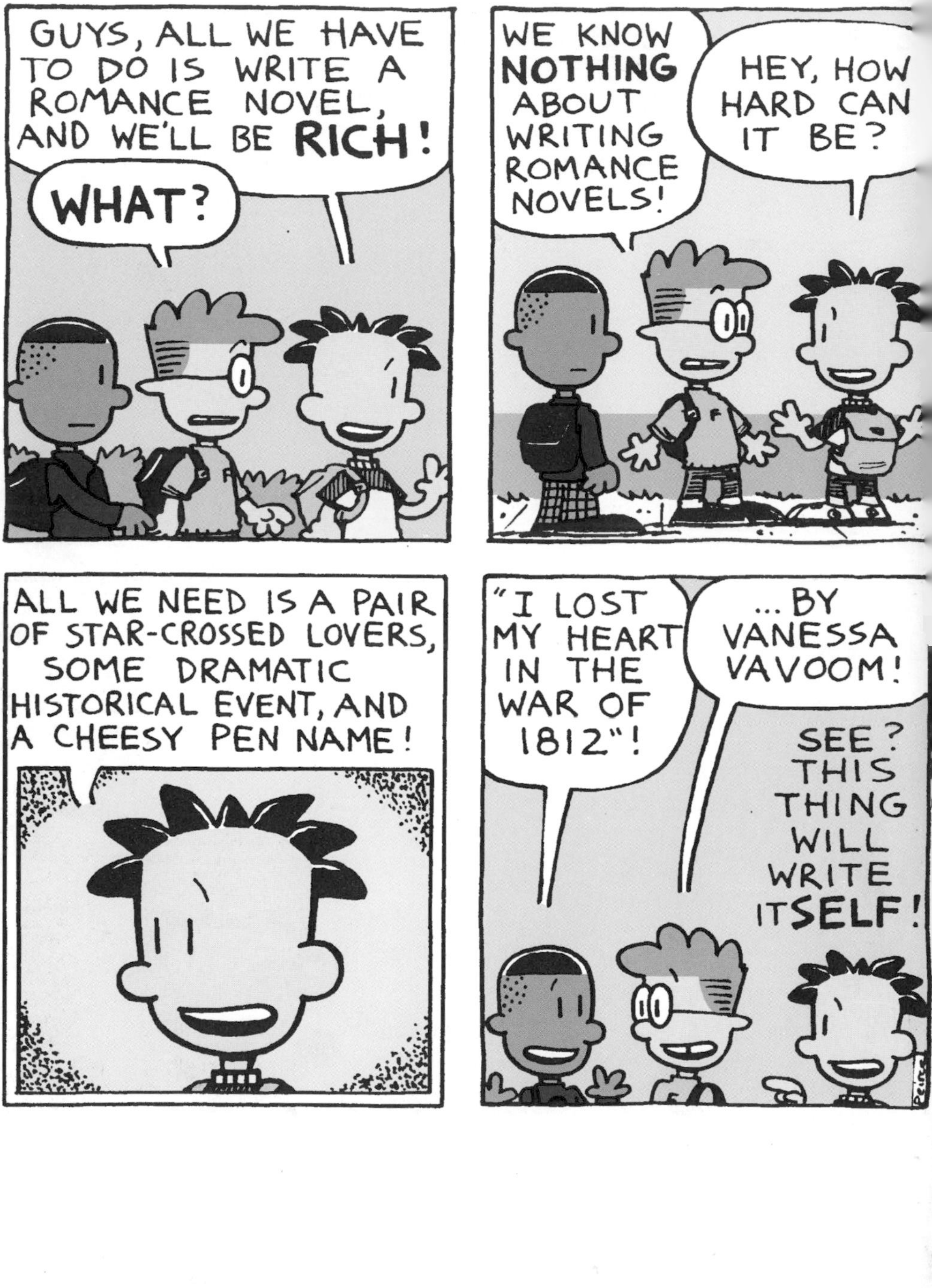
GUYS, ALL WE HAVE TO DO IS WRITE A ROMANCE NOVEL, AND WE'LL BE RICH!
WHAT?
WE KNOW NOTHING ABOUT WRITING ROMANCE NOVELS!
HEY, HOW HARD CAN IT BE?
ALL WE NEED IS A PAIR OF STAR-CROSSED LOVERS, SOME DRAMATIC HISTORICAL EVENT, AND A CHEESY PEN NAME!
"I LOST MY HEART IN THE WAR OF 1812"!
...BY VANESSA VAVOOM!
SEE? THIS THING WILL WRITE ITSELF!

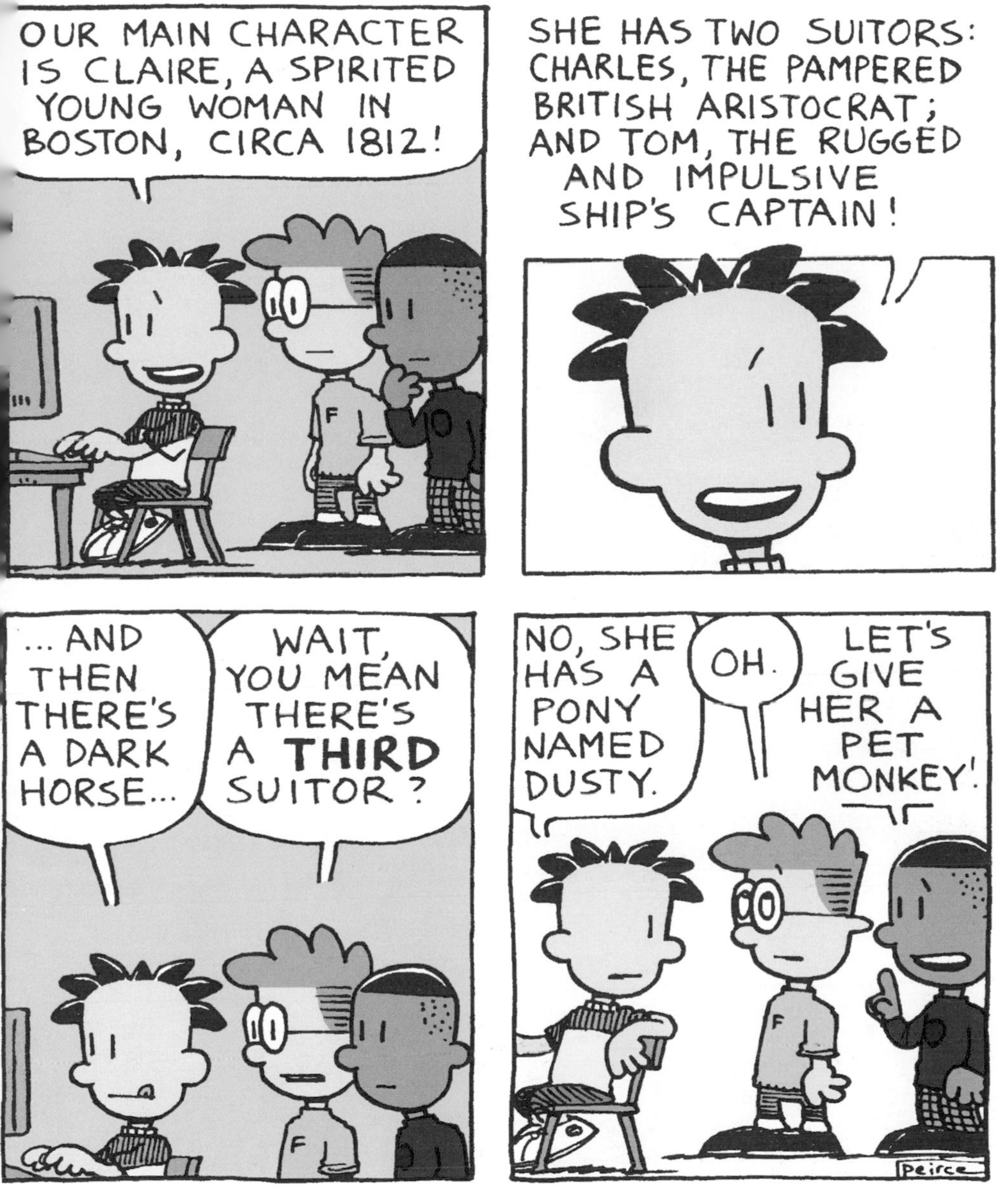
OUR MAIN CHARACTER IS CLAIRE, A SPIRITED YOUNG WOMAN IN BOSTON, CIRCA 1812!
SHE HAS TWO SUITORS: CHARLES, THE PAMPERED BRITISH ARISTOCRAT; AND TOM, THE RUGGED AND IMPULSIVE SHIP'S CAPTAIN!
... AND THEN THERE'S A DARK HORSE...
WAIT, YOU MEAN THERE'S A **THIRD** SUITOR?
NO, SHE HAS A PONY NAMED DUSTY.
OH.
LET'S GIVE HER A PET MONKEY!
Peirce

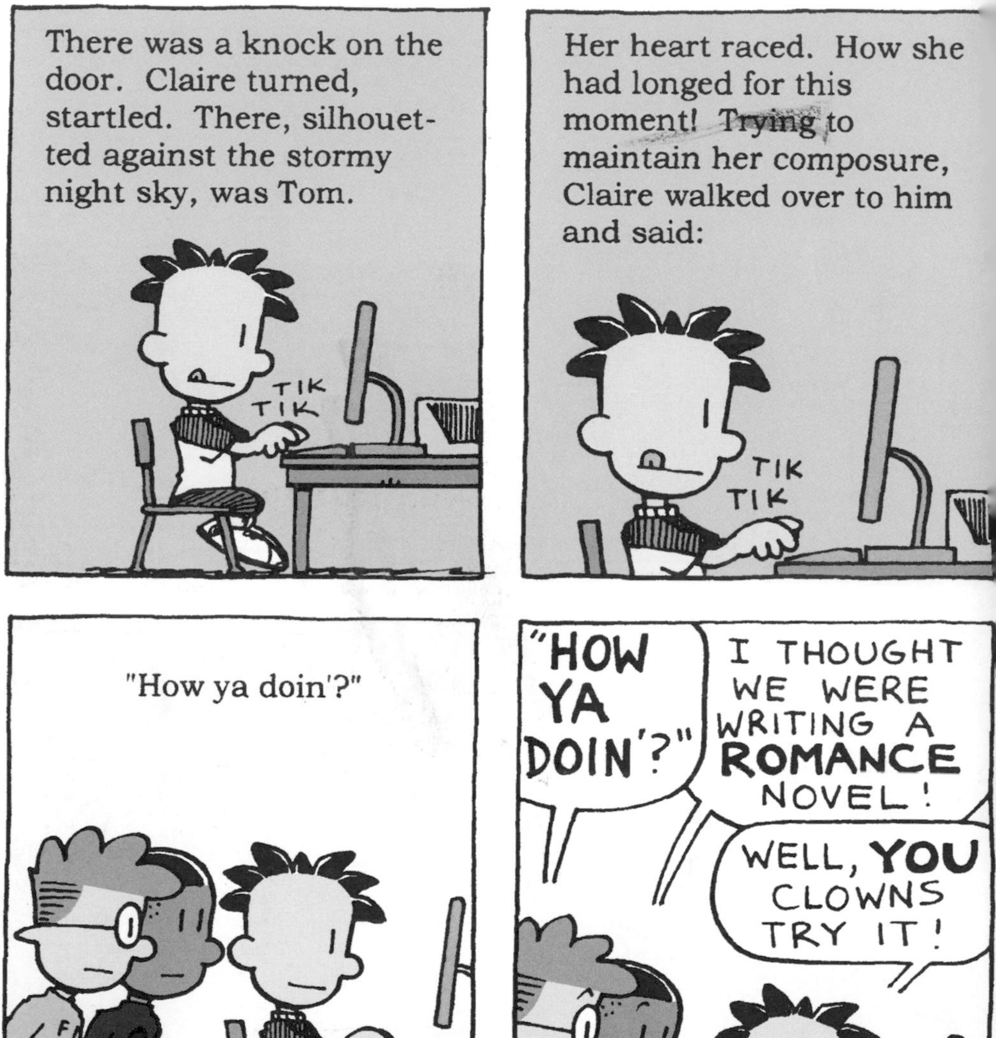
There was a knock on the door. Claire turned, startled. There, silhouetted against the stormy night sky, was Tom.
TIK TIK
Her heart raced. How she had longed for this moment! Trying to maintain her composure, Claire walked over to him and said:
TIK TIK
"How ya doin'?"
"HOW YA DOIN'?"
I THOUGHT WE WERE WRITING A ROMANCE NOVEL!
WELL, YOU CLOWNS TRY IT!

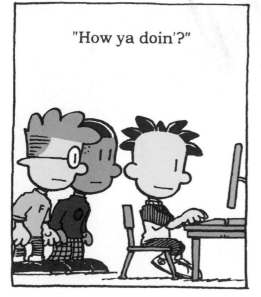

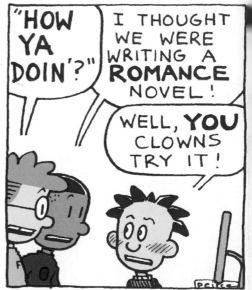

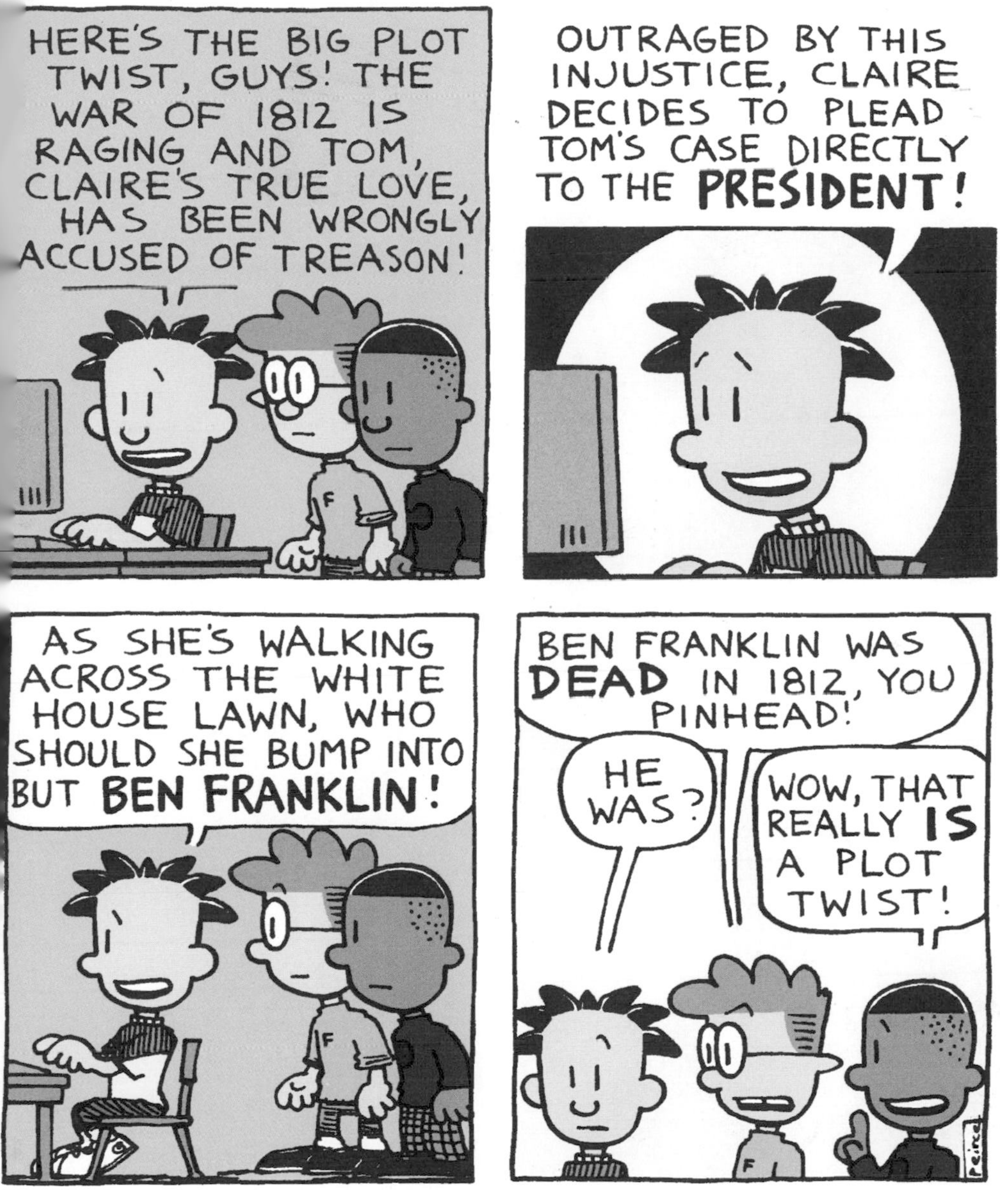
HERE'S THE BIG PLOT TWIST, GUYS! THE WAR OF 1812 IS RAGING AND TOM, CLAIRE'S TRUE LOVE, HAS BEEN WRONGLY ACCUSED OF TREASON!
OUTRAGED BY THIS INJUSTICE, CLAIRE DECIDES TO PLEAD TOM'S CASE DIRECTLY TO THE **PRESIDENT**!
AS SHE'S WALKING ACROSS THE WHITE HOUSE LAWN, WHO SHOULD SHE BUMP INTO BUT **BEN FRANKLIN**!
BEN FRANKLIN WAS **DEAD** IN 1812, YOU PINHEAD!
HE WAS?
WOW, THAT REALLY **IS** A PLOT TWIST!
Peirce

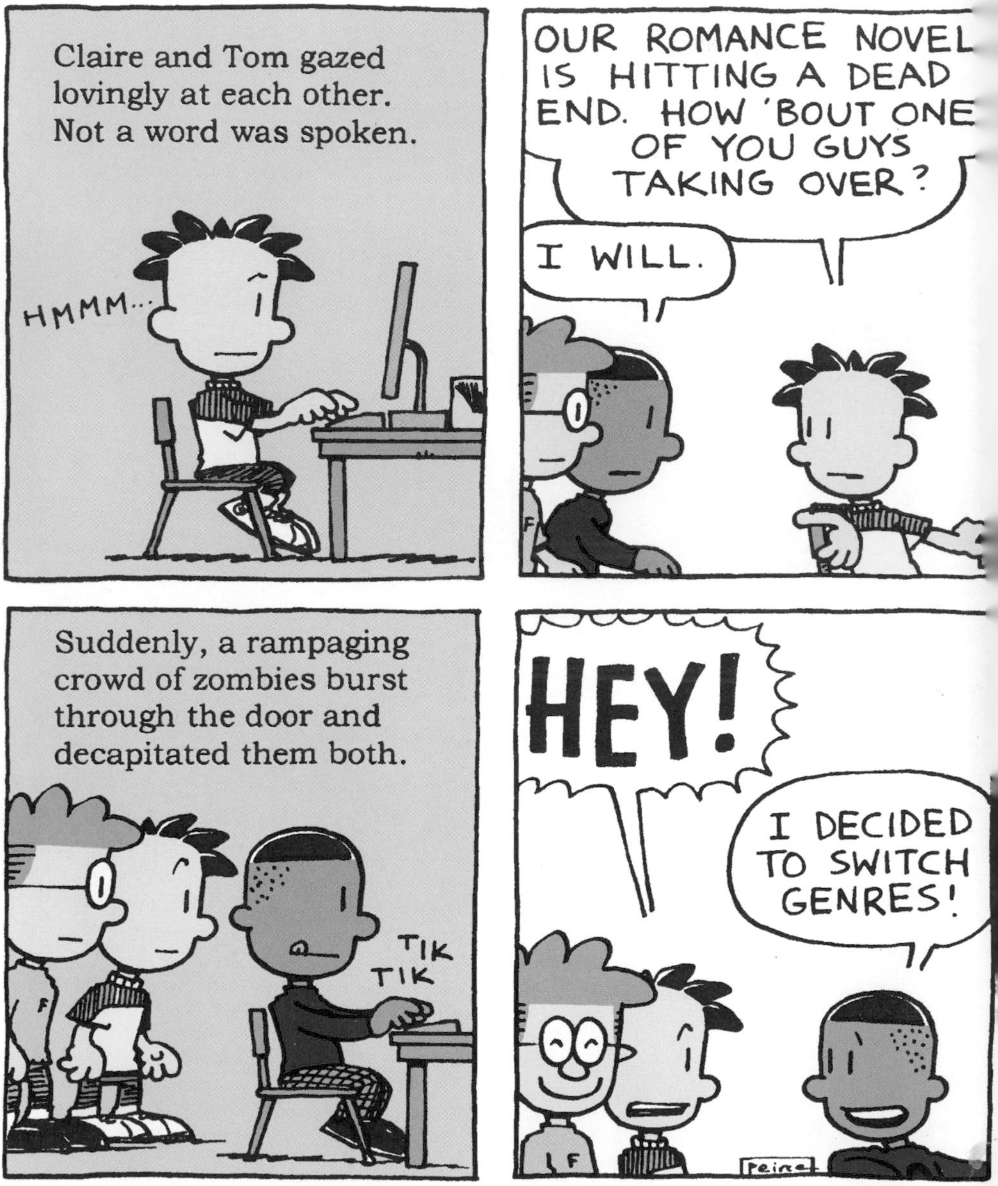
Claire and Tom gazed lovingly at each other. Not a word was spoken.
HMMM...
OUR ROMANCE NOVEL IS HITTING A DEAD END. HOW 'BOUT ONE OF YOU GUYS TAKING OVER?
I WILL.
Suddenly, a rampaging crowd of zombies burst through the door and decapitated them both.
TIK TIK
HEY!
I DECIDED TO SWITCH GENRES!
Peirce

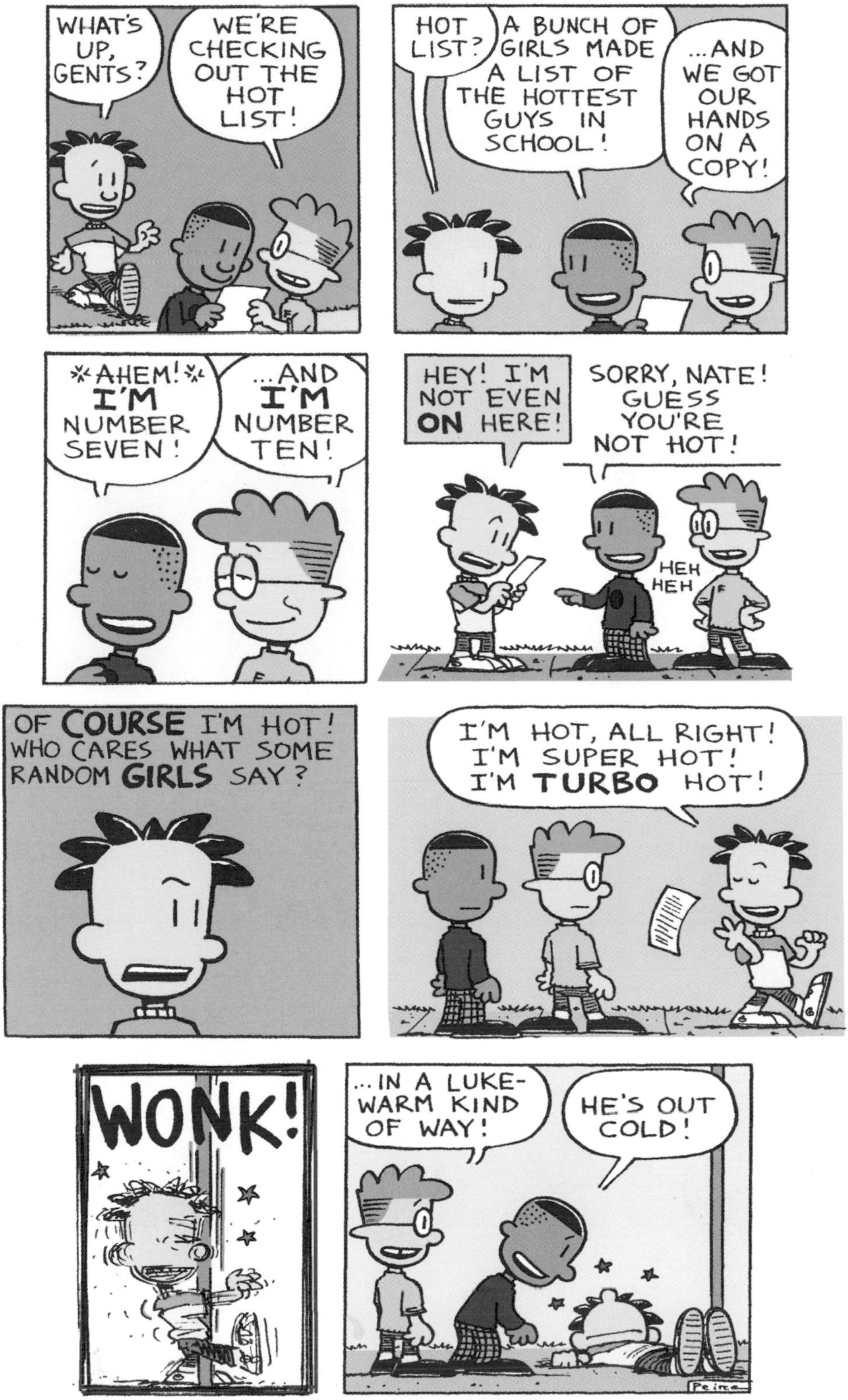
WHAT'S UP, GENTS?
WE'RE CHECKING OUT THE HOT LIST!
HOT LIST?
A BUNCH OF GIRLS MADE A LIST OF THE HOTTEST GUYS IN SCHOOL!
...AND WE GOT OUR HANDS ON A COPY!
AHEM! I'M NUMBER SEVEN!
...AND I'M NUMBER TEN!
HEY! I'M NOT EVEN ON HERE!
SORRY, NATE! GUESS YOU'RE NOT HOT!
HEH HEH
OF COURSE I'M HOT! WHO CARES WHAT SOME RANDOM GIRLS SAY?
I'M HOT, ALL RIGHT! I'M SUPER HOT! I'M TURBO HOT!
WONK!
...IN A LUKE-WARM KIND OF WAY!
HE'S OUT COLD!
Peirce

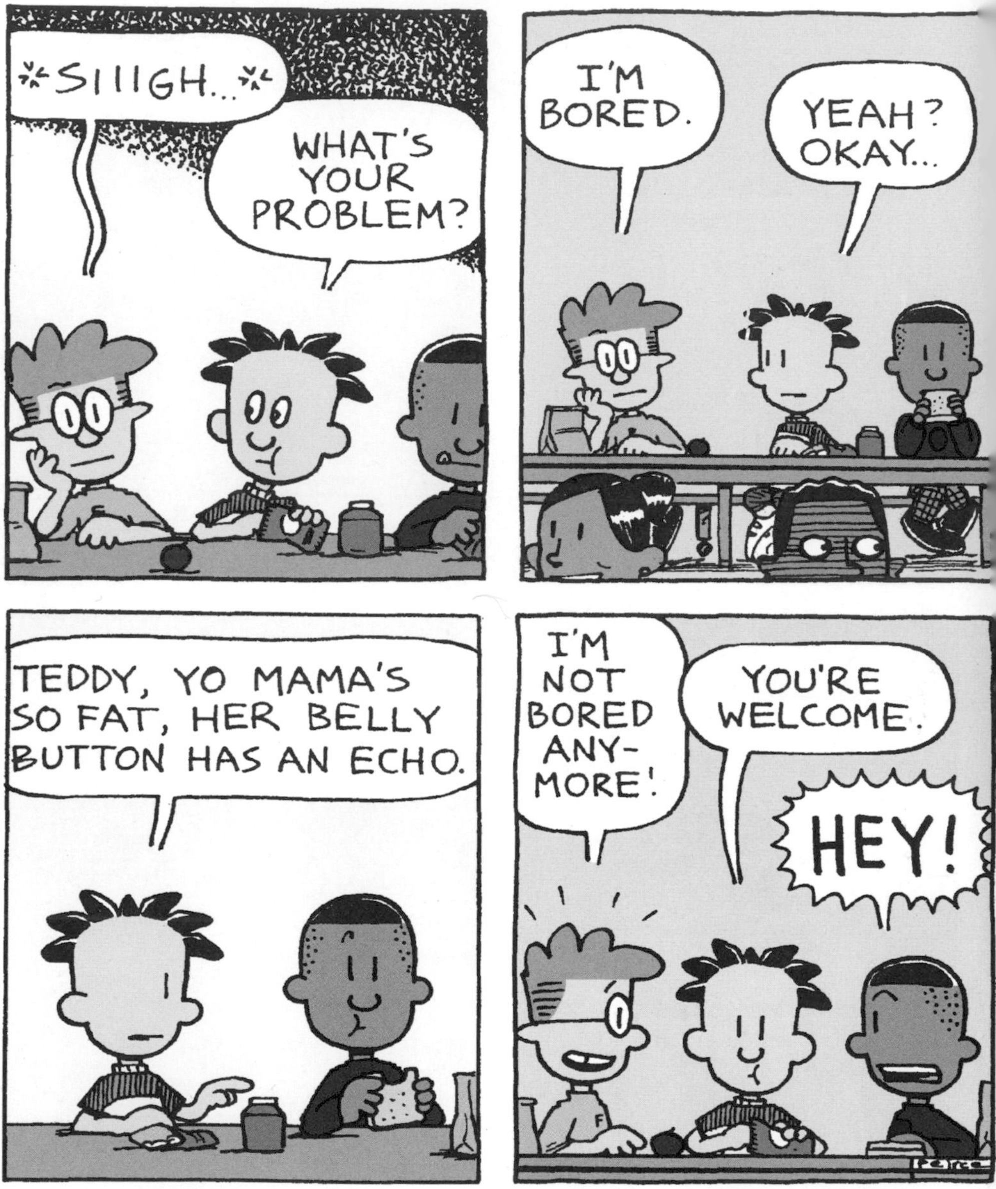
SIIIGH...
WHAT'S YOUR PROBLEM?
I'M BORED.
YEAH? OKAY...
TEDDY, YO MAMA'S SO FAT, HER BELLY BUTTON HAS AN ECHO.
I'M NOT BORED ANY-MORE!
YOU'RE WELCOME.
HEY!
peirce

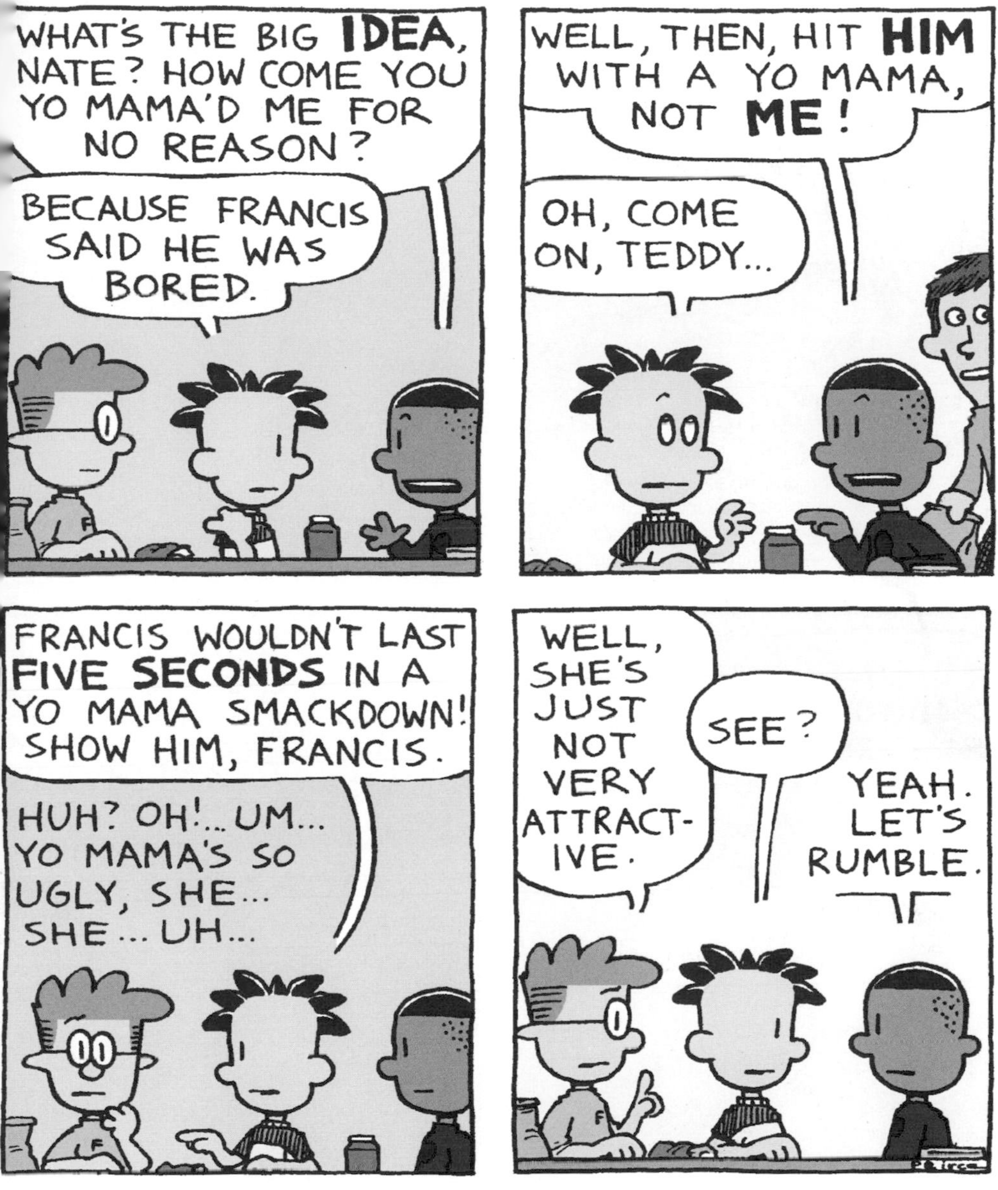
WHAT'S THE BIG IDEA, NATE? HOW COME YOU YO MAMA'D ME FOR NO REASON?
BECAUSE FRANCIS SAID HE WAS BORED.
WELL, THEN, HIT HIM WITH A YO MAMA, NOT ME!
OH, COME ON, TEDDY...
FRANCIS WOULDN'T LAST FIVE SECONDS IN A YO MAMA SMACKDOWN! SHOW HIM, FRANCIS.
HUH? OH!... UM... YO MAMA'S SO UGLY, SHE... SHE... UH...
WELL, SHE'S JUST NOT VERY ATTRACT-IVE.
SEE?
YEAH. LET'S RUMBLE.

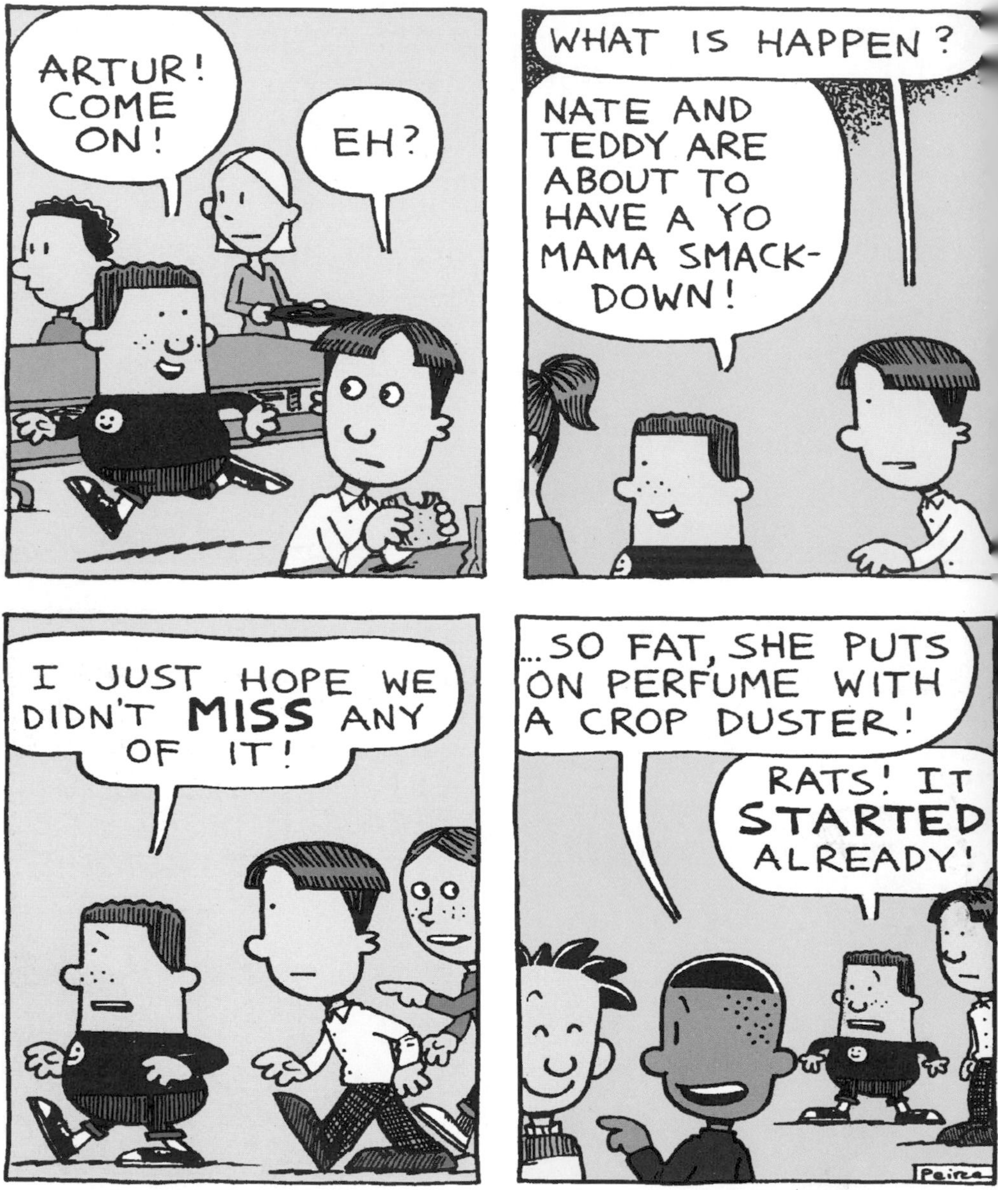
ARTUR! COME ON!
EH?
WHAT IS HAPPEN?
NATE AND TEDDY ARE ABOUT TO HAVE A YO MAMA SMACK-DOWN!
I JUST HOPE WE DIDN'T MISS ANY OF IT!
...SO FAT, SHE PUTS ON PERFUME WITH A CROP DUSTER!
RATS! IT STARTED ALREADY!
Peirce

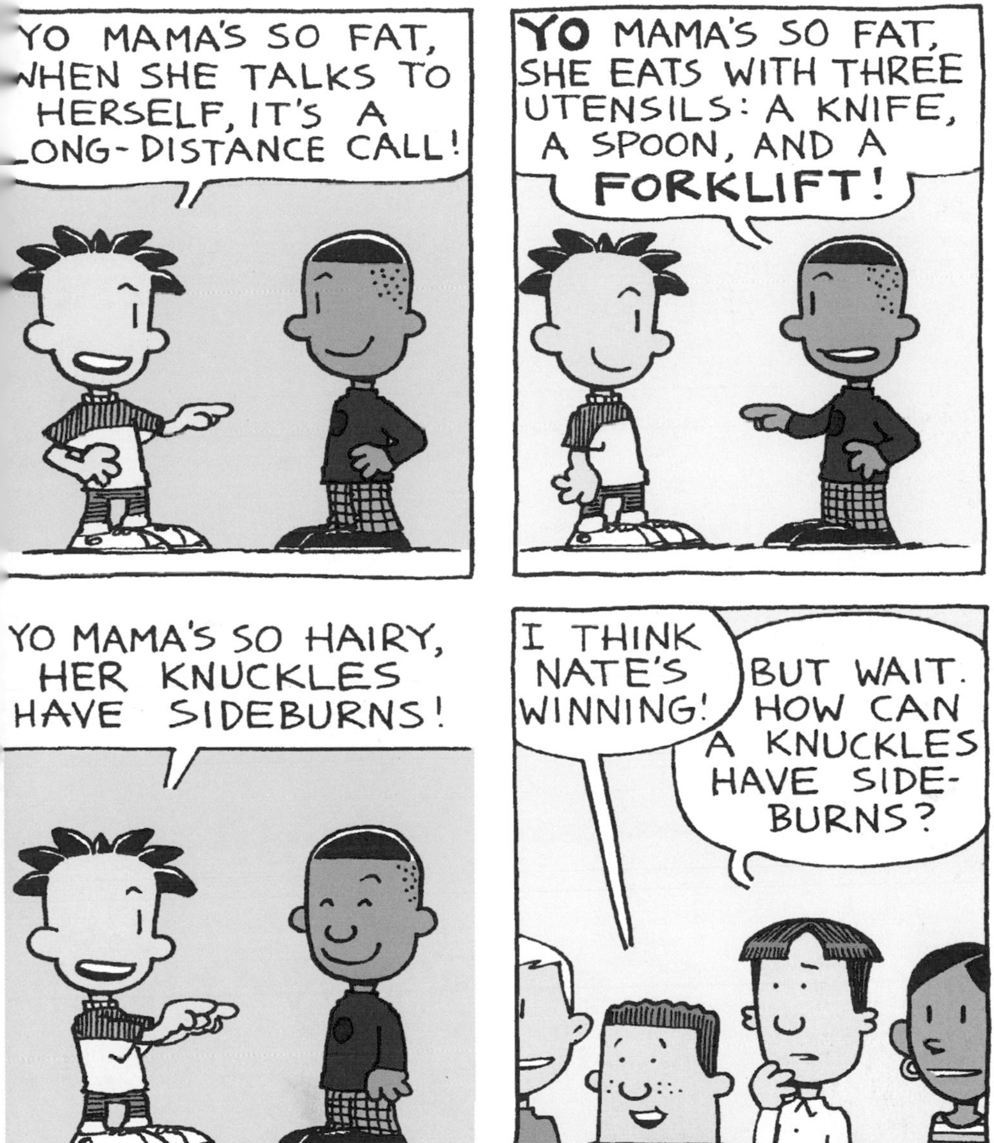
YO MAMA'S SO FAT, WHEN SHE TALKS TO HERSELF, IT'S A LONG-DISTANCE CALL!
YO MAMA'S SO FAT, SHE EATS WITH THREE UTENSILS: A KNIFE, A SPOON, AND A FORKLIFT!
YO MAMA'S SO HAIRY, HER KNUCKLES HAVE SIDEBURNS!
I THINK NATE'S WINNING!
BUT WAIT. HOW CAN A KNUCKLES HAVE SIDE-BURNS?
Peirce

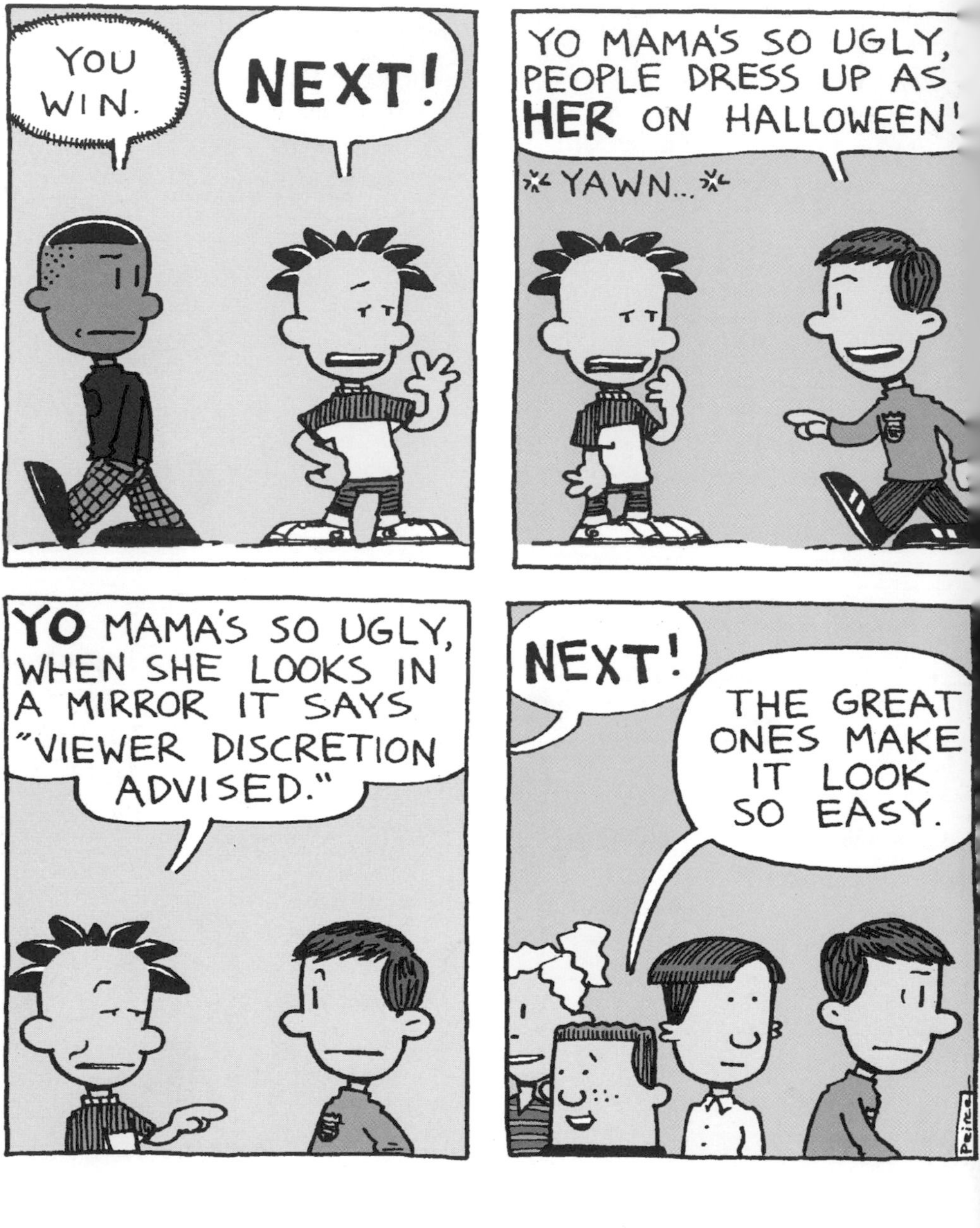
YOU WIN.
NEXT!
YO MAMA'S SO UGLY, PEOPLE DRESS UP AS HER ON HALLOWEEN!
YAWN...
YO MAMA'S SO UGLY, WHEN SHE LOOKS IN A MIRROR IT SAYS "VIEWER DISCRETION ADVISED."
NEXT!
THE GREAT ONES MAKE IT LOOK SO EASY.
Peirce

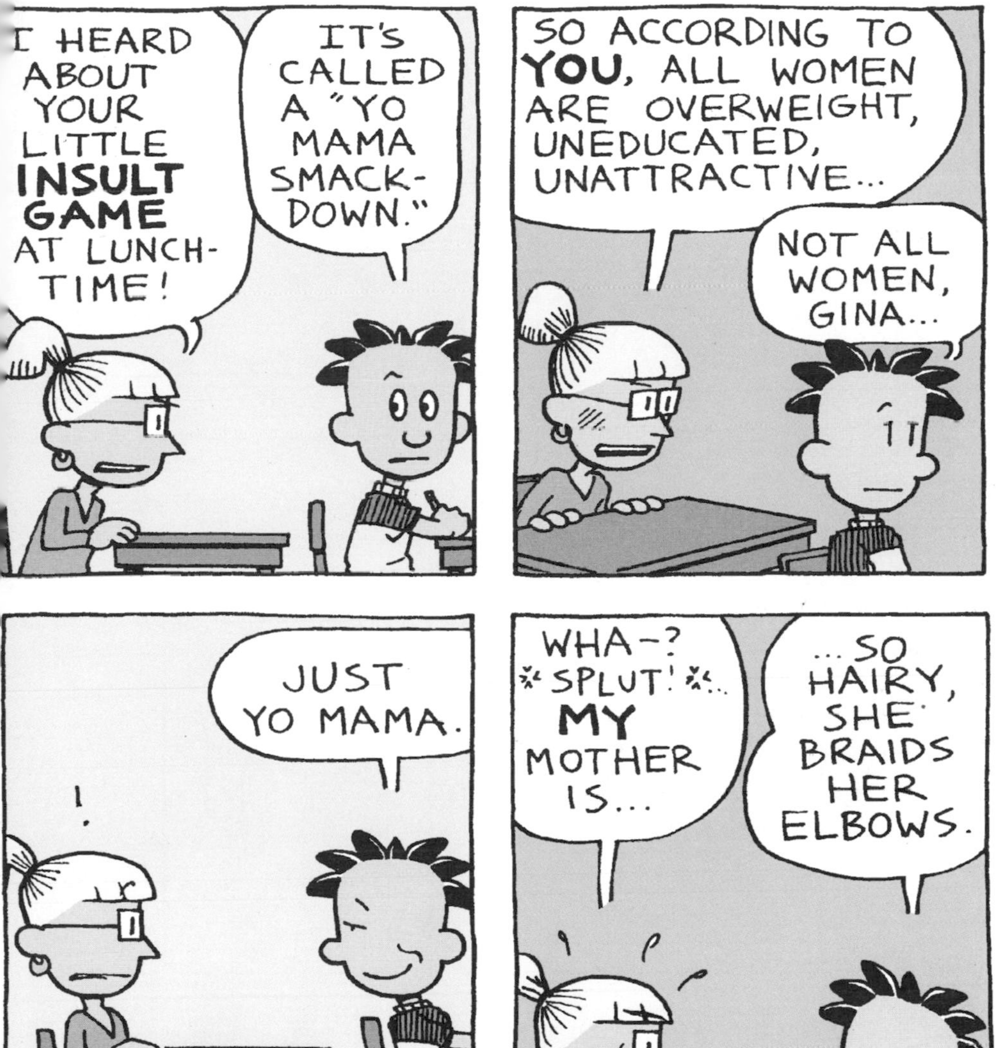
I HEARD ABOUT YOUR LITTLE **INSULT GAME** AT LUNCH-TIME!
IT'S CALLED A "YO MAMA SMACK-DOWN."
SO ACCORDING TO **YOU**, ALL WOMEN ARE OVERWEIGHT, UNEDUCATED, UNATTRACTIVE...
NOT ALL WOMEN, GINA...
JUST YO MAMA.
!
WHA-? SPLUT! **MY** MOTHER IS...
...SO HAIRY, SHE BRAIDS HER ELBOWS.
Peirce

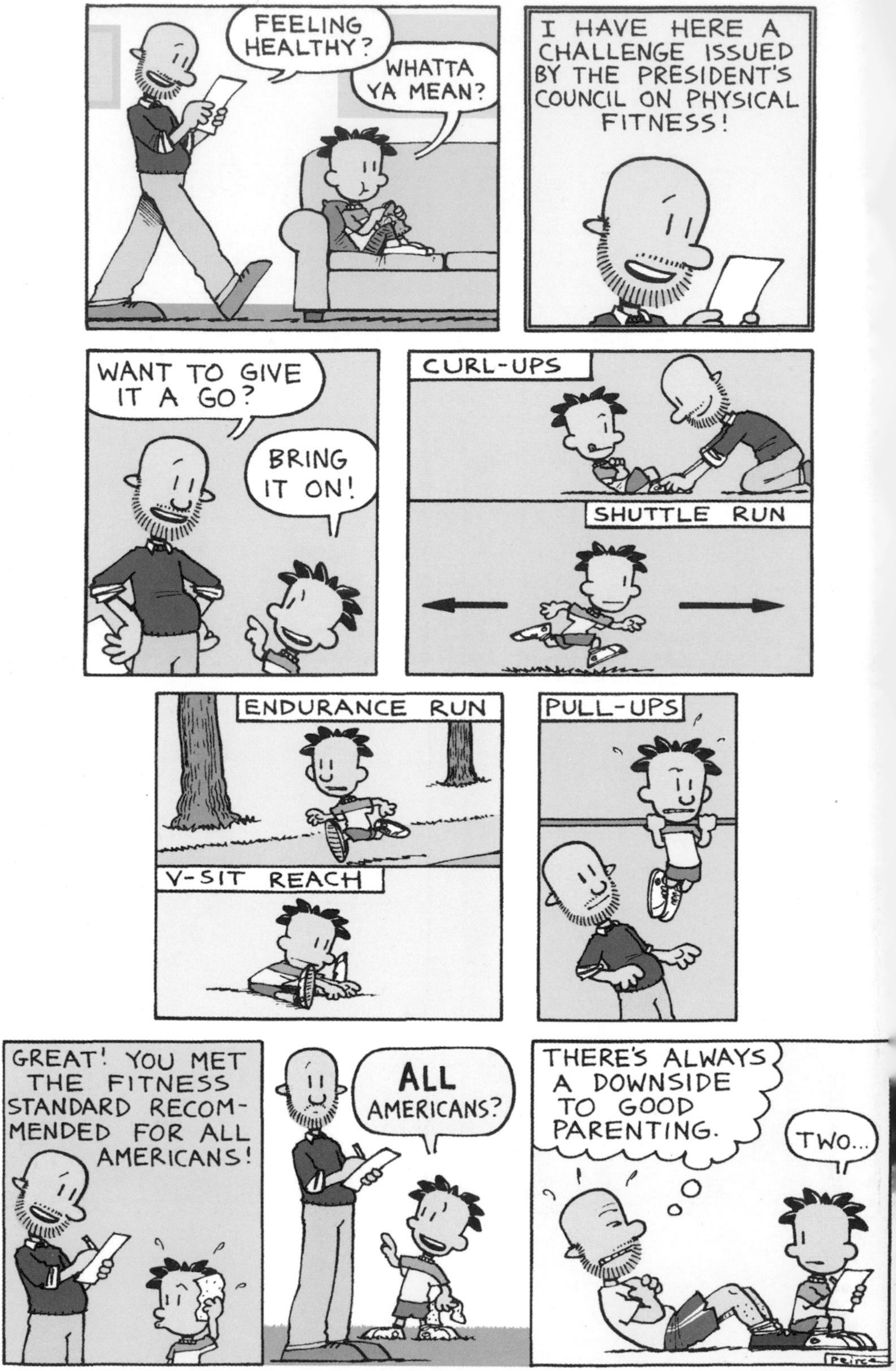
FEELING HEALTHY?
WHATTA YA MEAN?
I HAVE HERE A CHALLENGE ISSUED BY THE PRESIDENT'S COUNCIL ON PHYSICAL FITNESS!
WANT TO GIVE IT A GO?
BRING IT ON!
CURL-UPS
SHUTTLE RUN
ENDURANCE RUN
PULL-UPS
V-SIT REACH
GREAT! YOU MET THE FITNESS STANDARD RECOMMENDED FOR ALL AMERICANS!
ALL AMERICANS?
THERE'S ALWAYS A DOWNSIDE TO GOOD PARENTING.
TWO...
PEIRCE

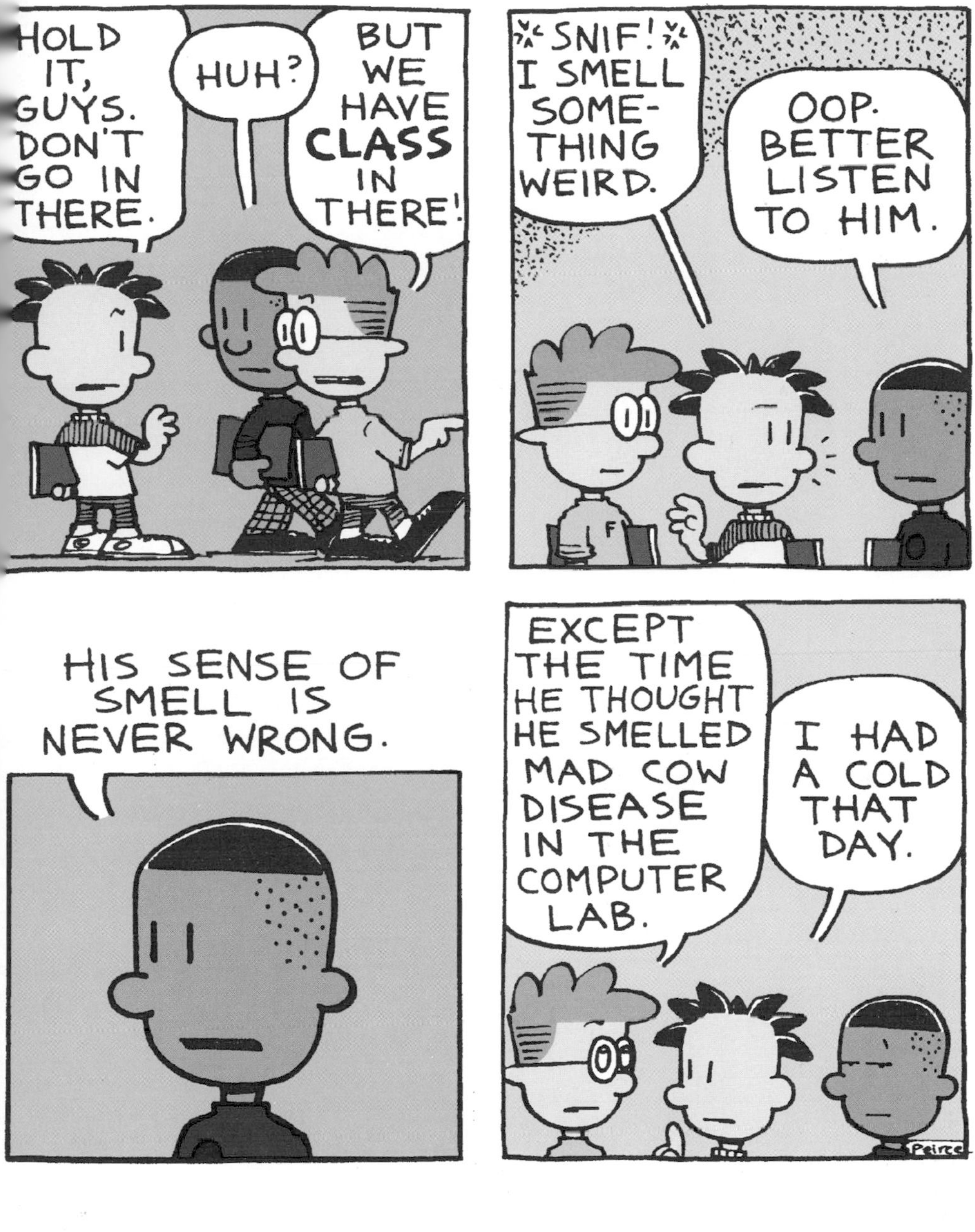
HOLD IT, GUYS. DON'T GO IN THERE.
HUH?
BUT WE HAVE **CLASS** IN THERE!
SNIF! I SMELL SOMETHING WEIRD.
OOP. BETTER LISTEN TO HIM.
HIS SENSE OF SMELL IS NEVER WRONG.
EXCEPT THE TIME HE THOUGHT HE SMELLED MAD COW DISEASE IN THE COMPUTER LAB.
I HAD A COLD THAT DAY.
Peirce

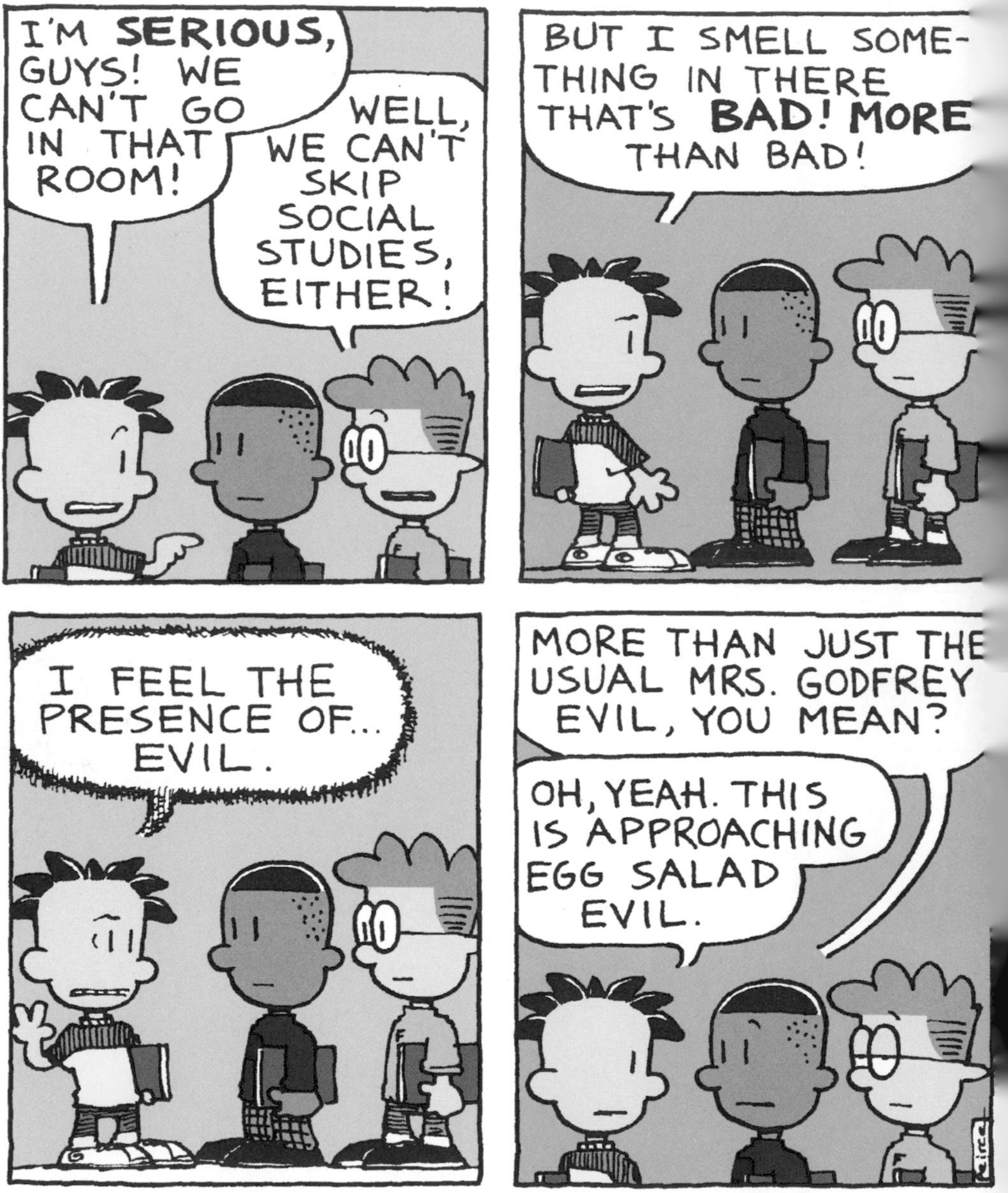
I'M SERIOUS, GUYS! WE CAN'T GO IN THAT ROOM!
WELL, WE CAN'T SKIP SOCIAL STUDIES, EITHER!
BUT I SMELL SOME-THING IN THERE THAT'S BAD! MORE THAN BAD!
I FEEL THE PRESENCE OF... EVIL.
MORE THAN JUST THE USUAL MRS. GODFREY EVIL, YOU MEAN?
OH, YEAH. THIS IS APPROACHING EGG SALAD EVIL.

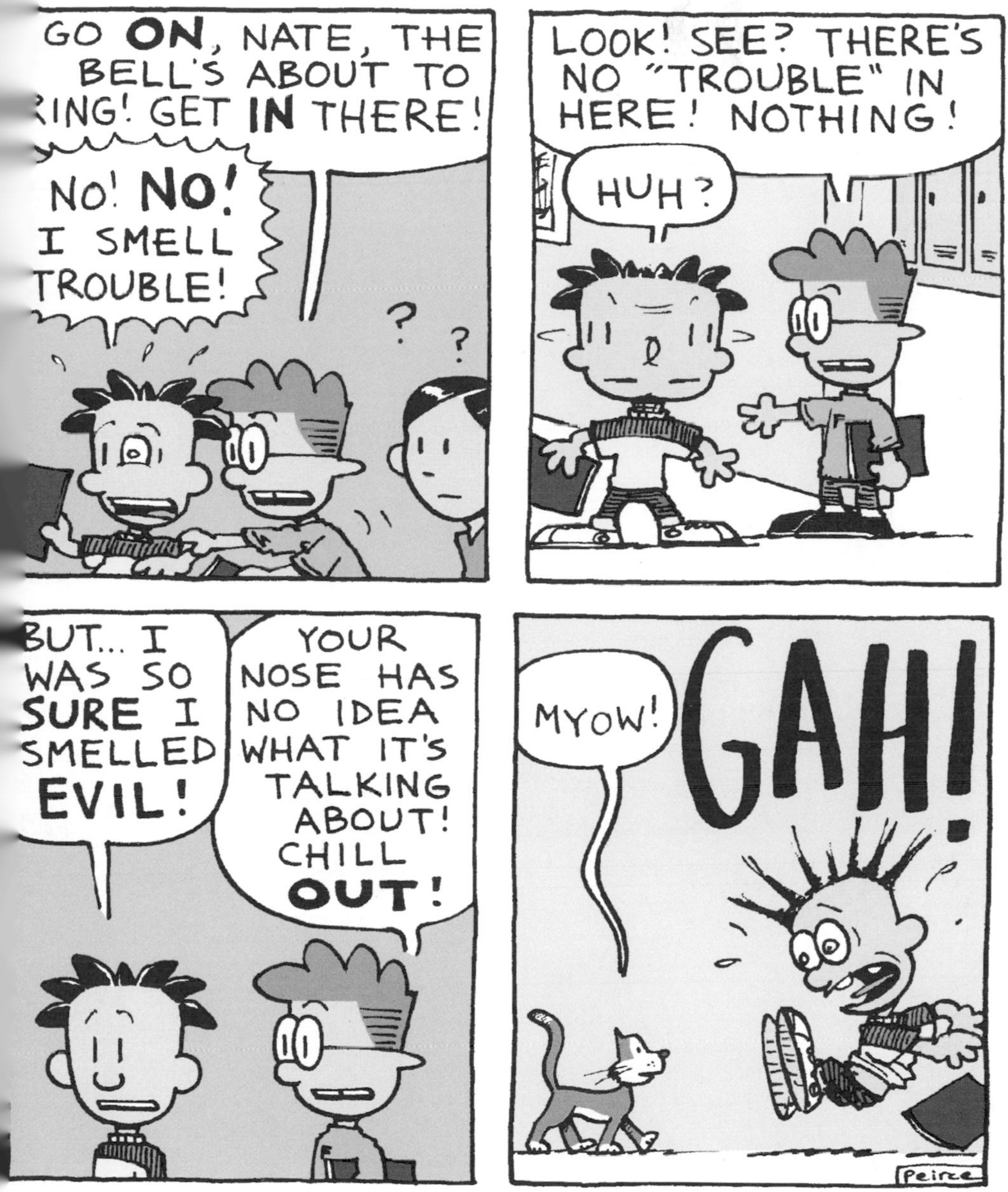
GO ON, NATE, THE BELL'S ABOUT TO RING! GET IN THERE!
NO! NO! I SMELL TROUBLE!
? ?
LOOK! SEE? THERE'S NO "TROUBLE" IN HERE! NOTHING!
HUH?
BUT... I WAS SO SURE I SMELLED EVIL!
YOUR NOSE HAS NO IDEA WHAT IT'S TALKING ABOUT! CHILL OUT!
MYOW!
GAH!
Peirce

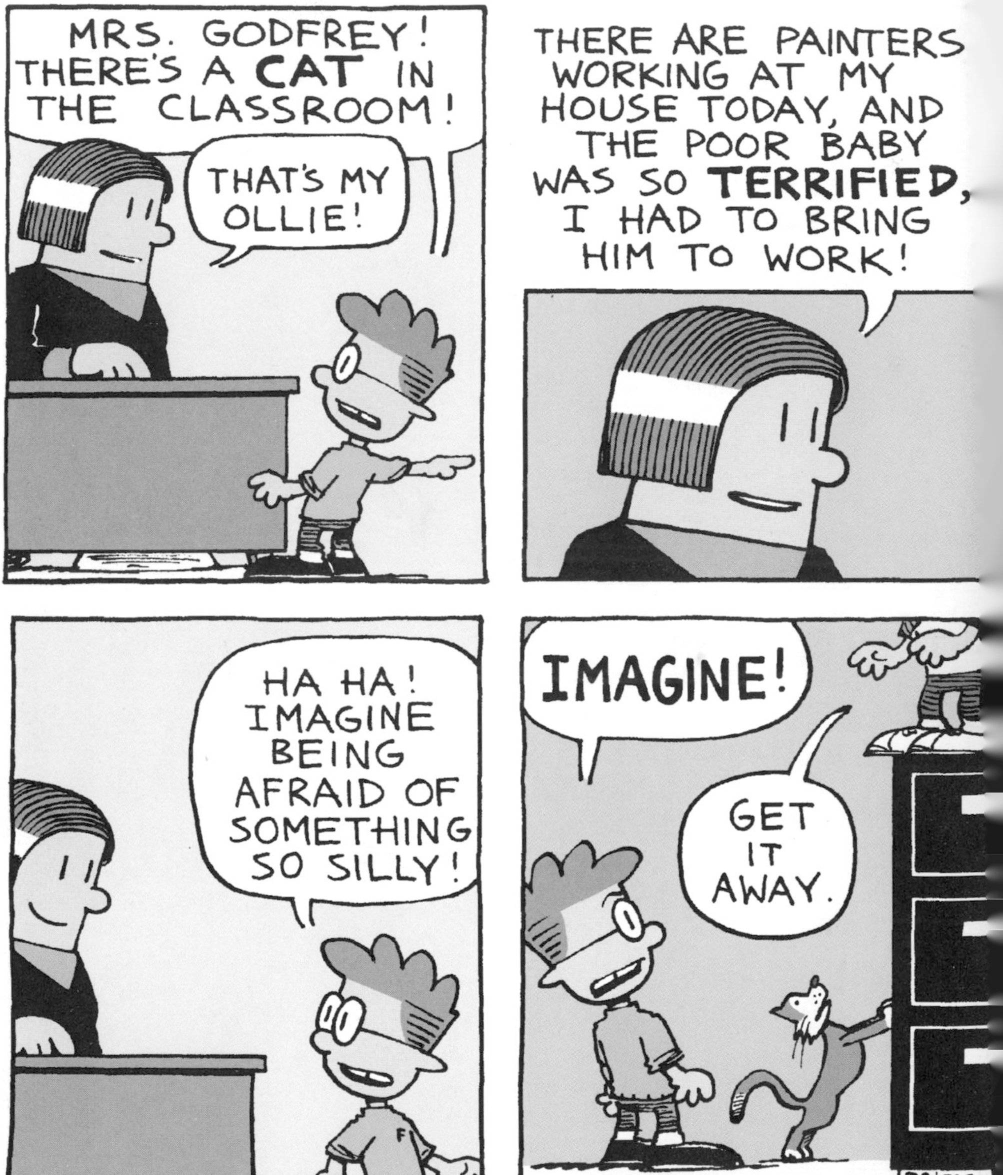
MRS. GODFREY! THERE'S A CAT IN THE CLASSROOM!
THAT'S MY OLLIE!
THERE ARE PAINTERS WORKING AT MY HOUSE TODAY, AND THE POOR BABY WAS SO TERRIFIED, I HAD TO BRING HIM TO WORK!
HA HA! IMAGINE BEING AFRAID OF SOMETHING SO SILLY!
IMAGINE!
GET IT AWAY.
peirce

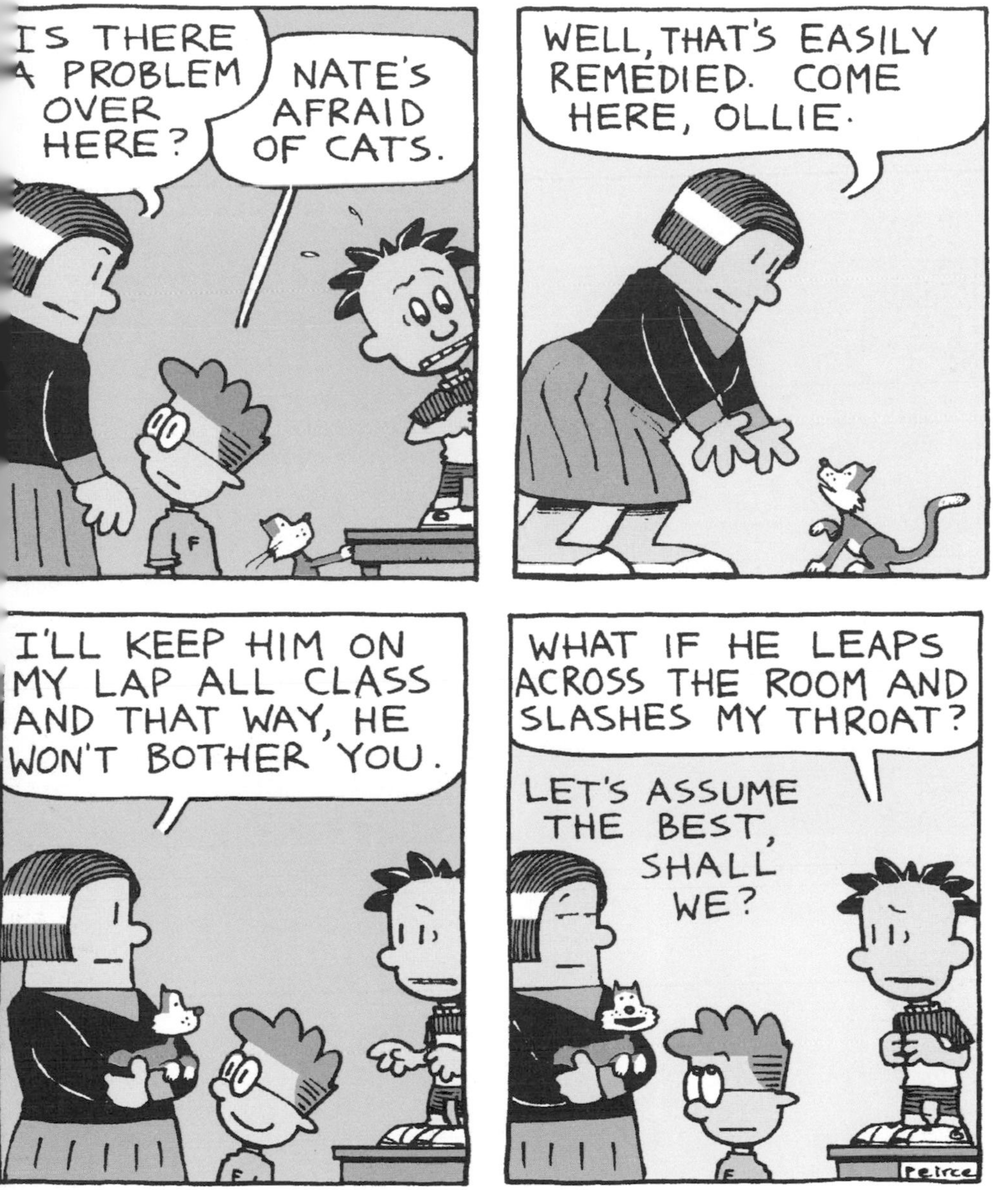
IS THERE A PROBLEM OVER HERE?
NATE'S AFRAID OF CATS.
WELL, THAT'S EASILY REMEDIED. COME HERE, OLLIE.
I'LL KEEP HIM ON MY LAP ALL CLASS AND THAT WAY, HE WON'T BOTHER YOU.
WHAT IF HE LEAPS ACROSS THE ROOM AND SLASHES MY THROAT?
LET'S ASSUME THE BEST, SHALL WE?
PEIRCE

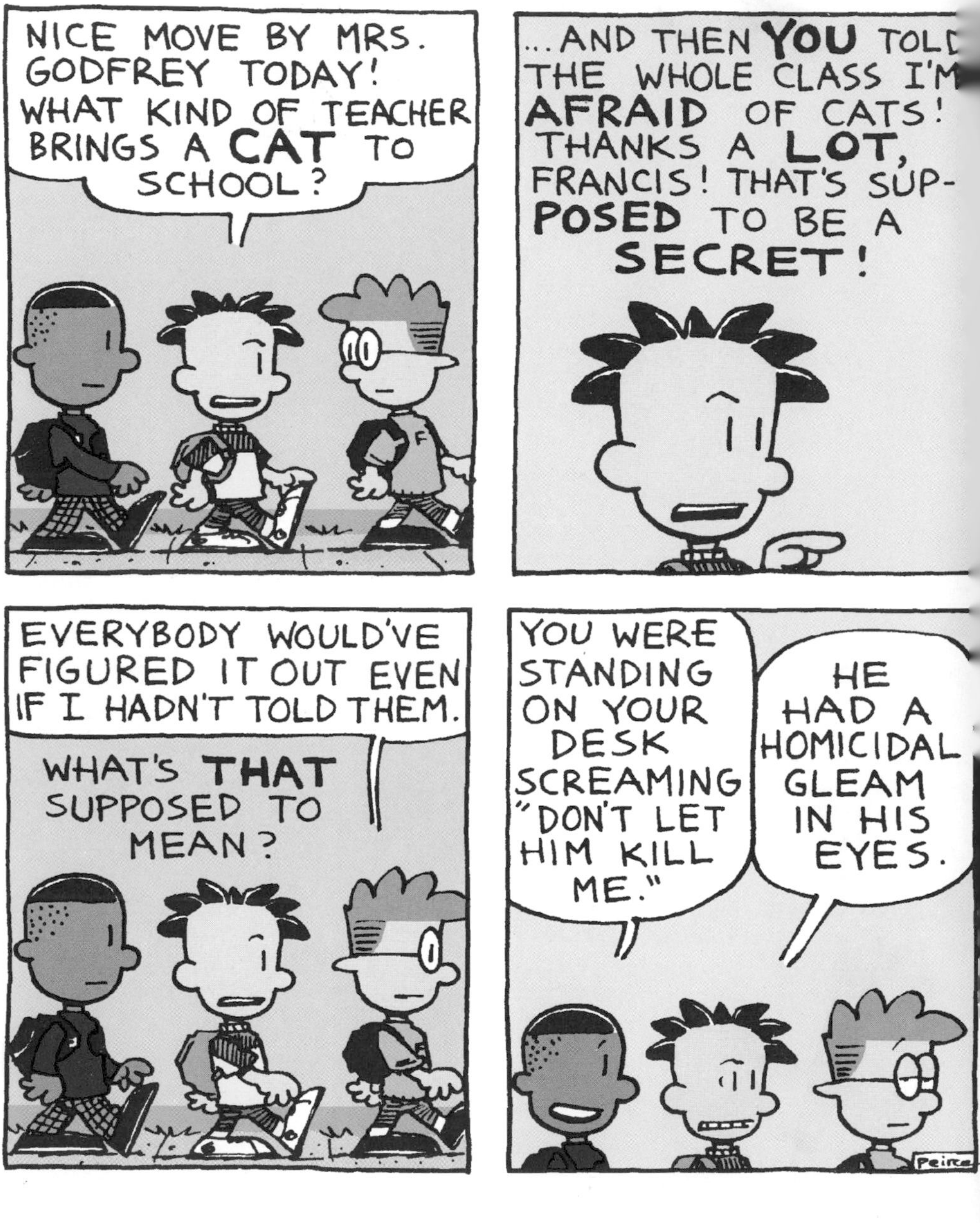
NICE MOVE BY MRS. GODFREY TODAY! WHAT KIND OF TEACHER BRINGS A CAT TO SCHOOL?
...AND THEN YOU TOLD THE WHOLE CLASS I'M AFRAID OF CATS! THANKS A LOT, FRANCIS! THAT'S SUPPOSED TO BE A SECRET!
EVERYBODY WOULD'VE FIGURED IT OUT EVEN IF I HADN'T TOLD THEM.
WHAT'S THAT SUPPOSED TO MEAN?
YOU WERE STANDING ON YOUR DESK SCREAMING "DON'T LET HIM KILL ME."
HE HAD A HOMICIDAL GLEAM IN HIS EYES.
Peirce

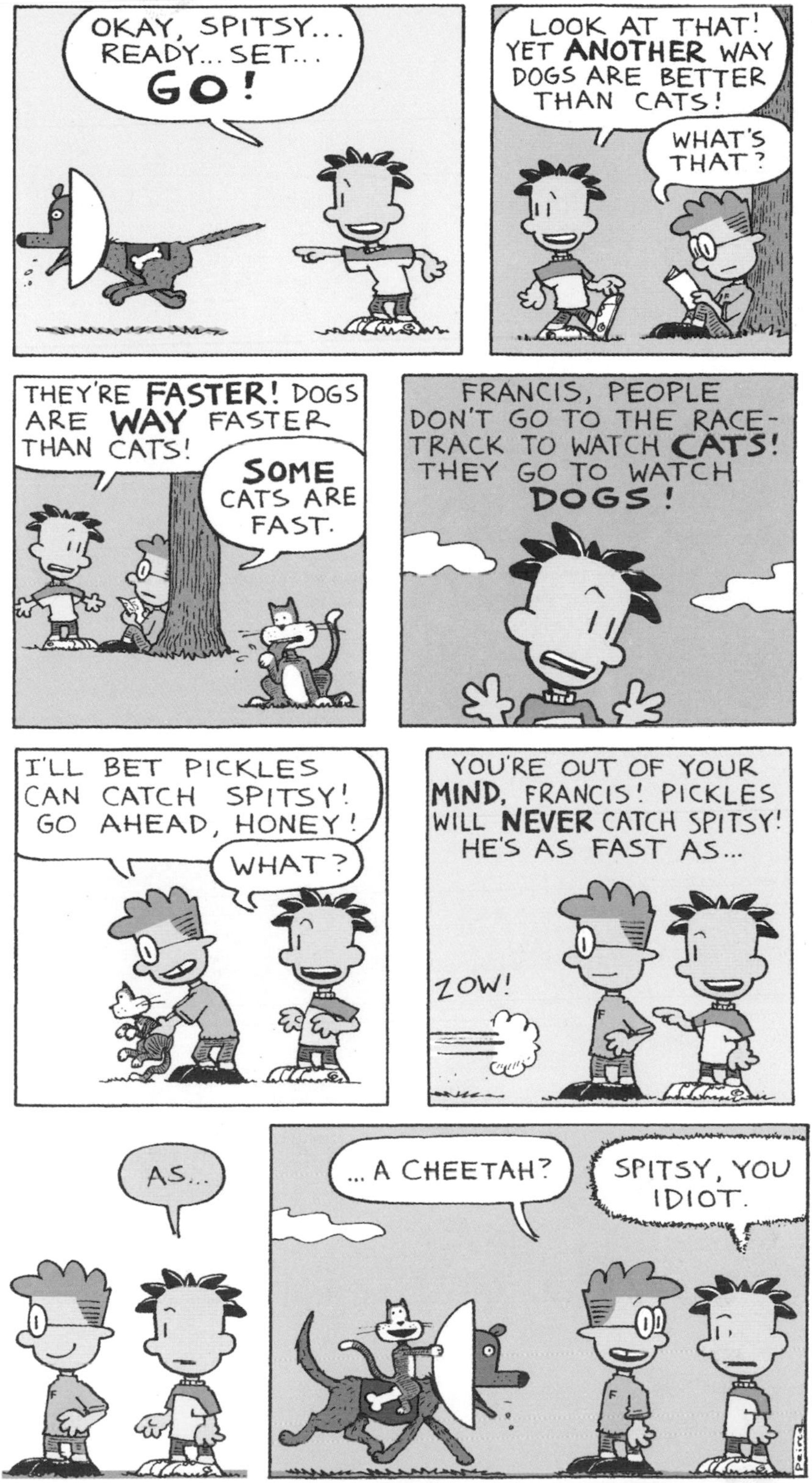
OKAY, SPITSY... READY... SET... GO!
LOOK AT THAT! YET ANOTHER WAY DOGS ARE BETTER THAN CATS!
WHAT'S THAT?
THEY'RE FASTER! DOGS ARE WAY FASTER THAN CATS!
SOME CATS ARE FAST.
FRANCIS, PEOPLE DON'T GO TO THE RACE-TRACK TO WATCH CATS! THEY GO TO WATCH DOGS!
I'LL BET PICKLES CAN CATCH SPITSY! GO AHEAD, HONEY!
WHAT?
YOU'RE OUT OF YOUR MIND, FRANCIS! PICKLES WILL NEVER CATCH SPITSY! HE'S AS FAST AS...
ZOW!
AS...
... A CHEETAH?
SPITSY, YOU IDIOT.
Peirce

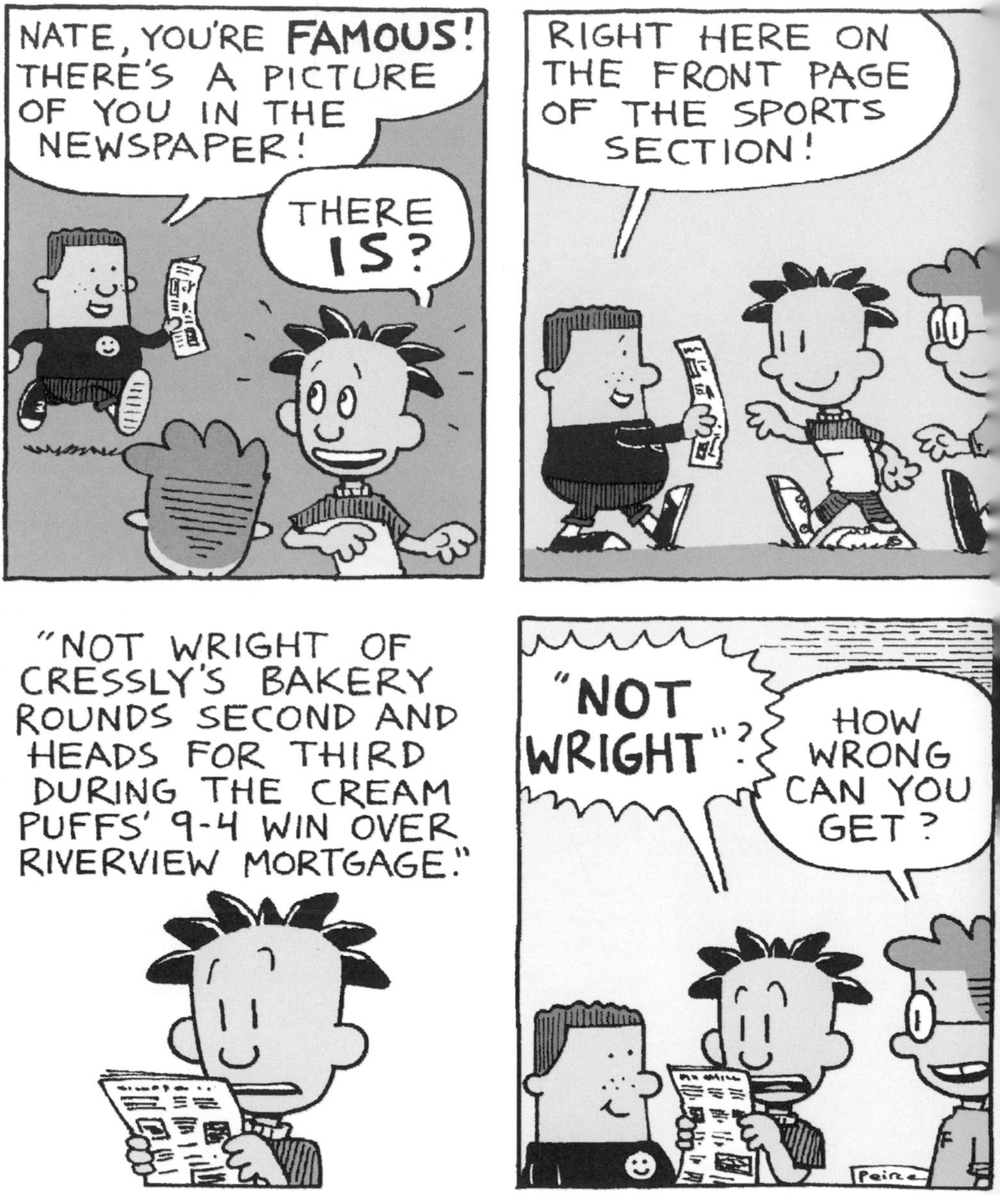
NATE, YOU'RE **FAMOUS**! THERE'S A PICTURE OF YOU IN THE NEWSPAPER!
THERE **IS**?
RIGHT HERE ON THE FRONT PAGE OF THE SPORTS SECTION!
"NOT WRIGHT OF CRESSLY'S BAKERY ROUNDS SECOND AND HEADS FOR THIRD DURING THE CREAM PUFFS' 9-4 WIN OVER RIVERVIEW MORTGAGE."
"**NOT WRIGHT**"?
HOW WRONG CAN YOU GET?
Peirce

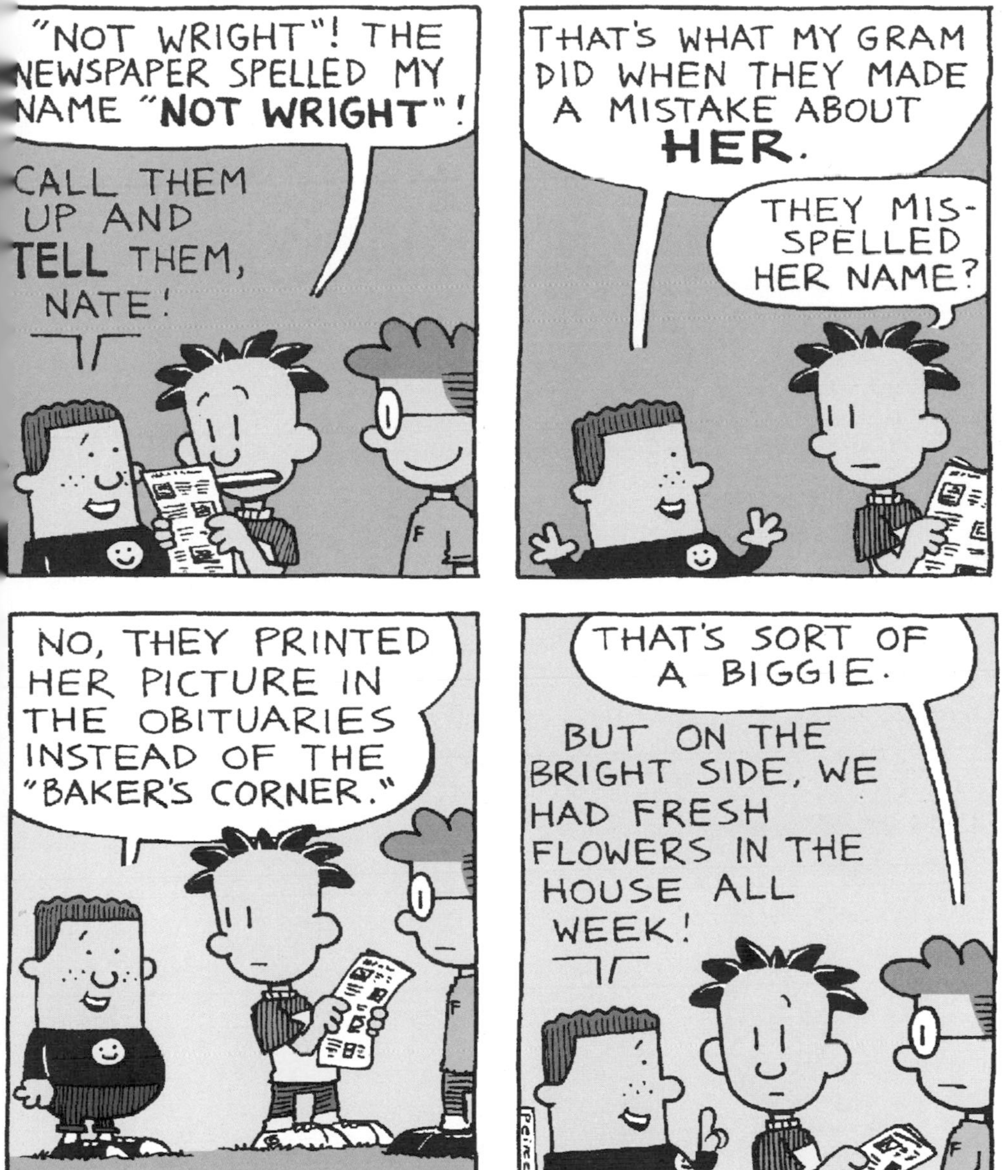
"NOT WRIGHT"! THE NEWSPAPER SPELLED MY NAME "**NOT WRIGHT**"!
CALL THEM UP AND **TELL** THEM, NATE!
THAT'S WHAT MY GRAM DID WHEN THEY MADE A MISTAKE ABOUT **HER**.
THEY MIS-SPELLED HER NAME?
NO, THEY PRINTED HER PICTURE IN THE OBITUARIES INSTEAD OF THE "BAKER'S CORNER."
THAT'S SORT OF A BIGGIE.
BUT ON THE BRIGHT SIDE, WE HAD FRESH FLOWERS IN THE HOUSE ALL WEEK!
PEIRCE

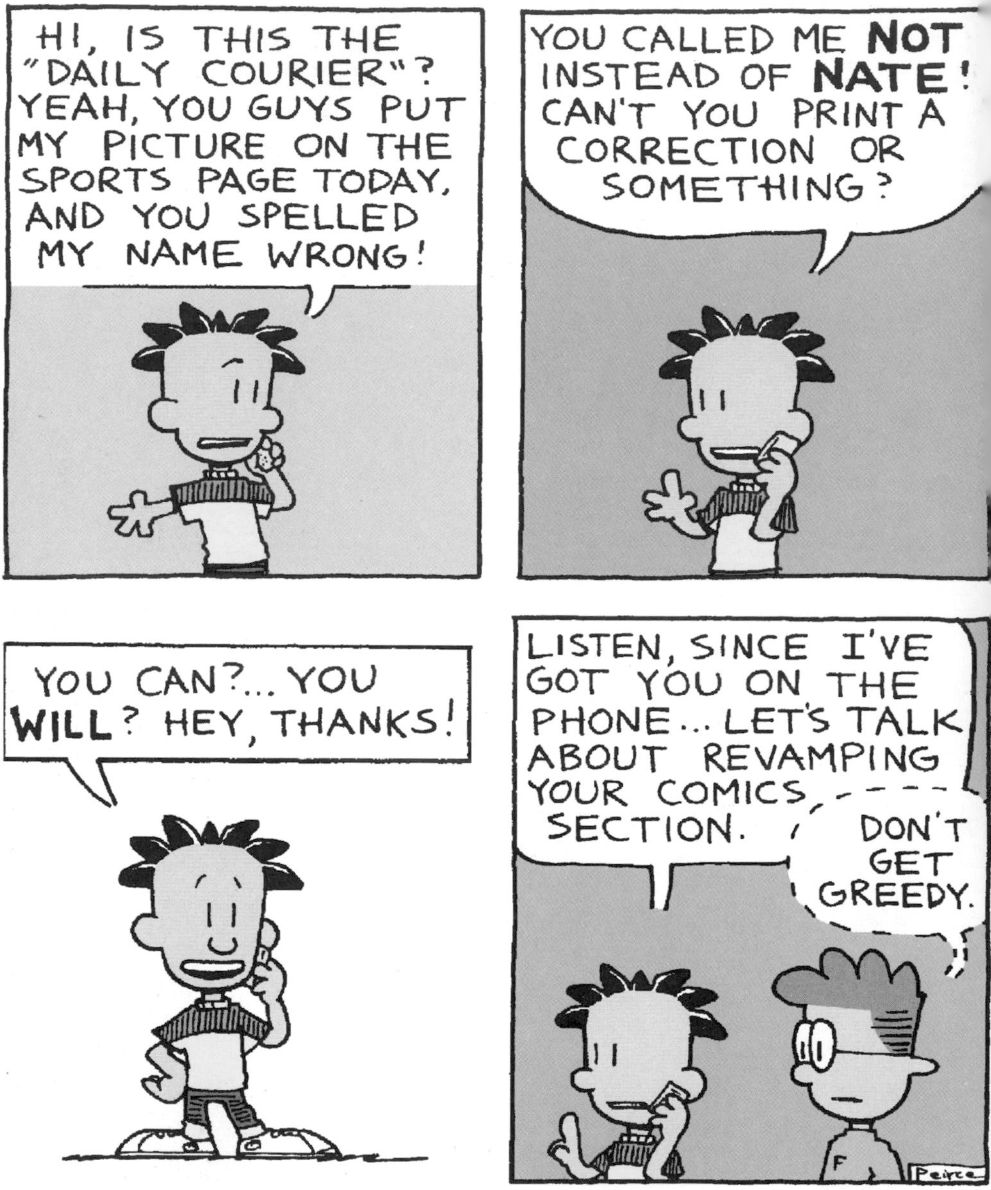
HI, IS THIS THE "DAILY COURIER"? YEAH, YOU GUYS PUT MY PICTURE ON THE SPORTS PAGE TODAY, AND YOU SPELLED MY NAME WRONG!
YOU CALLED ME **NOT** INSTEAD OF **NATE**! CAN'T YOU PRINT A CORRECTION OR SOMETHING?
YOU CAN?... YOU **WILL**? HEY, THANKS!
LISTEN, SINCE I'VE GOT YOU ON THE PHONE... LET'S TALK ABOUT REVAMPING YOUR COMICS SECTION.
DON'T GET GREEDY.
F
Peirce

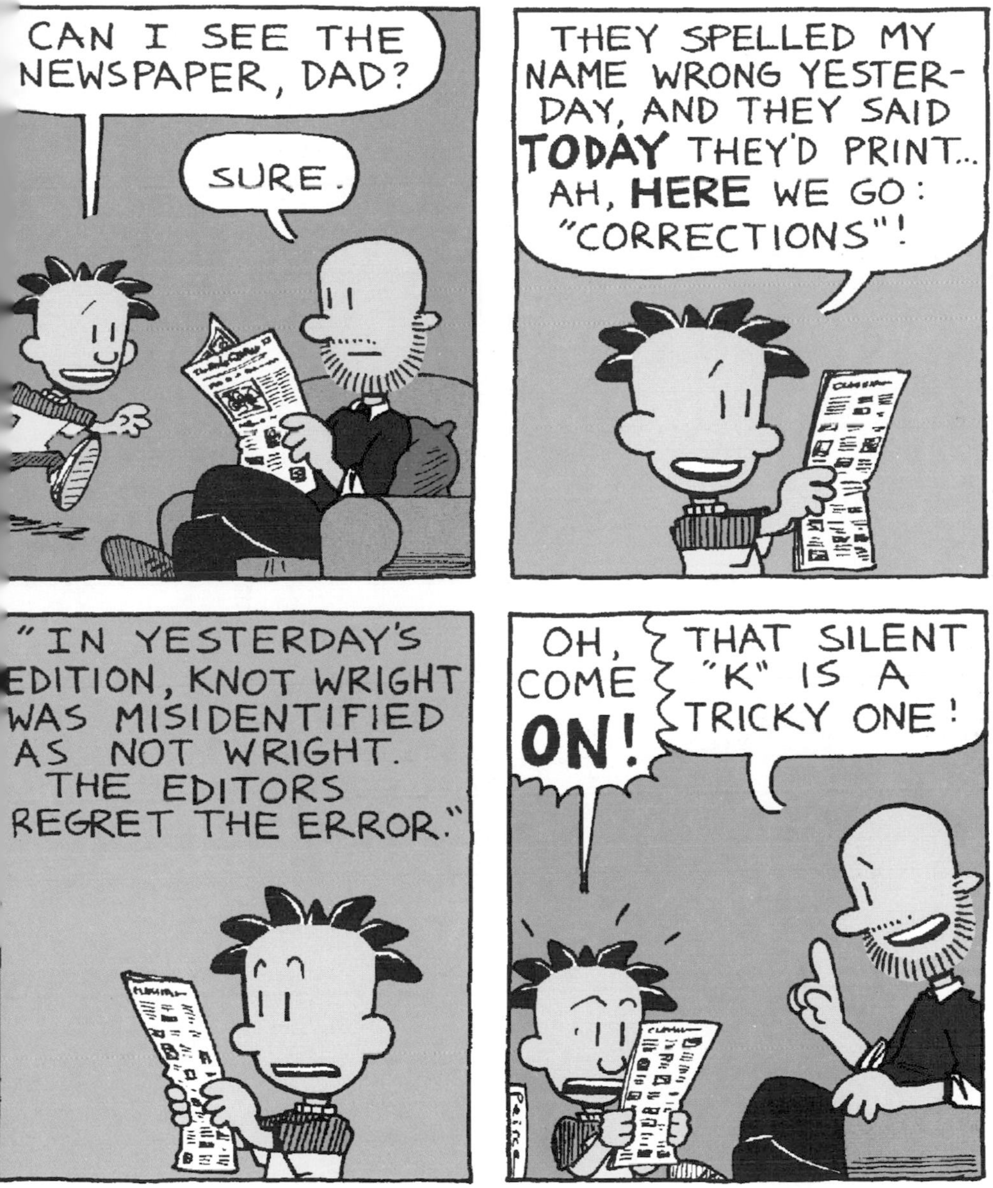
CAN I SEE THE NEWSPAPER, DAD?
SURE.
THEY SPELLED MY NAME WRONG YESTERDAY, AND THEY SAID TODAY THEY'D PRINT... AH, HERE WE GO: "CORRECTIONS"!
"IN YESTERDAY'S EDITION, KNOT WRIGHT WAS MISIDENTIFIED AS NOT WRIGHT. THE EDITORS REGRET THE ERROR."
OH, COME ON!
THAT SILENT "K" IS A TRICKY ONE!

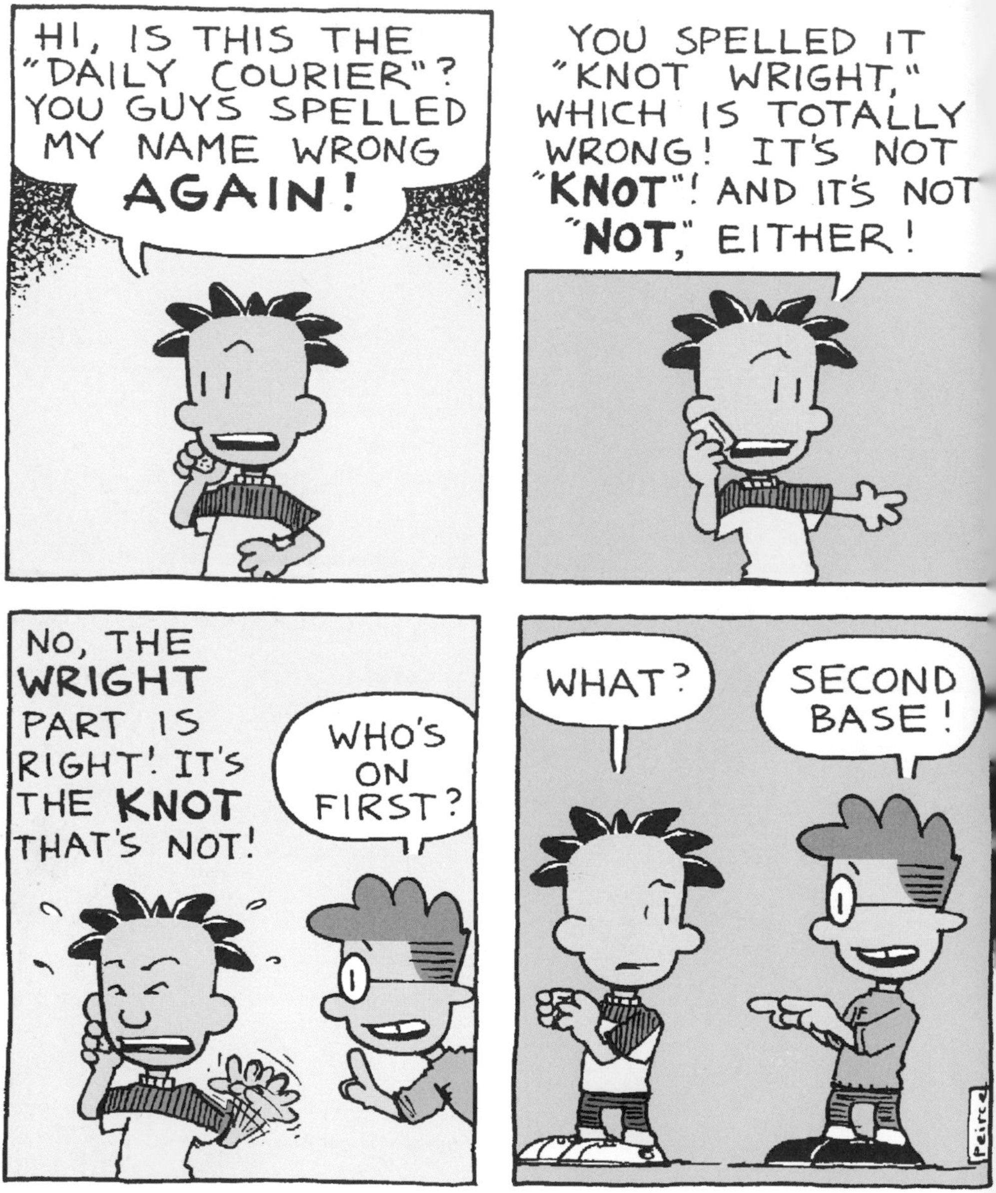

HI, IS THIS THE "DAILY COURIER"? YOU GUYS SPELLED MY NAME WRONG **AGAIN**!
YOU SPELLED IT "KNOT WRIGHT," WHICH IS TOTALLY WRONG! IT'S NOT "**KNOT**"! AND IT'S NOT "**NOT**," EITHER!
NO, THE **WRIGHT** PART IS RIGHT! IT'S THE **KNOT** THAT'S NOT!
WHO'S ON FIRST?
WHAT?
SECOND BASE!
Peirce

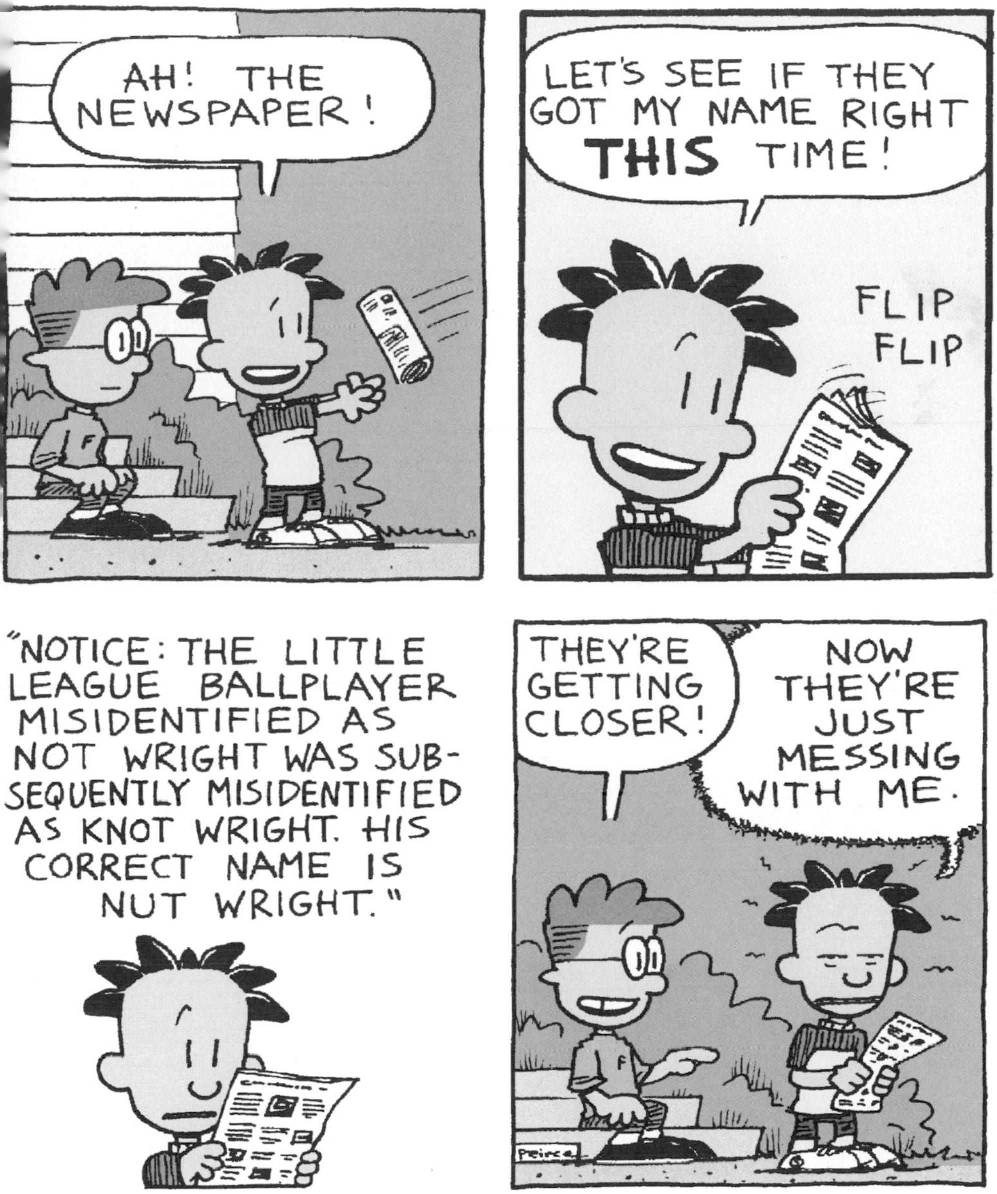
AH! THE NEWSPAPER!
LET'S SEE IF THEY GOT MY NAME RIGHT **THIS** TIME!
FLIP FLIP
"NOTICE: THE LITTLE LEAGUE BALLPLAYER MISIDENTIFIED AS NOT WRIGHT WAS SUBSEQUENTLY MISIDENTIFIED AS KNOT WRIGHT. HIS CORRECT NAME IS NUT WRIGHT."
THEY'RE GETTING CLOSER!
NOW THEY'RE JUST MESSING WITH ME.

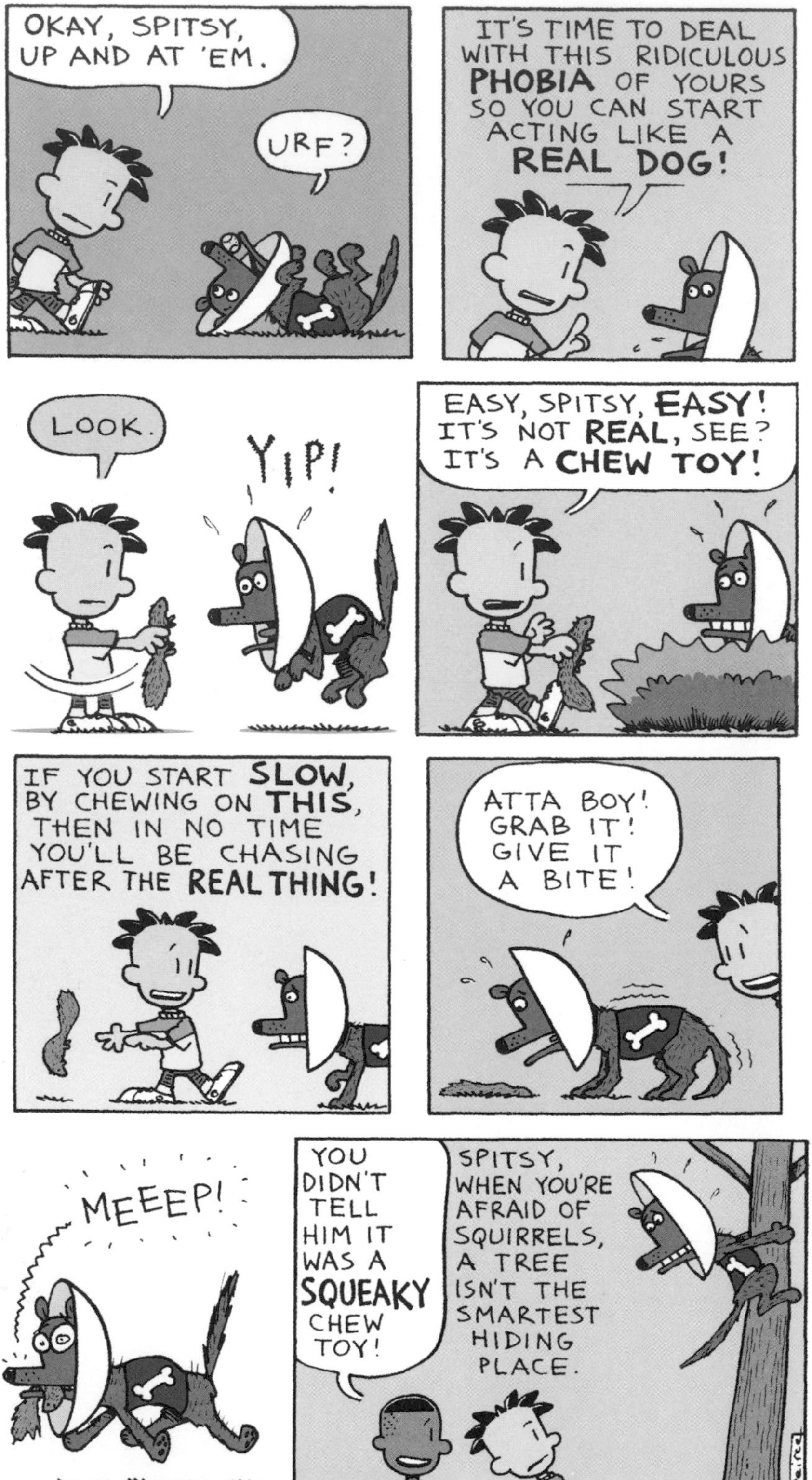
OKAY, SPITSY, UP AND AT 'EM.
URF?
IT'S TIME TO DEAL WITH THIS RIDICULOUS PHOBIA OF YOURS SO YOU CAN START ACTING LIKE A REAL DOG!
LOOK.
YIP!
EASY, SPITSY, EASY! IT'S NOT REAL, SEE? IT'S A CHEW TOY!
IF YOU START SLOW, BY CHEWING ON THIS, THEN IN NO TIME YOU'LL BE CHASING AFTER THE REAL THING!
ATTA BOY! GRAB IT! GIVE IT A BITE!
MEEEP!
YOU DIDN'T TELL HIM IT WAS A SQUEAKY CHEW TOY!
SPITSY, WHEN YOU'RE AFRAID OF SQUIRRELS, A TREE ISN'T THE SMARTEST HIDING PLACE.
Peirce

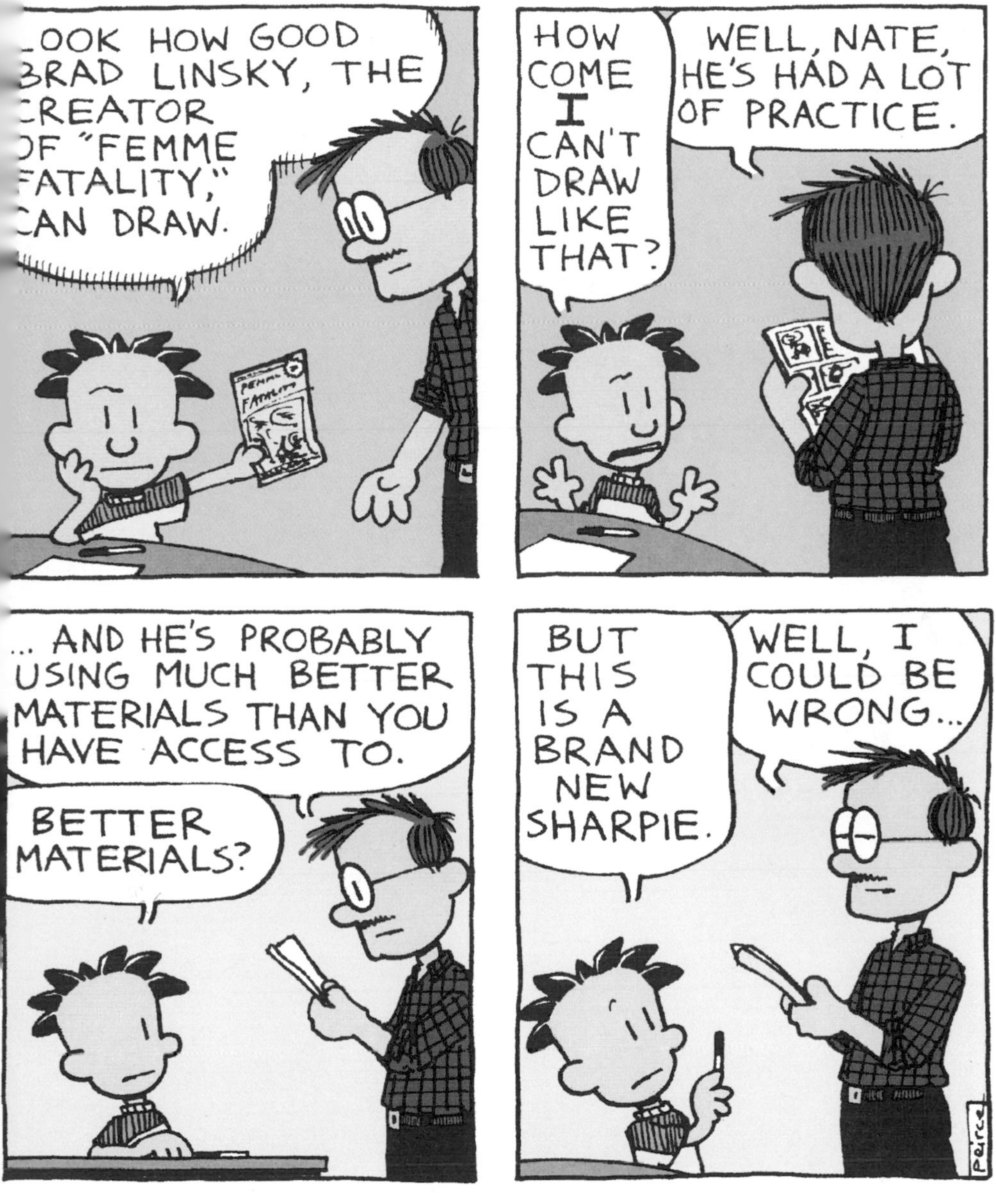
LOOK HOW GOOD BRAD LINSKY, THE CREATOR OF "FEMME FATALITY," CAN DRAW.
HOW COME I CAN'T DRAW LIKE THAT?
WELL, NATE, HE'S HAD A LOT OF PRACTICE.
... AND HE'S PROBABLY USING MUCH BETTER MATERIALS THAN YOU HAVE ACCESS TO.
BETTER MATERIALS?
BUT THIS IS A BRAND NEW SHARPIE.
WELL, I COULD BE WRONG...
peirce

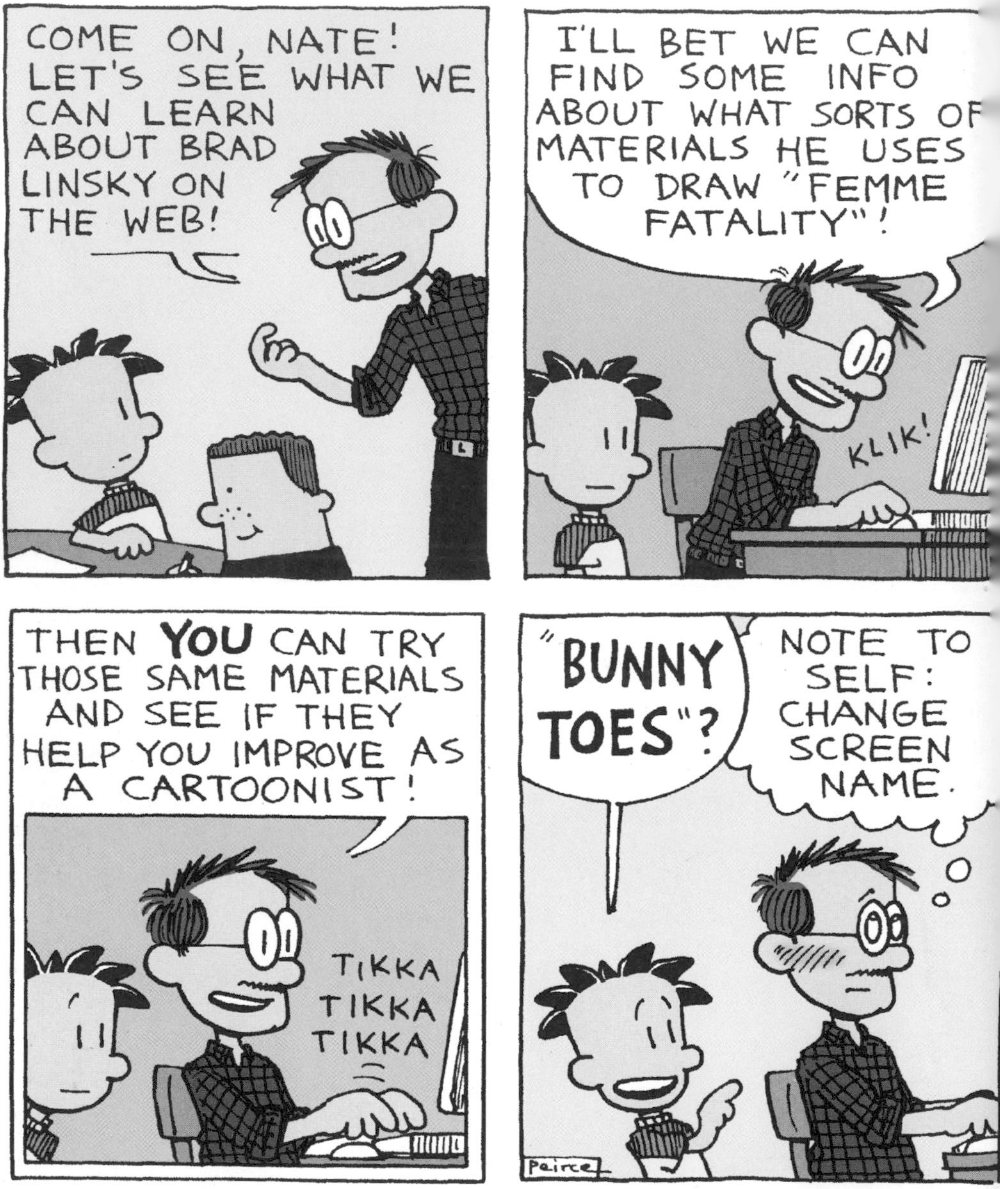
COME ON, NATE! LET'S SEE WHAT WE CAN LEARN ABOUT BRAD LINSKY ON THE WEB!
I'LL BET WE CAN FIND SOME INFO ABOUT WHAT SORTS OF MATERIALS HE USES TO DRAW "FEMME FATALITY"!
KLIK!
THEN **YOU** CAN TRY THOSE SAME MATERIALS AND SEE IF THEY HELP YOU IMPROVE AS A CARTOONIST!
TIKKA TIKKA TIKKA
"BUNNY TOES"?
NOTE TO SELF: CHANGE SCREEN NAME.
Peirce

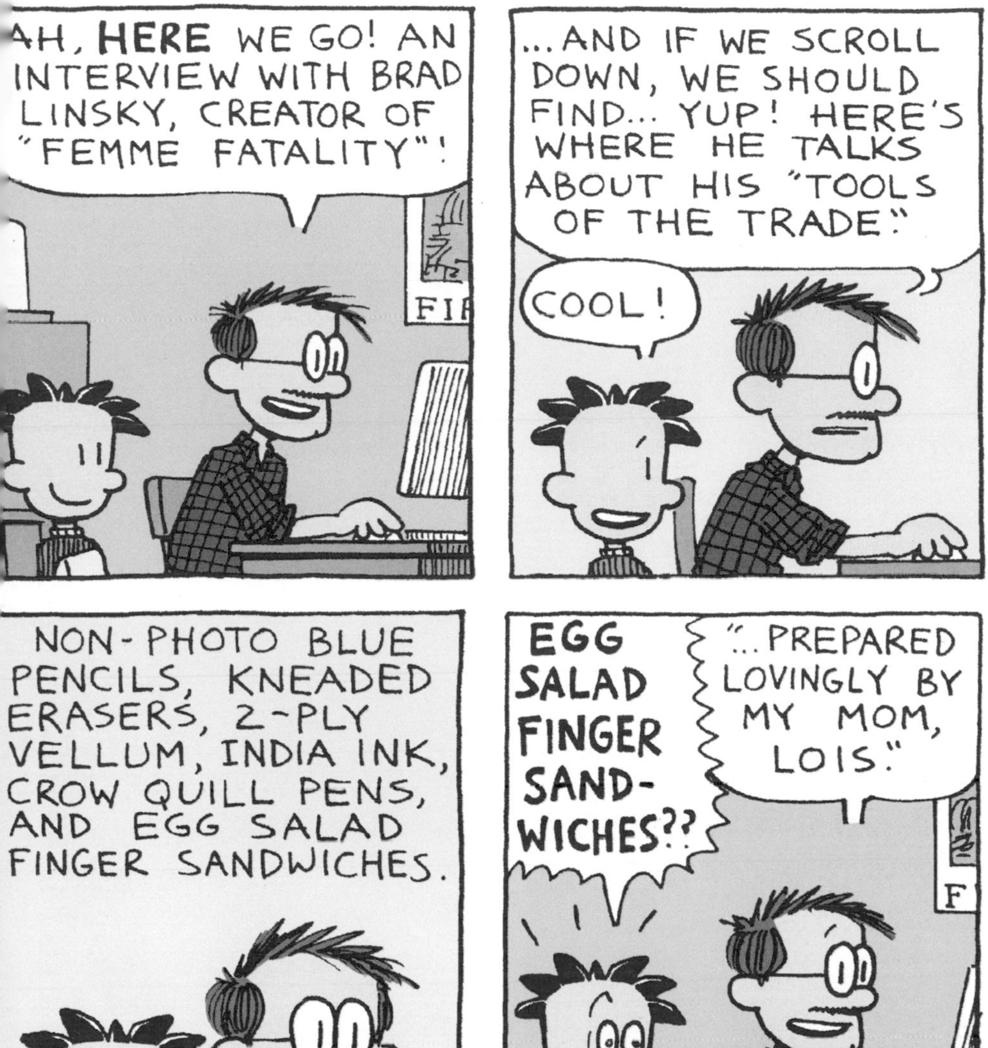
AH, **HERE** WE GO! AN INTERVIEW WITH BRAD LINSKY, CREATOR OF "FEMME FATALITY"!
...AND IF WE SCROLL DOWN, WE SHOULD FIND... YUP! HERE'S WHERE HE TALKS ABOUT HIS "TOOLS OF THE TRADE."
COOL!
NON-PHOTO BLUE PENCILS, KNEADED ERASERS, 2-PLY VELLUM, INDIA INK, CROW QUILL PENS, AND EGG SALAD FINGER SANDWICHES.
EGG SALAD FINGER SAND-WICHES??
"...PREPARED LOVINGLY BY MY MOM, LOIS."

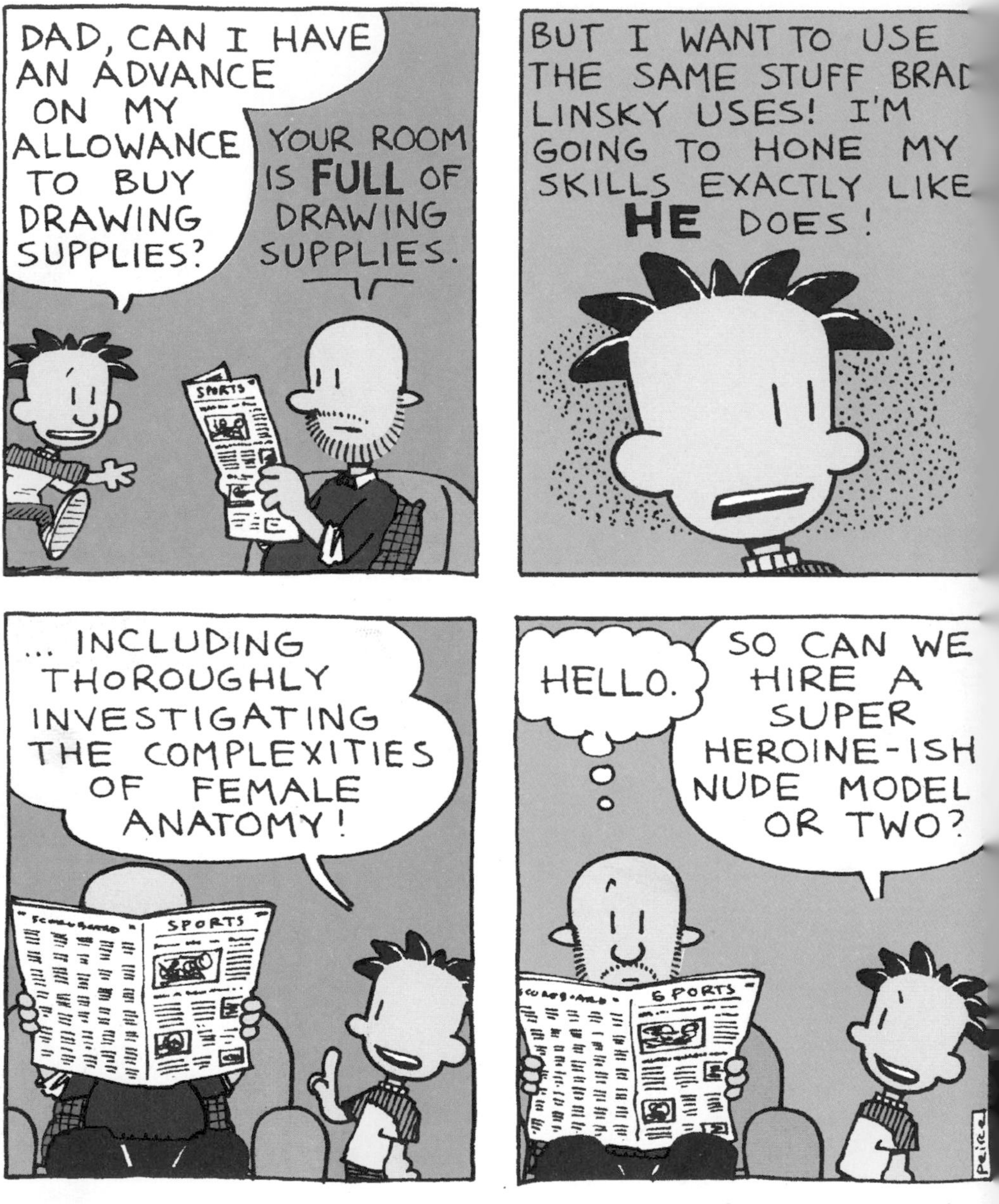
DAD, CAN I HAVE AN ADVANCE ON MY ALLOWANCE TO BUY DRAWING SUPPLIES?
YOUR ROOM IS **FULL** OF DRAWING SUPPLIES.
SPORTS
BUT I WANT TO USE THE SAME STUFF BRAD LINSKY USES! I'M GOING TO HONE MY SKILLS EXACTLY LIKE **HE** DOES!
... INCLUDING THOROUGHLY INVESTIGATING THE COMPLEXITIES OF FEMALE ANATOMY!
SPORTS
HELLO.
SO CAN WE HIRE A SUPER HEROINE-ISH NUDE MODEL OR TWO?
SPORTS
peirce

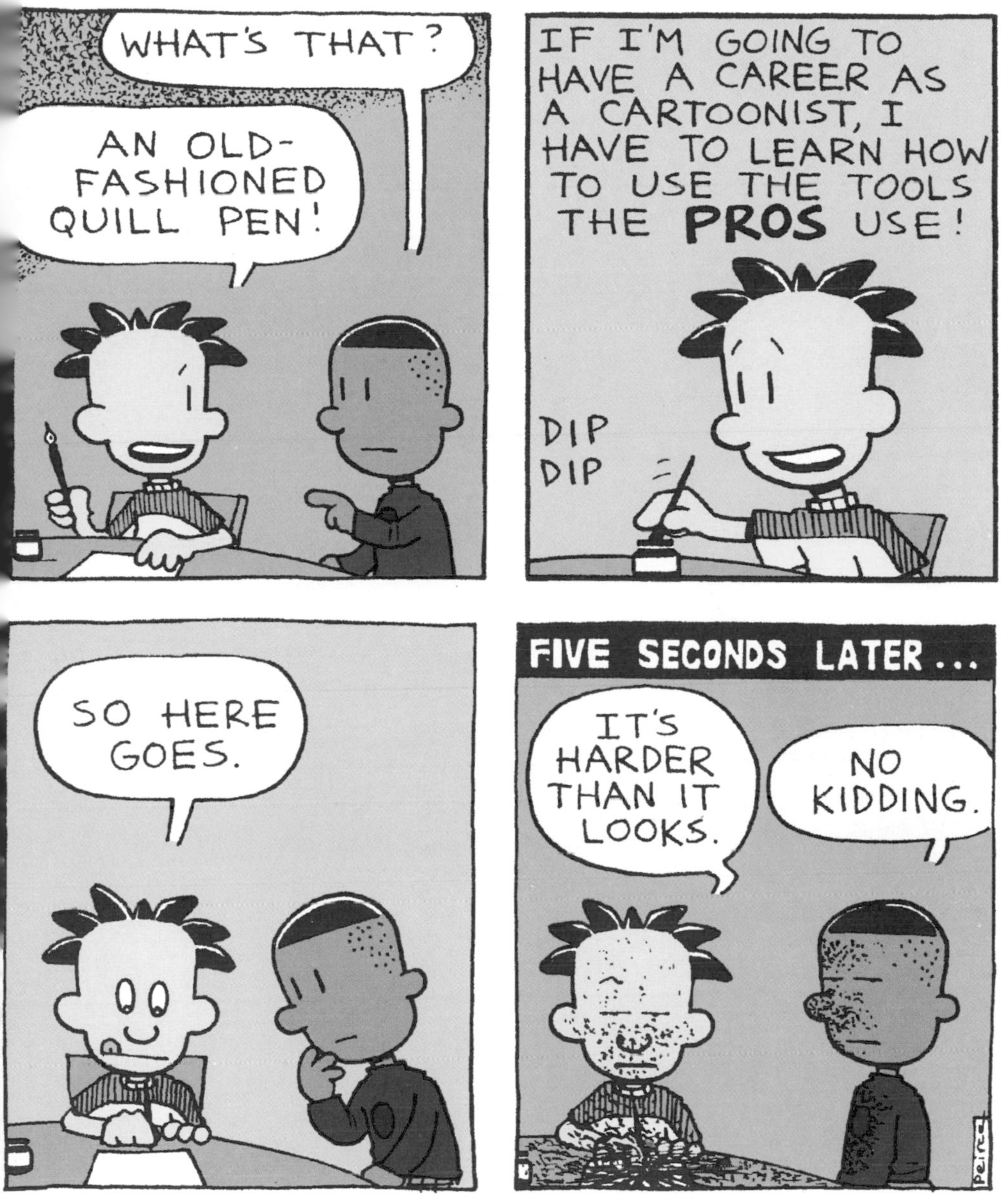
WHAT'S THAT?
AN OLD-FASHIONED QUILL PEN!
IF I'M GOING TO HAVE A CAREER AS A CARTOONIST, I HAVE TO LEARN HOW TO USE THE TOOLS THE **PROS** USE!
DIP DIP
SO HERE GOES.
FIVE SECONDS LATER...
IT'S HARDER THAN IT LOOKS.
NO KIDDING.
Peirce

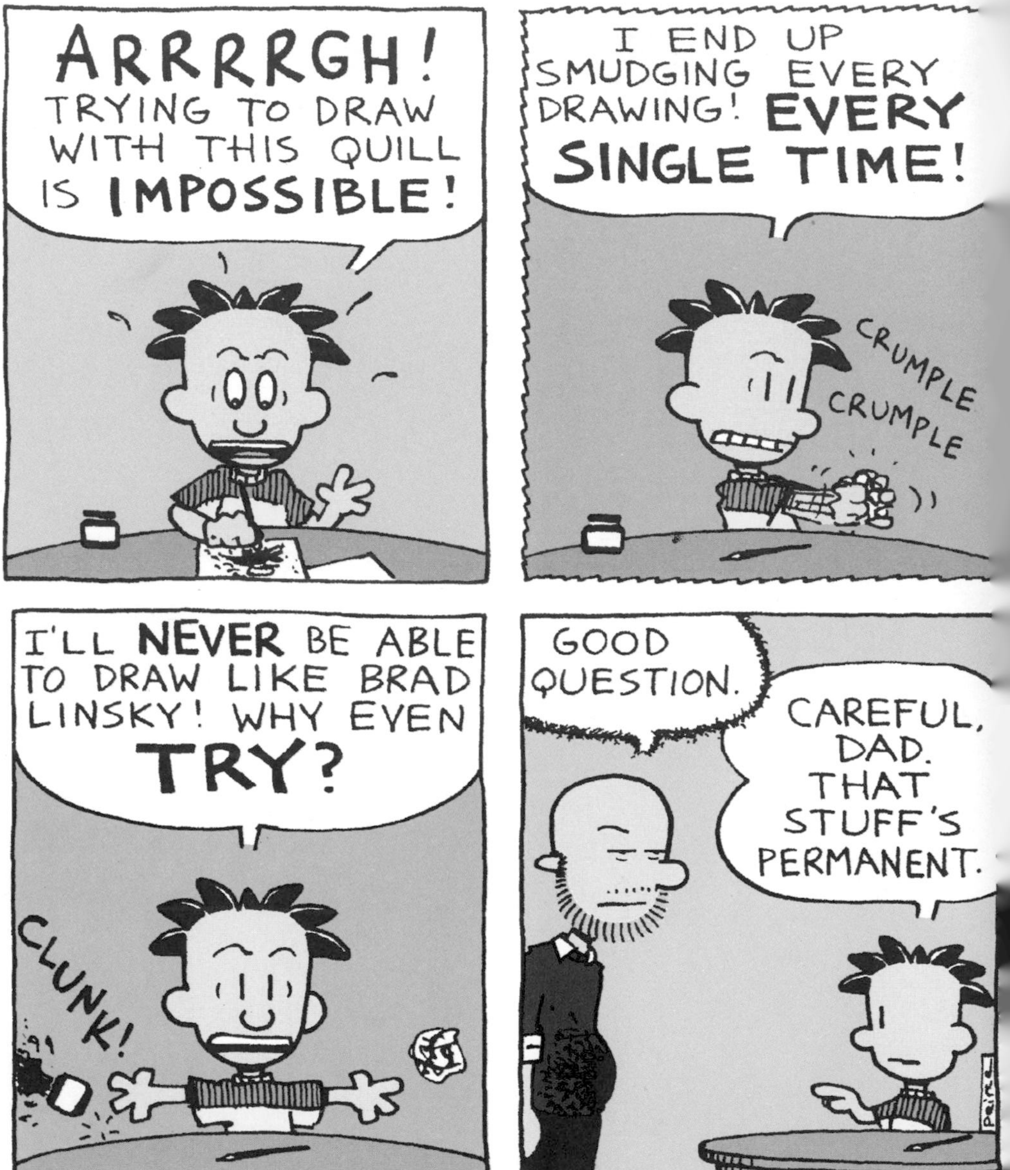
ARRRRRGH! TRYING TO DRAW WITH THIS QUILL IS IMPOSSIBLE!
I END UP SMUDGING EVERY DRAWING! EVERY SINGLE TIME!
CRUMPLE
CRUMPLE
I'LL NEVER BE ABLE TO DRAW LIKE BRAD LINSKY! WHY EVEN TRY?
CLUNK!
GOOD QUESTION.
CAREFUL, DAD. THAT STUFF'S PERMANENT.

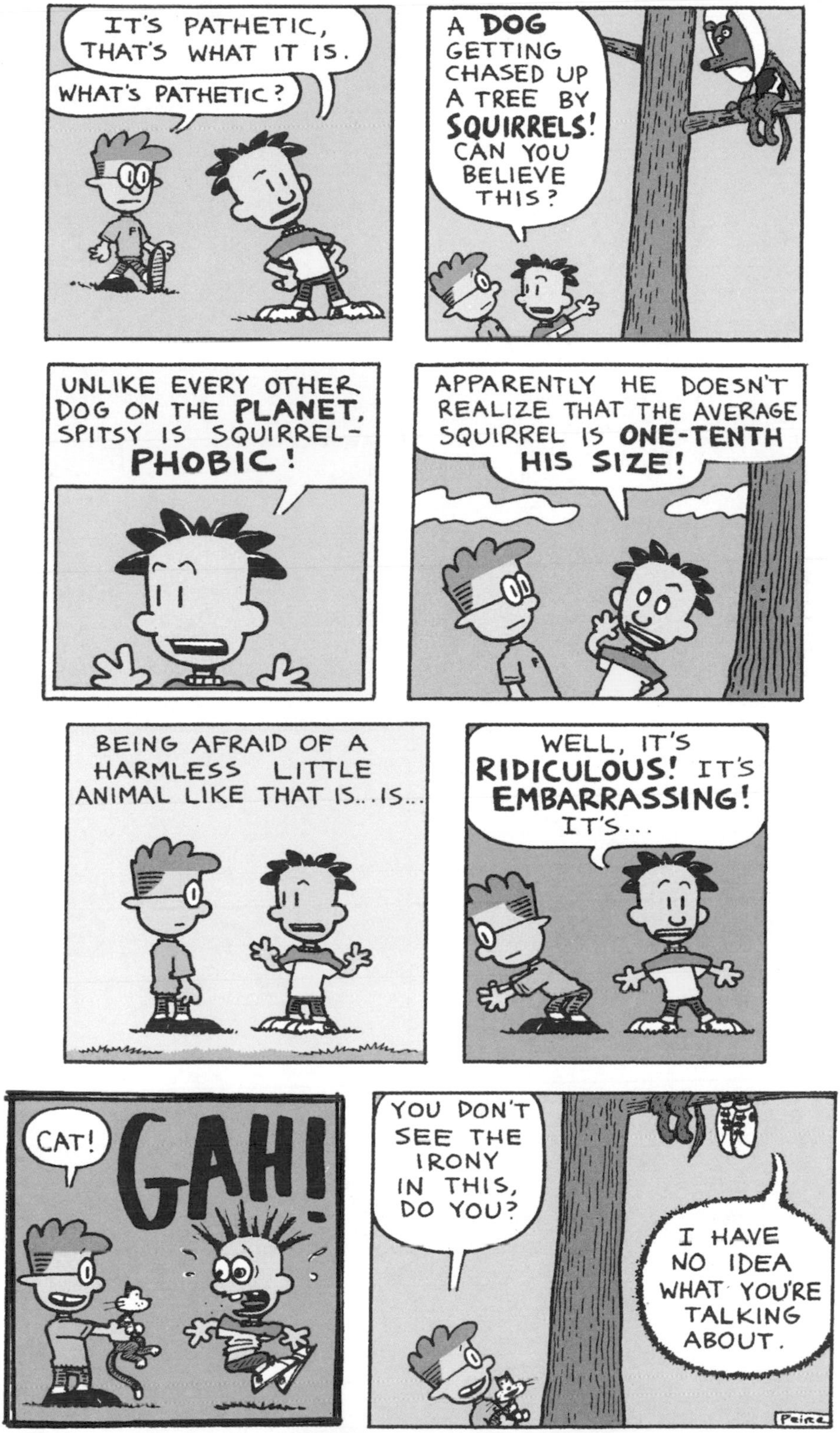
IT'S PATHETIC, THAT'S WHAT IT IS.
WHAT'S PATHETIC?
A DOG GETTING CHASED UP A TREE BY SQUIRRELS! CAN YOU BELIEVE THIS?
UNLIKE EVERY OTHER DOG ON THE PLANET, SPITSY IS SQUIRREL-PHOBIC!
APPARENTLY HE DOESN'T REALIZE THAT THE AVERAGE SQUIRREL IS ONE-TENTH HIS SIZE!
BEING AFRAID OF A HARMLESS LITTLE ANIMAL LIKE THAT IS... IS...
WELL, IT'S RIDICULOUS! IT'S EMBARRASSING! IT'S...
CAT!
GAH!
YOU DON'T SEE THE IRONY IN THIS, DO YOU?
I HAVE NO IDEA WHAT YOU'RE TALKING ABOUT.
Peirce

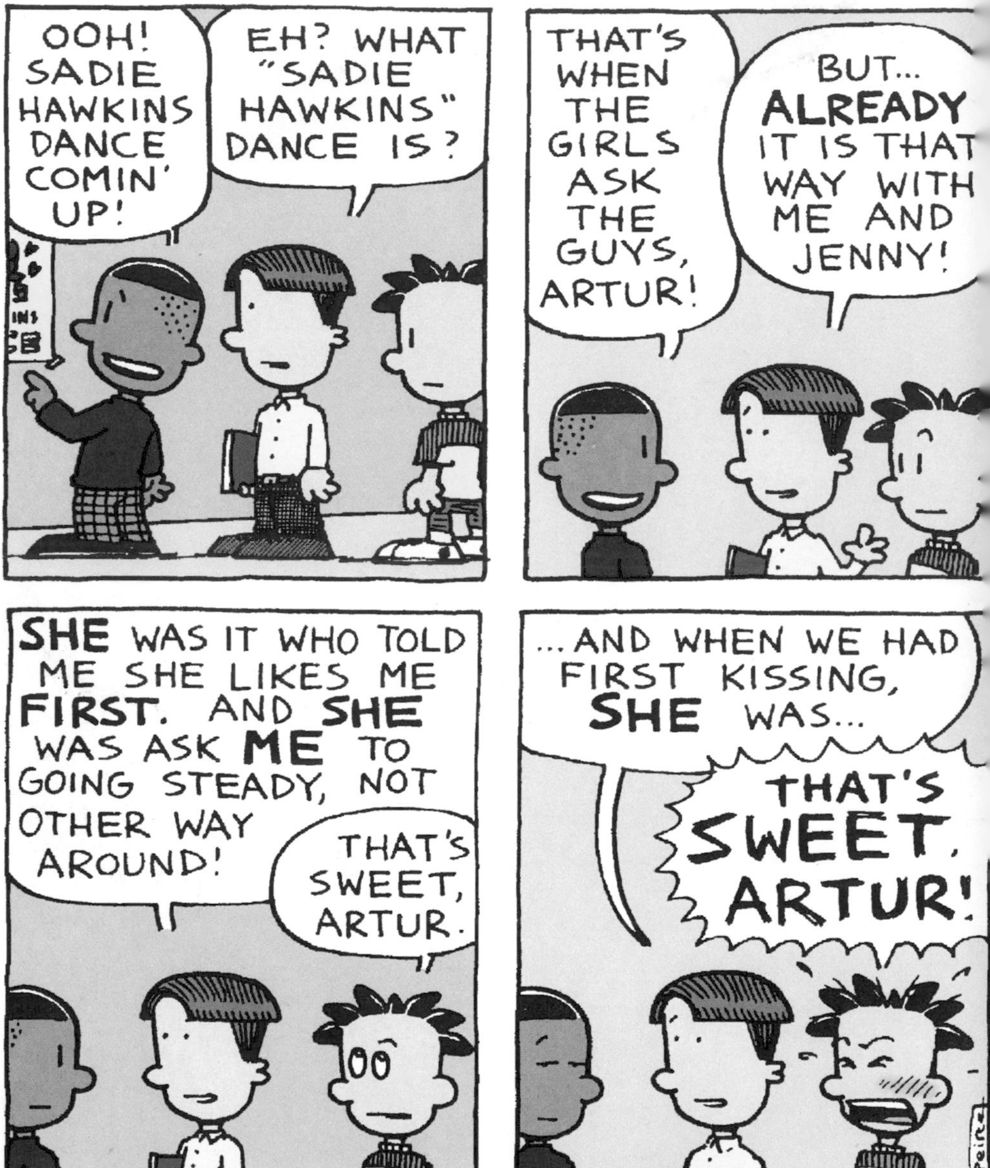
OOH! SADIE HAWKINS DANCE COMIN' UP!
EH? WHAT "SADIE HAWKINS" DANCE IS?
THAT'S WHEN THE GIRLS ASK THE GUYS, ARTUR!
BUT... ALREADY IT IS THAT WAY WITH ME AND JENNY!
SHE WAS IT WHO TOLD ME SHE LIKES ME FIRST. AND SHE WAS ASK ME TO GOING STEADY, NOT OTHER WAY AROUND!
THAT'S SWEET, ARTUR.
...AND WHEN WE HAD FIRST KISSING, SHE WAS...
THAT'S SWEET, ARTUR!

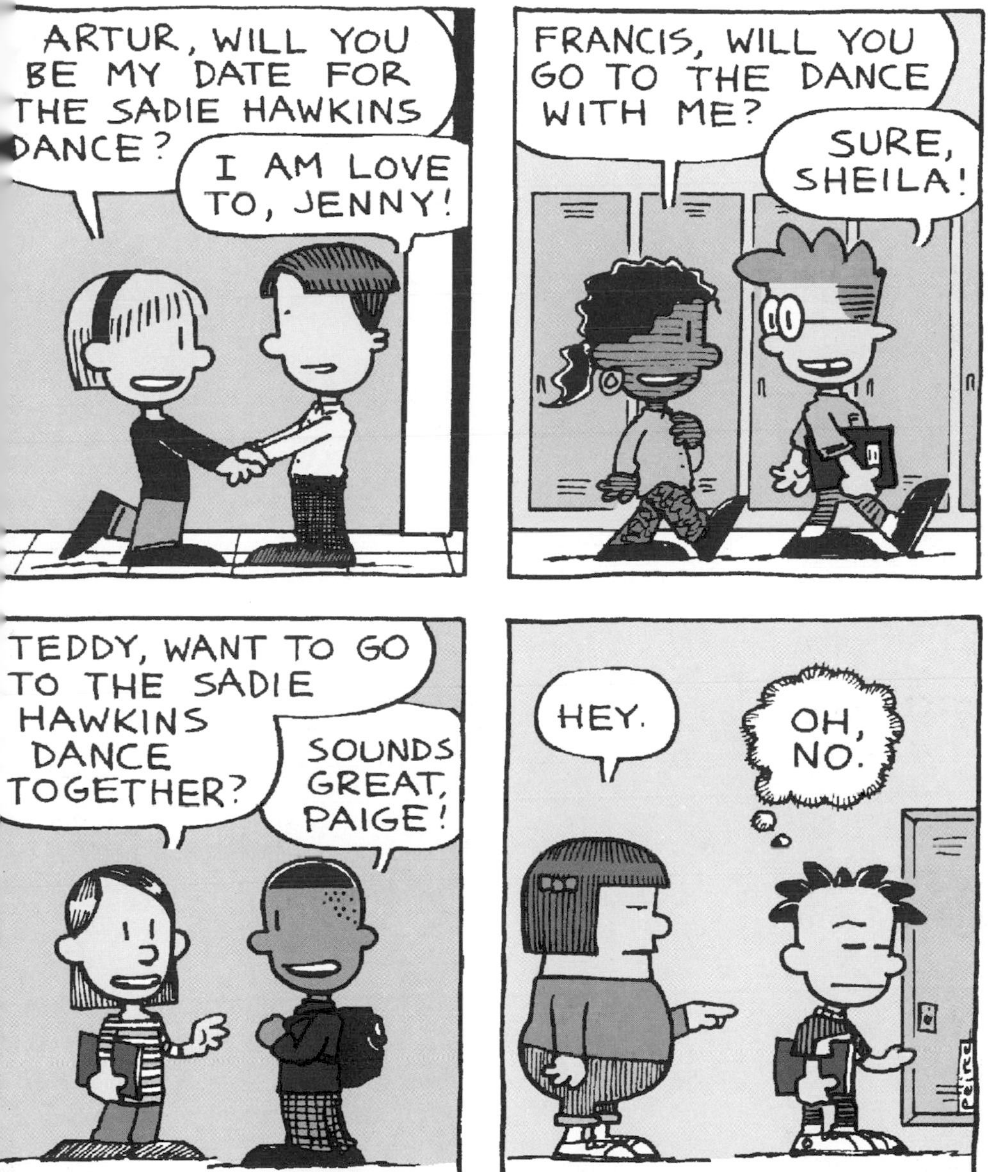
ARTUR, WILL YOU BE MY DATE FOR THE SADIE HAWKINS DANCE?
I AM LOVE TO, JENNY!
FRANCIS, WILL YOU GO TO THE DANCE WITH ME?
SURE, SHEILA!
TEDDY, WANT TO GO TO THE SADIE HAWKINS DANCE TOGETHER?
SOUNDS GREAT, PAIGE!
HEY.
OH, NO.
peirce

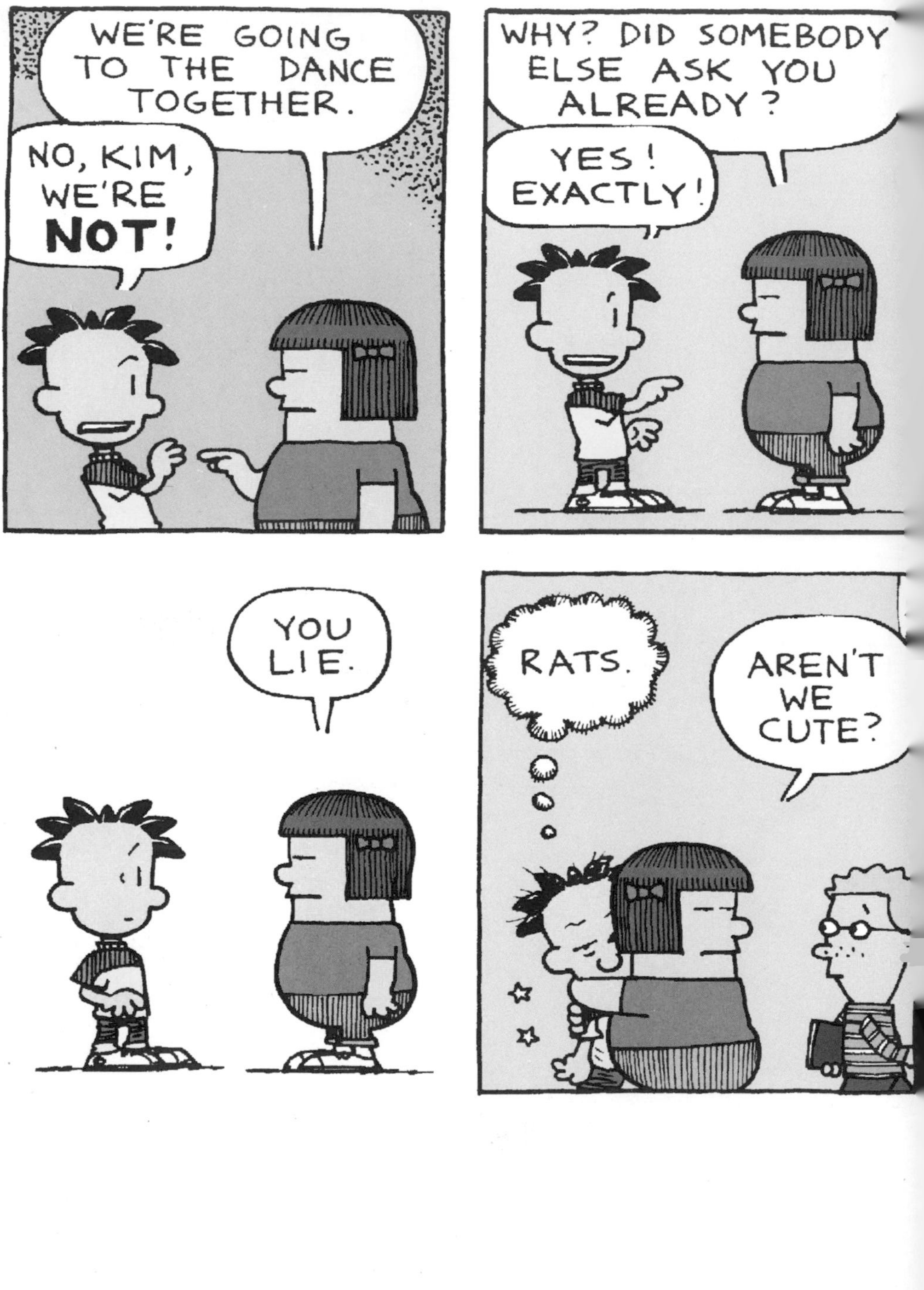
WE'RE GOING TO THE DANCE TOGETHER.
NO, KIM, WE'RE **NOT**!
WHY? DID SOMEBODY ELSE ASK YOU ALREADY?
YES! EXACTLY!
YOU LIE.
RATS.
AREN'T WE CUTE?

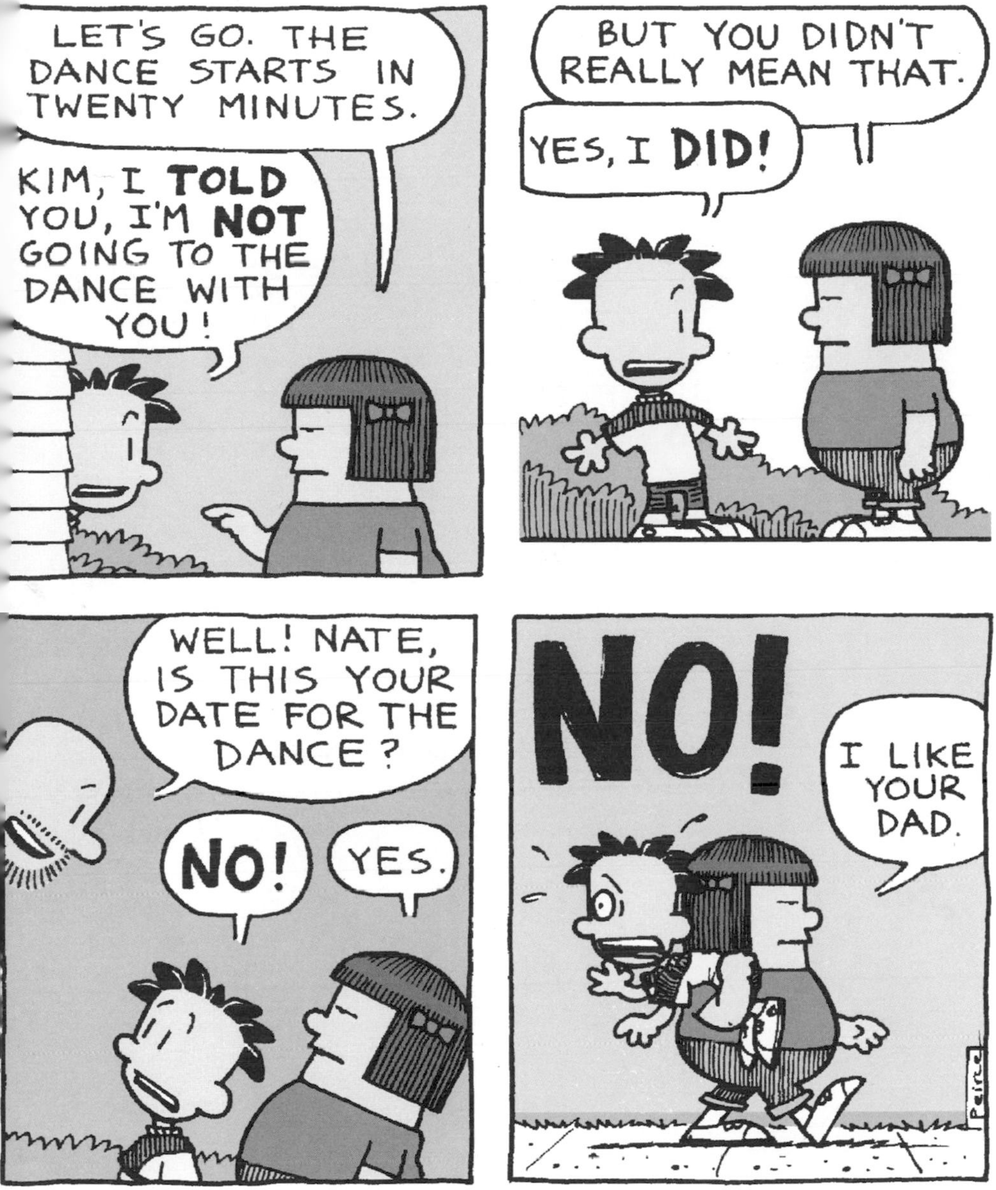
LET'S GO. THE DANCE STARTS IN TWENTY MINUTES.
KIM, I **TOLD** YOU, I'M **NOT** GOING TO THE DANCE WITH YOU!
BUT YOU DIDN'T REALLY MEAN THAT.
YES, I **DID**!
WELL! NATE, IS THIS YOUR DATE FOR THE DANCE?
NO!
YES.
NO!
I LIKE YOUR DAD.
Peirce

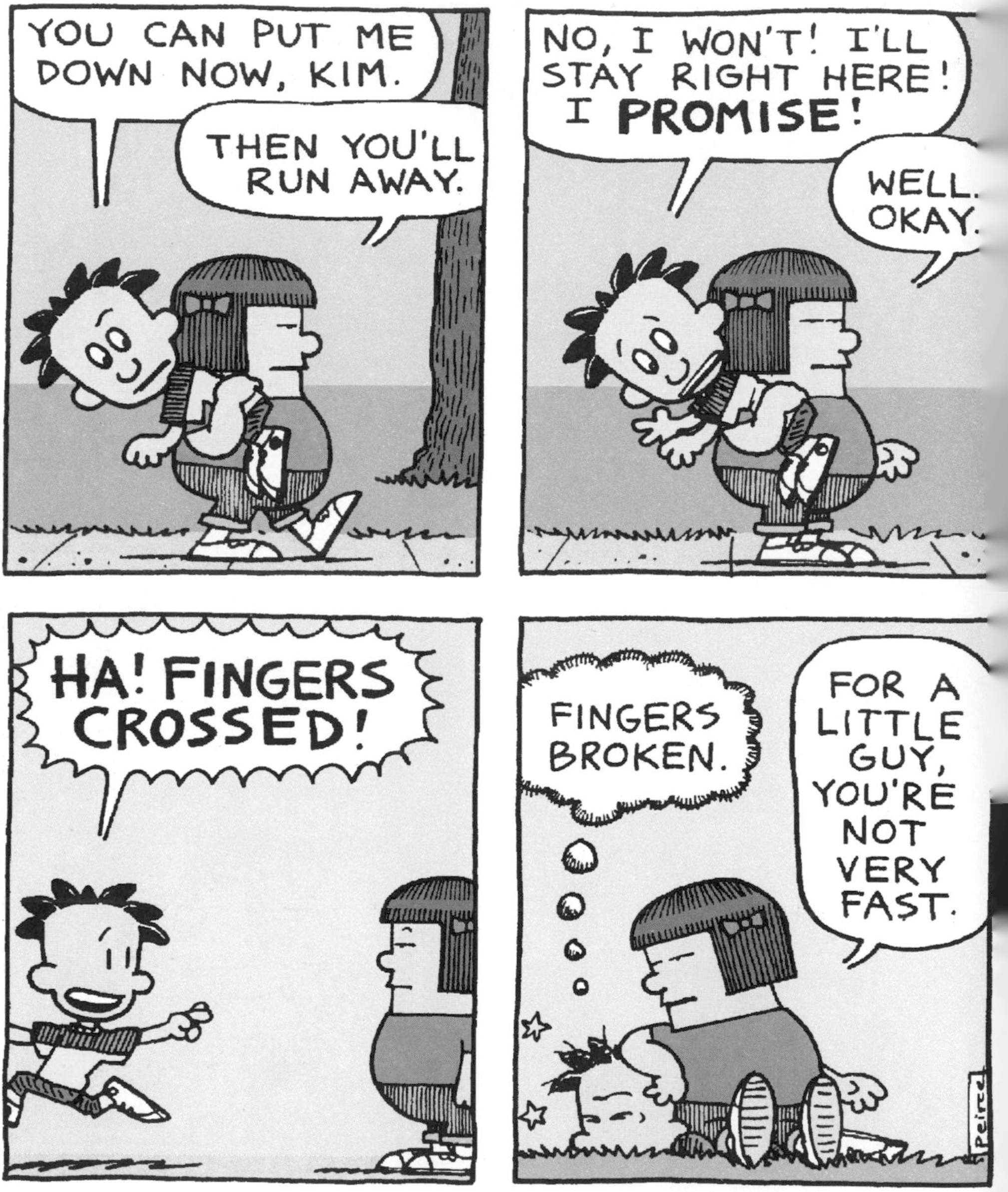
YOU CAN PUT ME DOWN NOW, KIM.
THEN YOU'LL RUN AWAY.
NO, I WON'T! I'LL STAY RIGHT HERE! I **PROMISE**!
WELL. OKAY.
HA! FINGERS CROSSED!
FINGERS BROKEN.
FOR A LITTLE GUY, YOU'RE NOT VERY FAST.
Peirce

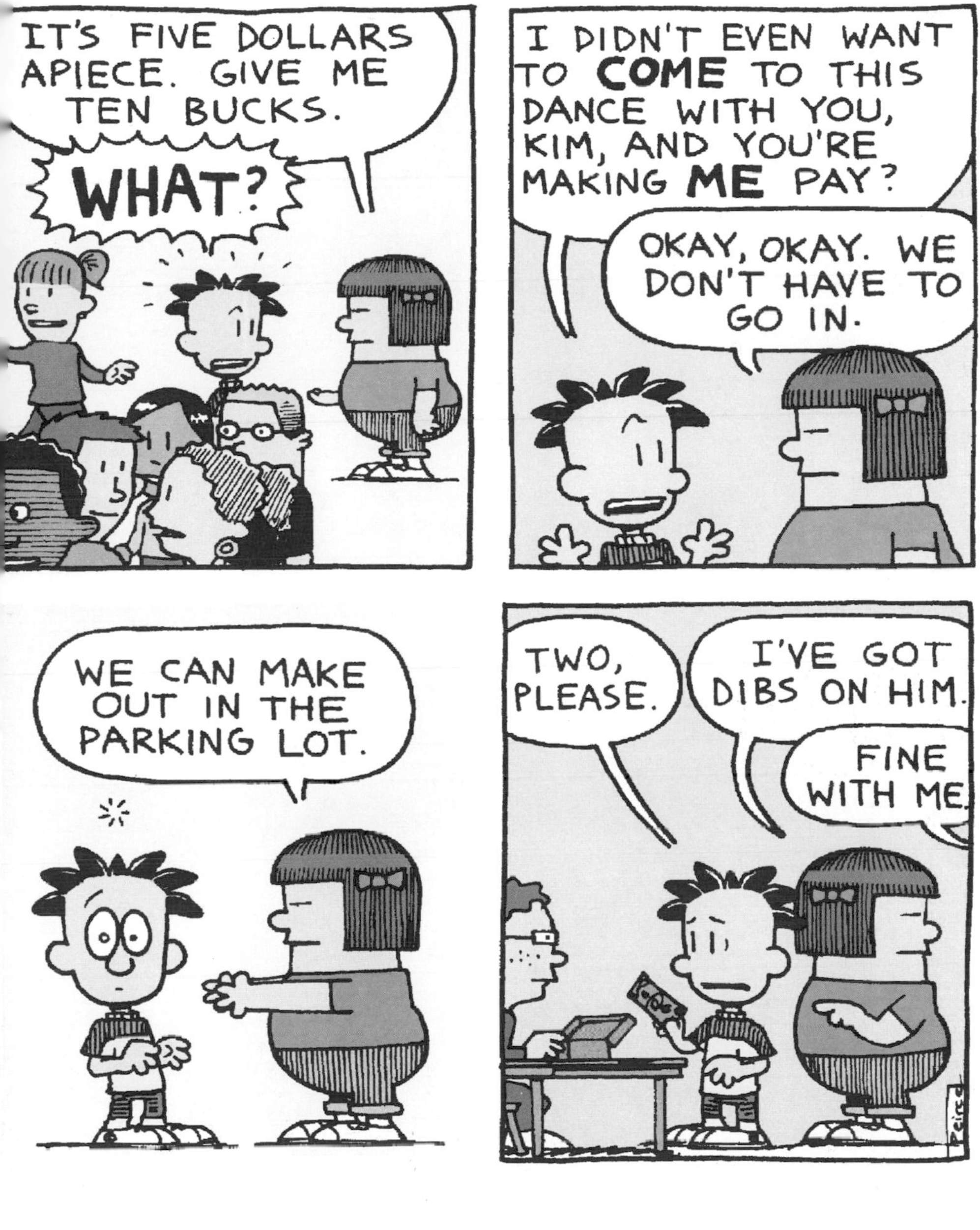
IT'S FIVE DOLLARS APIECE. GIVE ME TEN BUCKS.
WHAT?
I DIDN'T EVEN WANT TO COME TO THIS DANCE WITH YOU, KIM, AND YOU'RE MAKING ME PAY?
OKAY, OKAY. WE DON'T HAVE TO GO IN.
WE CAN MAKE OUT IN THE PARKING LOT.
TWO, PLEASE.
I'VE GOT DIBS ON HIM.
FINE WITH ME.

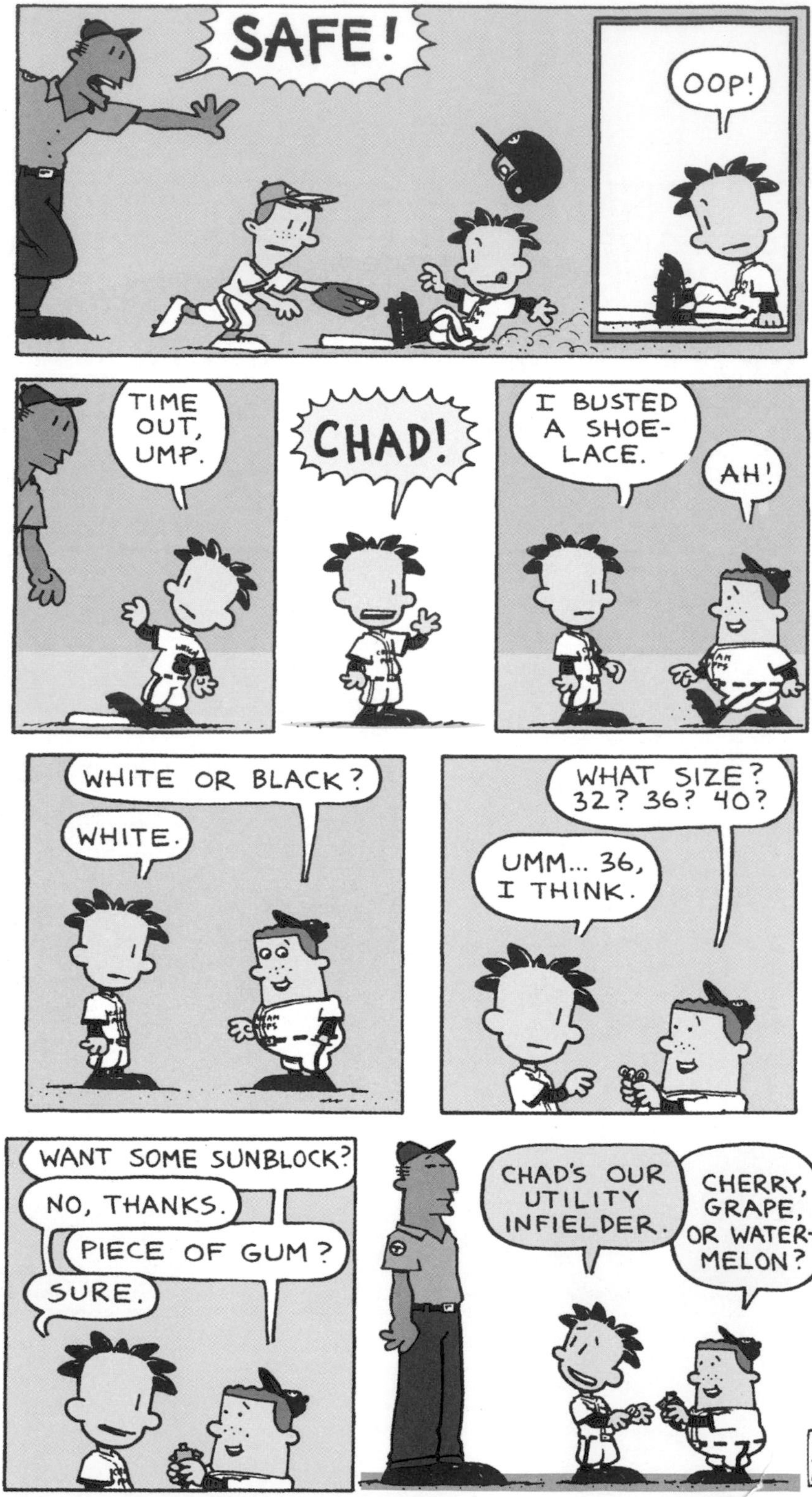
SAFE!
OOP!
TIME OUT, UMP.
CHAD!
I BUSTED A SHOE-LACE.
AH!
WHITE OR BLACK?
WHITE.
WHAT SIZE? 32? 36? 40?
UMM... 36, I THINK.
WANT SOME SUNBLOCK?
NO, THANKS.
PIECE OF GUM?
SURE.
CHAD'S OUR UTILITY INFIELDER.
CHERRY, GRAPE, OR WATER-MELON?
Peirce

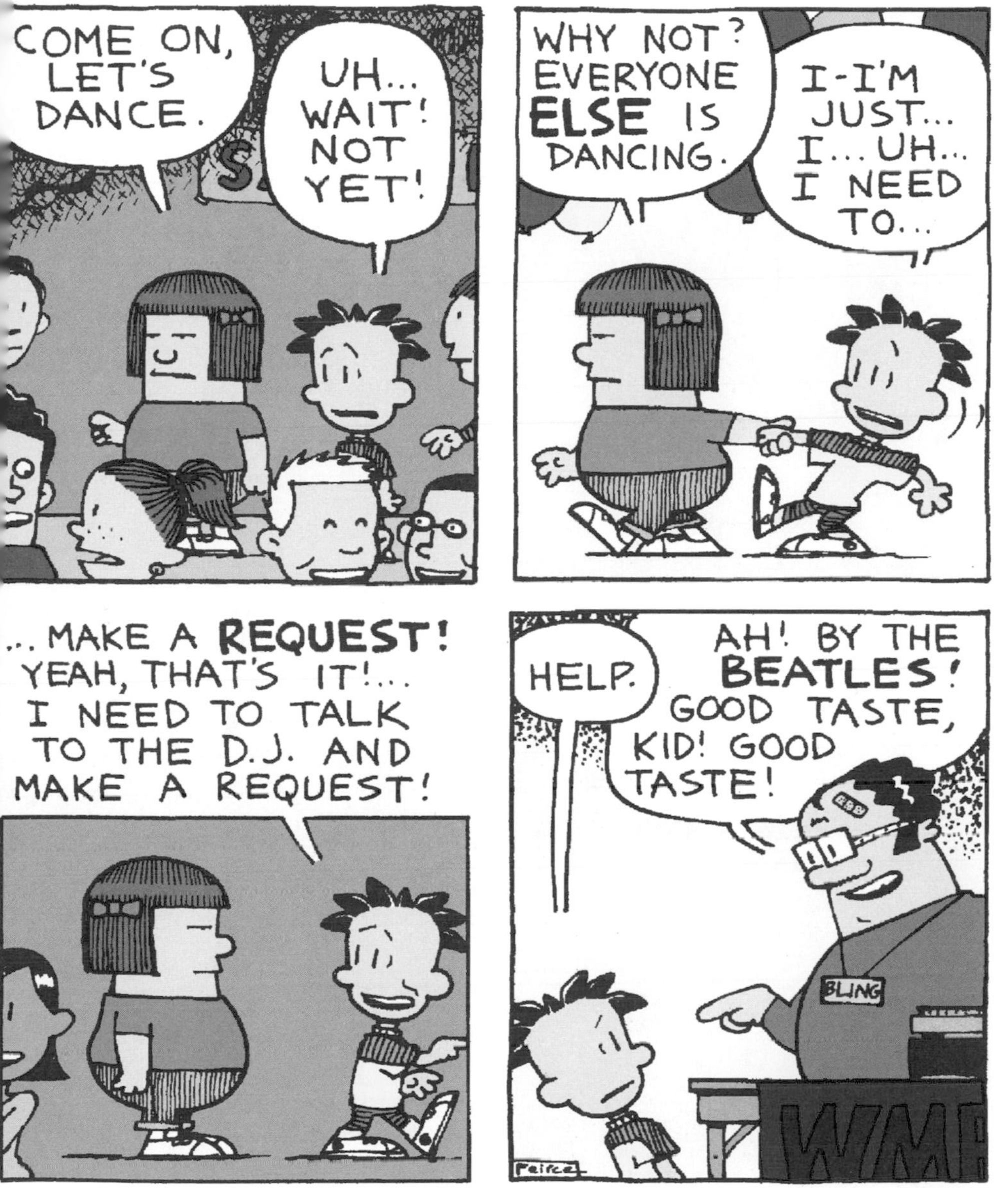
COME ON, LET'S DANCE.
UH... WAIT! NOT YET!
WHY NOT? EVERYONE **ELSE** IS DANCING.
I-I'M JUST... I... UH... I NEED TO...
... MAKE A **REQUEST!** YEAH, THAT'S IT!... I NEED TO TALK TO THE D.J. AND MAKE A REQUEST!
HELP.
AH! BY THE **BEATLES!** GOOD TASTE, KID! GOOD TASTE!
BLING
Peirce

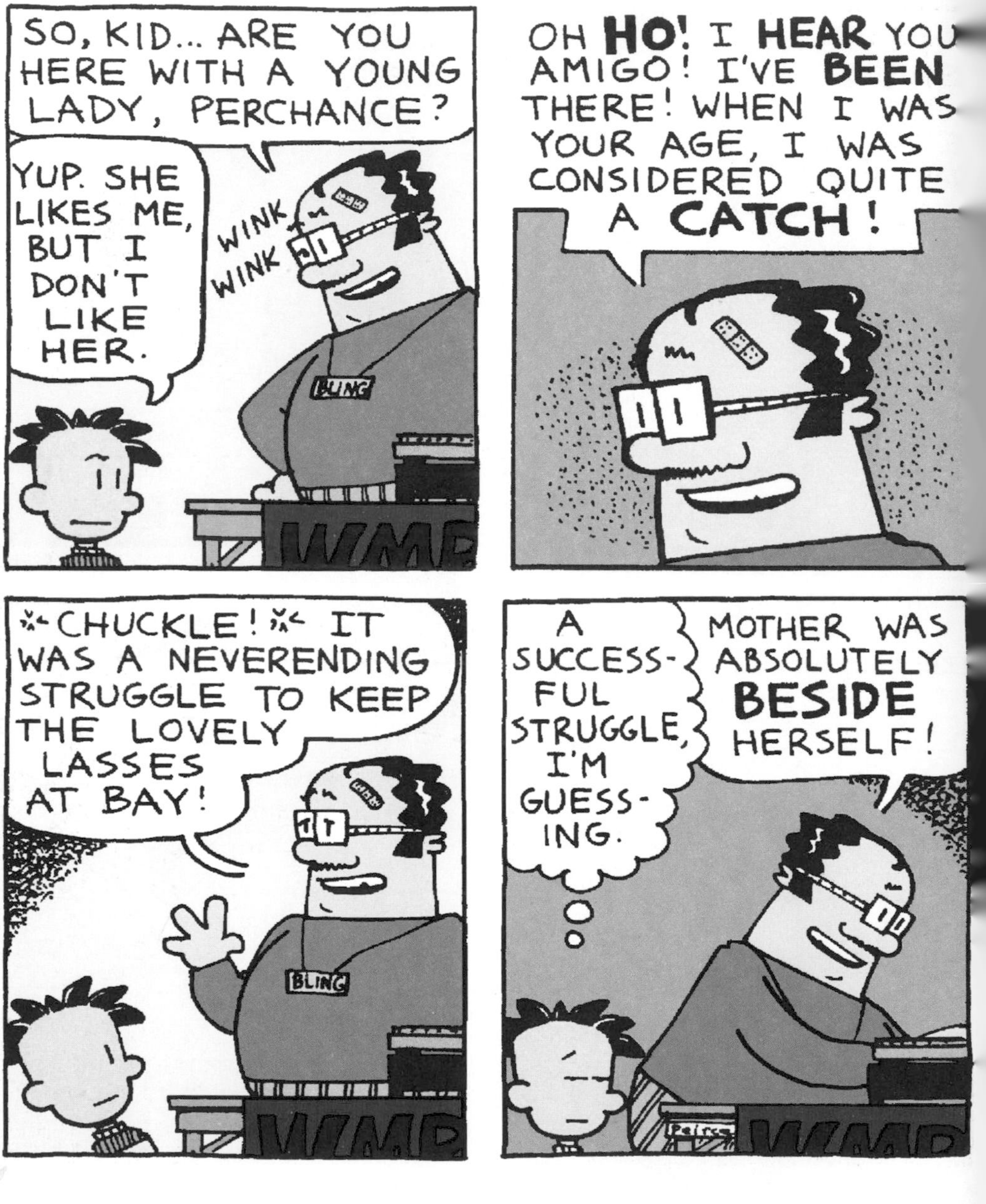
SO, KID... ARE YOU HERE WITH A YOUNG LADY, PERCHANCE?
YUP. SHE LIKES ME, BUT I DON'T LIKE HER.
WINK WINK
BLING
OH HO! I HEAR YOU AMIGO! I'VE BEEN THERE! WHEN I WAS YOUR AGE, I WAS CONSIDERED QUITE A CATCH!
CHUCKLE! IT WAS A NEVERENDING STRUGGLE TO KEEP THE LOVELY LASSES AT BAY!
BLING
A SUCCESSFUL STRUGGLE, I'M GUESSING.
MOTHER WAS ABSOLUTELY BESIDE HERSELF!

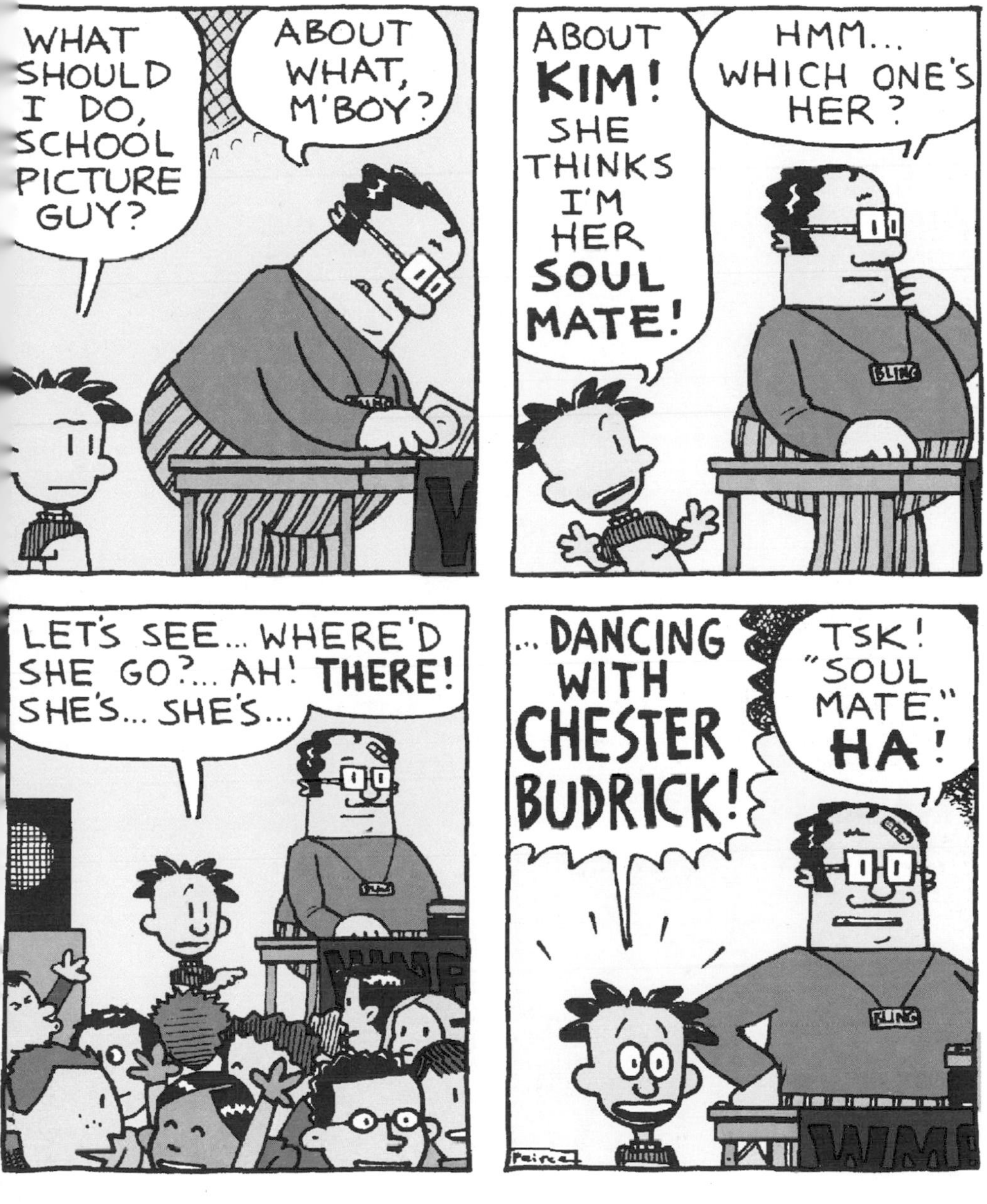
WHAT SHOULD I DO, SCHOOL PICTURE GUY?
ABOUT WHAT, M'BOY?
ABOUT KIM! SHE THINKS I'M HER SOUL MATE!
HMM... WHICH ONE'S HER?
LET'S SEE... WHERE'D SHE GO?... AH! THERE! SHE'S... SHE'S...
...DANCING WITH CHESTER BUDRICK!
TSK! "SOUL MATE." HA!
BLING
WIMP
Peirce

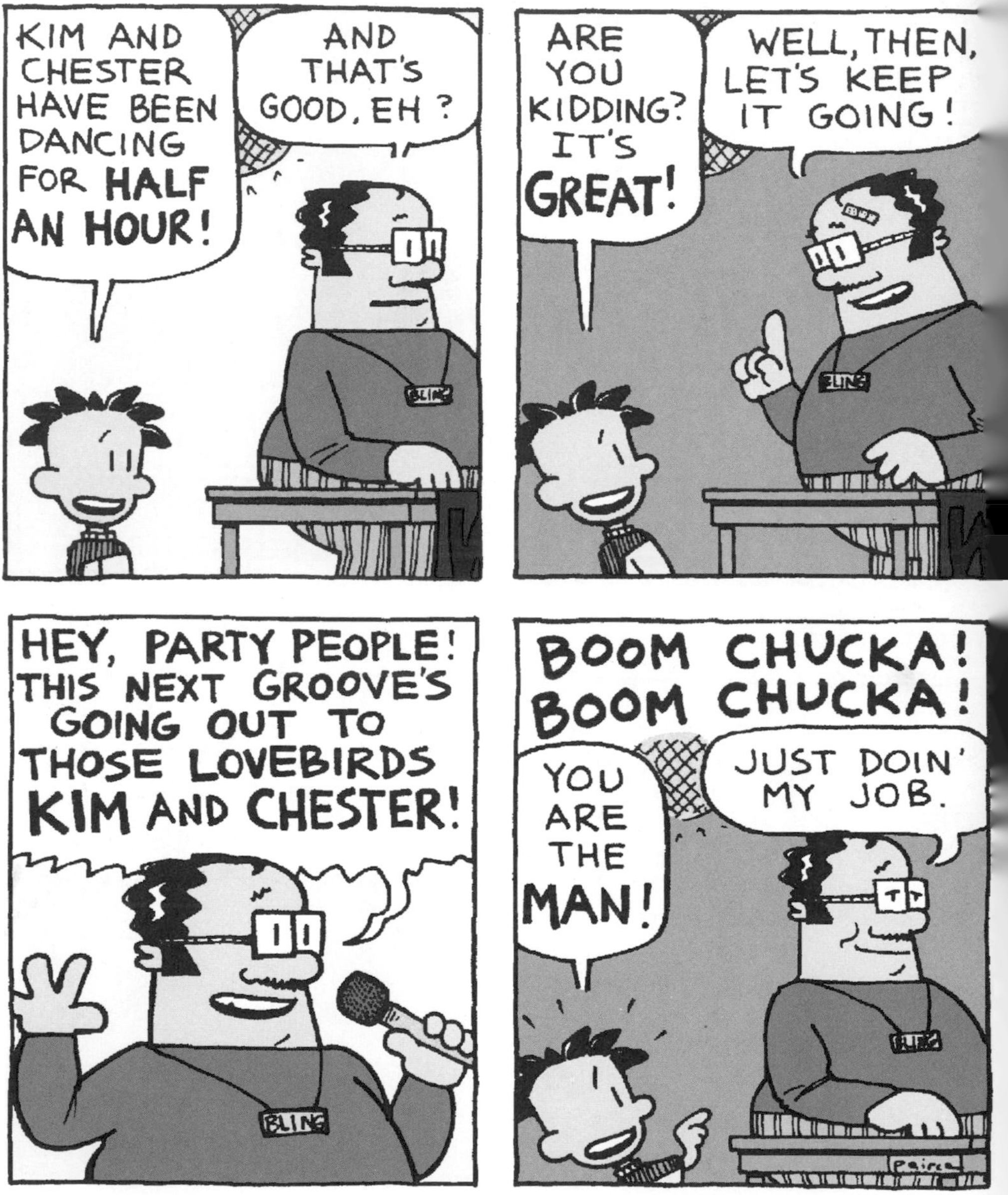
KIM AND CHESTER HAVE BEEN DANCING FOR HALF AN HOUR!
AND THAT'S GOOD, EH?
BLING
ARE YOU KIDDING? IT'S GREAT!
WELL, THEN, LET'S KEEP IT GOING!
BLING
HEY, PARTY PEOPLE! THIS NEXT GROOVE'S GOING OUT TO THOSE LOVEBIRDS KIM AND CHESTER!
BLING
BOOM CHUCKA! BOOM CHUCKA!
YOU ARE THE MAN!
JUST DOIN' MY JOB.
BLING

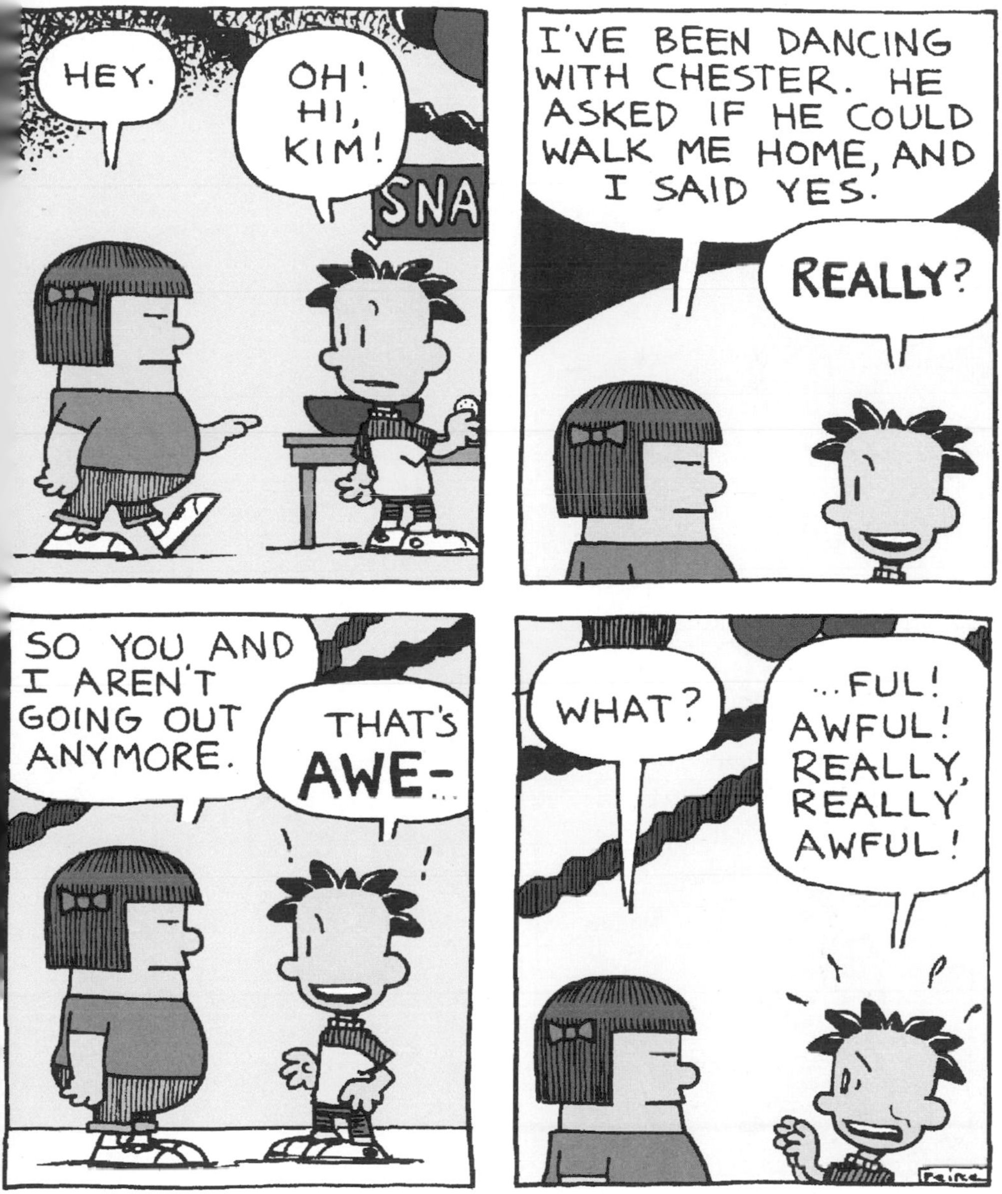
HEY.
OH! HI, KIM!
SNA
I'VE BEEN DANCING WITH CHESTER. HE ASKED IF HE COULD WALK ME HOME, AND I SAID YES.
REALLY?
SO YOU AND I AREN'T GOING OUT ANYMORE.
THAT'S AWE-...
WHAT?
...FUL! AWFUL! REALLY, REALLY AWFUL!

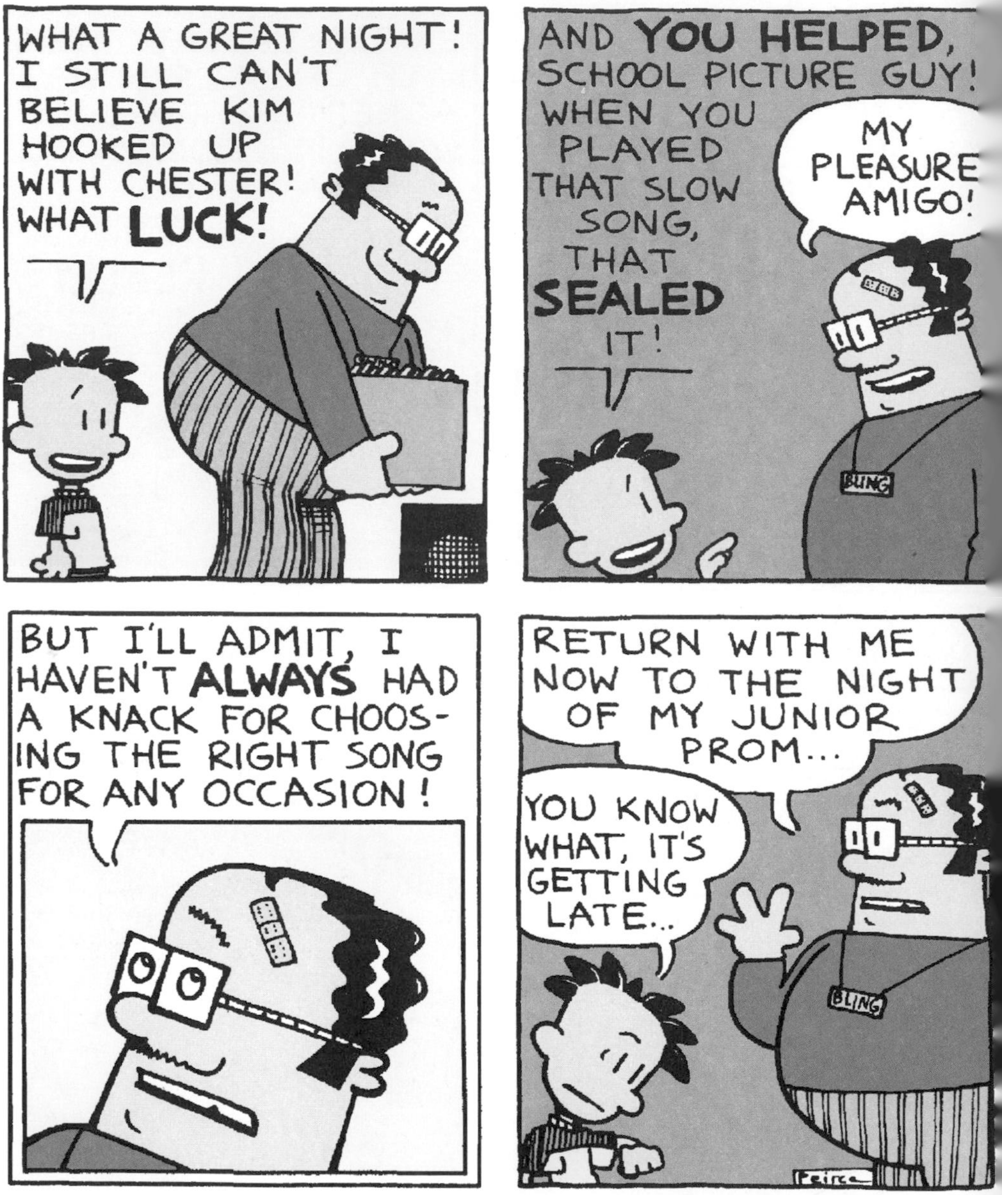
WHAT A GREAT NIGHT! I STILL CAN'T BELIEVE KIM HOOKED UP WITH CHESTER! WHAT LUCK!
AND YOU HELPED, SCHOOL PICTURE GUY! WHEN YOU PLAYED THAT SLOW SONG, THAT SEALED IT!
MY PLEASURE AMIGO!
BLING
BUT I'LL ADMIT, I HAVEN'T ALWAYS HAD A KNACK FOR CHOOSING THE RIGHT SONG FOR ANY OCCASION!
RETURN WITH ME NOW TO THE NIGHT OF MY JUNIOR PROM...
YOU KNOW WHAT, IT'S GETTING LATE...
BLING
Peirce

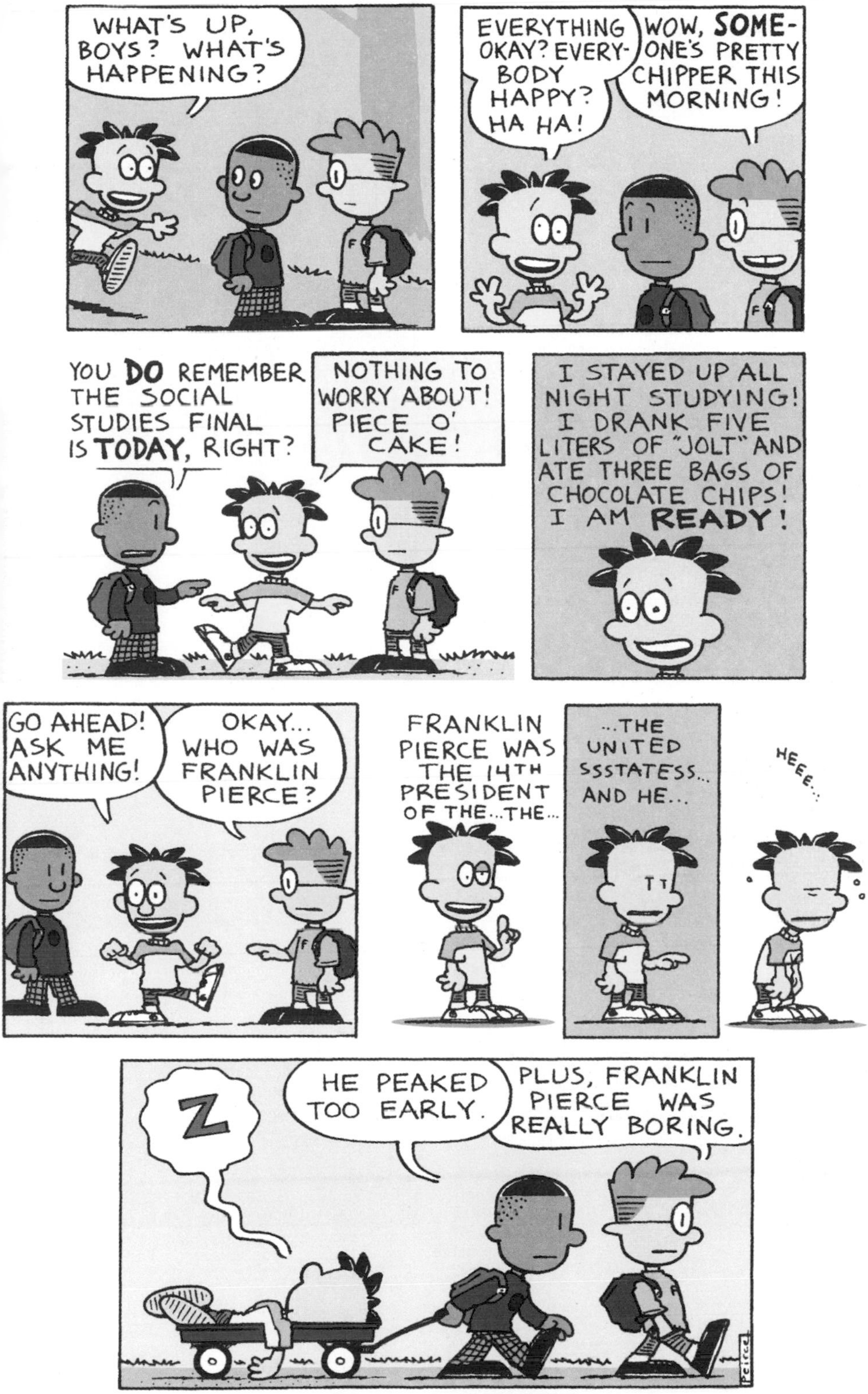
WHAT'S UP, BOYS? WHAT'S HAPPENING?
EVERYTHING OKAY? EVERY-BODY HAPPY? HA HA!
WOW, SOME-ONE'S PRETTY CHIPPER THIS MORNING!
YOU DO REMEMBER THE SOCIAL STUDIES FINAL IS TODAY, RIGHT?
NOTHING TO WORRY ABOUT! PIECE O' CAKE!
I STAYED UP ALL NIGHT STUDYING! I DRANK FIVE LITERS OF "JOLT" AND ATE THREE BAGS OF CHOCOLATE CHIPS! I AM READY!
GO AHEAD! ASK ME ANYTHING!
OKAY... WHO WAS FRANKLIN PIERCE?
FRANKLIN PIERCE WAS THE 14TH PRESIDENT OF THE...THE...
...THE UNITED SSSTATESS... AND HE...
HEEE...
Z
HE PEAKED TOO EARLY.
PLUS, FRANKLIN PIERCE WAS REALLY BORING.
Peirce

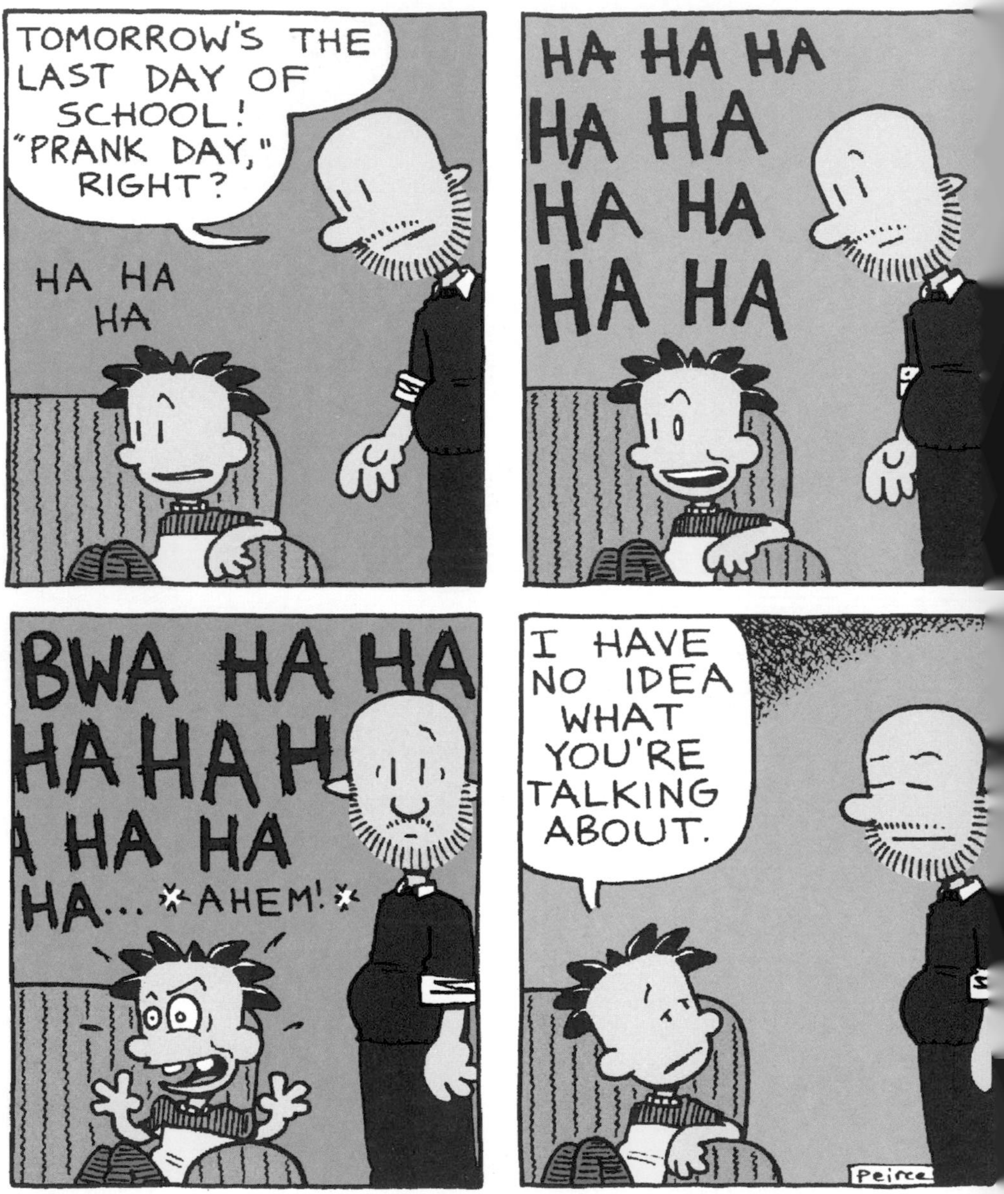
TOMORROW'S THE LAST DAY OF SCHOOL! "PRANK DAY," RIGHT?
HA HA HA
HA HA HA HA HA HA HA HA HA HA
BWA HA HA HA HA HA HA HA HA... *AHEM!*
I HAVE NO IDEA WHAT YOU'RE TALKING ABOUT.
Peirce

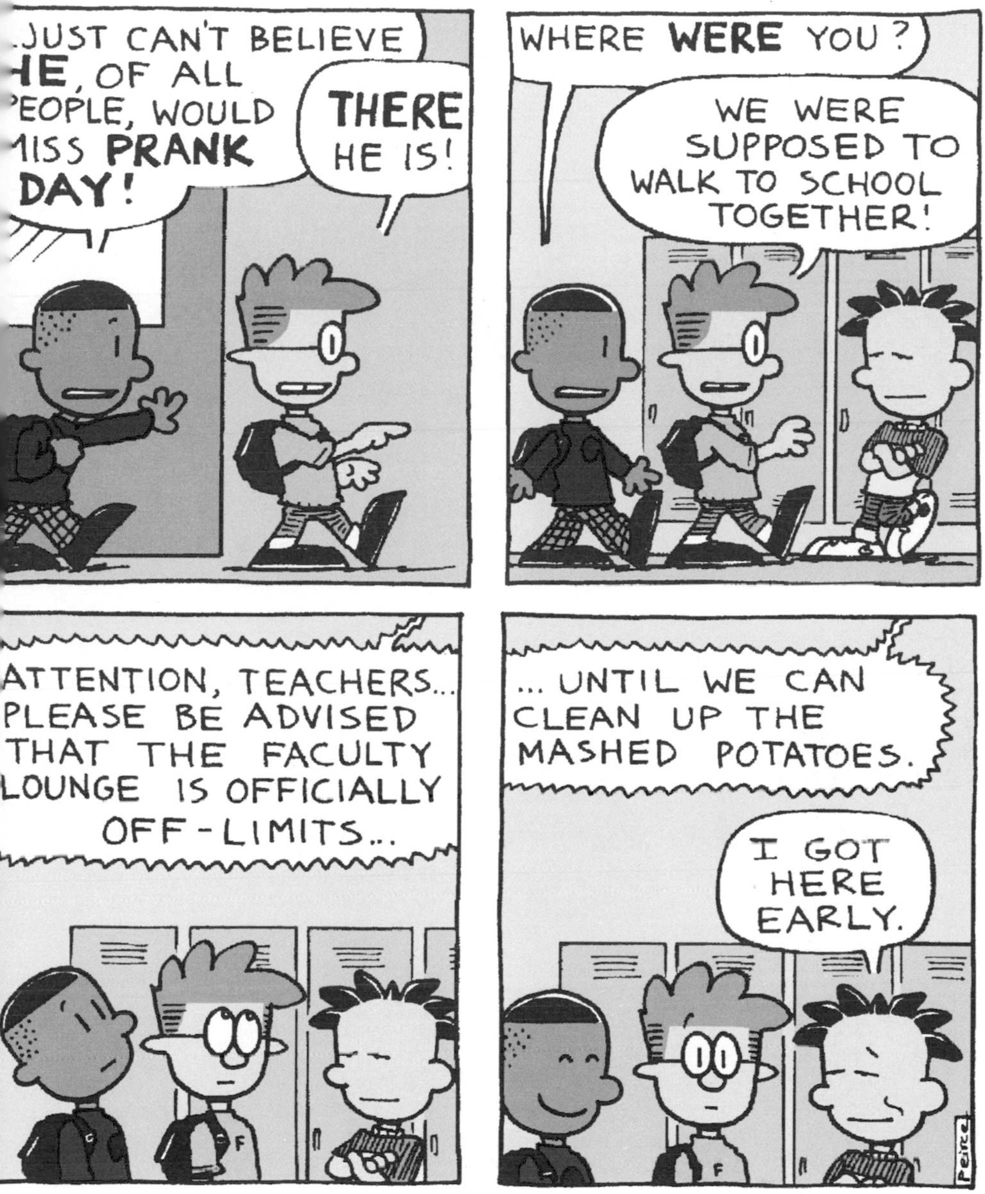
JUST CAN'T BELIEVE HE, OF ALL PEOPLE, WOULD MISS PRANK DAY!
THERE HE IS!
WHERE WERE YOU?
WE WERE SUPPOSED TO WALK TO SCHOOL TOGETHER!
ATTENTION, TEACHERS... PLEASE BE ADVISED THAT THE FACULTY LOUNGE IS OFFICIALLY OFF-LIMITS...
... UNTIL WE CAN CLEAN UP THE MASHED POTATOES.
I GOT HERE EARLY.
PEIRCE

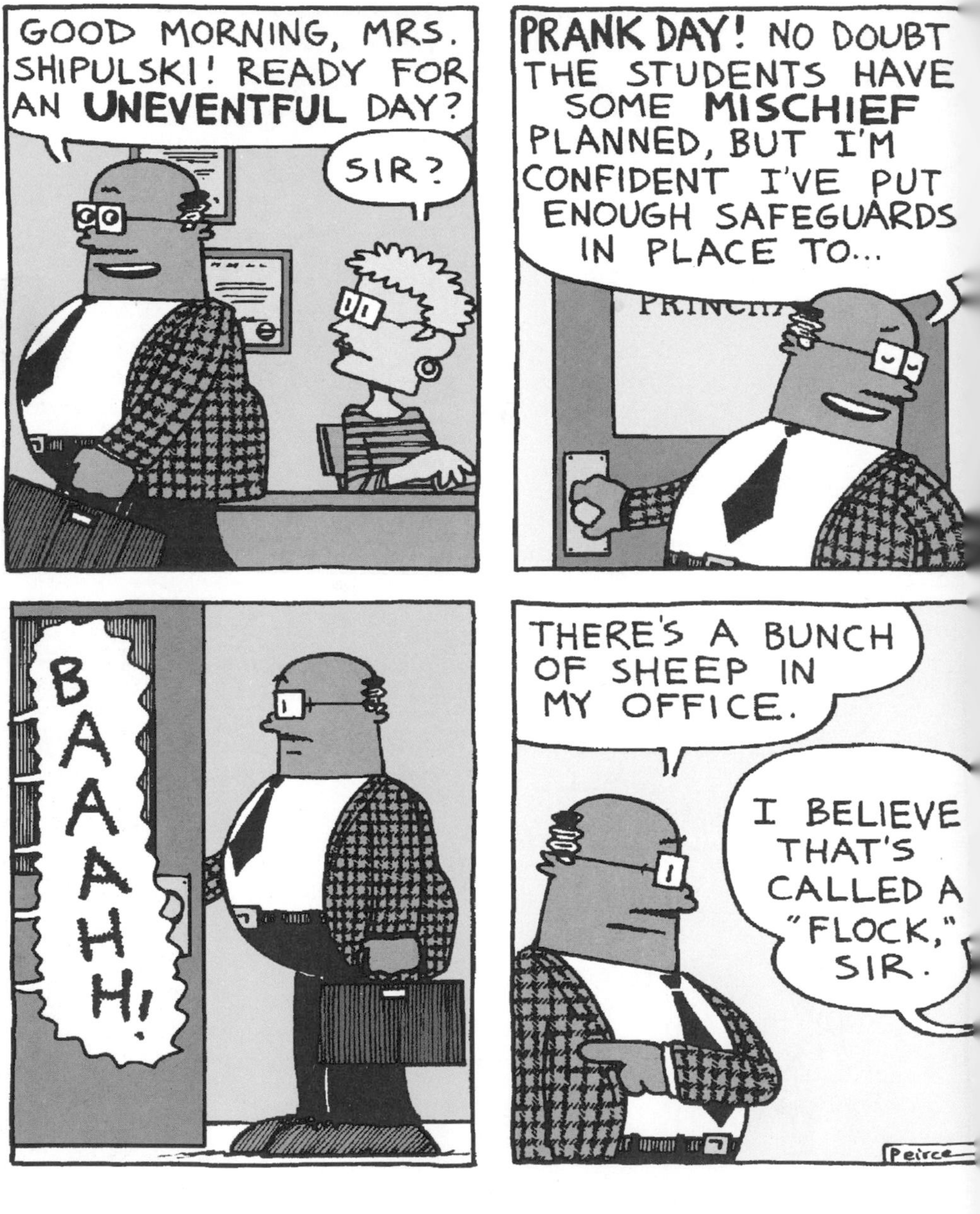
GOOD MORNING, MRS. SHIPULSKI! READY FOR AN **UNEVENTFUL** DAY?
SIR?
PRANK DAY! NO DOUBT THE STUDENTS HAVE SOME **MISCHIEF** PLANNED, BUT I'M CONFIDENT I'VE PUT ENOUGH SAFEGUARDS IN PLACE TO...
PRINCIPA
BAAAHH!
THERE'S A BUNCH OF SHEEP IN MY OFFICE.
I BELIEVE THAT'S CALLED A "FLOCK," SIR.
Peirce

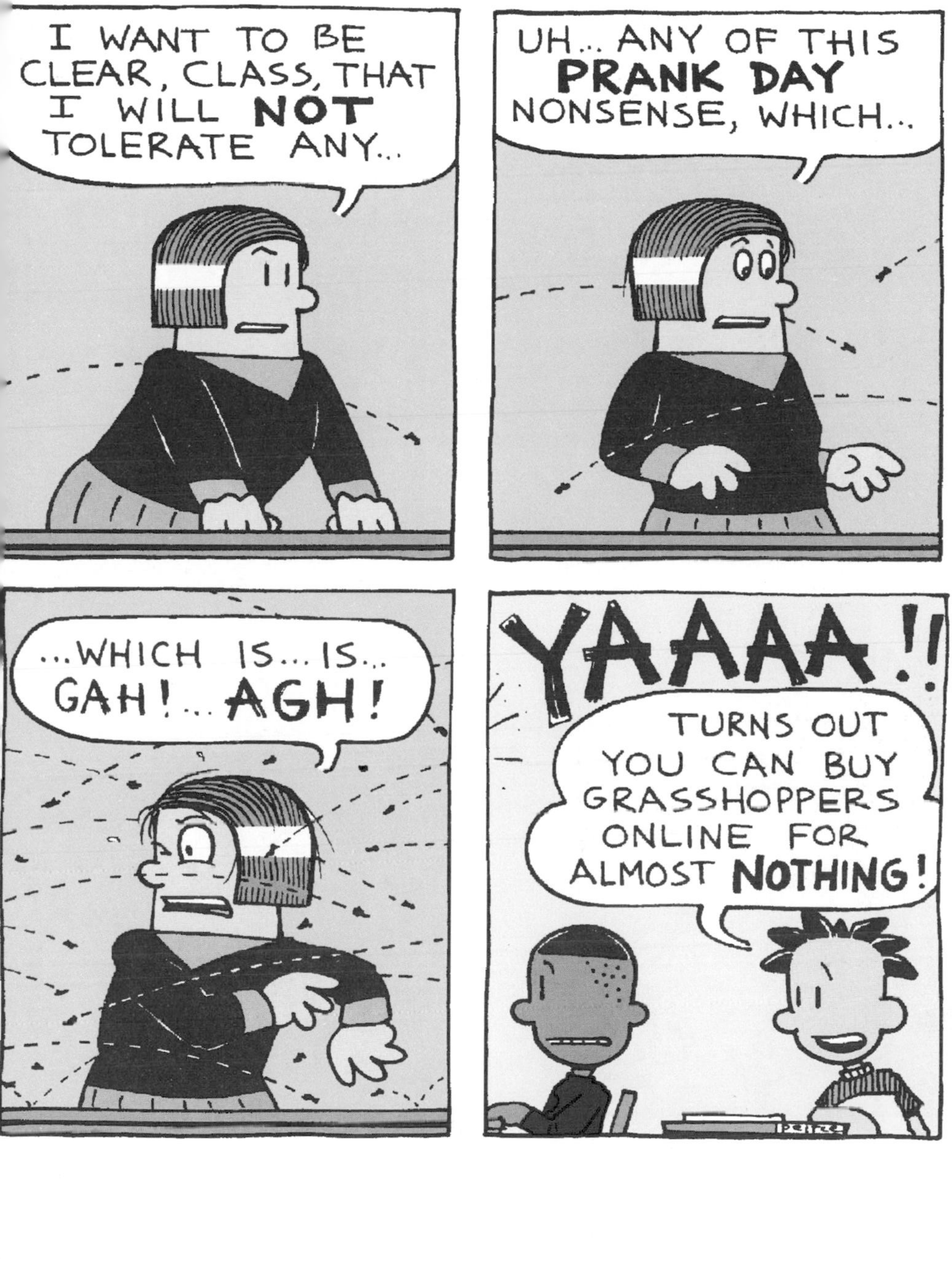
I WANT TO BE CLEAR, CLASS, THAT I WILL NOT TOLERATE ANY...
UH... ANY OF THIS PRANK DAY NONSENSE, WHICH...
...WHICH IS... IS... GAH!... AGH!
YAAAA!!
TURNS OUT YOU CAN BUY GRASSHOPPERS ONLINE FOR ALMOST NOTHING!

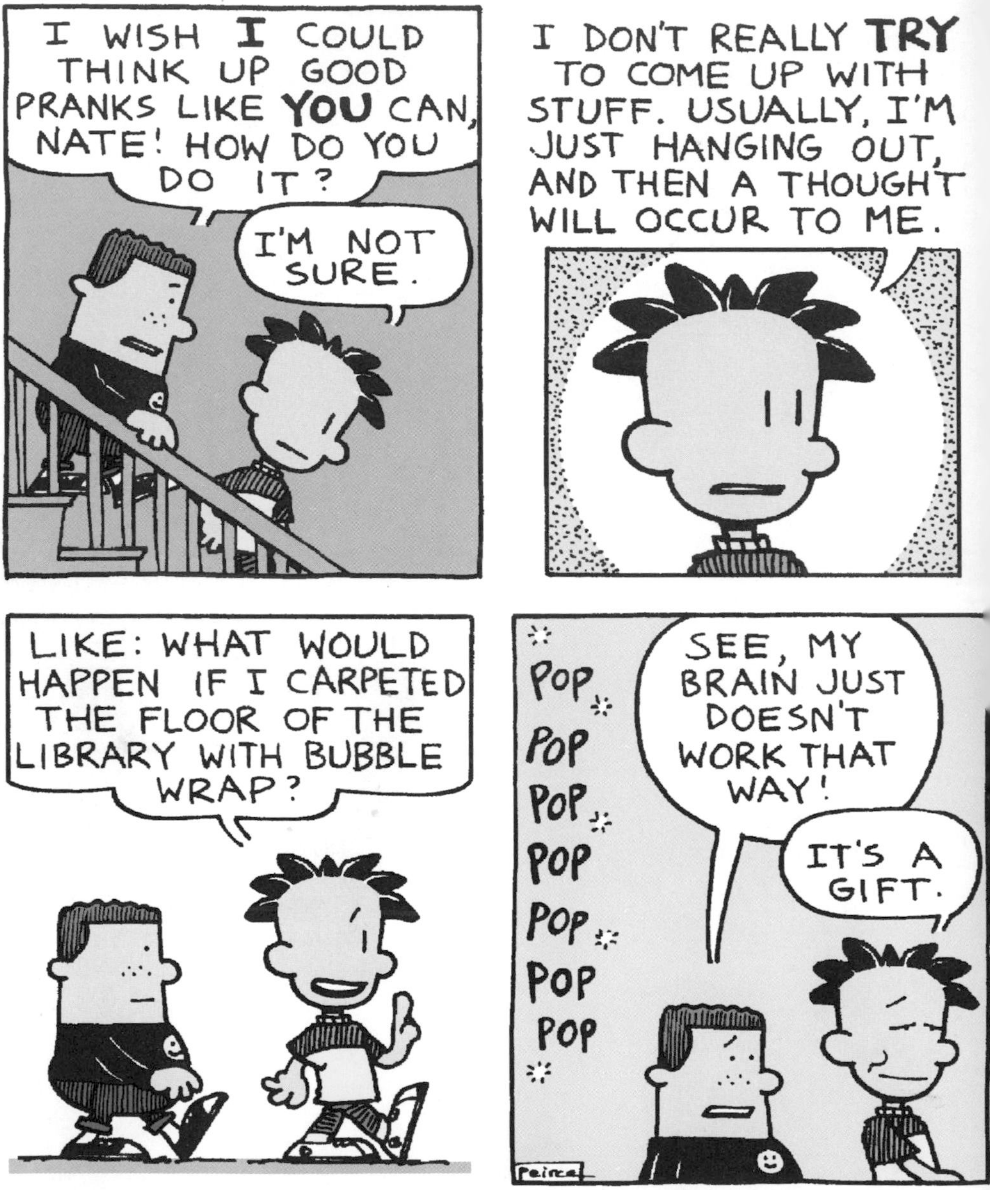
I WISH I COULD THINK UP GOOD PRANKS LIKE YOU CAN, NATE! HOW DO YOU DO IT?
I'M NOT SURE.
I DON'T REALLY TRY TO COME UP WITH STUFF. USUALLY, I'M JUST HANGING OUT, AND THEN A THOUGHT WILL OCCUR TO ME.
LIKE: WHAT WOULD HAPPEN IF I CARPETED THE FLOOR OF THE LIBRARY WITH BUBBLE WRAP?
POP
POP
POP
POP
POP
POP
POP
SEE, MY BRAIN JUST DOESN'T WORK THAT WAY!
IT'S A GIFT.
Peirce

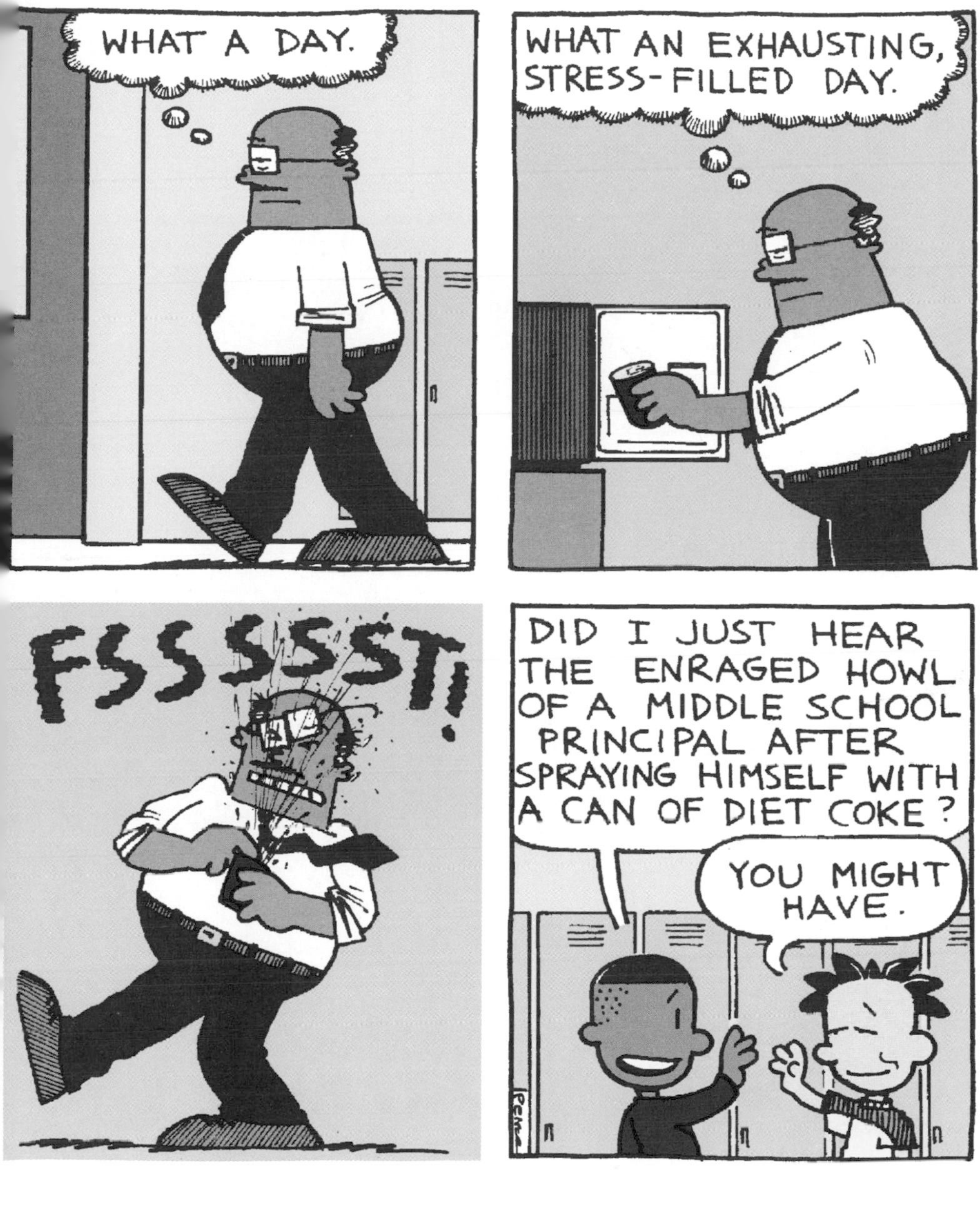
WHAT A DAY.
WHAT AN EXHAUSTING, STRESS-FILLED DAY.
FSSSSST!
DID I JUST HEAR THE ENRAGED HOWL OF A MIDDLE SCHOOL PRINCIPAL AFTER SPRAYING HIMSELF WITH A CAN OF DIET COKE?
YOU MIGHT HAVE.

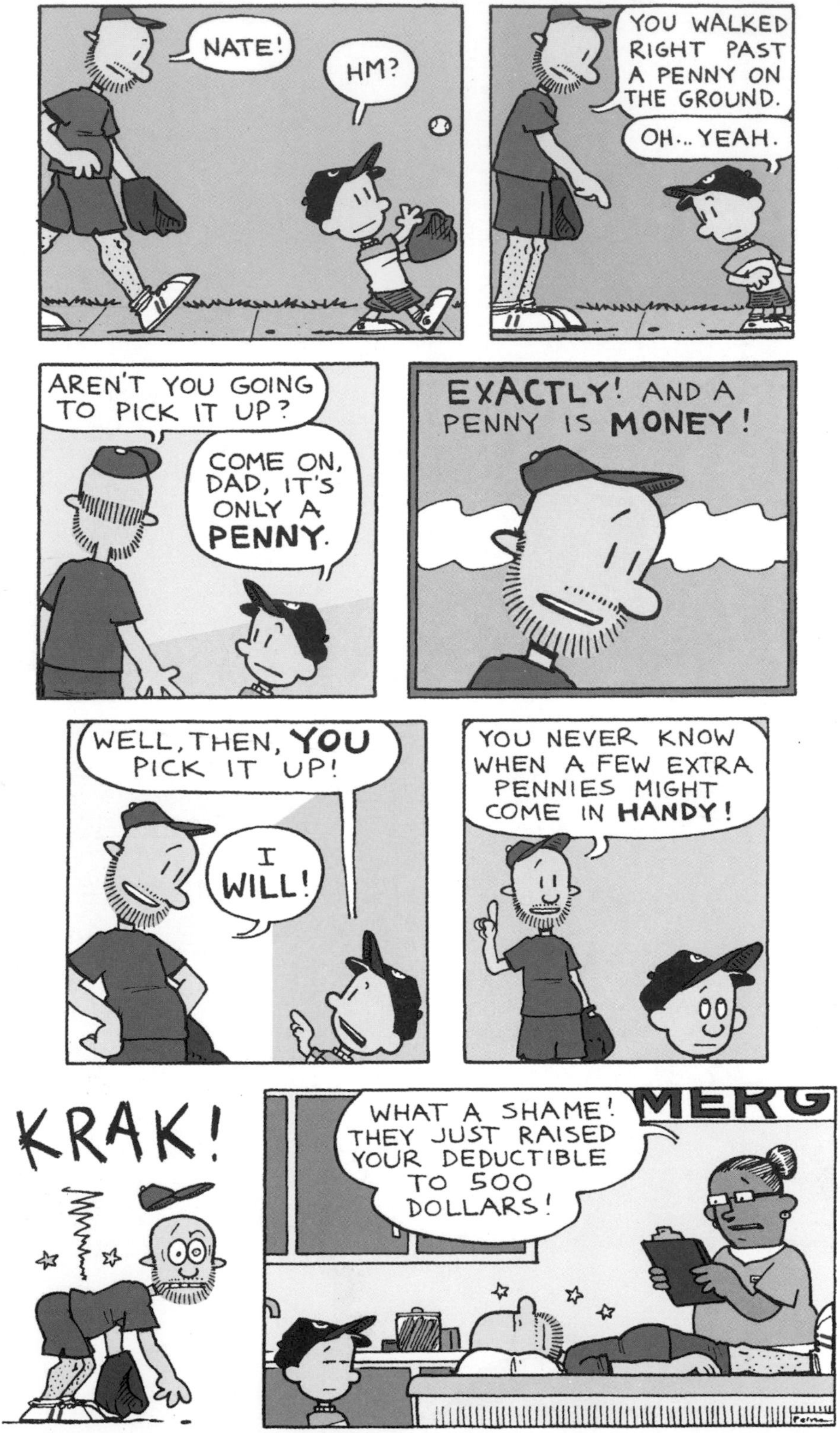
NATE!
HM?
YOU WALKED RIGHT PAST A PENNY ON THE GROUND.
OH... YEAH.
AREN'T YOU GOING TO PICK IT UP?
COME ON, DAD, IT'S ONLY A PENNY.
EXACTLY! AND A PENNY IS MONEY!
WELL, THEN, YOU PICK IT UP!
I WILL!
YOU NEVER KNOW WHEN A FEW EXTRA PENNIES MIGHT COME IN HANDY!
KRAK!
WHAT A SHAME! THEY JUST RAISED YOUR DEDUCTIBLE TO 500 DOLLARS!
MERG

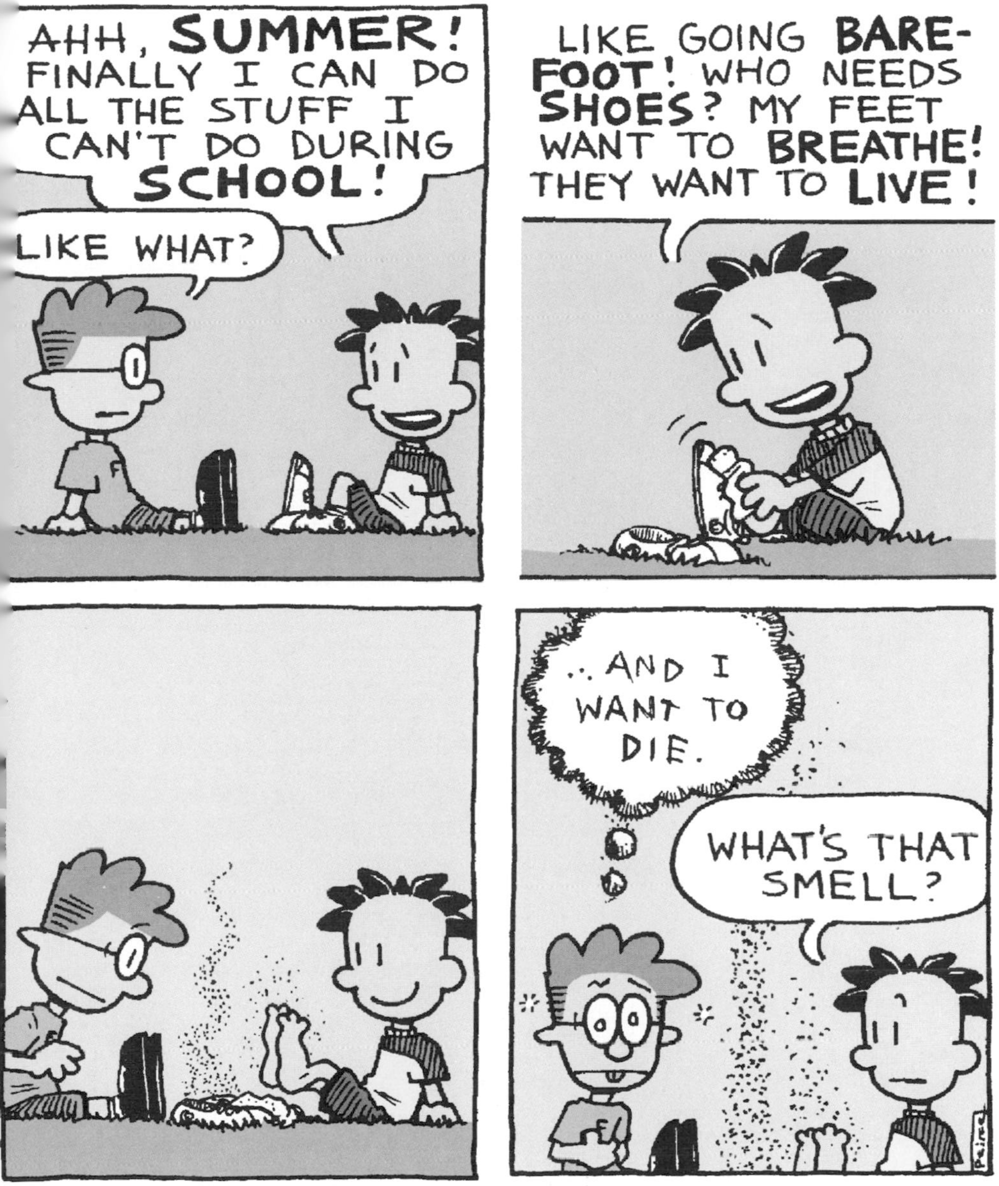
AHH, SUMMER! FINALLY I CAN DO ALL THE STUFF I CAN'T DO DURING SCHOOL!
LIKE WHAT?
LIKE GOING BAREFOOT! WHO NEEDS SHOES? MY FEET WANT TO BREATHE! THEY WANT TO LIVE!
...AND I WANT TO DIE.
WHAT'S THAT SMELL?

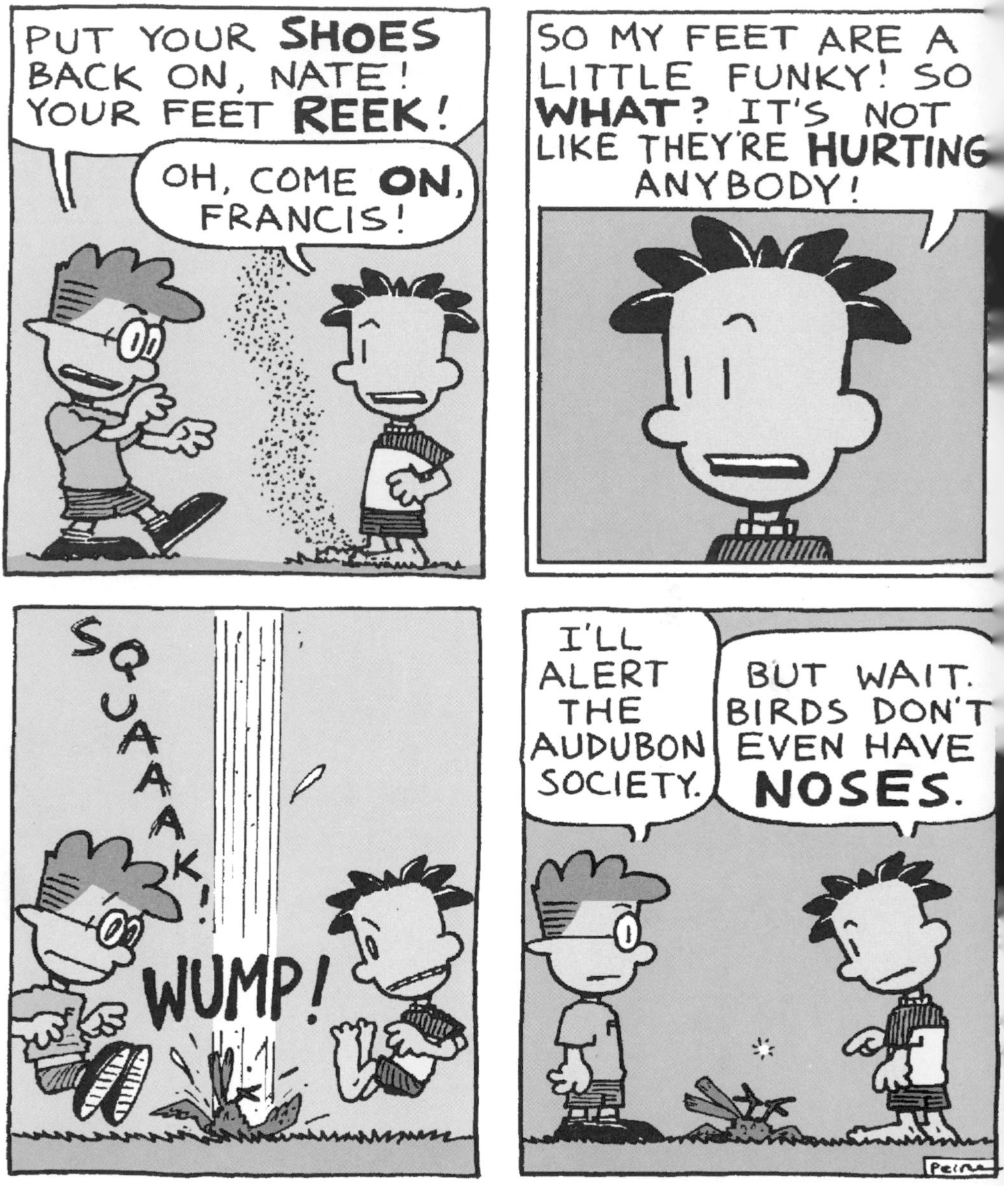
PUT YOUR SHOES BACK ON, NATE! YOUR FEET REEK!
OH, COME ON, FRANCIS!
SO MY FEET ARE A LITTLE FUNKY! SO WHAT? IT'S NOT LIKE THEY'RE HURTING ANYBODY!
SQUAAAK!
WUMP!
I'LL ALERT THE AUDUBON SOCIETY.
BUT WAIT. BIRDS DON'T EVEN HAVE NOSES.

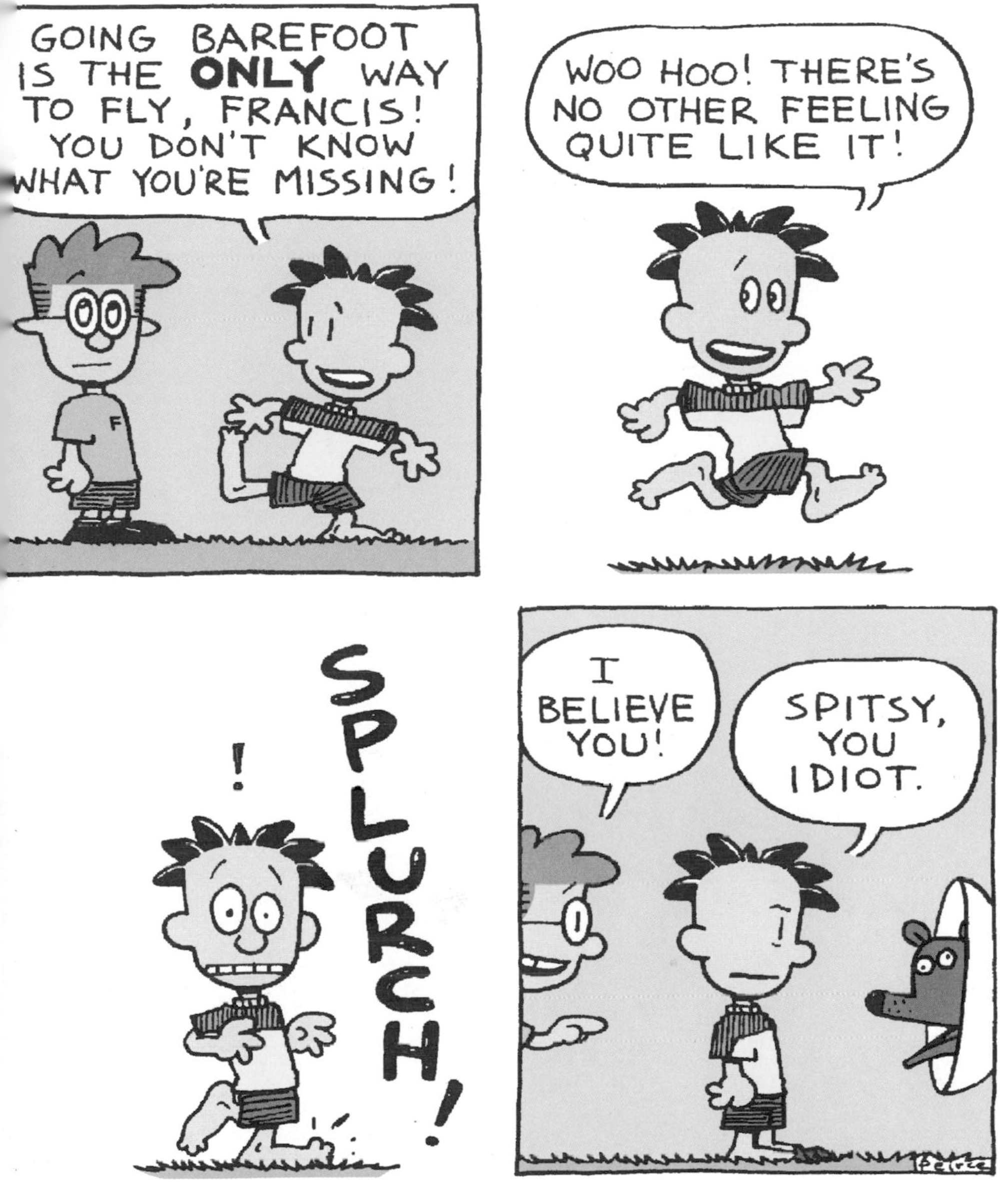
GOING BAREFOOT IS THE **ONLY** WAY TO FLY, FRANCIS! YOU DON'T KNOW WHAT YOU'RE MISSING!
WOO HOO! THERE'S NO OTHER FEELING QUITE LIKE IT!
!
SPLURCH!
I BELIEVE YOU!
SPITSY, YOU IDIOT.

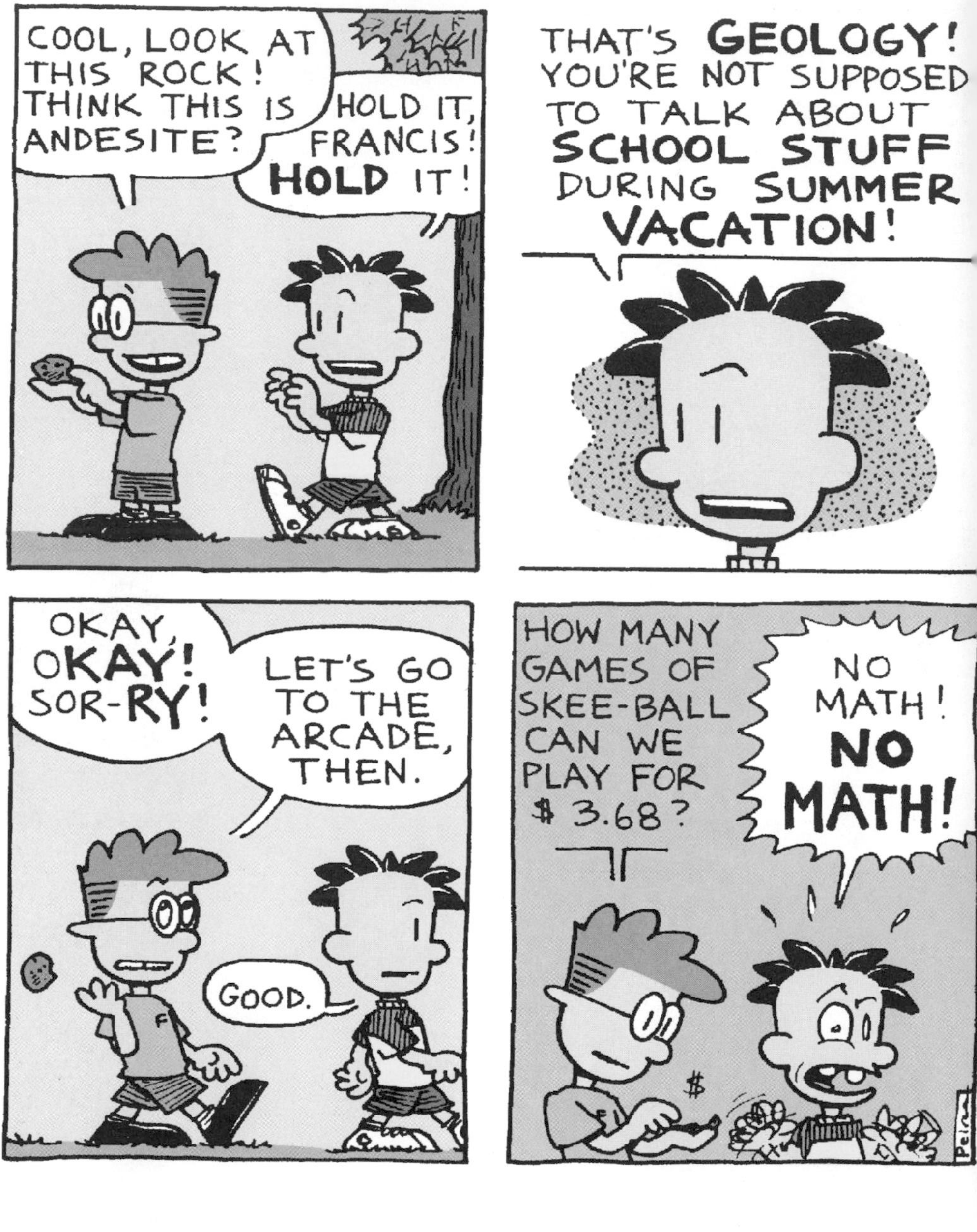
COOL, LOOK AT THIS ROCK! THINK THIS IS ANDESITE?
HOLD IT, FRANCIS! **HOLD** IT!
THAT'S **GEOLOGY**! YOU'RE NOT SUPPOSED TO TALK ABOUT **SCHOOL STUFF** DURING **SUMMER VACATION**!
OKAY, O**KAY**! SOR-**RY**!
LET'S GO TO THE ARCADE, THEN.
GOOD.
HOW MANY GAMES OF SKEE-BALL CAN WE PLAY FOR $ 3.68?
NO MATH! **NO MATH!**
Peirce

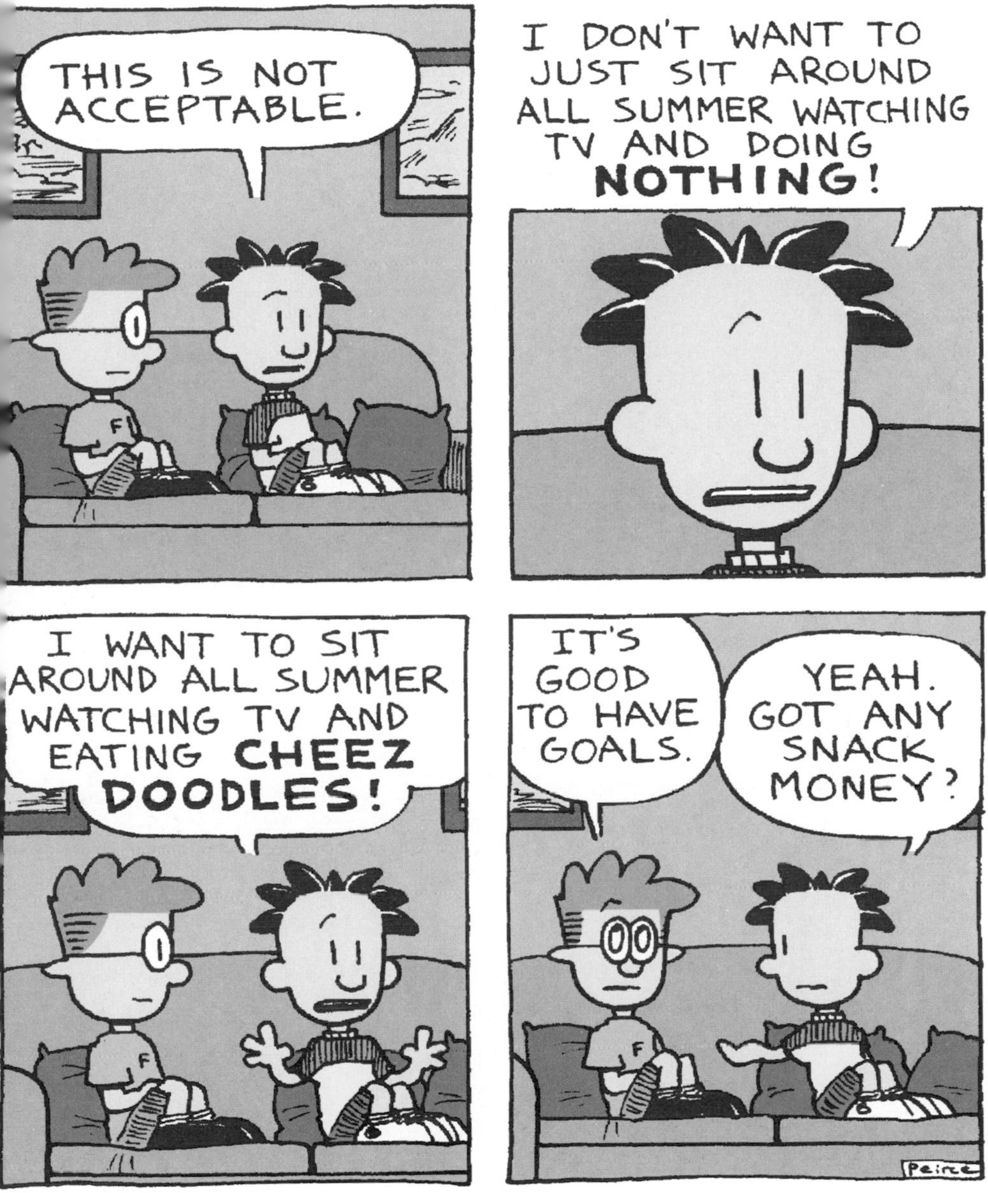
THIS IS NOT ACCEPTABLE.
I DON'T WANT TO JUST SIT AROUND ALL SUMMER WATCHING TV AND DOING NOTHING!
I WANT TO SIT AROUND ALL SUMMER WATCHING TV AND EATING CHEEZ DOODLES!
IT'S GOOD TO HAVE GOALS.
YEAH. GOT ANY SNACK MONEY?
Peirce

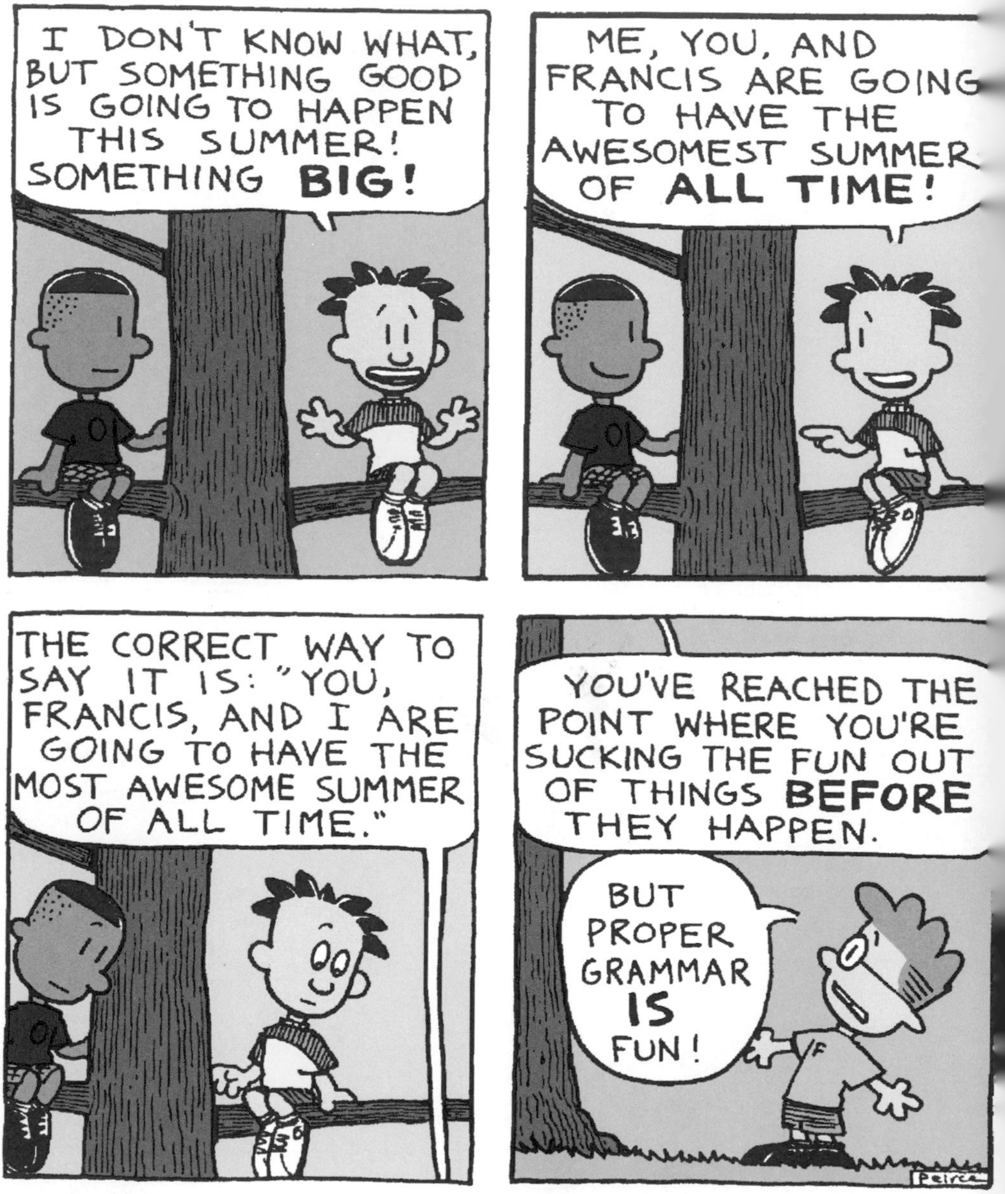
I DON'T KNOW WHAT, BUT SOMETHING GOOD IS GOING TO HAPPEN THIS SUMMER! SOMETHING **BIG**!
ME, YOU, AND FRANCIS ARE GOING TO HAVE THE AWESOMEST SUMMER OF **ALL TIME**!
THE CORRECT WAY TO SAY IT IS: "YOU, FRANCIS, AND I ARE GOING TO HAVE THE MOST AWESOME SUMMER OF ALL TIME."
YOU'VE REACHED THE POINT WHERE YOU'RE SUCKING THE FUN OUT OF THINGS **BEFORE** THEY HAPPEN.
BUT PROPER GRAMMAR **IS** FUN!
Peirce

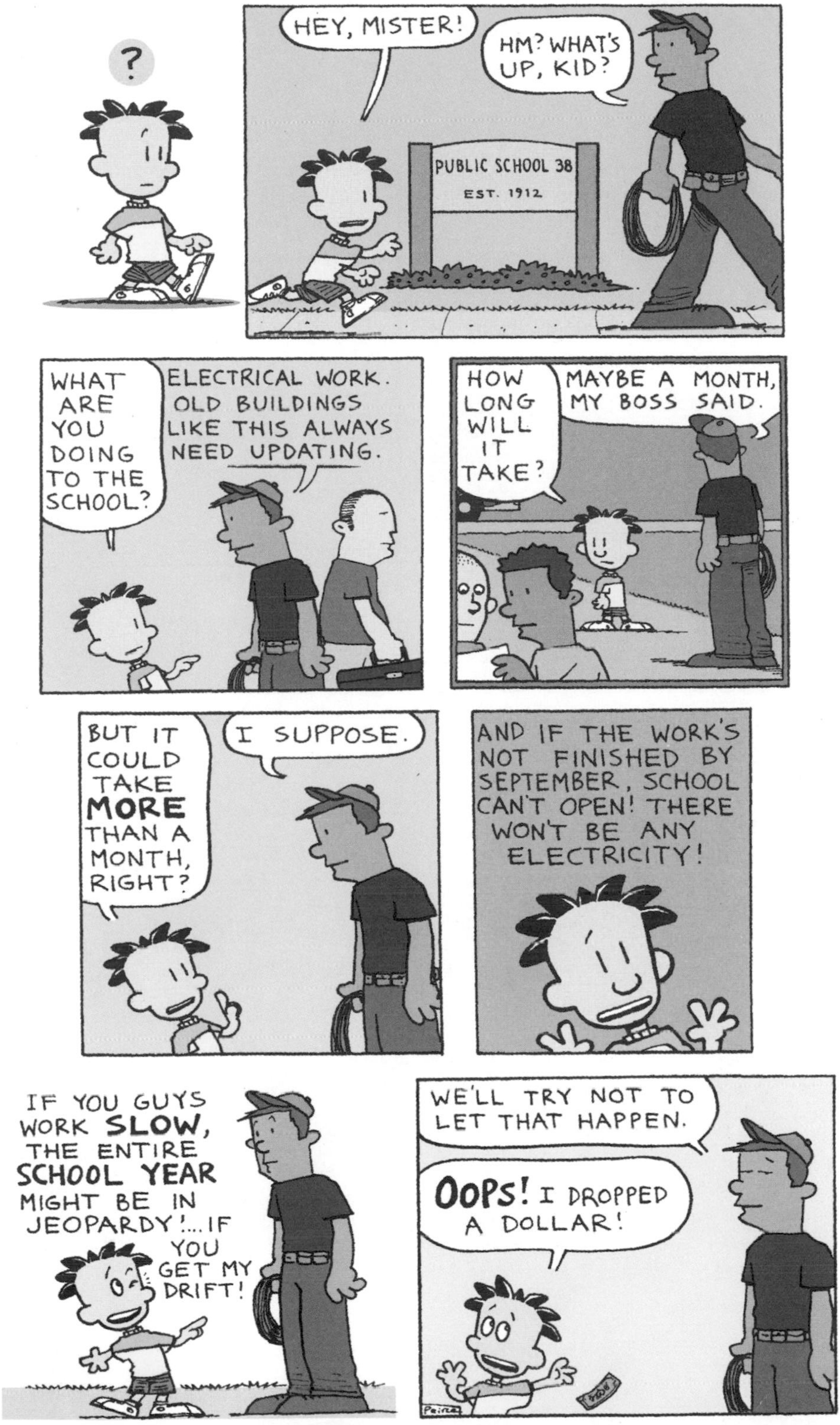
?
HEY, MISTER!
HM? WHAT'S UP, KID?
PUBLIC SCHOOL 38
EST. 1912
WHAT ARE YOU DOING TO THE SCHOOL?
ELECTRICAL WORK. OLD BUILDINGS LIKE THIS ALWAYS NEED UPDATING.
HOW LONG WILL IT TAKE?
MAYBE A MONTH, MY BOSS SAID.
BUT IT COULD TAKE **MORE** THAN A MONTH, RIGHT?
I SUPPOSE.
AND IF THE WORK'S NOT FINISHED BY SEPTEMBER, SCHOOL CAN'T OPEN! THERE WON'T BE ANY ELECTRICITY!
IF YOU GUYS WORK **SLOW**, THE ENTIRE **SCHOOL YEAR** MIGHT BE IN JEOPARDY!... IF YOU GET MY DRIFT!
WE'LL TRY NOT TO LET THAT HAPPEN.
OOPS! I DROPPED A DOLLAR!

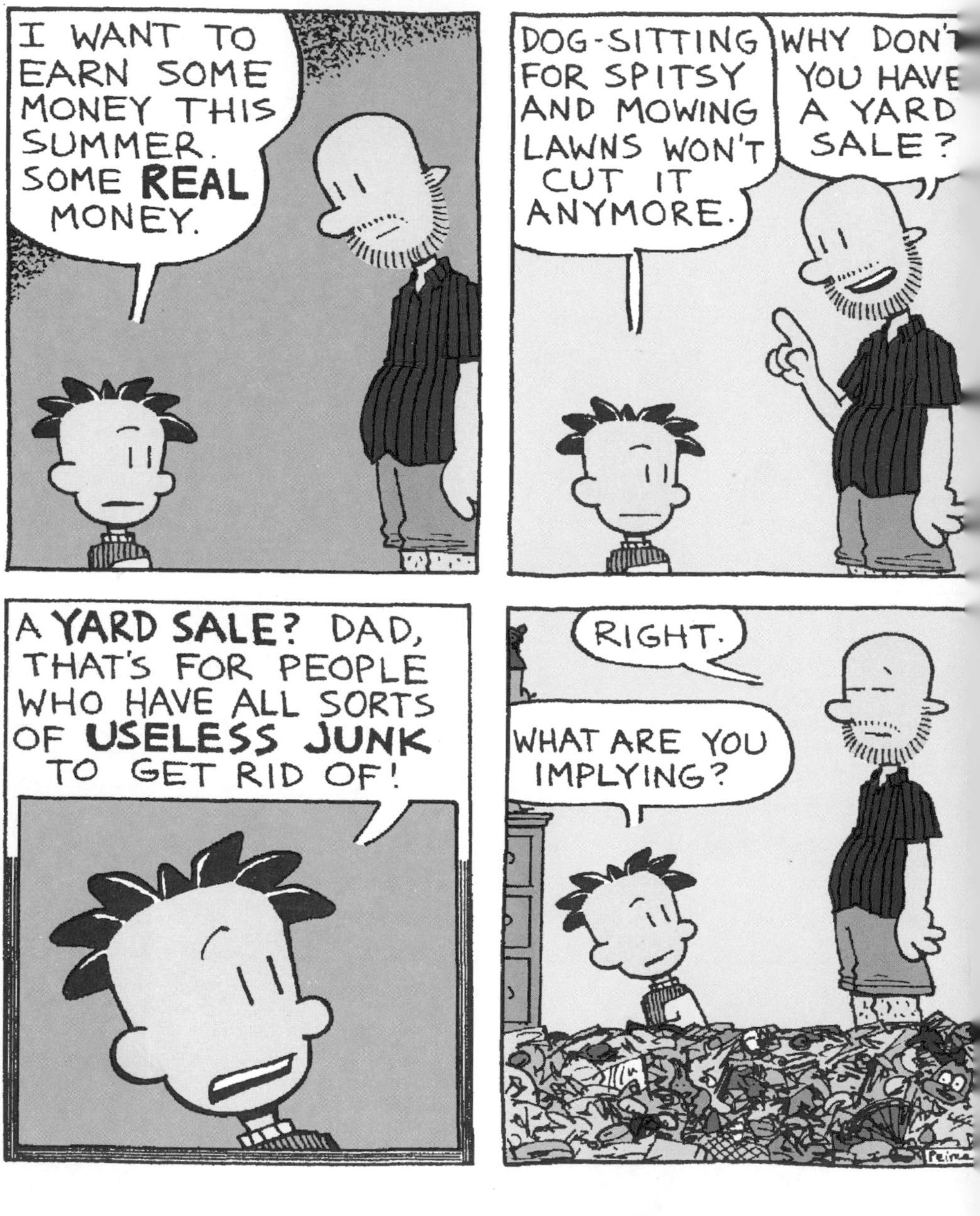
I WANT TO EARN SOME MONEY THIS SUMMER. SOME **REAL** MONEY.
DOG-SITTING FOR SPITSY AND MOWING LAWNS WON'T CUT IT ANYMORE.
WHY DON'T YOU HAVE A YARD SALE?
A **YARD SALE?** DAD, THAT'S FOR PEOPLE WHO HAVE ALL SORTS OF **USELESS JUNK** TO GET RID OF!
RIGHT.
WHAT ARE YOU IMPLYING?

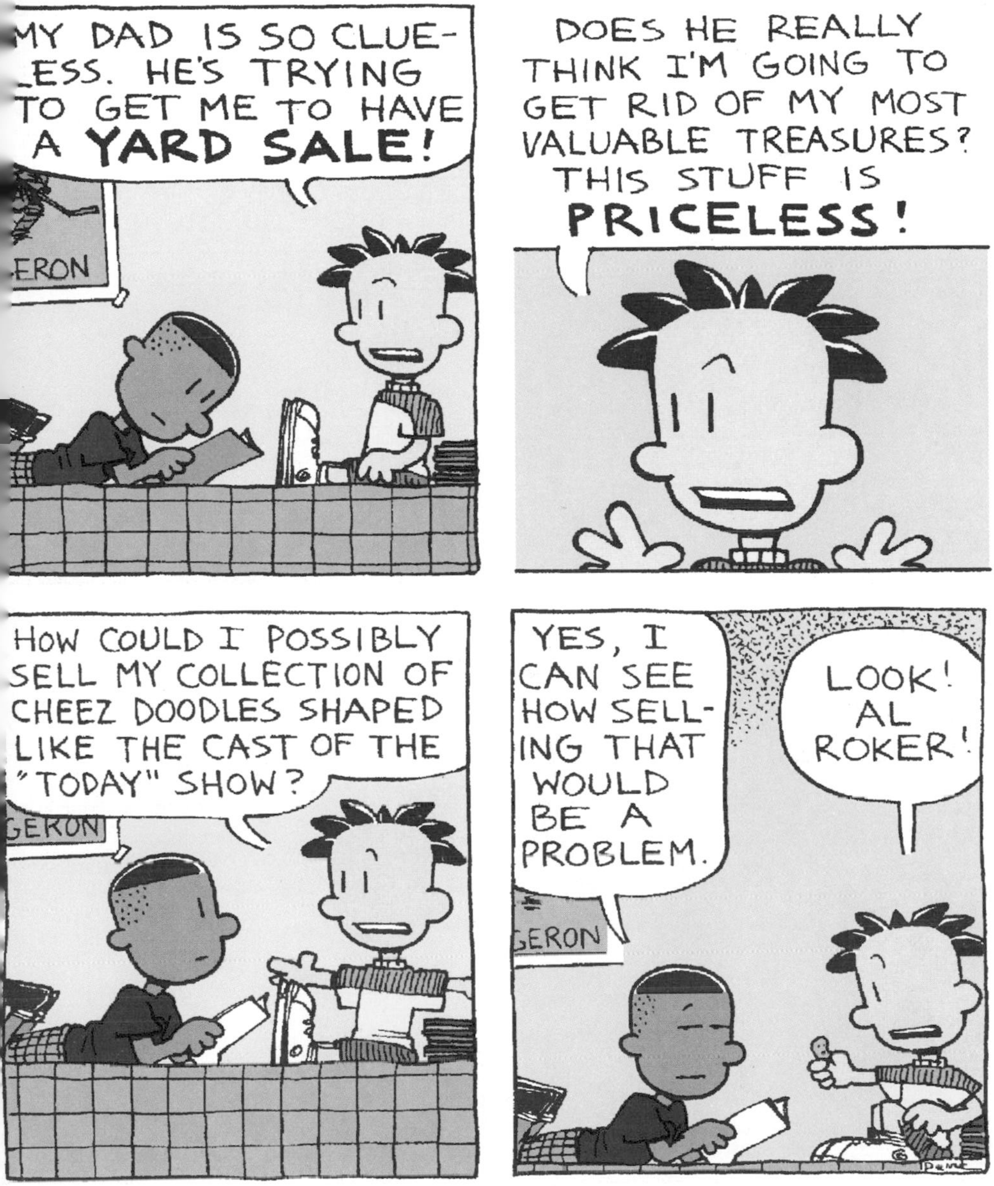
MY DAD IS SO CLUELESS. HE'S TRYING TO GET ME TO HAVE A **YARD SALE!**
DOES HE REALLY THINK I'M GOING TO GET RID OF MY MOST VALUABLE TREASURES? THIS STUFF IS **PRICELESS!**
HOW COULD I POSSIBLY SELL MY COLLECTION OF CHEEZ DOODLES SHAPED LIKE THE CAST OF THE "TODAY" SHOW?
YES, I CAN SEE HOW SELLING THAT WOULD BE A PROBLEM.
LOOK! AL ROKER!

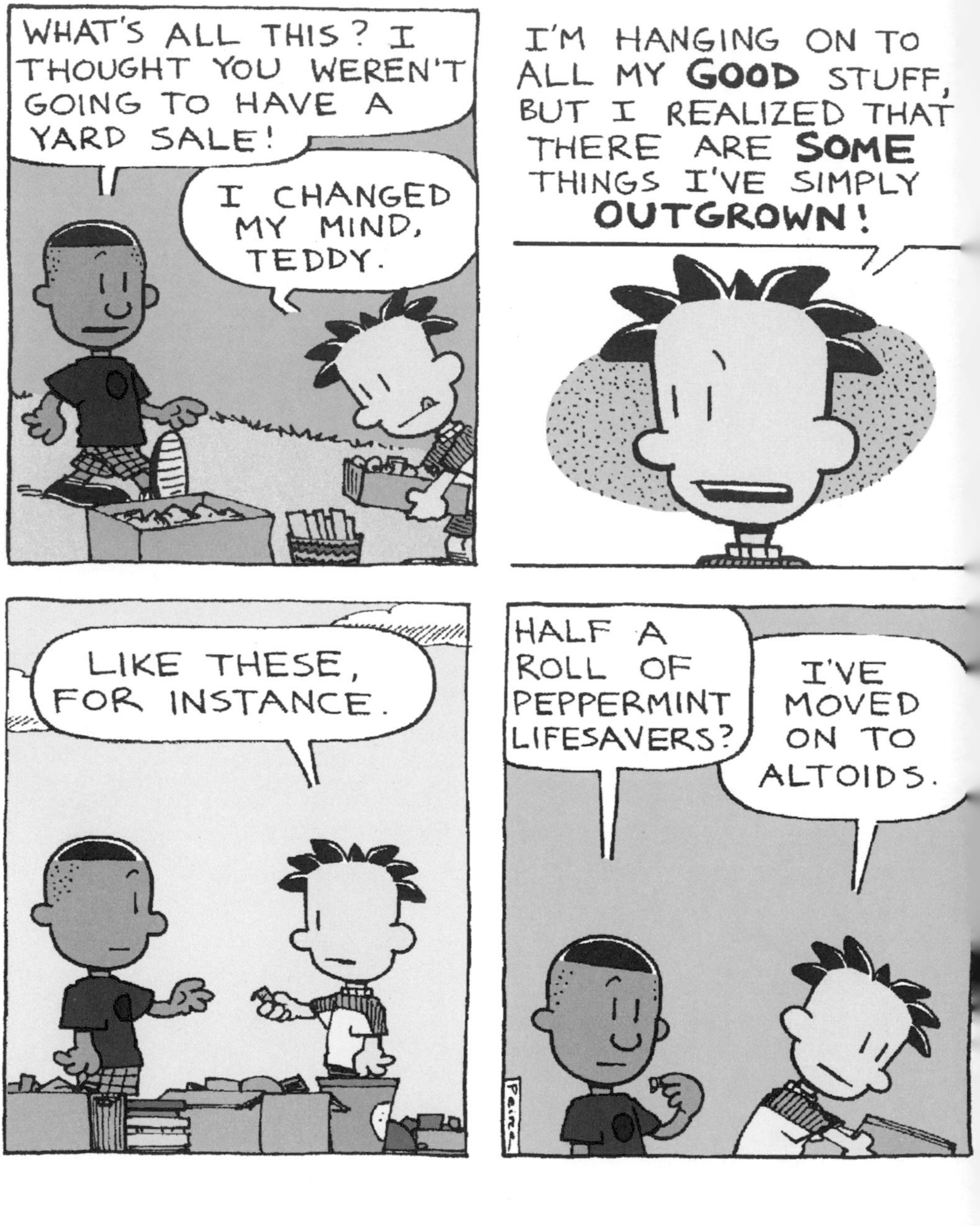
WHAT'S ALL THIS? I THOUGHT YOU WEREN'T GOING TO HAVE A YARD SALE!
I CHANGED MY MIND, TEDDY.
I'M HANGING ON TO ALL MY **GOOD** STUFF, BUT I REALIZED THAT THERE ARE **SOME** THINGS I'VE SIMPLY **OUTGROWN**!
LIKE THESE, FOR INSTANCE.
HALF A ROLL OF PEPPERMINT LIFESAVERS?
I'VE MOVED ON TO ALTOIDS.

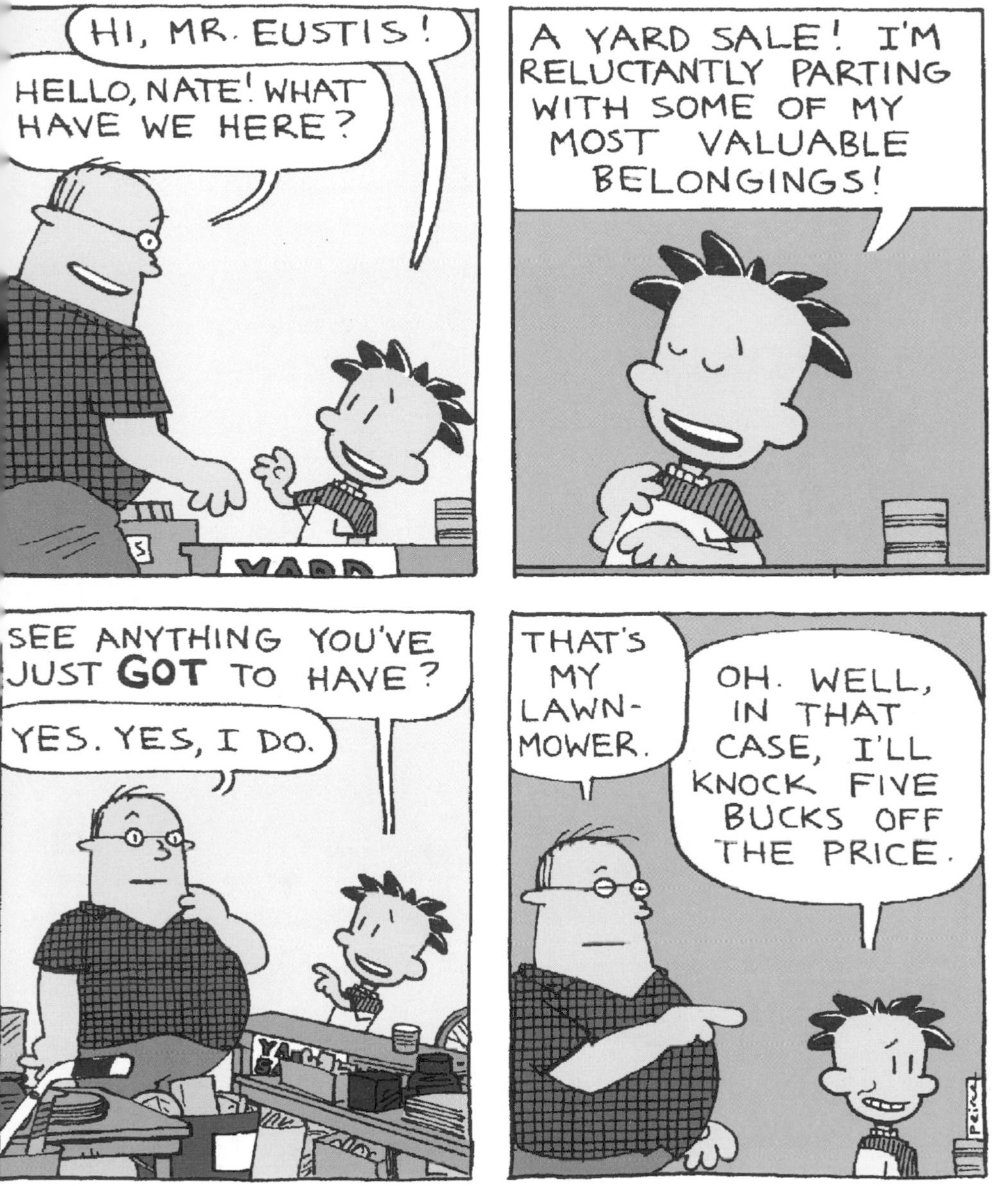
HI, MR. EUSTIS!
HELLO, NATE! WHAT HAVE WE HERE?
A YARD SALE! I'M RELUCTANTLY PARTING WITH SOME OF MY MOST VALUABLE BELONGINGS!
SEE ANYTHING YOU'VE JUST **GOT** TO HAVE?
YES. YES, I DO.
THAT'S MY LAWN-MOWER.
OH. WELL, IN THAT CASE, I'LL KNOCK FIVE BUCKS OFF THE PRICE.

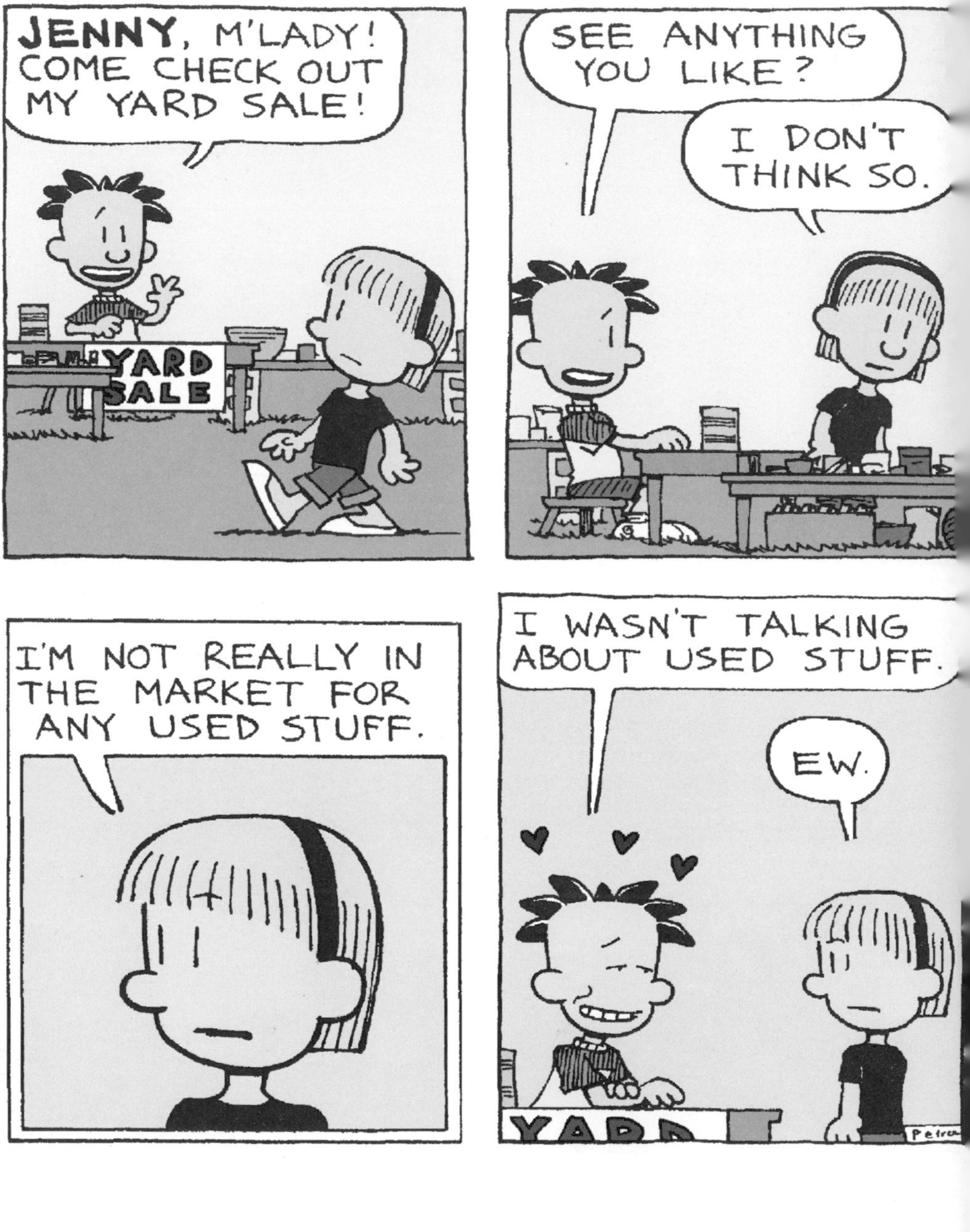
JENNY, M'LADY! COME CHECK OUT MY YARD SALE!
YARD SALE
SEE ANYTHING YOU LIKE?
I DON'T THINK SO.
I'M NOT REALLY IN THE MARKET FOR ANY USED STUFF.
I WASN'T TALKING ABOUT USED STUFF.
EW.

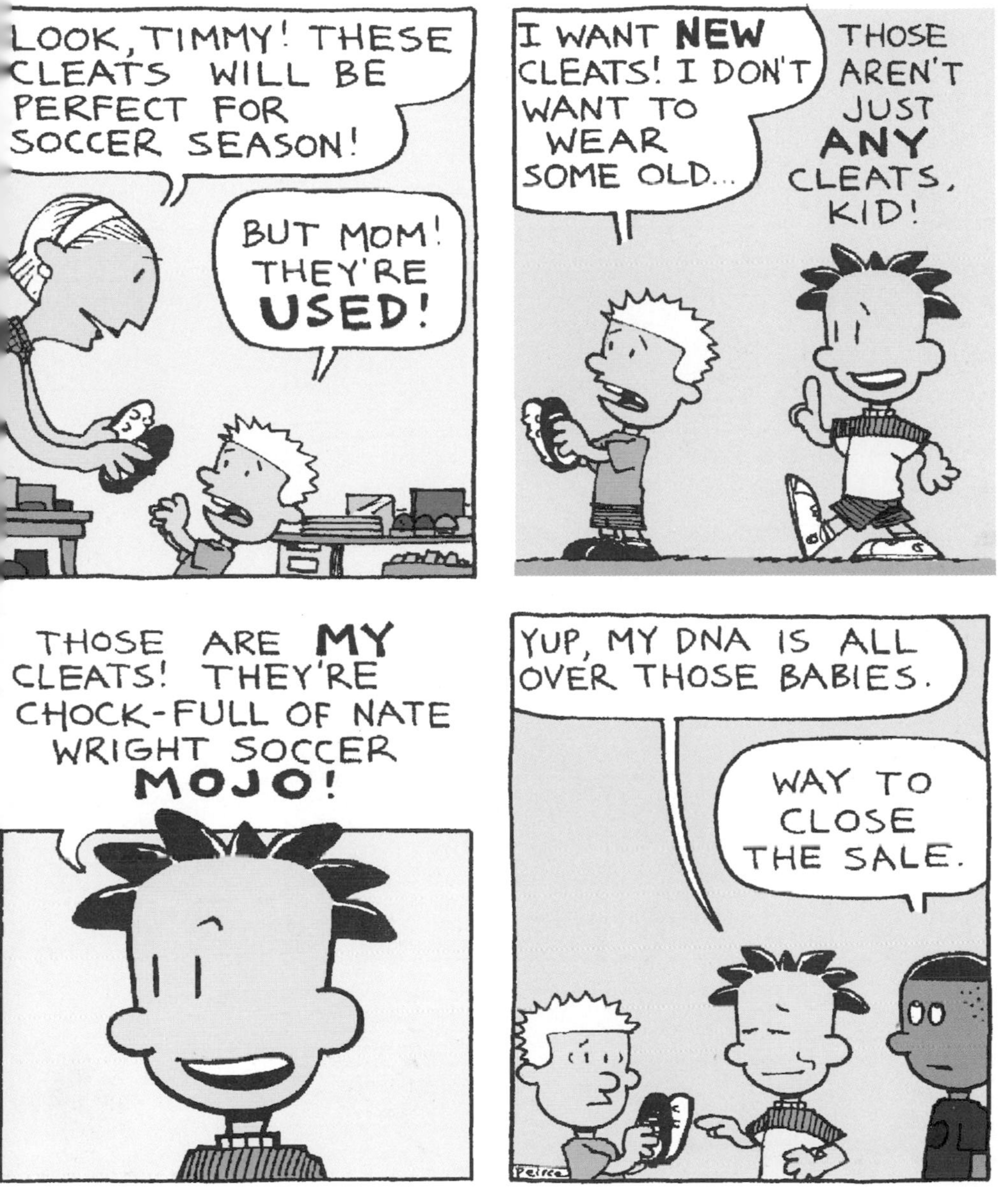
LOOK, TIMMY! THESE CLEATS WILL BE PERFECT FOR SOCCER SEASON!
BUT MOM! THEY'RE **USED**!
I WANT **NEW** CLEATS! I DON'T WANT TO WEAR SOME OLD...
THOSE AREN'T JUST **ANY** CLEATS, KID!
THOSE ARE **MY** CLEATS! THEY'RE CHOCK-FULL OF NATE WRIGHT SOCCER **MOJO**!
YUP, MY DNA IS ALL OVER THOSE BABIES.
WAY TO CLOSE THE SALE.
Peirce

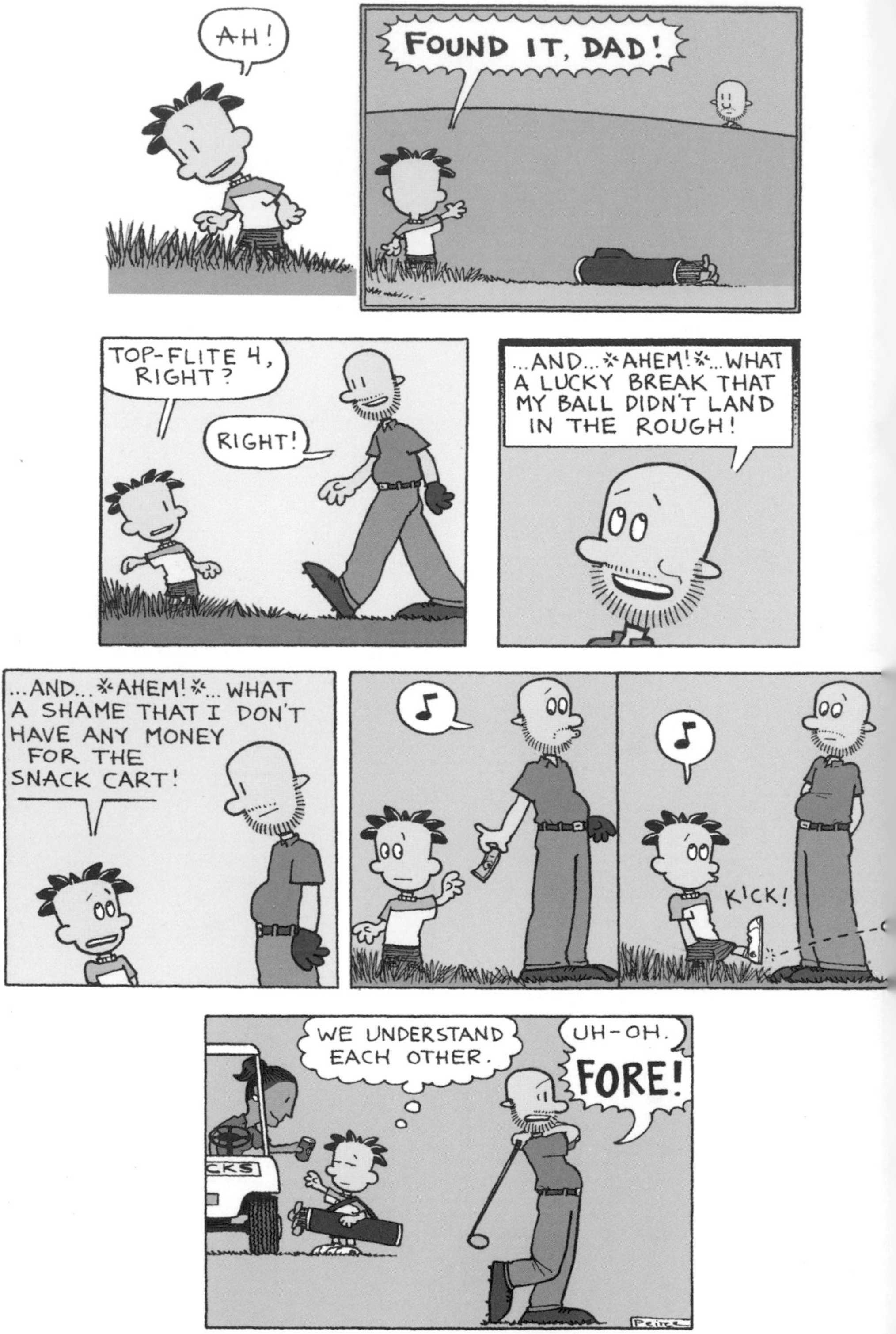
AH!
FOUND IT, DAD!
TOP-FLITE 4, RIGHT?
RIGHT!
...AND... *AHEM!* ...WHAT A LUCKY BREAK THAT MY BALL DIDN'T LAND IN THE ROUGH!
...AND... *AHEM!* ... WHAT A SHAME THAT I DON'T HAVE ANY MONEY FOR THE SNACK CART!
KICK!
WE UNDERSTAND EACH OTHER.
UH-OH.
FORE!
CKS
Peirce

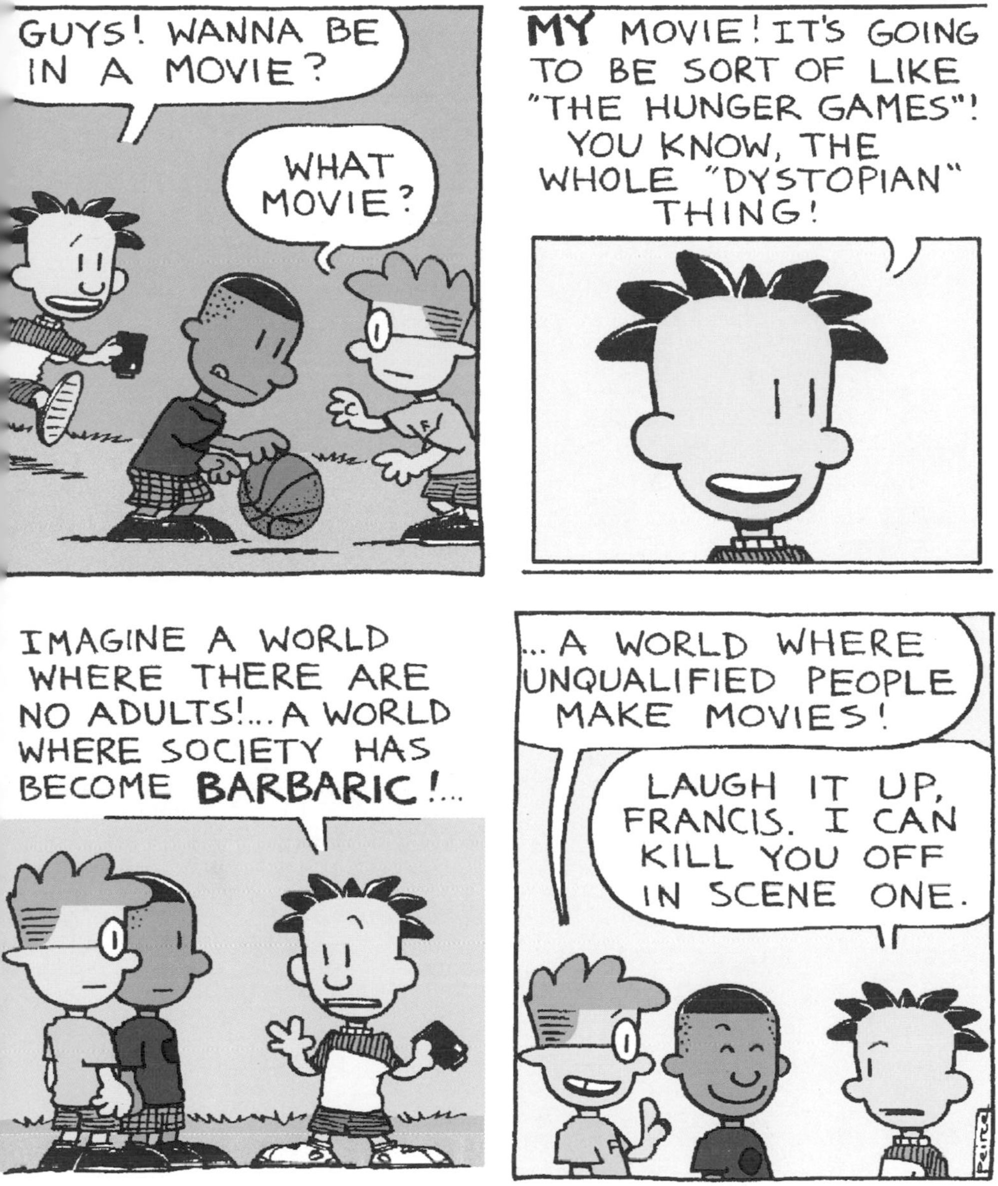
GUYS! WANNA BE IN A MOVIE?
WHAT MOVIE?
MY MOVIE! IT'S GOING TO BE SORT OF LIKE "THE HUNGER GAMES"! YOU KNOW, THE WHOLE "DYSTOPIAN" THING!
IMAGINE A WORLD WHERE THERE ARE NO ADULTS!... A WORLD WHERE SOCIETY HAS BECOME BARBARIC!...
... A WORLD WHERE UNQUALIFIED PEOPLE MAKE MOVIES!
LAUGH IT UP, FRANCIS. I CAN KILL YOU OFF IN SCENE ONE.
PEIRCE

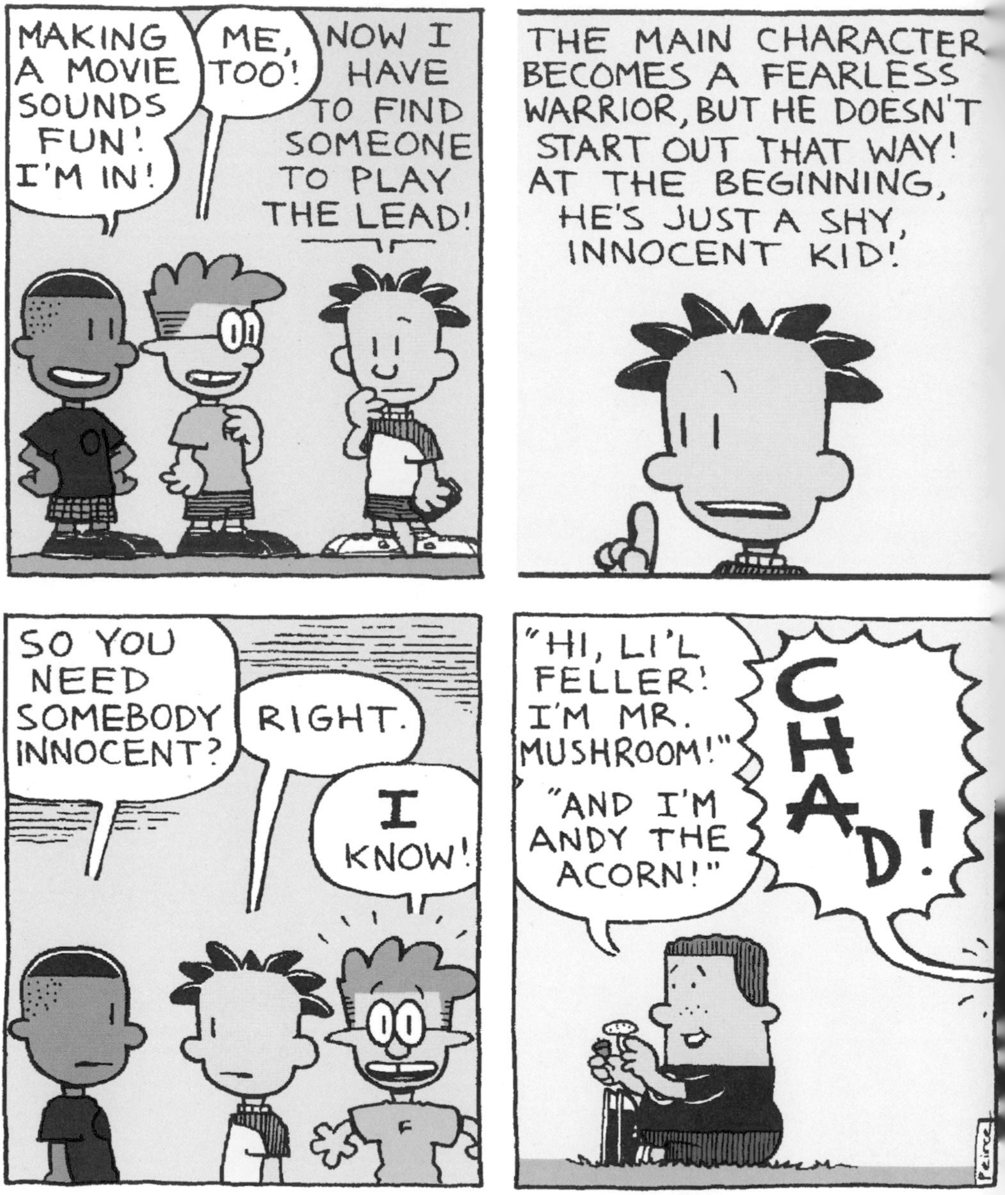
MAKING A MOVIE SOUNDS FUN! I'M IN!
ME, TOO!
NOW I HAVE TO FIND SOMEONE TO PLAY THE LEAD!
THE MAIN CHARACTER BECOMES A FEARLESS WARRIOR, BUT HE DOESN'T START OUT THAT WAY! AT THE BEGINNING, HE'S JUST A SHY, INNOCENT KID!
SO YOU NEED SOMEBODY INNOCENT?
RIGHT.
I KNOW!
"HI, LI'L FELLER! I'M MR. MUSHROOM!"
"AND I'M ANDY THE ACORN!"
CHAD!
Peirce

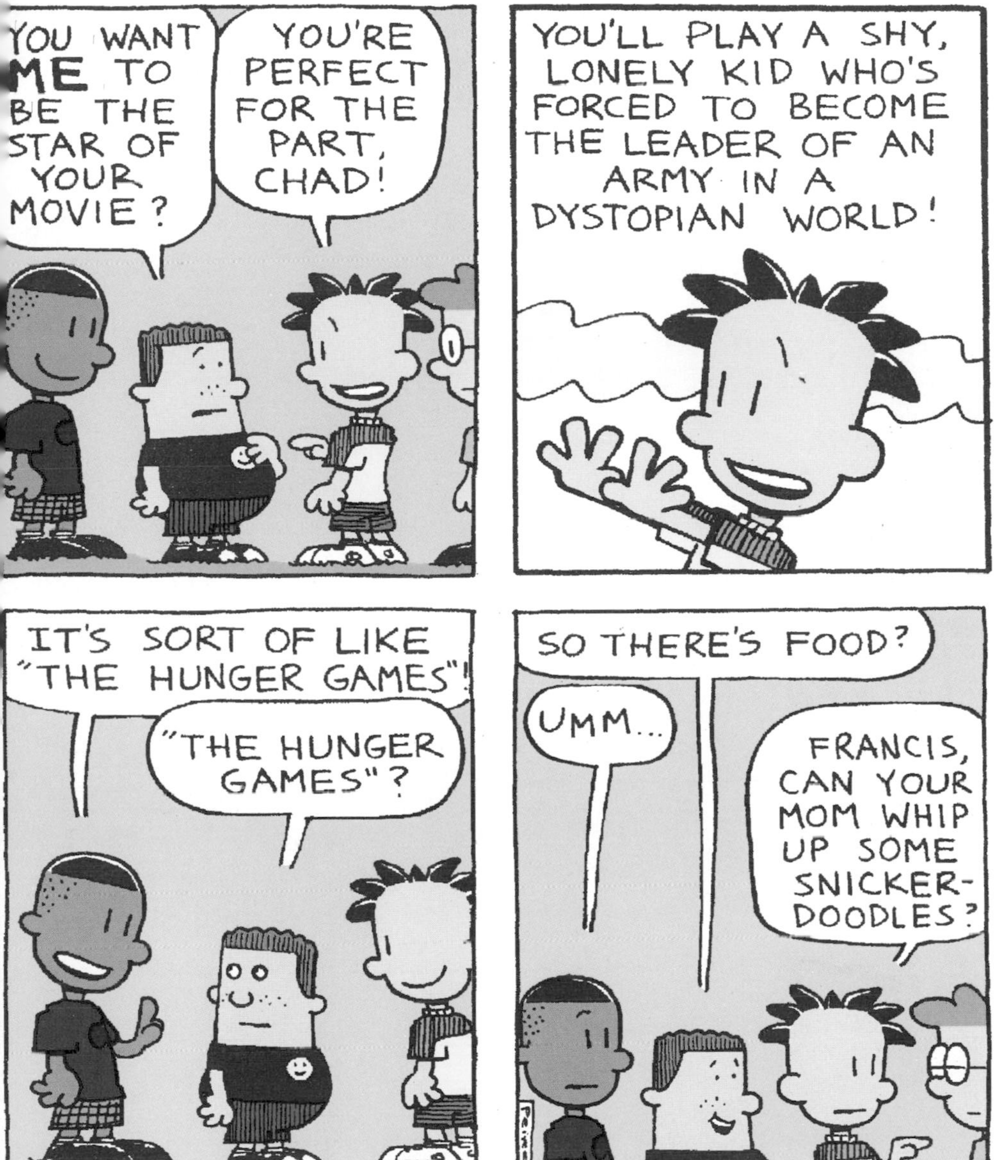
YOU WANT ME TO BE THE STAR OF YOUR MOVIE?
YOU'RE PERFECT FOR THE PART, CHAD!
YOU'LL PLAY A SHY, LONELY KID WHO'S FORCED TO BECOME THE LEADER OF AN ARMY IN A DYSTOPIAN WORLD!
IT'S SORT OF LIKE "THE HUNGER GAMES"!
"THE HUNGER GAMES"?
SO THERE'S FOOD?
UMM...
FRANCIS, CAN YOUR MOM WHIP UP SOME SNICKER-DOODLES?

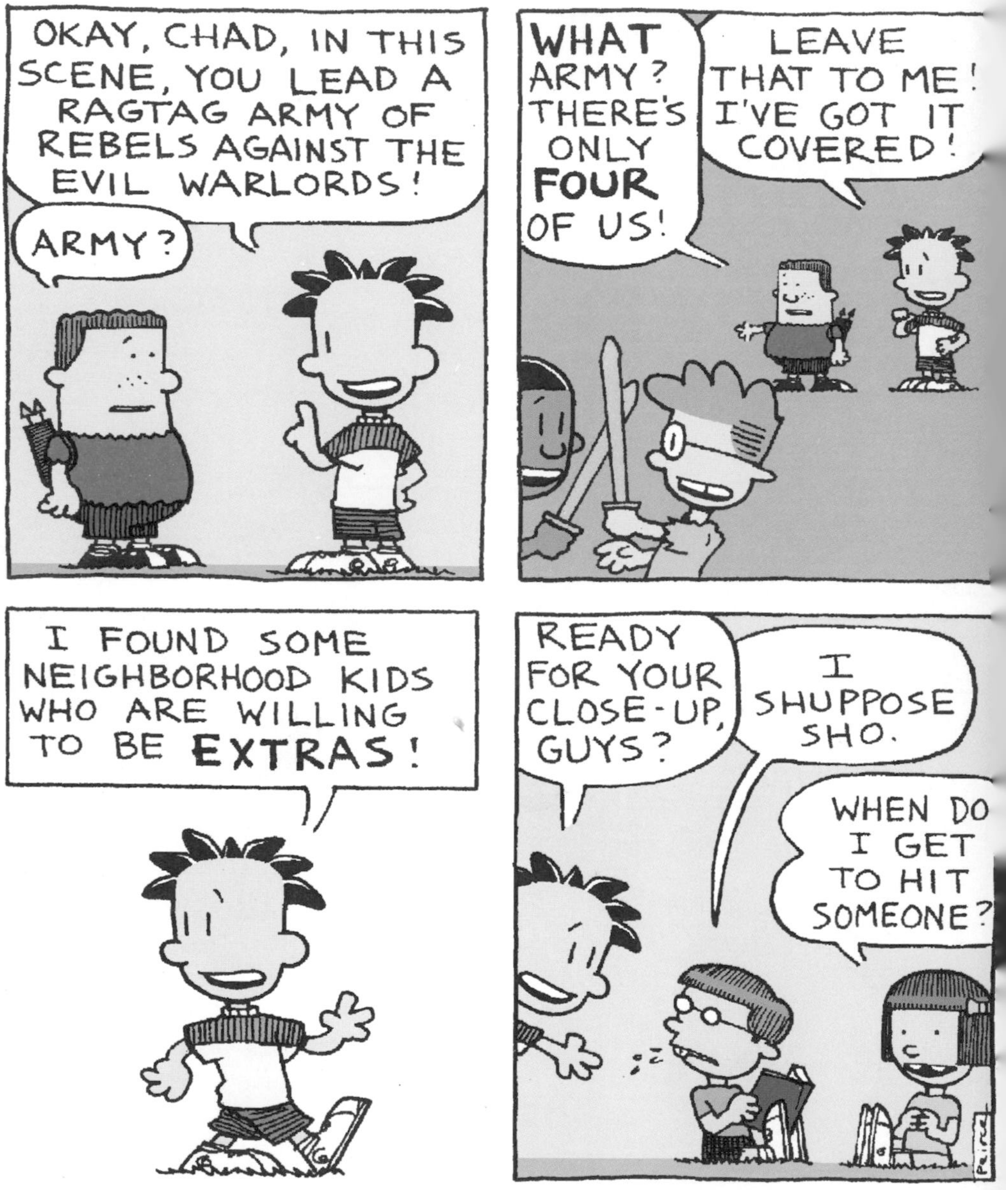
OKAY, CHAD, IN THIS SCENE, YOU LEAD A RAGTAG ARMY OF REBELS AGAINST THE EVIL WARLORDS!
ARMY?
WHAT ARMY? THERE'S ONLY **FOUR** OF US!
LEAVE THAT TO ME! I'VE GOT IT COVERED!
I FOUND SOME NEIGHBORHOOD KIDS WHO ARE WILLING TO BE **EXTRAS**!
READY FOR YOUR CLOSE-UP, GUYS?
I SHUPPOSE SHO.
WHEN DO I GET TO HIT SOMEONE?

CUT! CHAD, THIS IS THE SCENE WHERE YOUR OLDER BROTHER **DIES!** WHERE'S THE **EMOTION?** LET'S SEE SOME **TEARS!**

I CAN'T DO IT!

I MEAN, I KNOW FRANCIS ISN'T **REALLY** DYING, SO I DON'T **FEEL** ANYTHING!

OKAY, I GET IT. LET'S SEE HERE...

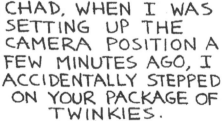

CHAD, WHEN I WAS SETTING UP THE CAMERA POSITION A FEW MINUTES AGO, I ACCIDENTALLY STEPPED ON YOUR PACKAGE OF TWINKIES.

W-WHAT?

ACTION!

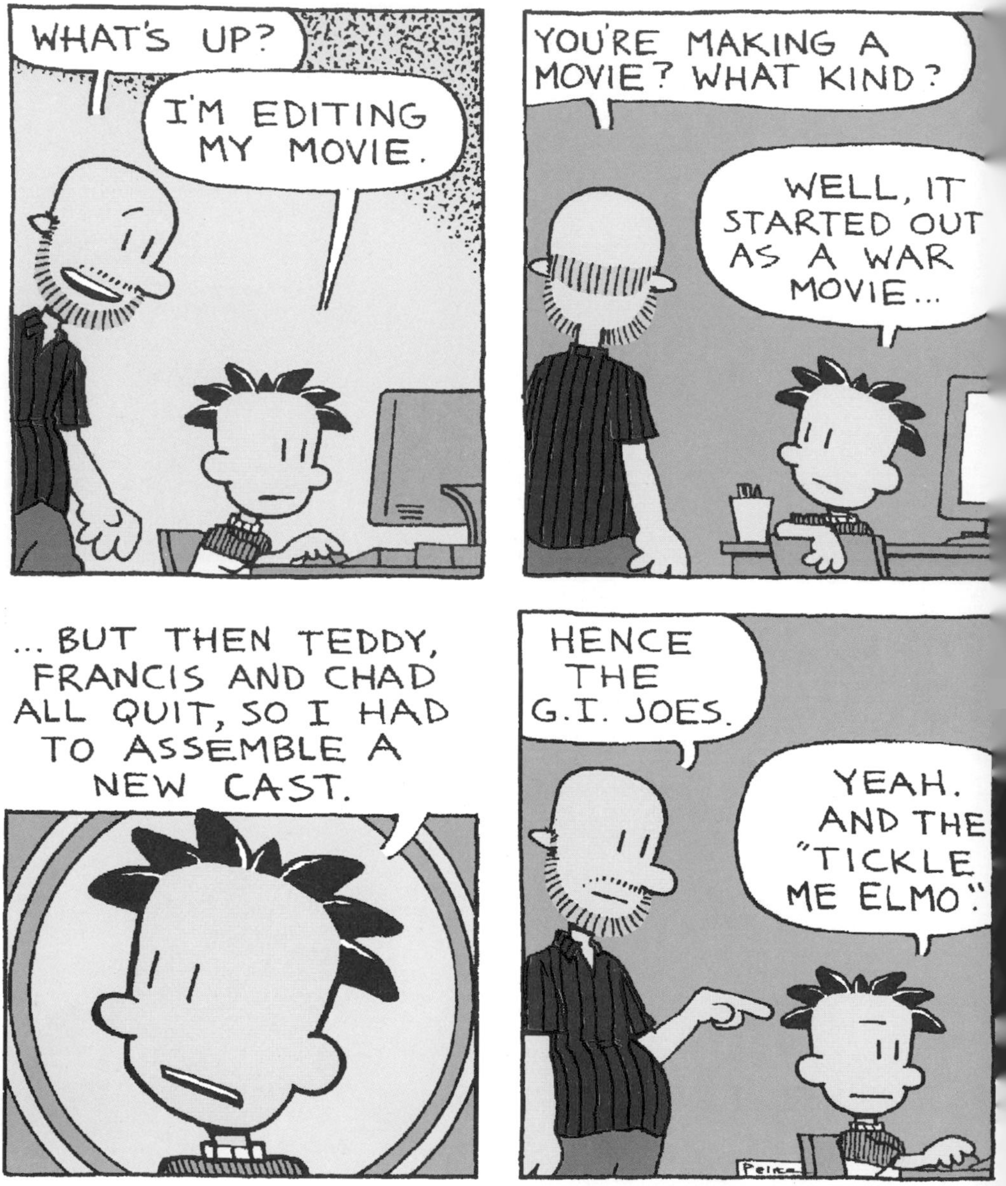
WHAT'S UP?
I'M EDITING MY MOVIE.
YOU'RE MAKING A MOVIE? WHAT KIND?
WELL, IT STARTED OUT AS A WAR MOVIE...
...BUT THEN TEDDY, FRANCIS AND CHAD ALL QUIT, SO I HAD TO ASSEMBLE A NEW CAST.
HENCE THE G.I. JOES.
YEAH. AND THE "TICKLE ME ELMO."
Peirce

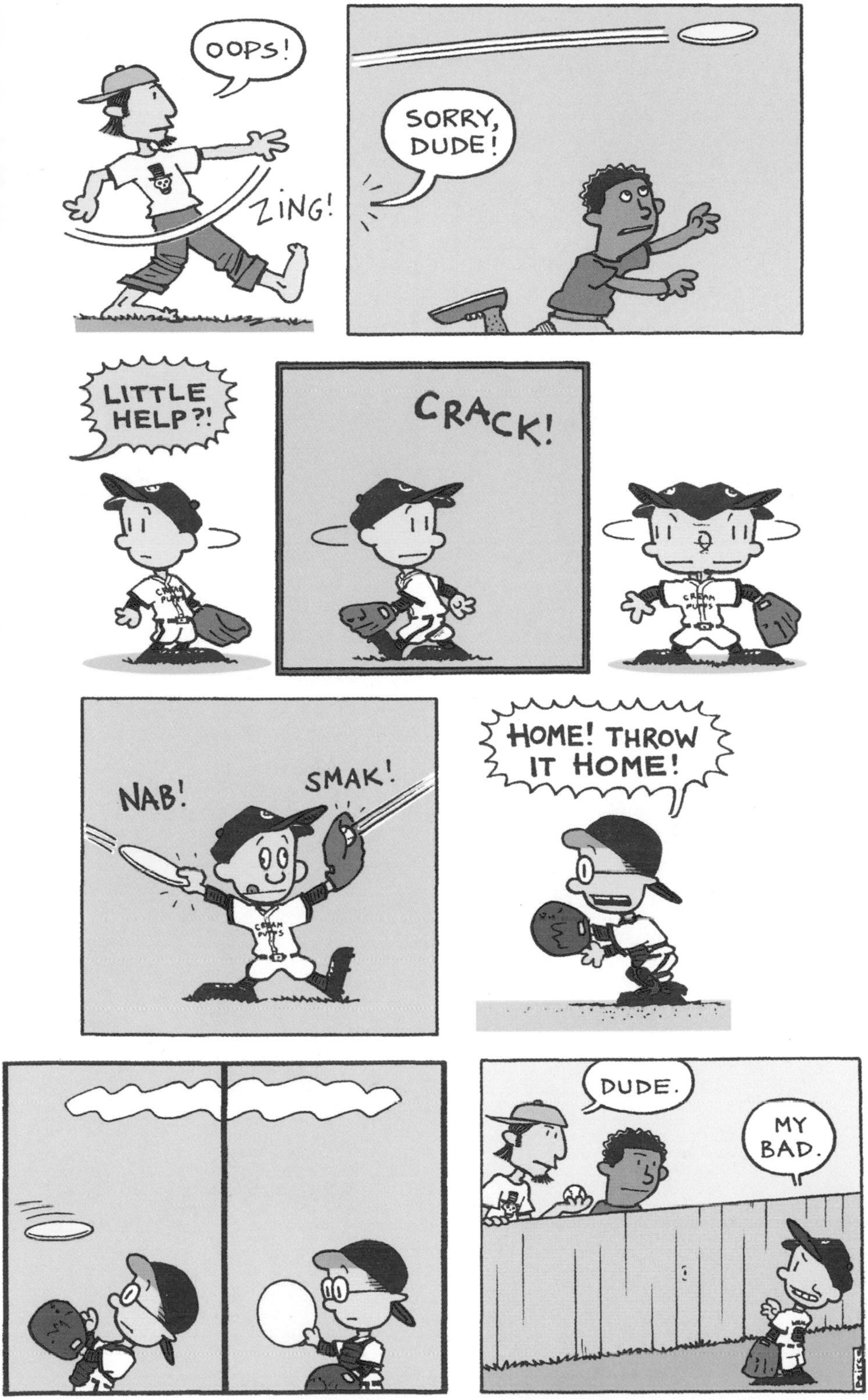
OOPS!
ZING!
SORRY, DUDE!
LITTLE HELP?!
CRACK!
NAB!
SMAK!
HOME! THROW IT HOME!
DUDE.
MY BAD.

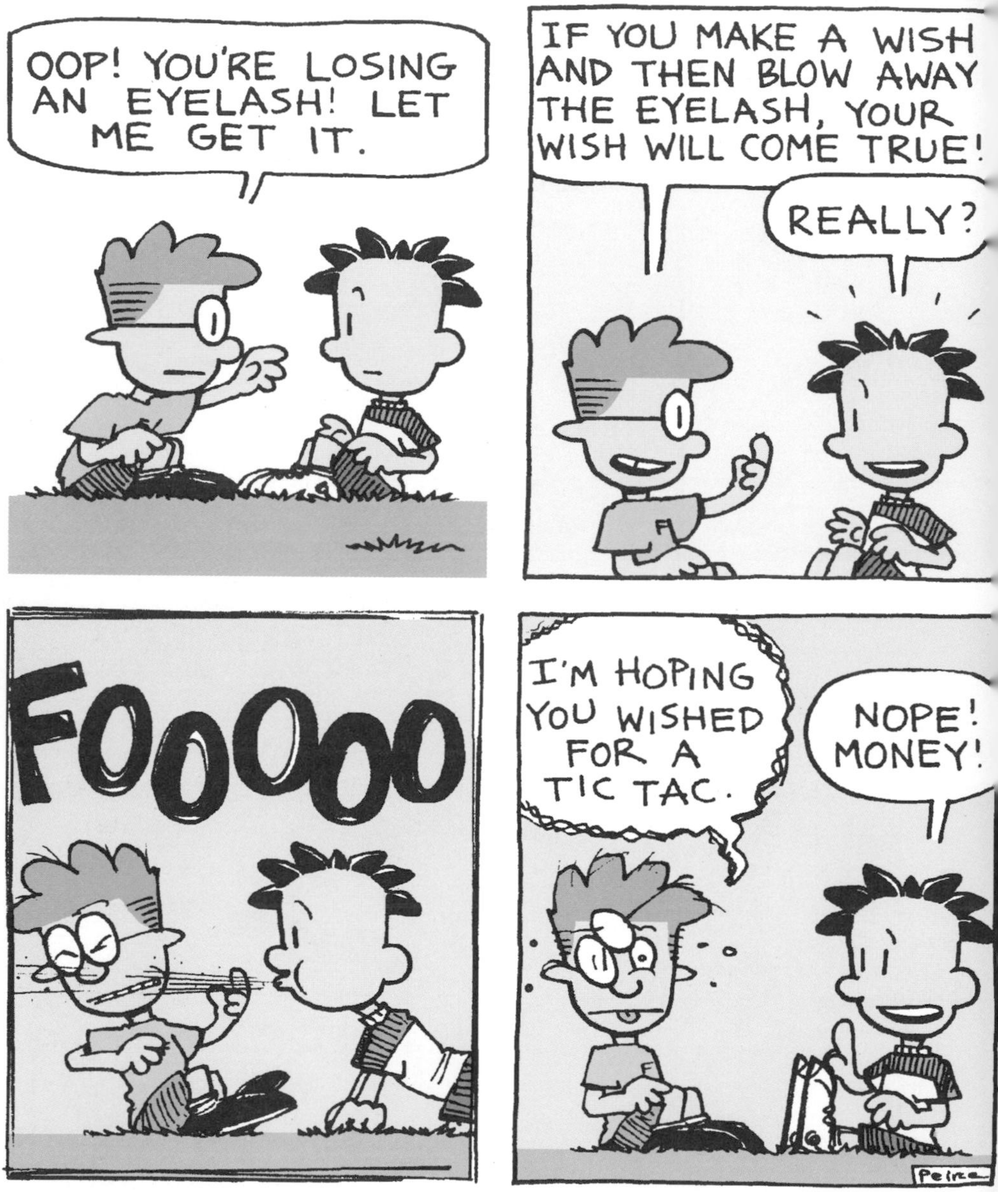
OOP! YOU'RE LOSING AN EYELASH! LET ME GET IT.
IF YOU MAKE A WISH AND THEN BLOW AWAY THE EYELASH, YOUR WISH WILL COME TRUE!
REALLY?
FOOOOO
I'M HOPING YOU WISHED FOR A TIC TAC.
NOPE! MONEY!
Peirce

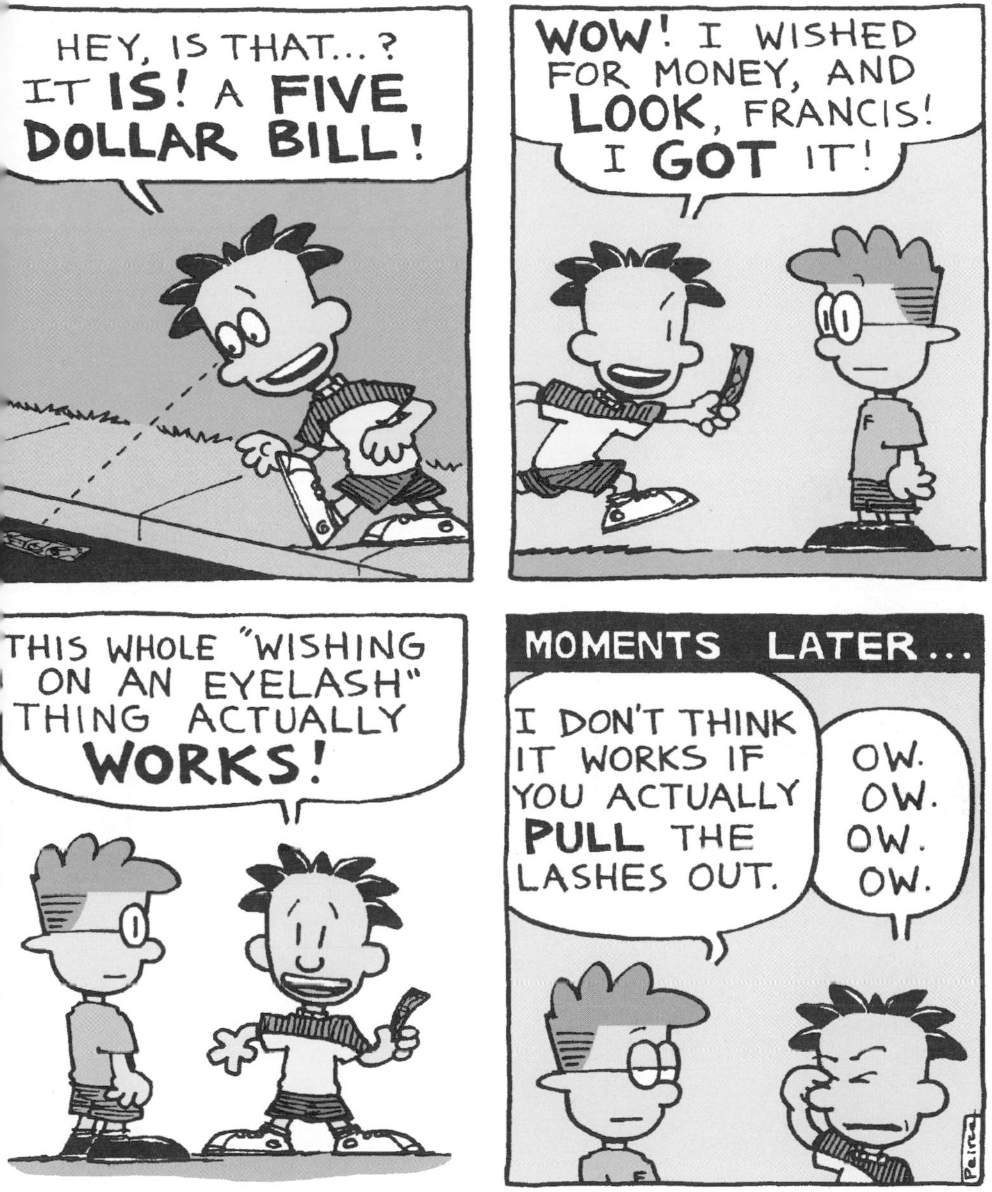
HEY, IS THAT...? IT IS! A FIVE DOLLAR BILL!
WOW! I WISHED FOR MONEY, AND LOOK, FRANCIS! I GOT IT!
THIS WHOLE "WISHING ON AN EYELASH" THING ACTUALLY WORKS!
MOMENTS LATER...
I DON'T THINK IT WORKS IF YOU ACTUALLY PULL THE LASHES OUT.
OW. OW. OW. OW.
Peirce

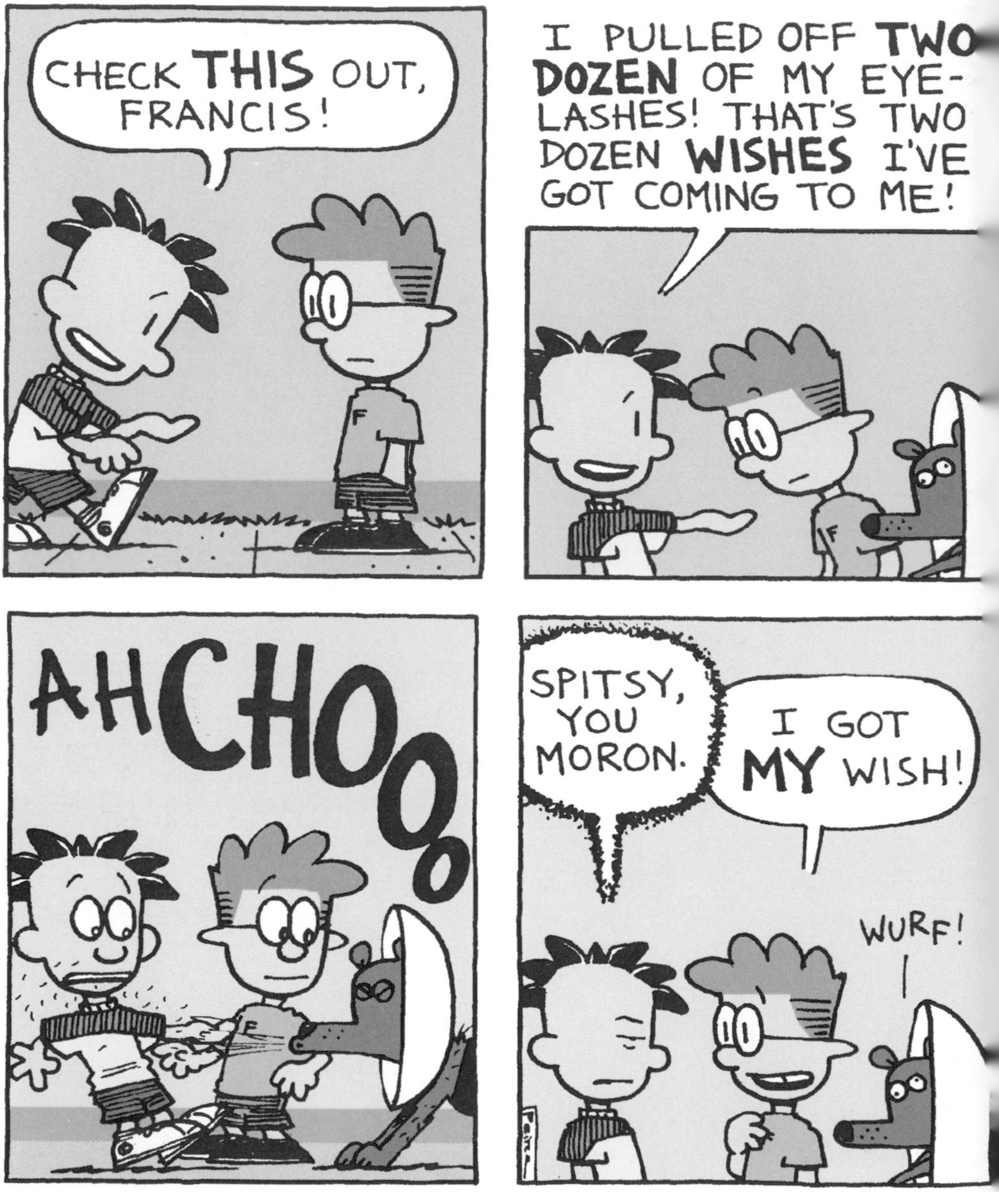
CHECK THIS OUT, FRANCIS!
I PULLED OFF TWO DOZEN OF MY EYE-LASHES! THAT'S TWO DOZEN WISHES I'VE GOT COMING TO ME!
AHCHOO
SPITSY, YOU MORON.
I GOT MY WISH!
WURF!

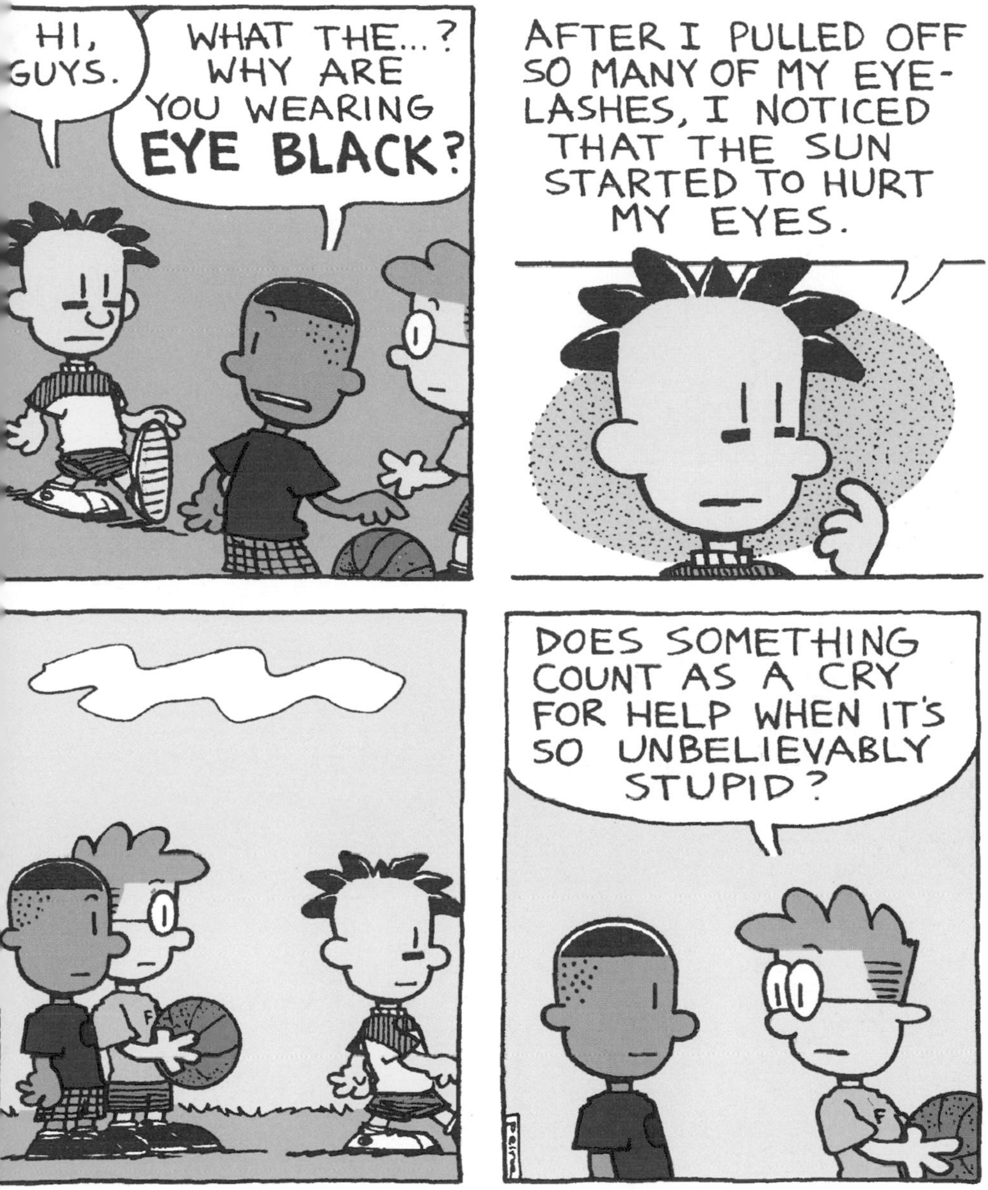
HI, GUYS.
WHAT THE...? WHY ARE YOU WEARING EYE BLACK?
AFTER I PULLED OFF SO MANY OF MY EYE-LASHES, I NOTICED THAT THE SUN STARTED TO HURT MY EYES.
DOES SOMETHING COUNT AS A CRY FOR HELP WHEN IT'S SO UNBELIEVABLY STUPID?

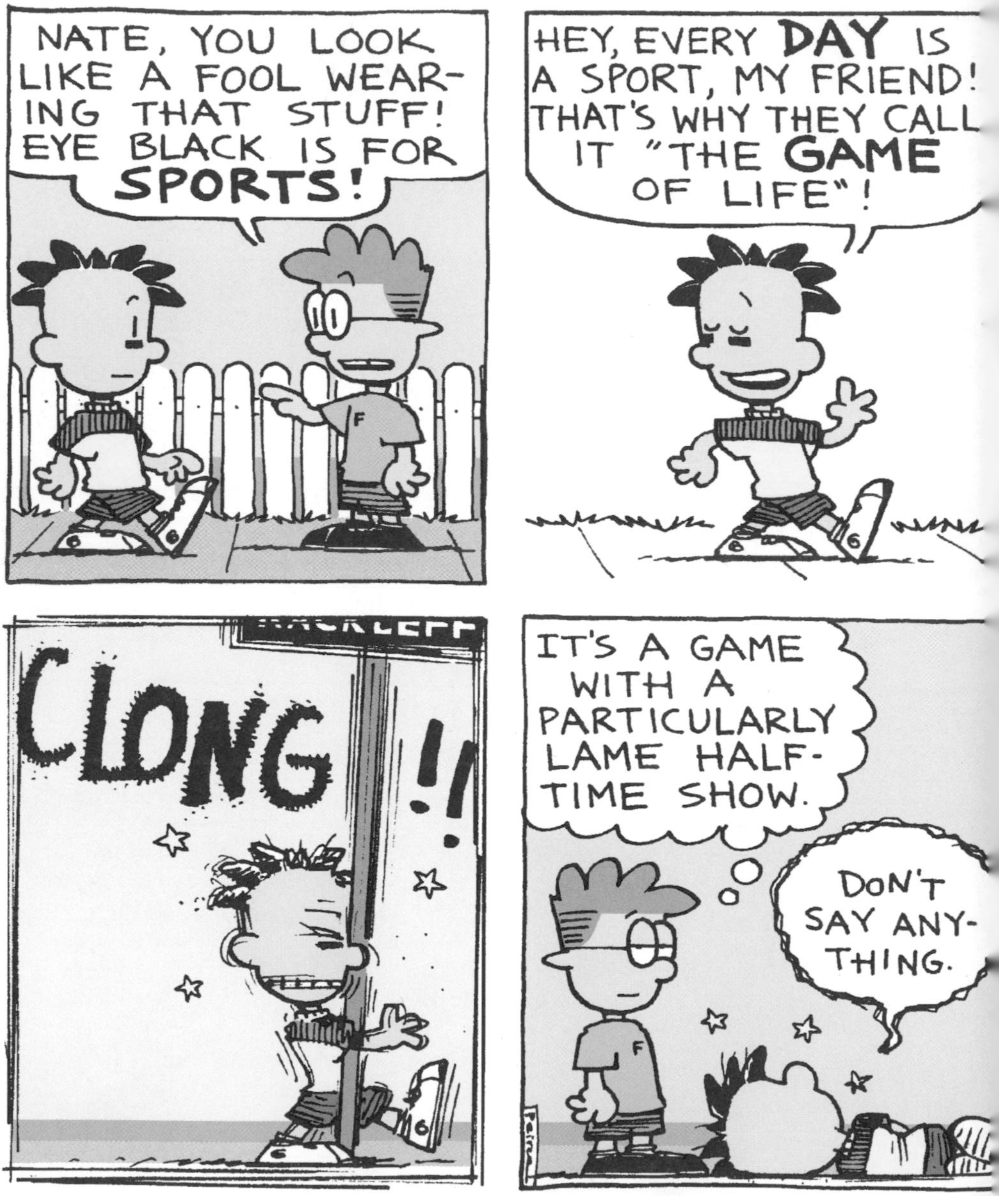
NATE, YOU LOOK LIKE A FOOL WEARING THAT STUFF! EYE BLACK IS FOR **SPORTS**!
HEY, EVERY **DAY** IS A SPORT, MY FRIEND! THAT'S WHY THEY CALL IT "THE **GAME** OF LIFE"!
CLONG!!
IT'S A GAME WITH A PARTICULARLY LAME HALF-TIME SHOW.
DON'T SAY ANYTHING.

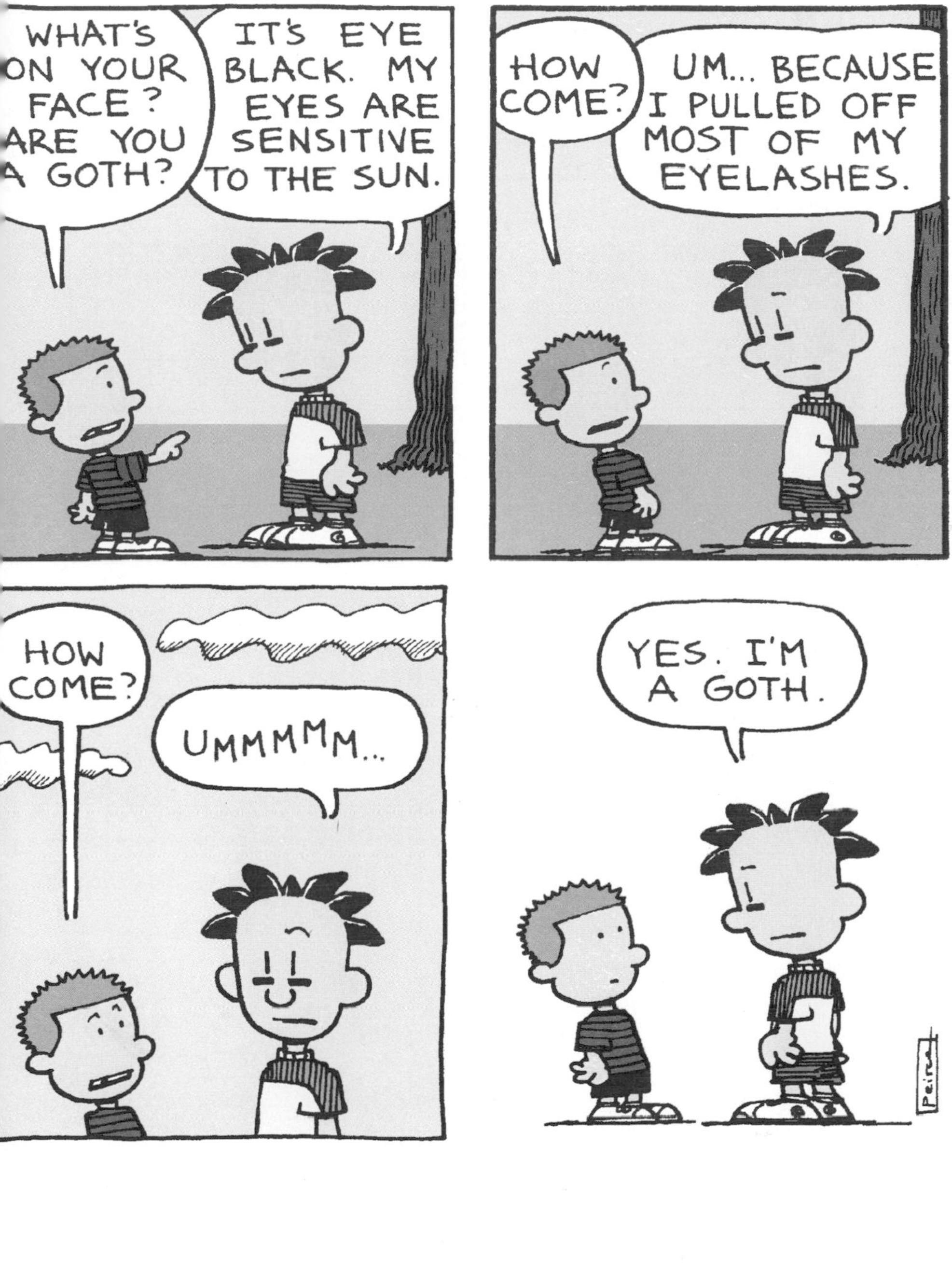
WHAT'S ON YOUR FACE? ARE YOU A GOTH?
IT'S EYE BLACK. MY EYES ARE SENSITIVE TO THE SUN.
HOW COME?
UM... BECAUSE I PULLED OFF MOST OF MY EYELASHES.
HOW COME?
UMMMMM...
YES. I'M A GOTH.
Peirce

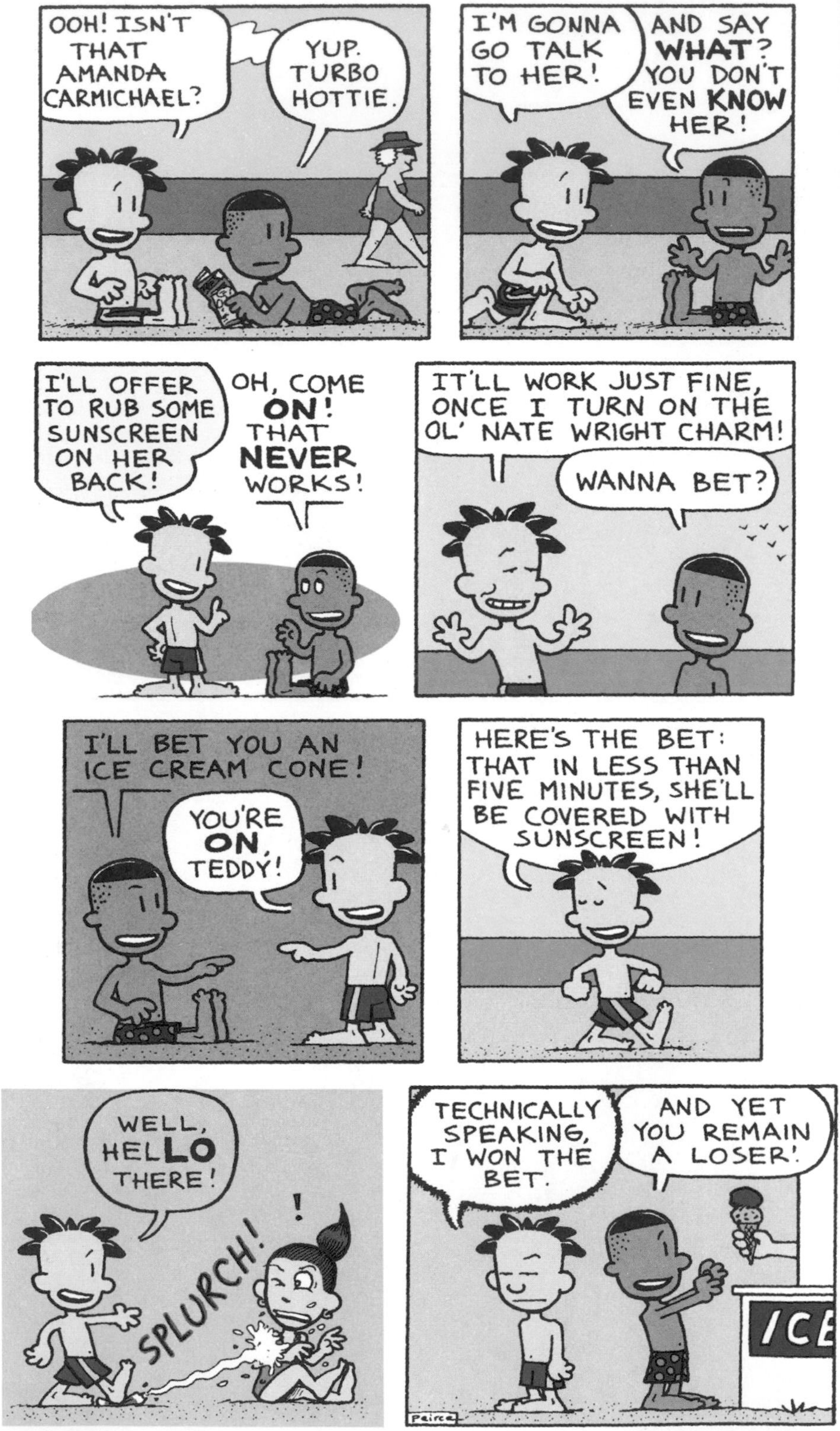
OOH! ISN'T THAT AMANDA CARMICHAEL?
YUP. TURBO HOTTIE.
I'M GONNA GO TALK TO HER!
AND SAY **WHAT**? YOU DON'T EVEN **KNOW** HER!
I'LL OFFER TO RUB SOME SUNSCREEN ON HER BACK!
OH, COME **ON**! THAT **NEVER** WORKS!
IT'LL WORK JUST FINE, ONCE I TURN ON THE OL' NATE WRIGHT CHARM!
WANNA BET?
I'LL BET YOU AN ICE CREAM CONE!
YOU'RE **ON**, TEDDY!
HERE'S THE BET: THAT IN LESS THAN FIVE MINUTES, SHE'LL BE COVERED WITH SUNSCREEN!
WELL, HEL**LO** THERE!
!
SPLURCH!
TECHNICALLY SPEAKING, I WON THE BET.
AND YET YOU REMAIN A LOSER!
ICE
Peirce

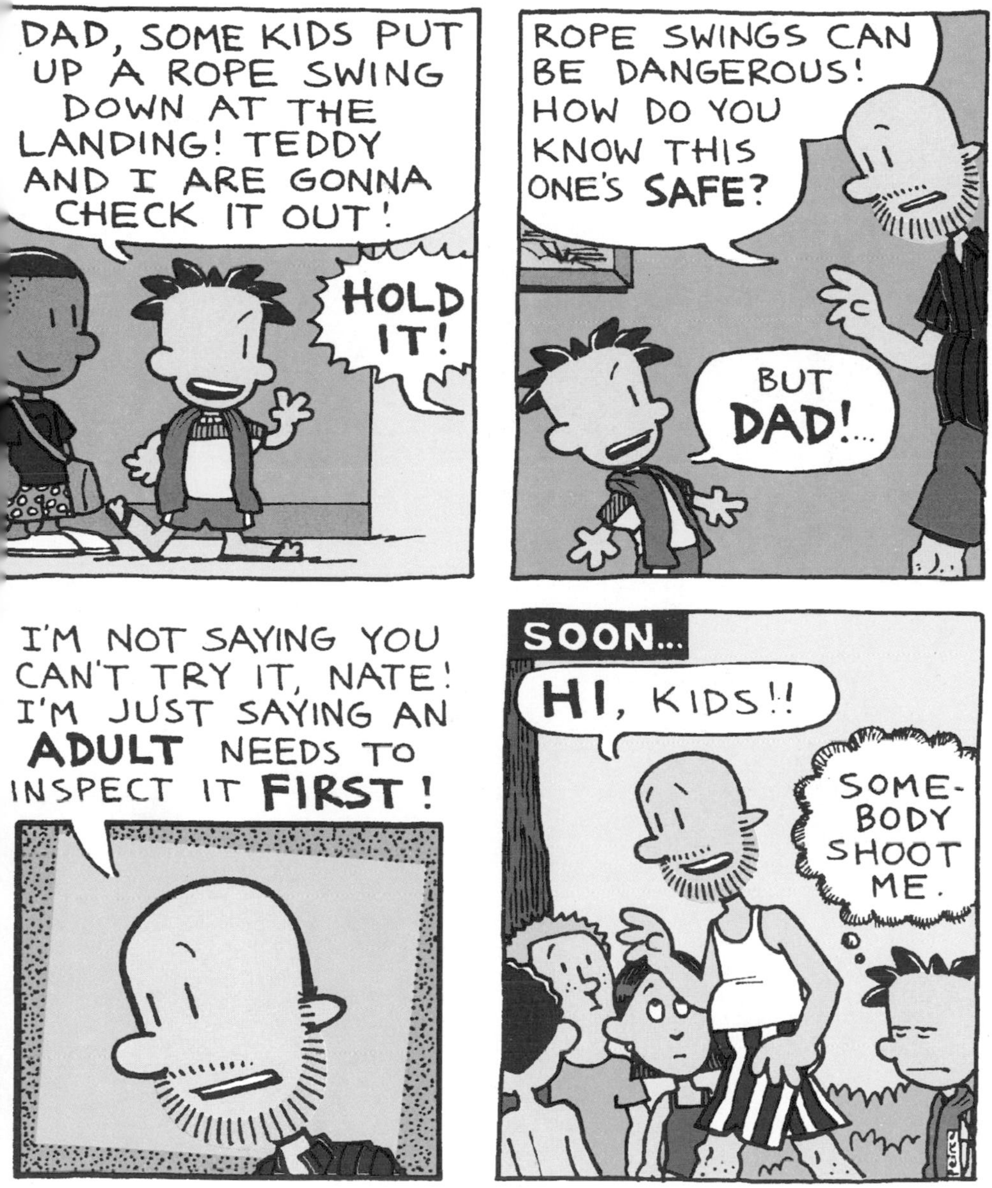
DAD, SOME KIDS PUT UP A ROPE SWING DOWN AT THE LANDING! TEDDY AND I ARE GONNA CHECK IT OUT!
HOLD IT!
ROPE SWINGS CAN BE DANGEROUS! HOW DO YOU KNOW THIS ONE'S SAFE?
BUT DAD!...
I'M NOT SAYING YOU CAN'T TRY IT, NATE! I'M JUST SAYING AN ADULT NEEDS TO INSPECT IT FIRST!
SOON...
HI, KIDS!!
SOME-BODY SHOOT ME.

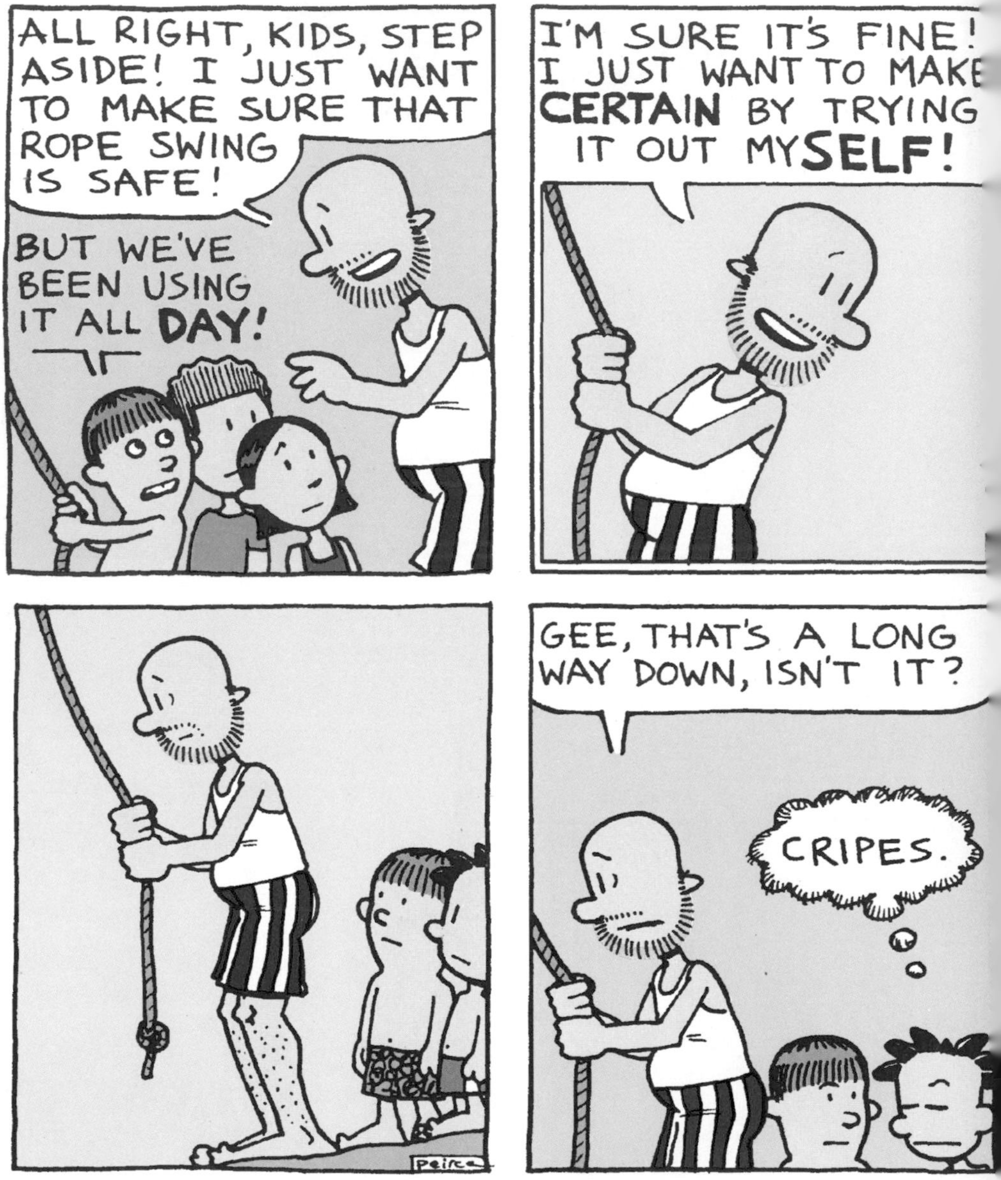
ALL RIGHT, KIDS, STEP ASIDE! I JUST WANT TO MAKE SURE THAT ROPE SWING IS SAFE!
BUT WE'VE BEEN USING IT ALL DAY!
I'M SURE IT'S FINE! I JUST WANT TO MAKE CERTAIN BY TRYING IT OUT MYSELF!
GEE, THAT'S A LONG WAY DOWN, ISN'T IT?
CRIPES.

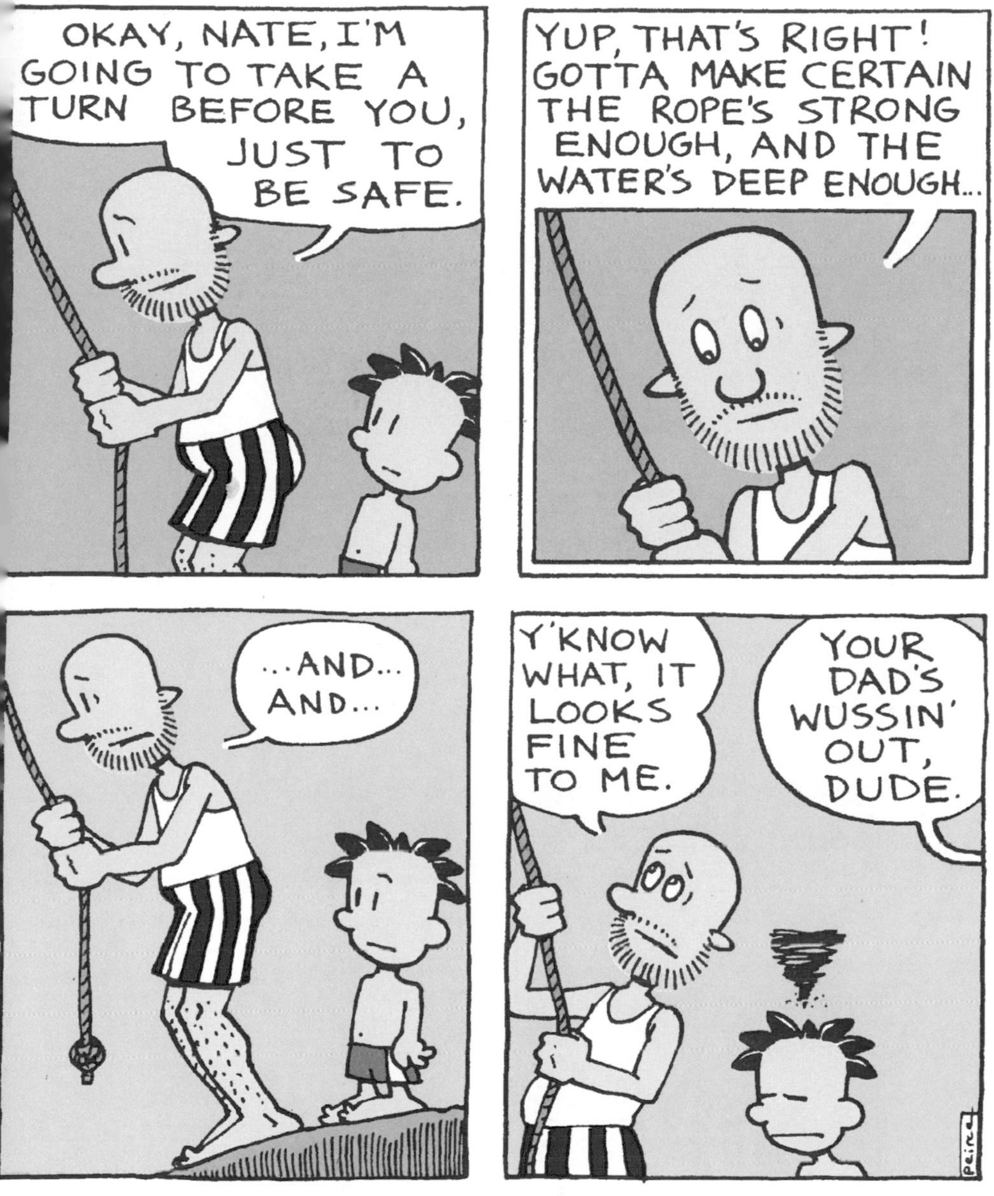
OKAY, NATE, I'M GOING TO TAKE A TURN BEFORE YOU, JUST TO BE SAFE.
YUP, THAT'S RIGHT! GOTTA MAKE CERTAIN THE ROPE'S STRONG ENOUGH, AND THE WATER'S DEEP ENOUGH...
...AND... AND...
Y'KNOW WHAT, IT LOOKS FINE TO ME.
YOUR DAD'S WUSSIN' OUT, DUDE.
PEIRCE

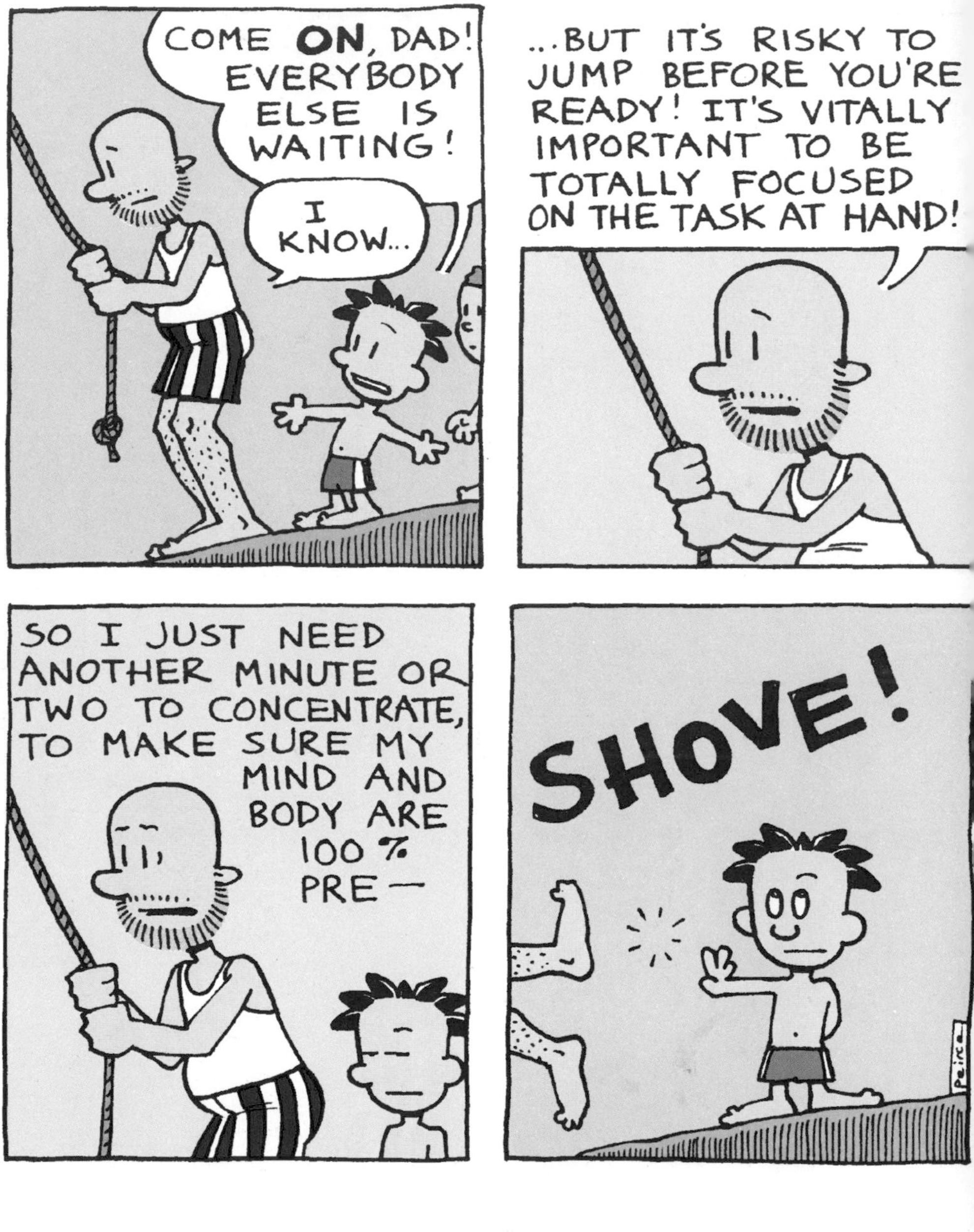
COME ON, DAD! EVERYBODY ELSE IS WAITING!
I KNOW...
...BUT IT'S RISKY TO JUMP BEFORE YOU'RE READY! IT'S VITALLY IMPORTANT TO BE TOTALLY FOCUSED ON THE TASK AT HAND!
SO I JUST NEED ANOTHER MINUTE OR TWO TO CONCENTRATE, TO MAKE SURE MY MIND AND BODY ARE 100% PRE—
SHOVE!
Peirce

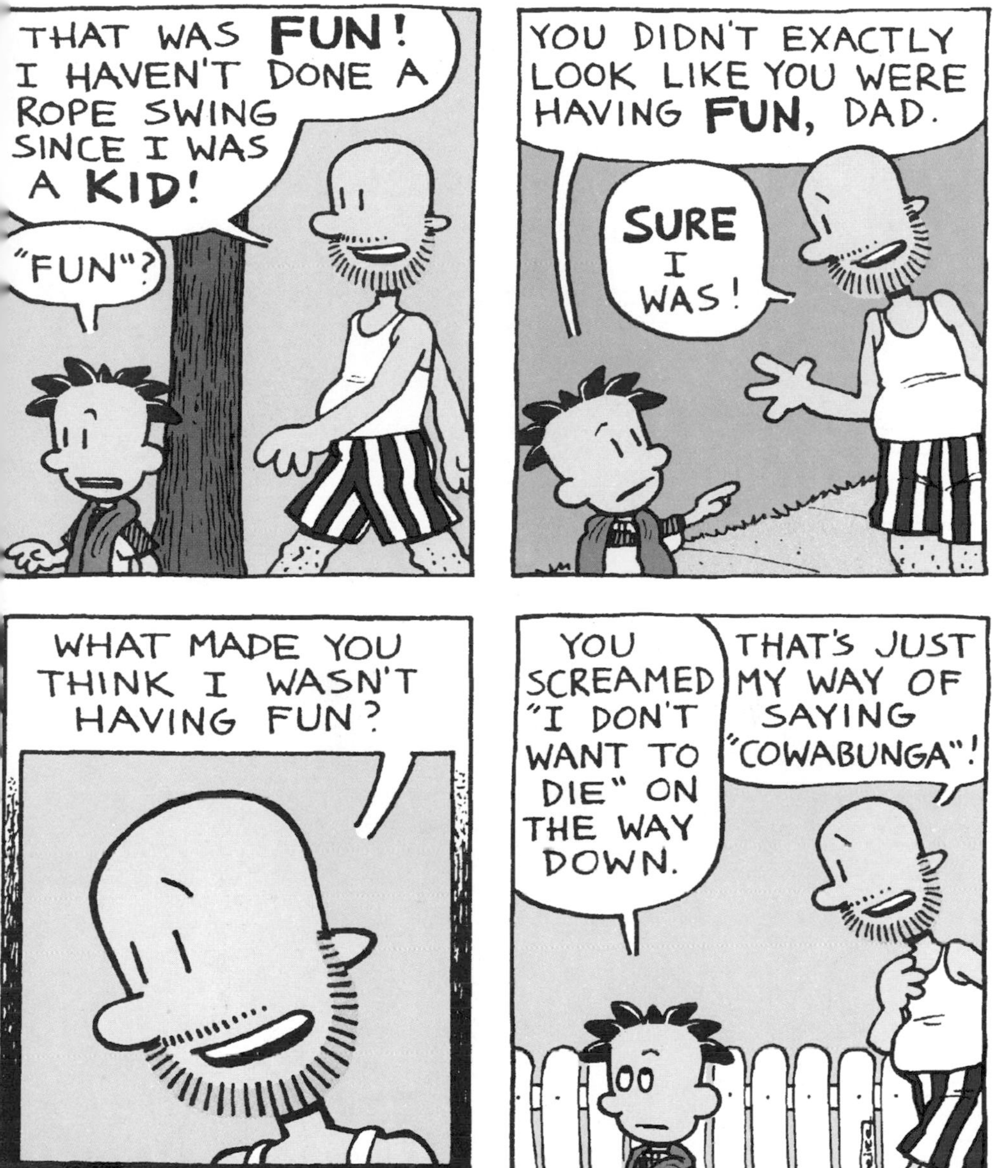
THAT WAS **FUN**! I HAVEN'T DONE A ROPE SWING SINCE I WAS A **KID**!
"FUN"?
YOU DIDN'T EXACTLY LOOK LIKE YOU WERE HAVING **FUN**, DAD.
SURE I WAS!
WHAT MADE YOU THINK I WASN'T HAVING FUN?
YOU SCREAMED "I DON'T WANT TO DIE" ON THE WAY DOWN.
THAT'S JUST MY WAY OF SAYING "COWABUNGA"!

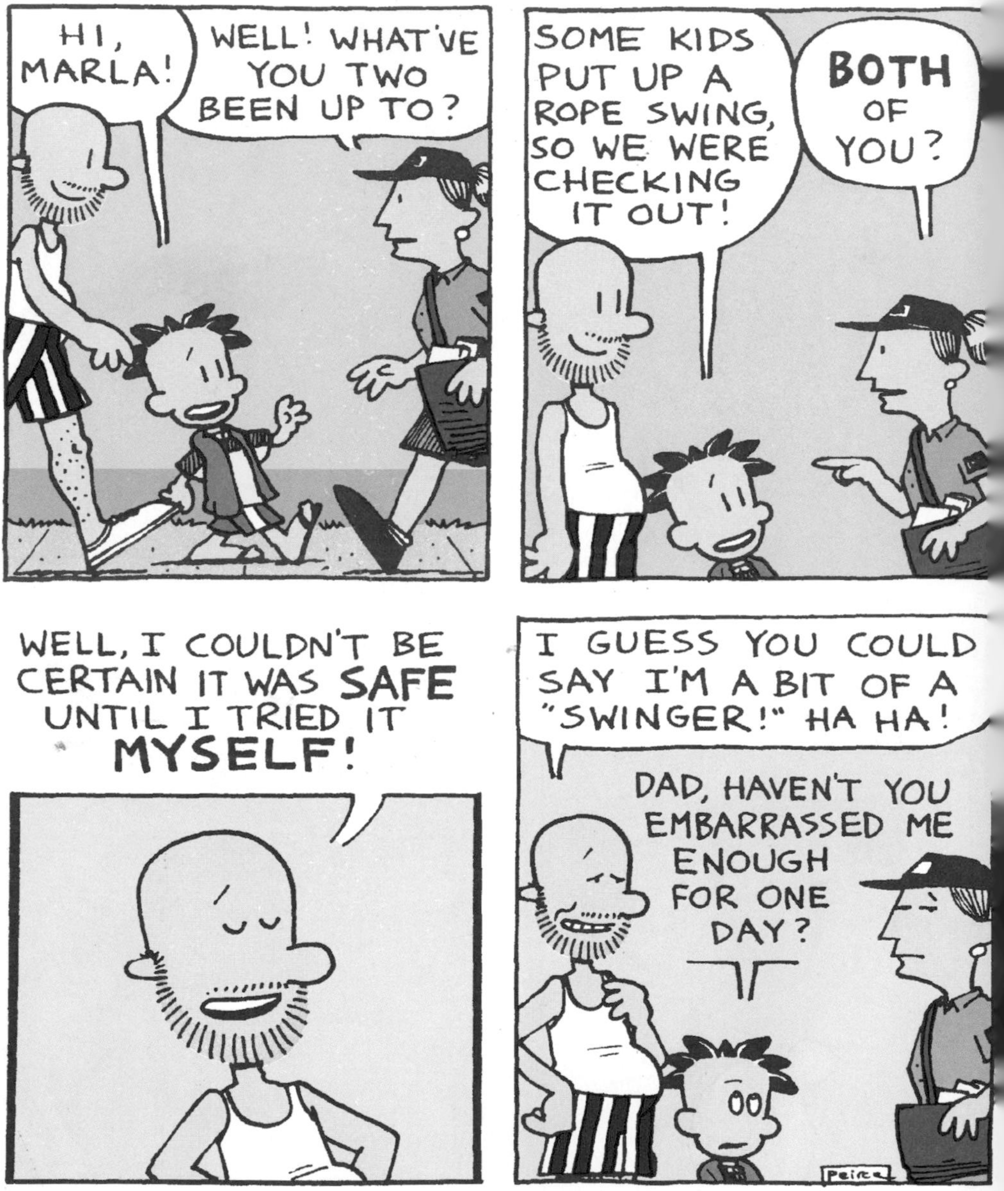
HI, MARLA!
WELL! WHAT'VE YOU TWO BEEN UP TO?
SOME KIDS PUT UP A ROPE SWING, SO WE WERE CHECKING IT OUT!
BOTH OF YOU?
WELL, I COULDN'T BE CERTAIN IT WAS SAFE UNTIL I TRIED IT MYSELF!
I GUESS YOU COULD SAY I'M A BIT OF A "SWINGER!" HA HA!
DAD, HAVEN'T YOU EMBARRASSED ME ENOUGH FOR ONE DAY?
Peirce

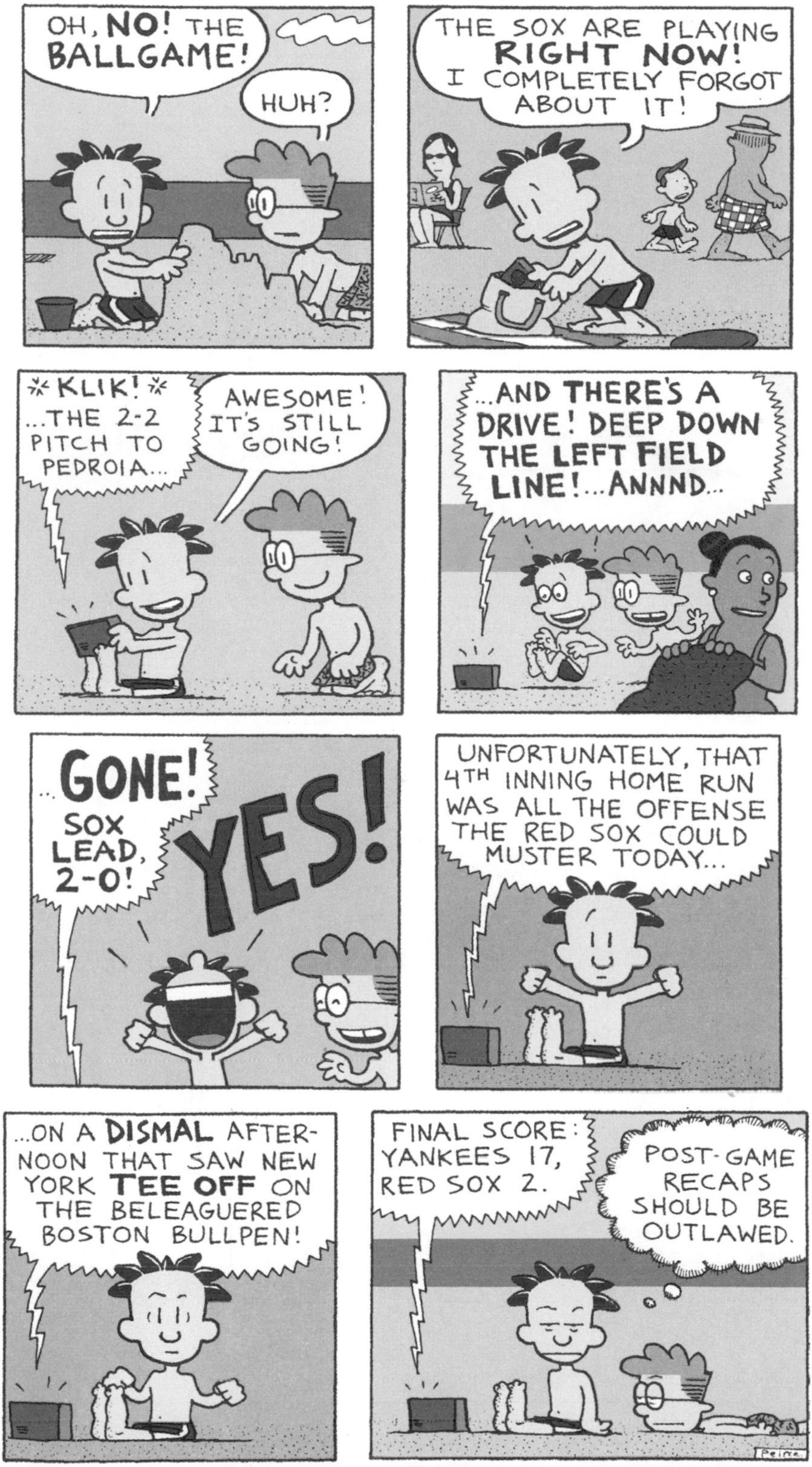
OH, NO! THE BALLGAME!
HUH?
THE SOX ARE PLAYING RIGHT NOW! I COMPLETELY FORGOT ABOUT IT!
KLIK! ...THE 2-2 PITCH TO PEDROIA...
AWESOME! IT'S STILL GOING!
...AND THERE'S A DRIVE! DEEP DOWN THE LEFT FIELD LINE!...ANNND...
...GONE! SOX LEAD, 2-0!
YES!
UNFORTUNATELY, THAT 4TH INNING HOME RUN WAS ALL THE OFFENSE THE RED SOX COULD MUSTER TODAY...
...ON A DISMAL AFTERNOON THAT SAW NEW YORK TEE OFF ON THE BELEAGUERED BOSTON BULLPEN!
FINAL SCORE: YANKEES 17, RED SOX 2.
POST-GAME RECAPS SHOULD BE OUTLAWED.
Peirce

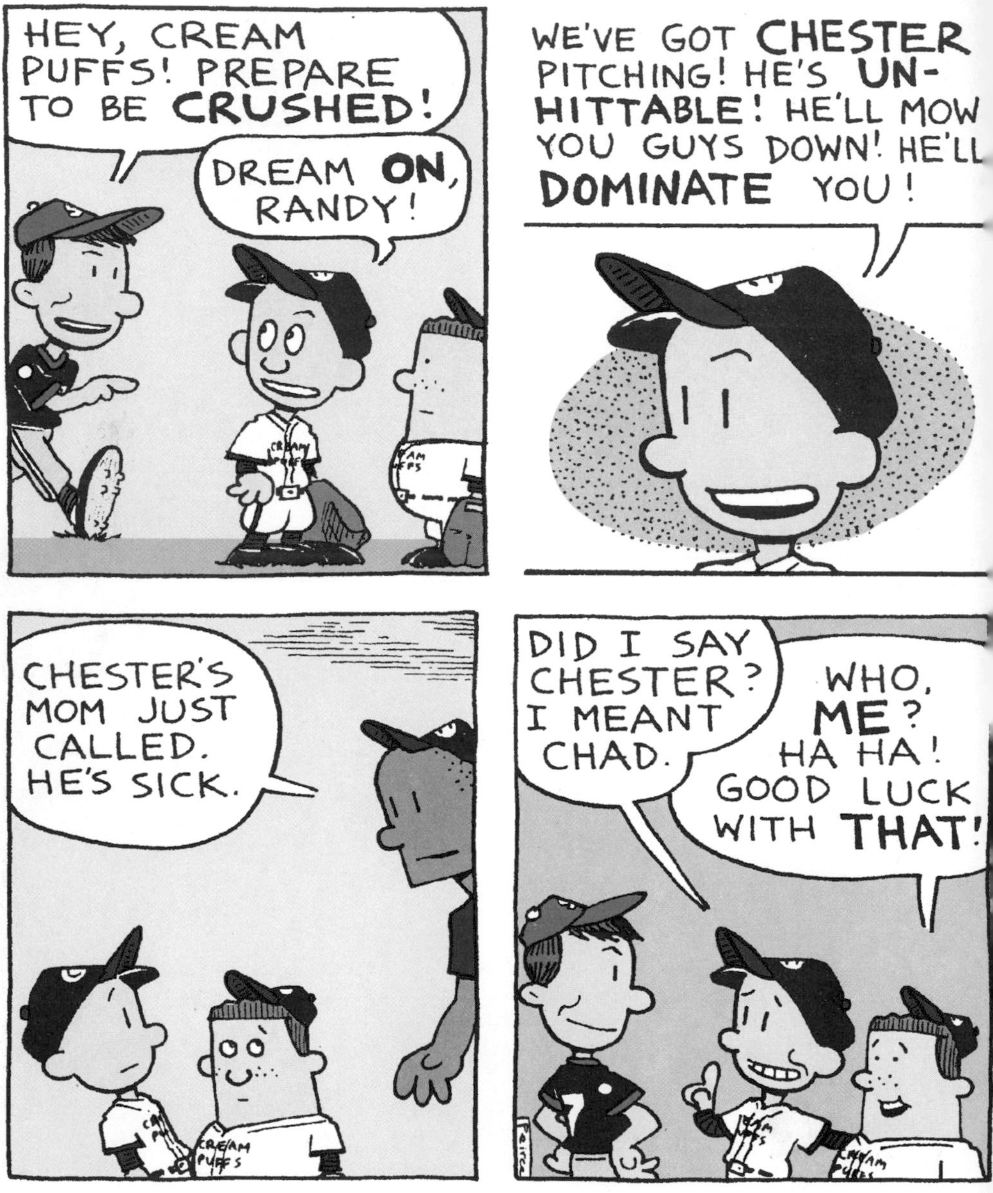

HEY, CREAM PUFFS! PREPARE TO BE **CRUSHED**!
DREAM **ON**, RANDY!
WE'VE GOT **CHESTER** PITCHING! HE'S **UN-HITTABLE**! HE'LL MOW YOU GUYS DOWN! HE'LL **DOMINATE** YOU!
CHESTER'S MOM JUST CALLED. HE'S SICK.
DID I SAY CHESTER? I MEANT CHAD.
WHO, **ME**? HA HA! GOOD LUCK WITH **THAT**!

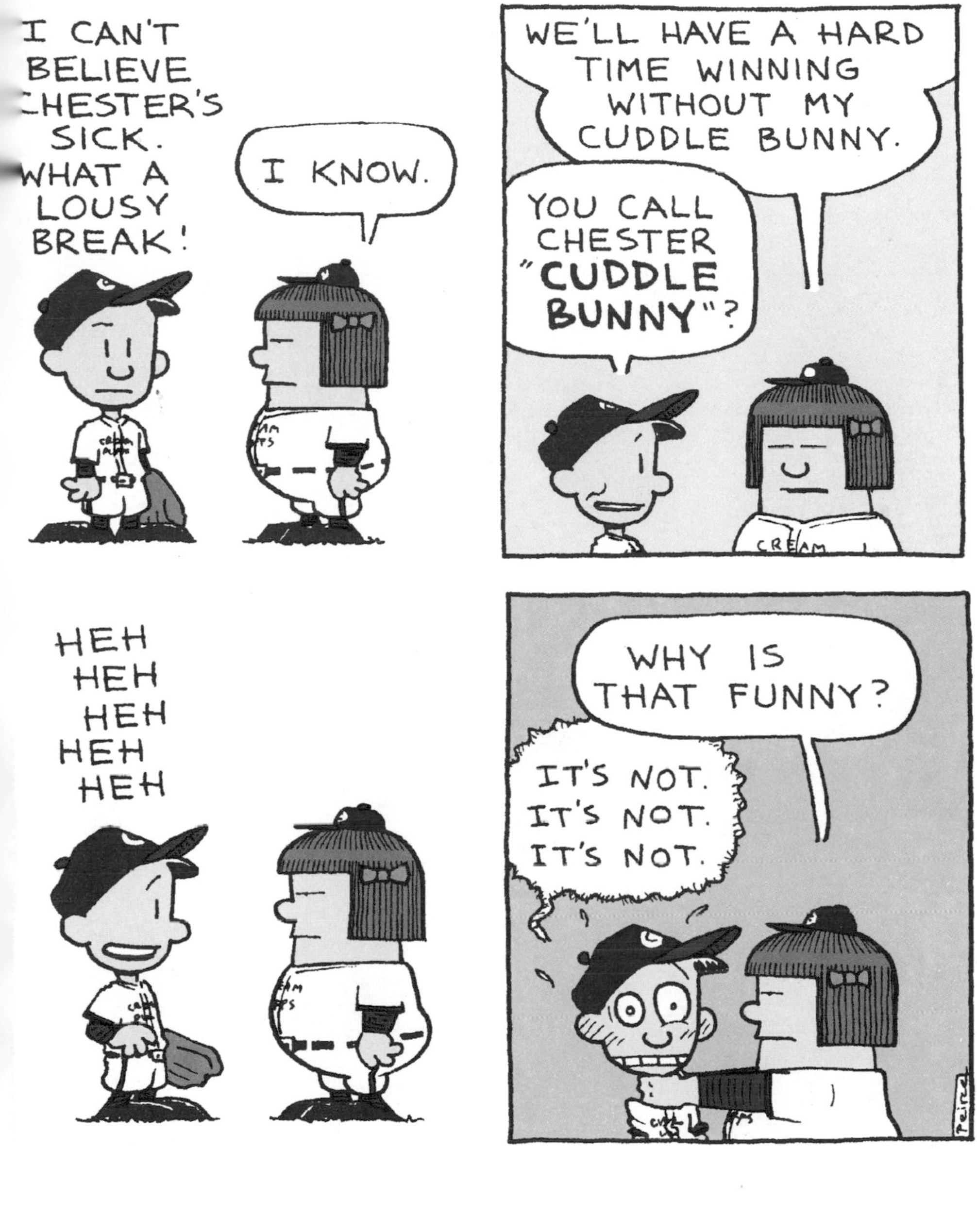
I CAN'T BELIEVE CHESTER'S SICK. WHAT A LOUSY BREAK!
I KNOW.
WE'LL HAVE A HARD TIME WINNING WITHOUT MY CUDDLE BUNNY.
YOU CALL CHESTER "CUDDLE BUNNY"?
CREAM
HEH HEH HEH HEH HEH
WHY IS THAT FUNNY?
IT'S NOT. IT'S NOT. IT'S NOT.
Peirce

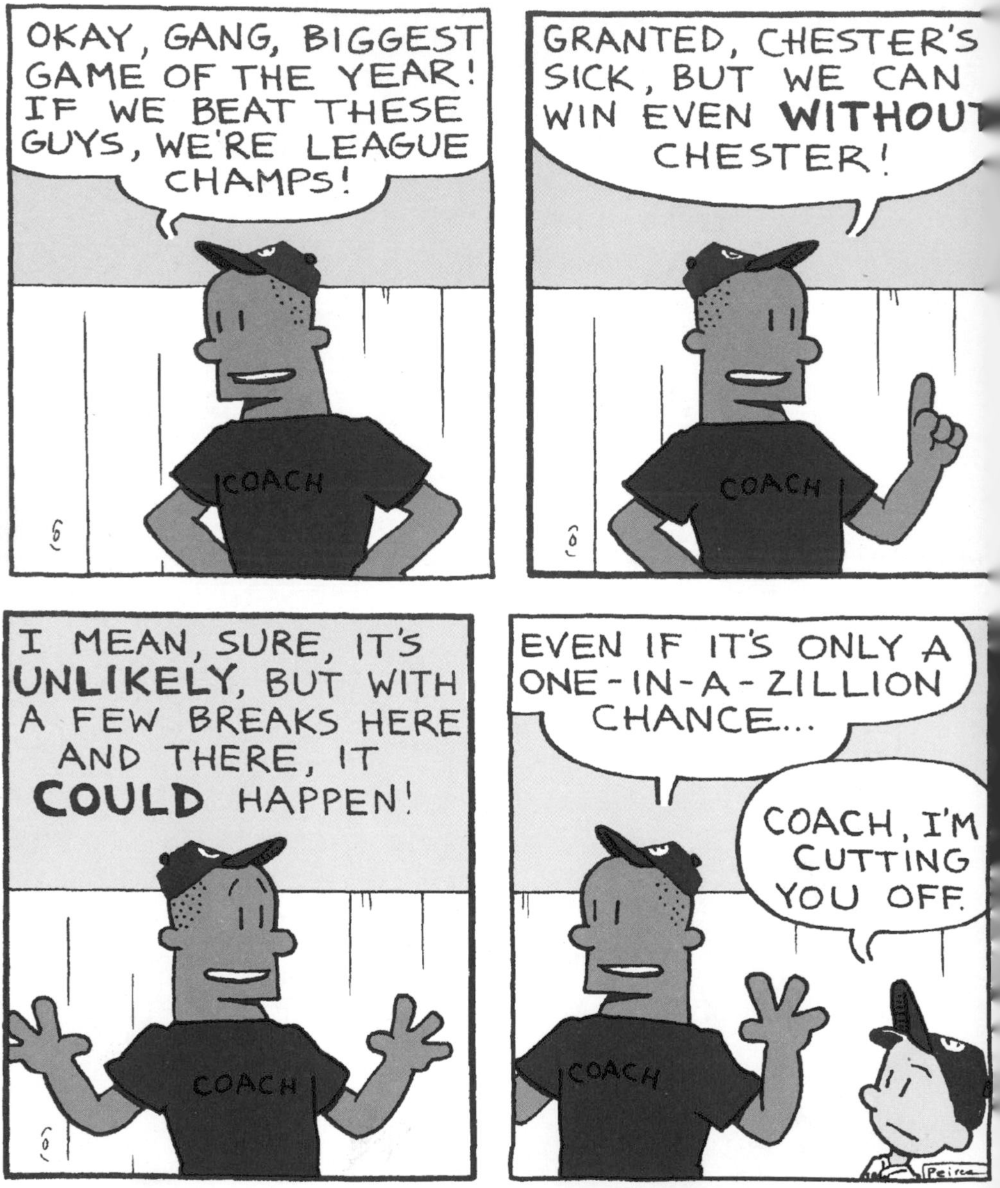
OKAY, GANG, BIGGEST GAME OF THE YEAR! IF WE BEAT THESE GUYS, WE'RE LEAGUE CHAMPS!
COACH
GRANTED, CHESTER'S SICK, BUT WE CAN WIN EVEN **WITHOUT** CHESTER!
COACH
I MEAN, SURE, IT'S **UNLIKELY**, BUT WITH A FEW BREAKS HERE AND THERE, IT **COULD** HAPPEN!
COACH
EVEN IF IT'S ONLY A ONE-IN-A-ZILLION CHANCE...
COACH, I'M CUTTING YOU OFF.
COACH
Peirce

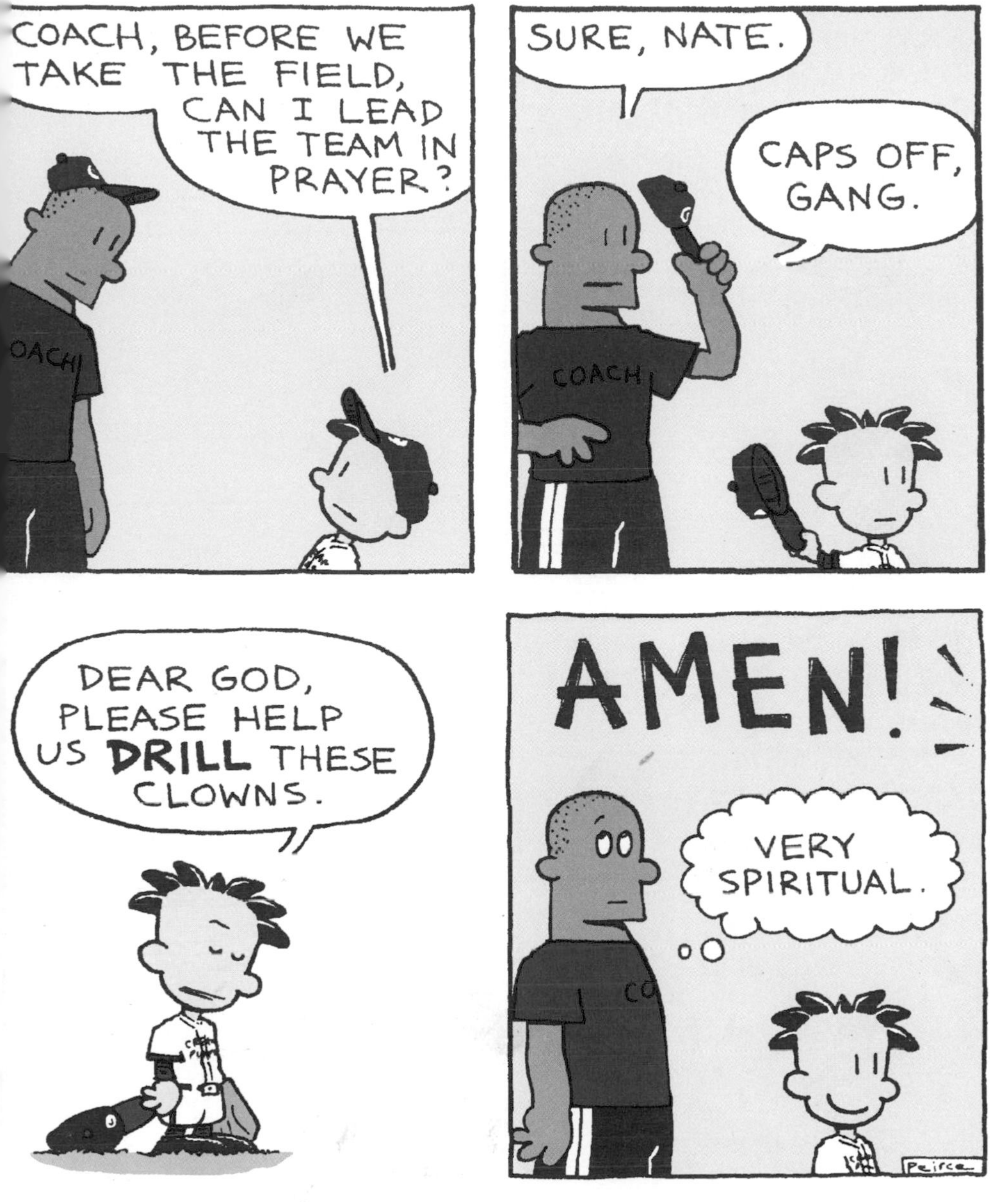
COACH, BEFORE WE TAKE THE FIELD, CAN I LEAD THE TEAM IN PRAYER?
SURE, NATE.
CAPS OFF, GANG.
DEAR GOD, PLEASE HELP US **DRILL** THESE CLOWNS.
AMEN!
VERY SPIRITUAL.
Peirce

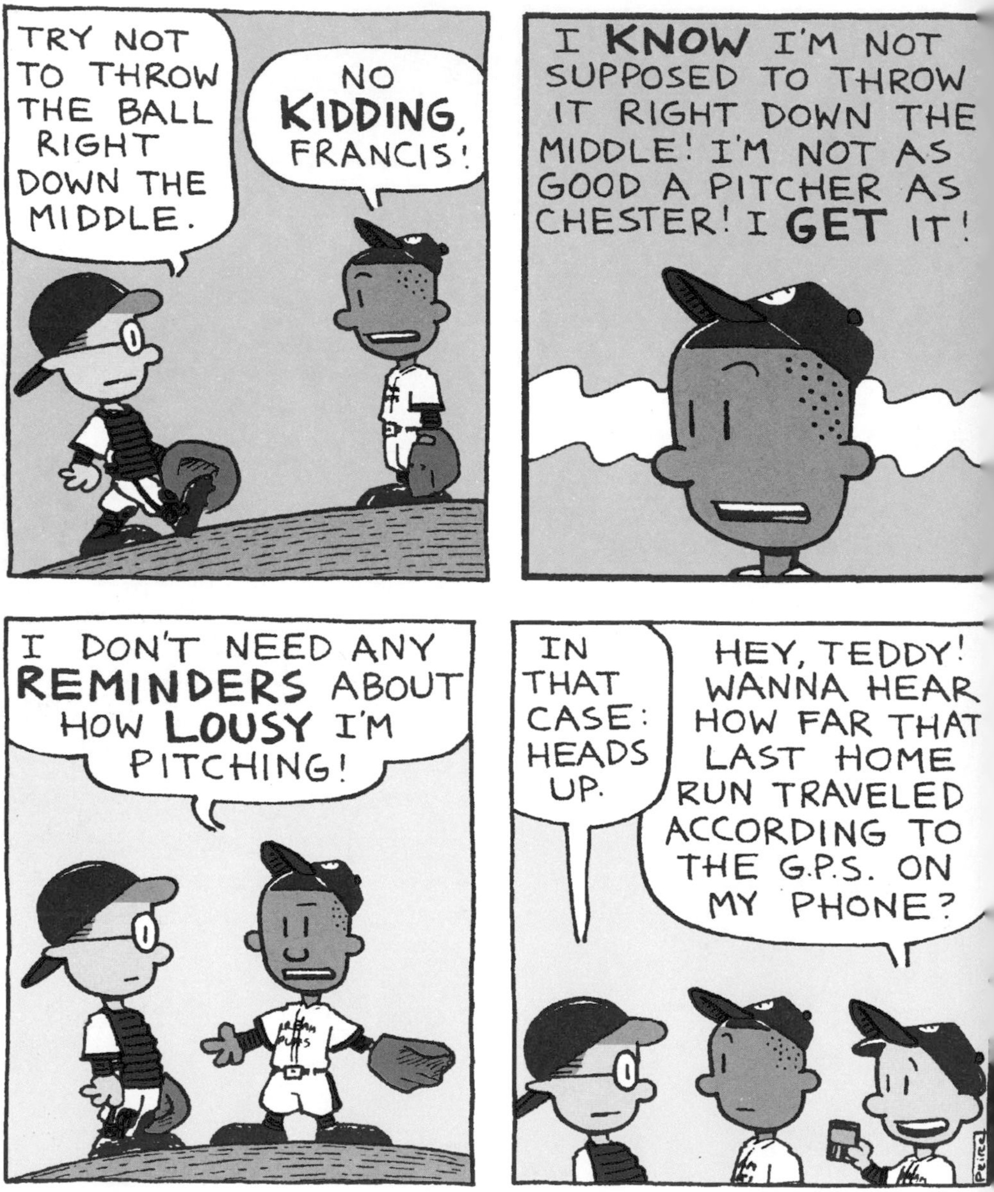
TRY NOT TO THROW THE BALL RIGHT DOWN THE MIDDLE.
NO **KIDDING**, FRANCIS!
I **KNOW** I'M NOT SUPPOSED TO THROW IT RIGHT DOWN THE MIDDLE! I'M NOT AS GOOD A PITCHER AS CHESTER! I **GET** IT!
I DON'T NEED ANY **REMINDERS** ABOUT HOW **LOUSY** I'M PITCHING!
HEY, TEDDY! WANNA HEAR HOW FAR THAT LAST HOME RUN TRAVELED ACCORDING TO THE G.P.S. ON MY PHONE?
IN THAT CASE: HEADS UP.
PEIRCE

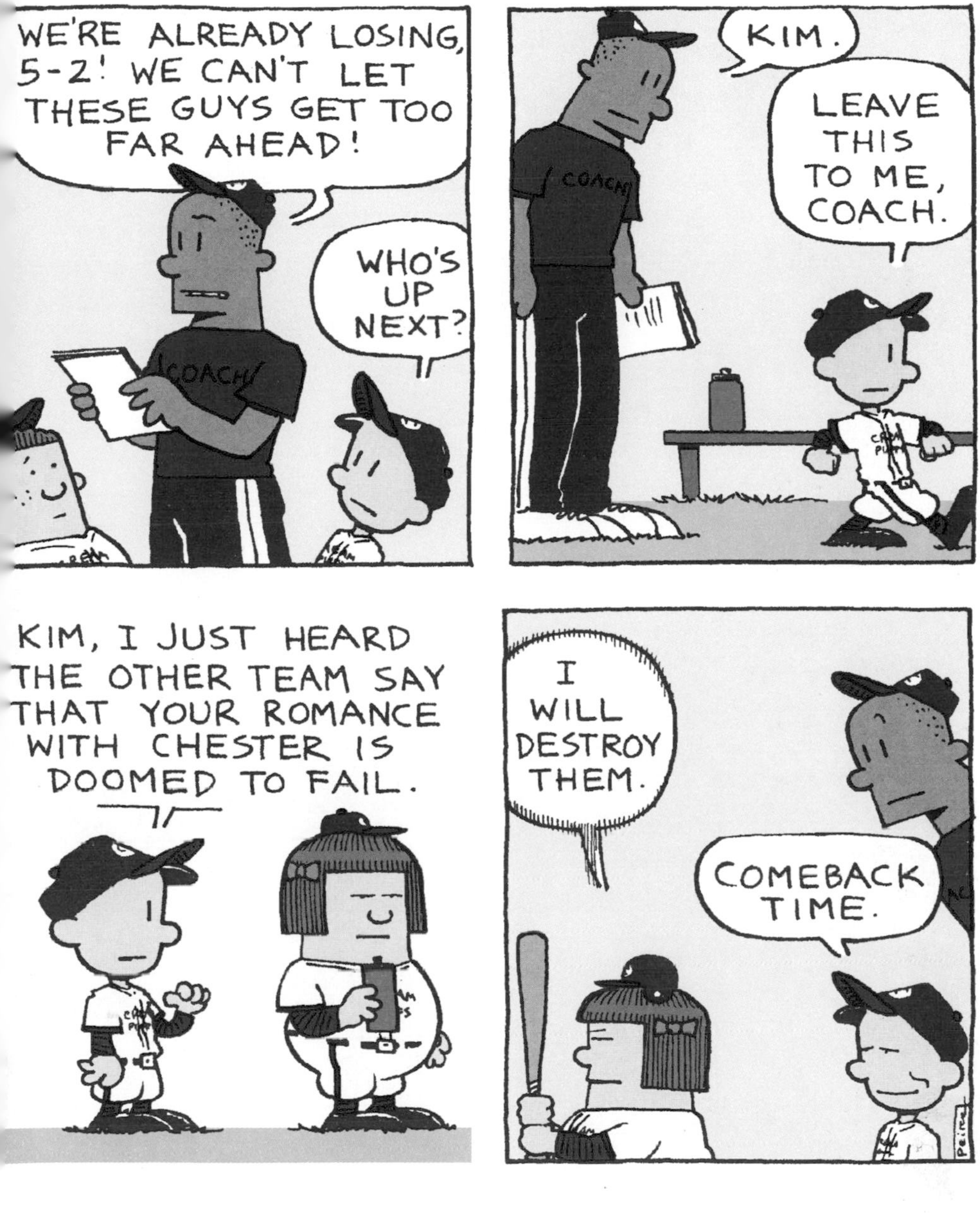
WE'RE ALREADY LOSING, 5-2! WE CAN'T LET THESE GUYS GET TOO FAR AHEAD!
WHO'S UP NEXT?
KIM.
LEAVE THIS TO ME, COACH.
KIM, I JUST HEARD THE OTHER TEAM SAY THAT YOUR ROMANCE WITH CHESTER IS DOOMED TO FAIL.
I WILL DESTROY THEM.
COMEBACK TIME.

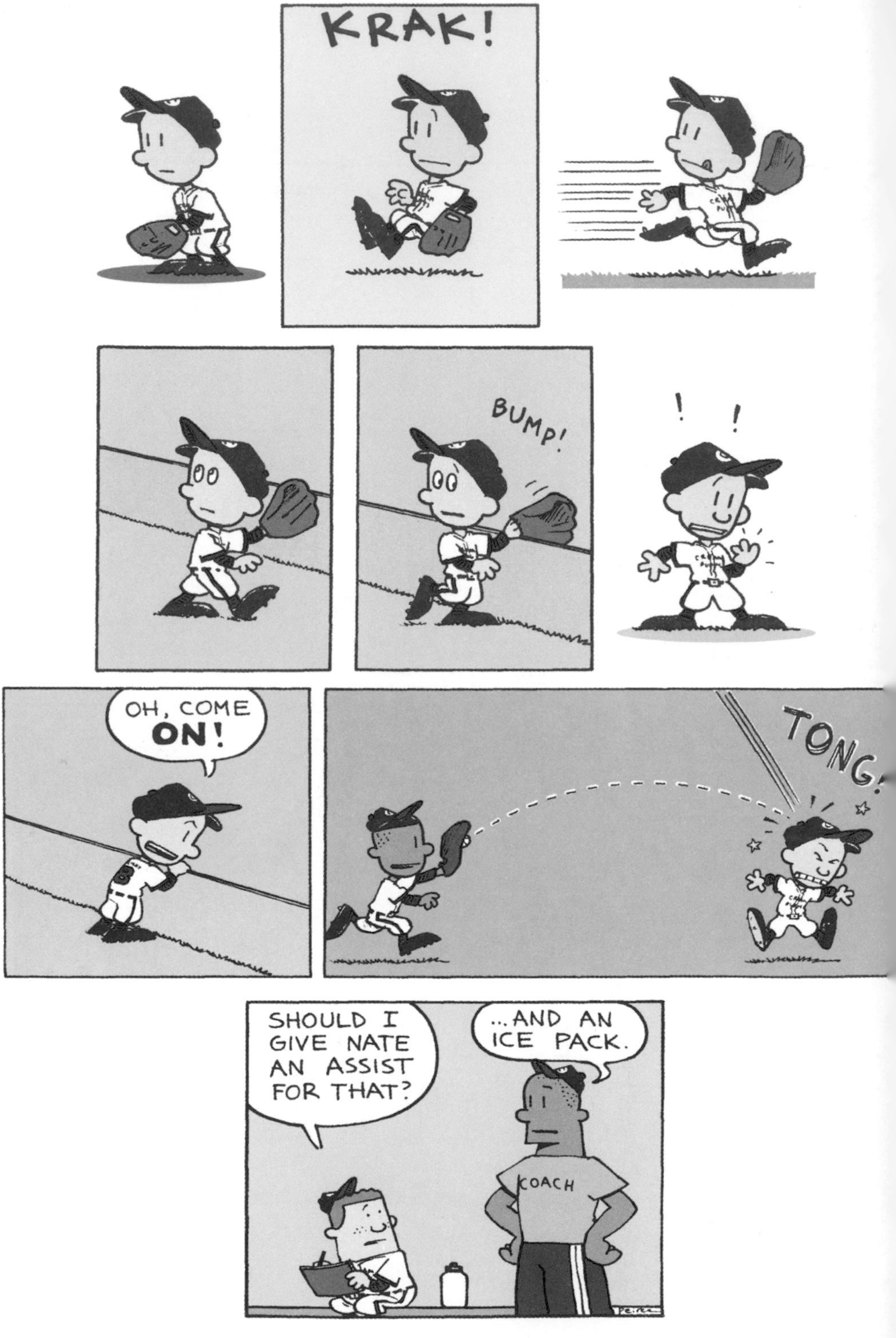
KRAK!
BUMP!
! !
OH, COME ON!
TONG!
SHOULD I GIVE NATE AN ASSIST FOR THAT?
...AND AN ICE PACK.
COACH

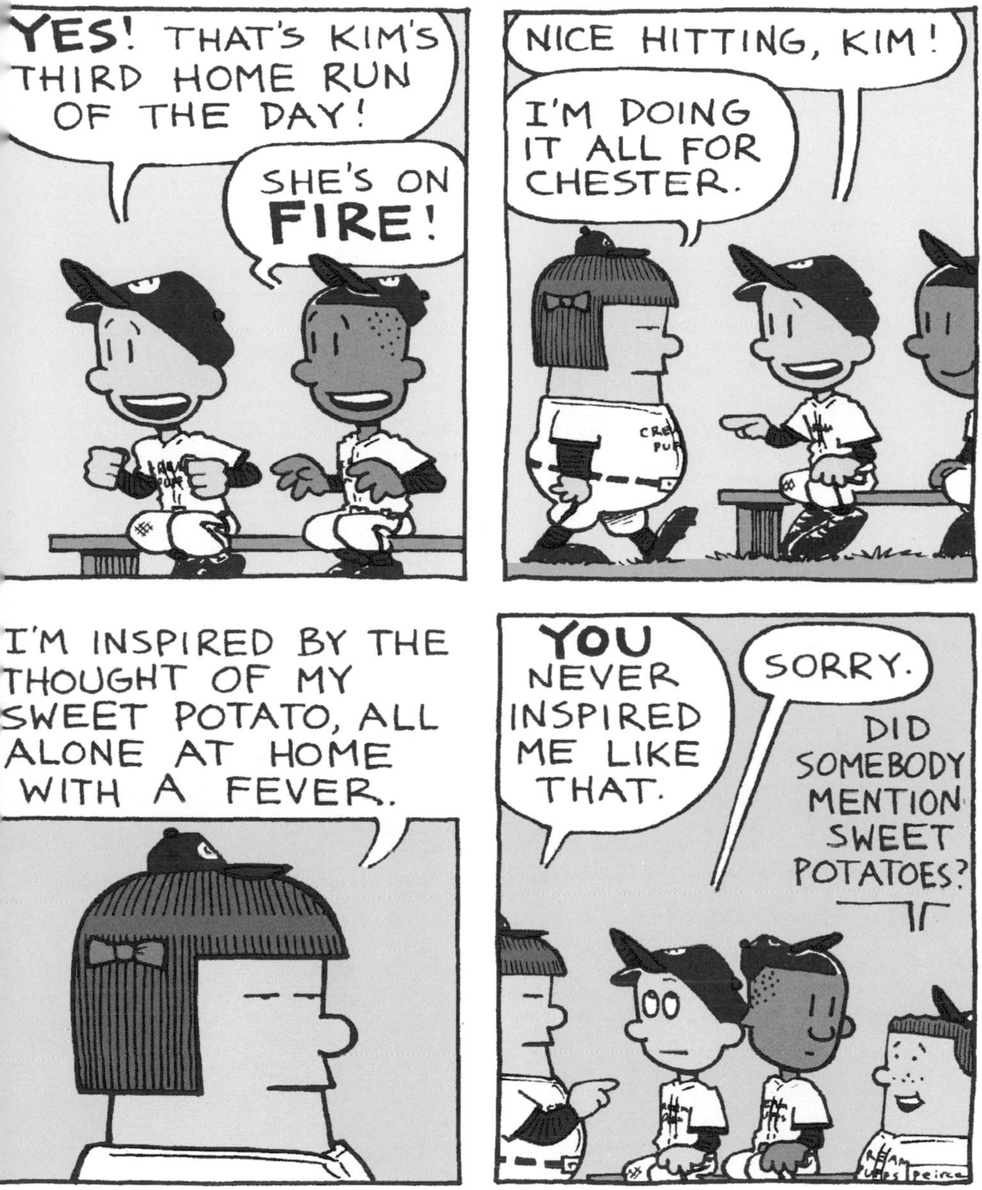
YES! THAT'S KIM'S THIRD HOME RUN OF THE DAY!
SHE'S ON FIRE!
NICE HITTING, KIM!
I'M DOING IT ALL FOR CHESTER.
I'M INSPIRED BY THE THOUGHT OF MY SWEET POTATO, ALL ALONE AT HOME WITH A FEVER.
YOU NEVER INSPIRED ME LIKE THAT.
SORRY.
DID SOMEBODY MENTION SWEET POTATOES?

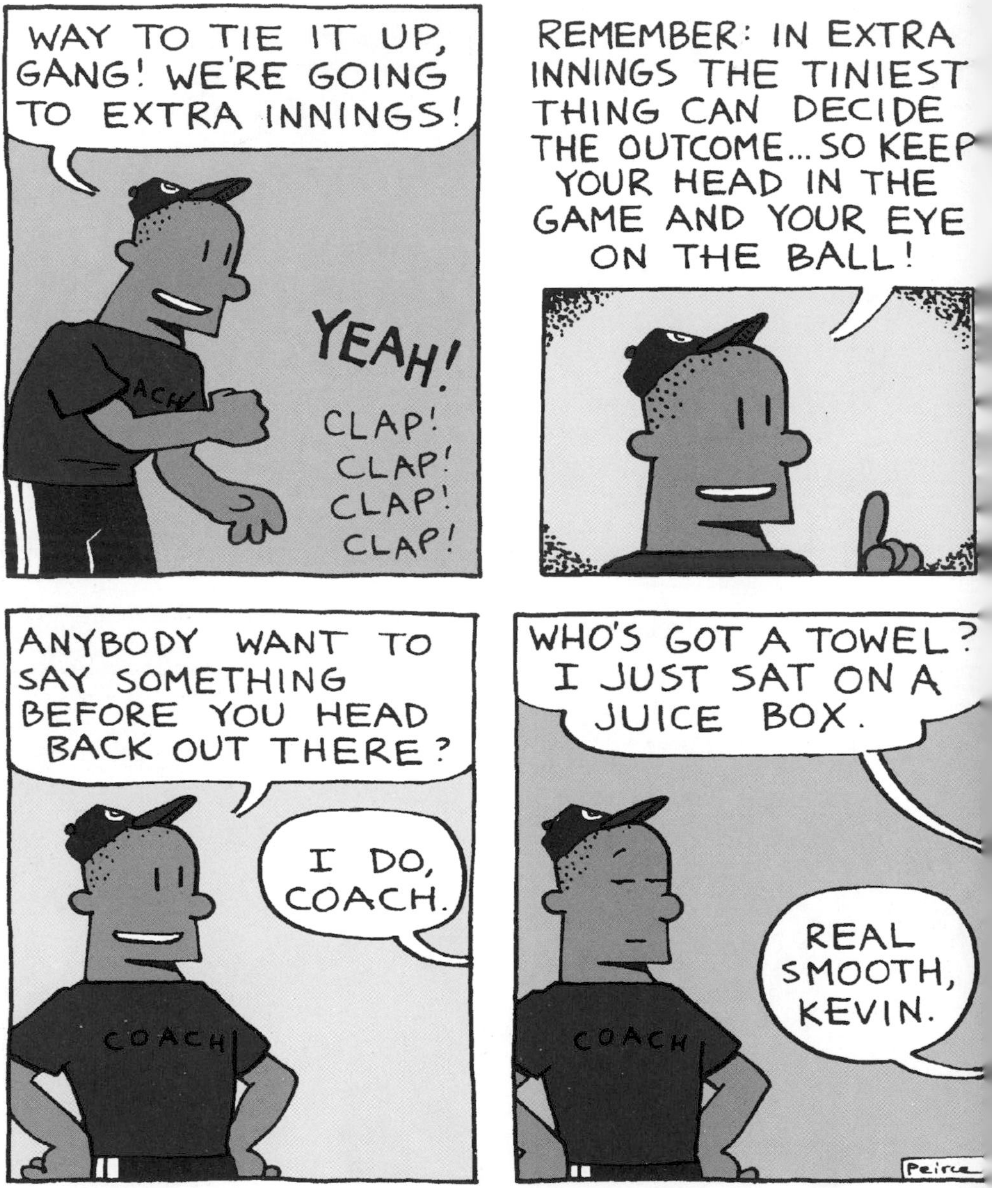
WAY TO TIE IT UP, GANG! WE'RE GOING TO EXTRA INNINGS!
ACH
YEAH!
CLAP! CLAP! CLAP! CLAP!
REMEMBER: IN EXTRA INNINGS THE TINIEST THING CAN DECIDE THE OUTCOME... SO KEEP YOUR HEAD IN THE GAME AND YOUR EYE ON THE BALL!
ANYBODY WANT TO SAY SOMETHING BEFORE YOU HEAD BACK OUT THERE?
I DO, COACH.
COACH
WHO'S GOT A TOWEL? I JUST SAT ON A JUICE BOX.
REAL SMOOTH, KEVIN.
COACH
Peirce

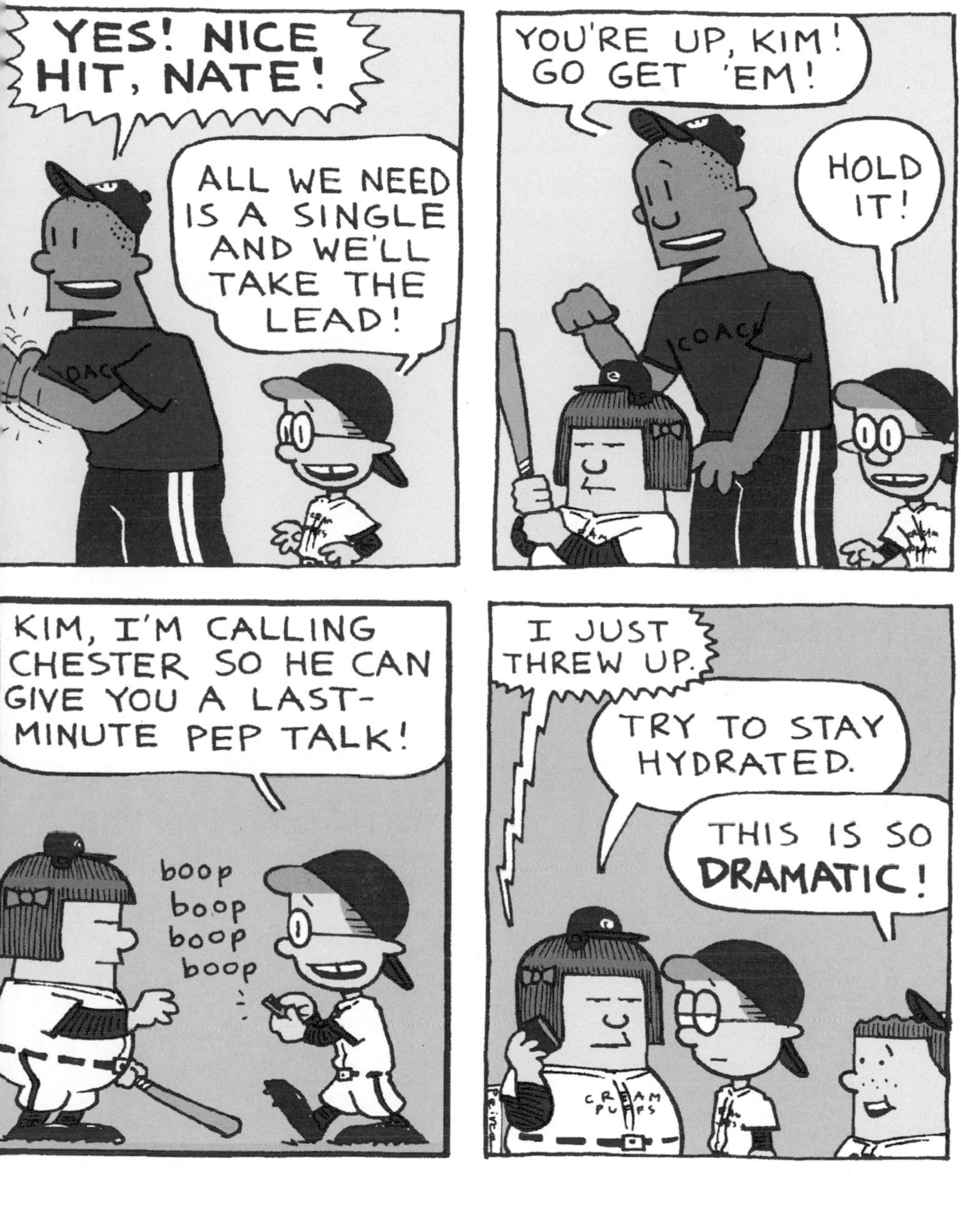
YES! NICE HIT, NATE!
ALL WE NEED IS A SINGLE AND WE'LL TAKE THE LEAD!
YOU'RE UP, KIM! GO GET 'EM!
HOLD IT!
KIM, I'M CALLING CHESTER SO HE CAN GIVE YOU A LAST-MINUTE PEP TALK!
boop boop boop boop
I JUST THREW UP.
TRY TO STAY HYDRATED.
THIS IS SO **DRAMATIC**!

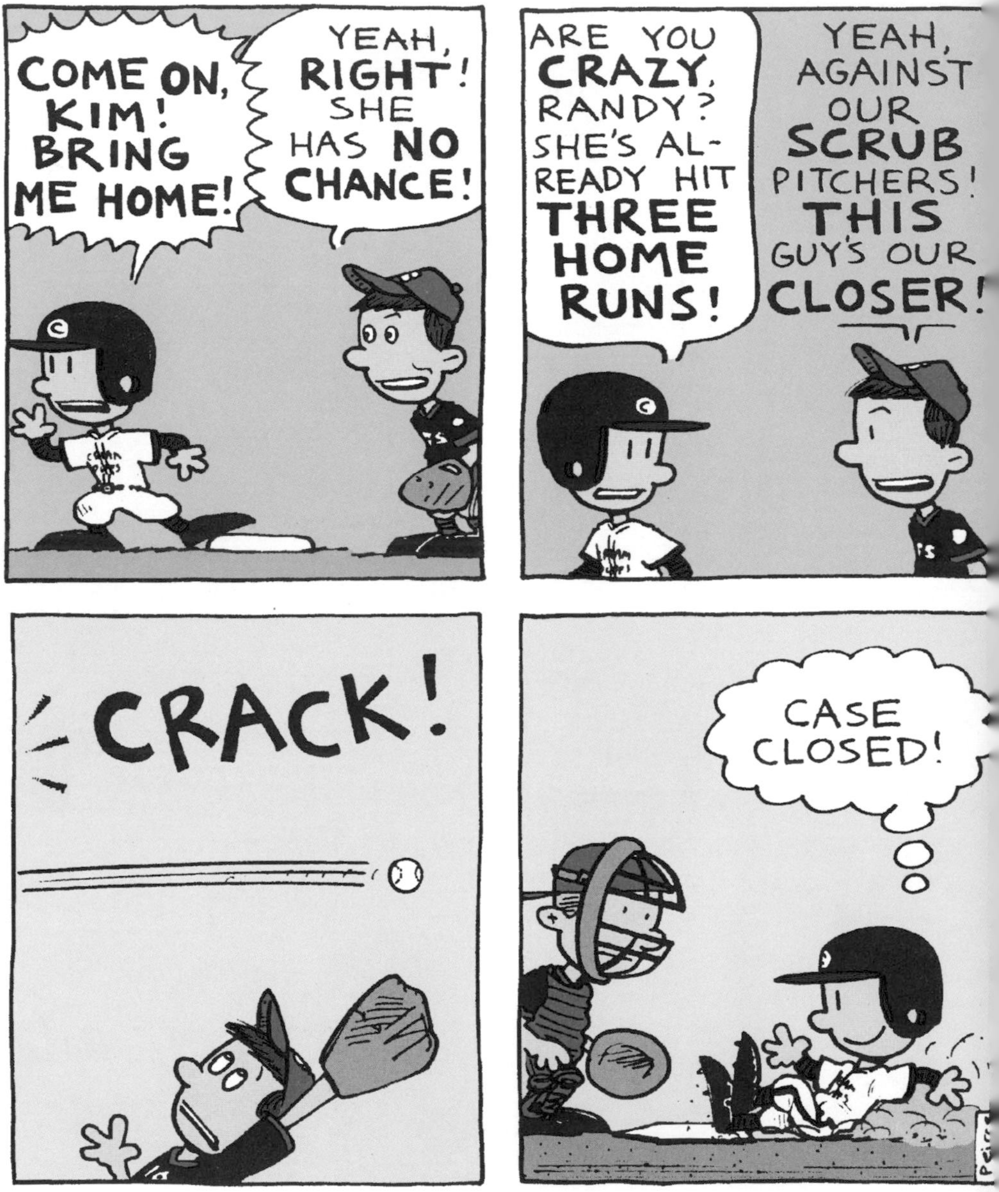
COME ON, KIM! BRING ME HOME!
YEAH, RIGHT! SHE HAS NO CHANCE!
ARE YOU CRAZY, RANDY? SHE'S ALREADY HIT THREE HOME RUNS!
YEAH, AGAINST OUR SCRUB PITCHERS! THIS GUY'S OUR CLOSER!
CRACK!
CASE CLOSED!

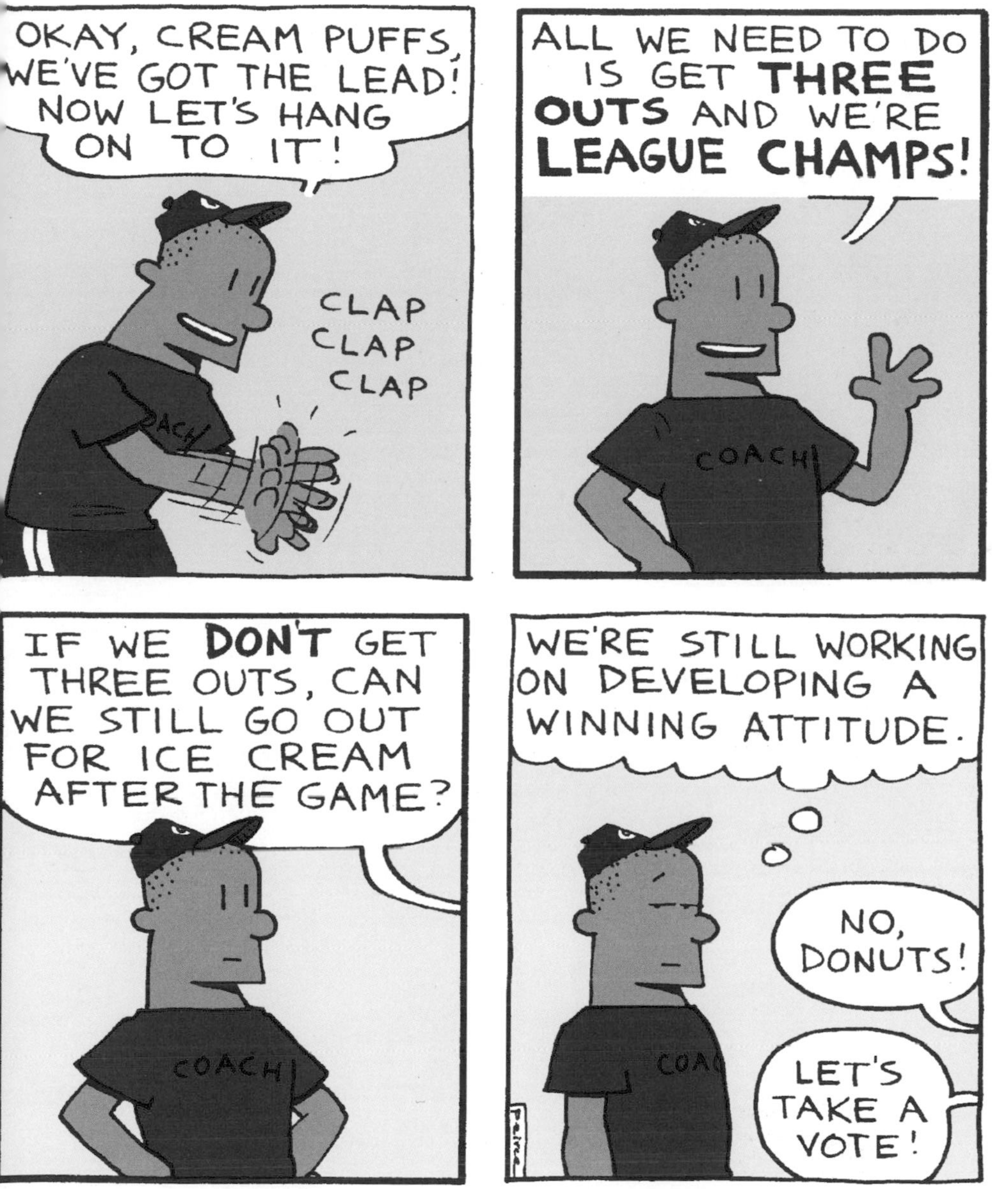
OKAY, CREAM PUFFS, WE'VE GOT THE LEAD! NOW LET'S HANG ON TO IT!
CLAP CLAP CLAP
COACH
ALL WE NEED TO DO IS GET THREE OUTS AND WE'RE LEAGUE CHAMPS!
COACH
IF WE DON'T GET THREE OUTS, CAN WE STILL GO OUT FOR ICE CREAM AFTER THE GAME?
COACH
WE'RE STILL WORKING ON DEVELOPING A WINNING ATTITUDE.
NO, DONUTS!
LET'S TAKE A VOTE!
Peirce

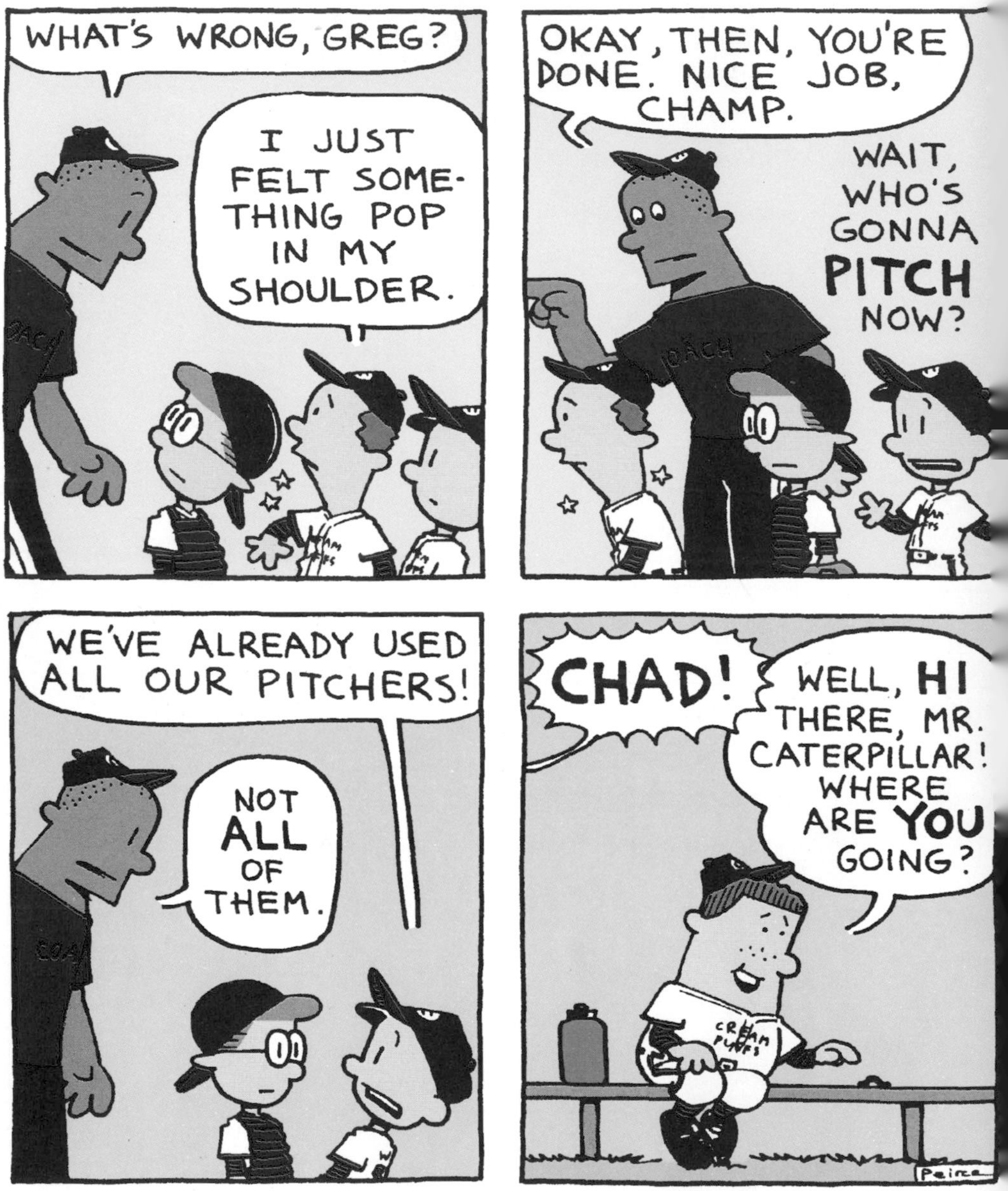
WHAT'S WRONG, GREG?
I JUST FELT SOMETHING POP IN MY SHOULDER.
OKAY, THEN, YOU'RE DONE. NICE JOB, CHAMP.
WAIT, WHO'S GONNA PITCH NOW?
WE'VE ALREADY USED ALL OUR PITCHERS!
NOT ALL OF THEM.
CHAD!
WELL, HI THERE, MR. CATERPILLAR! WHERE ARE YOU GOING?
CREAM PUFFS
Peirce

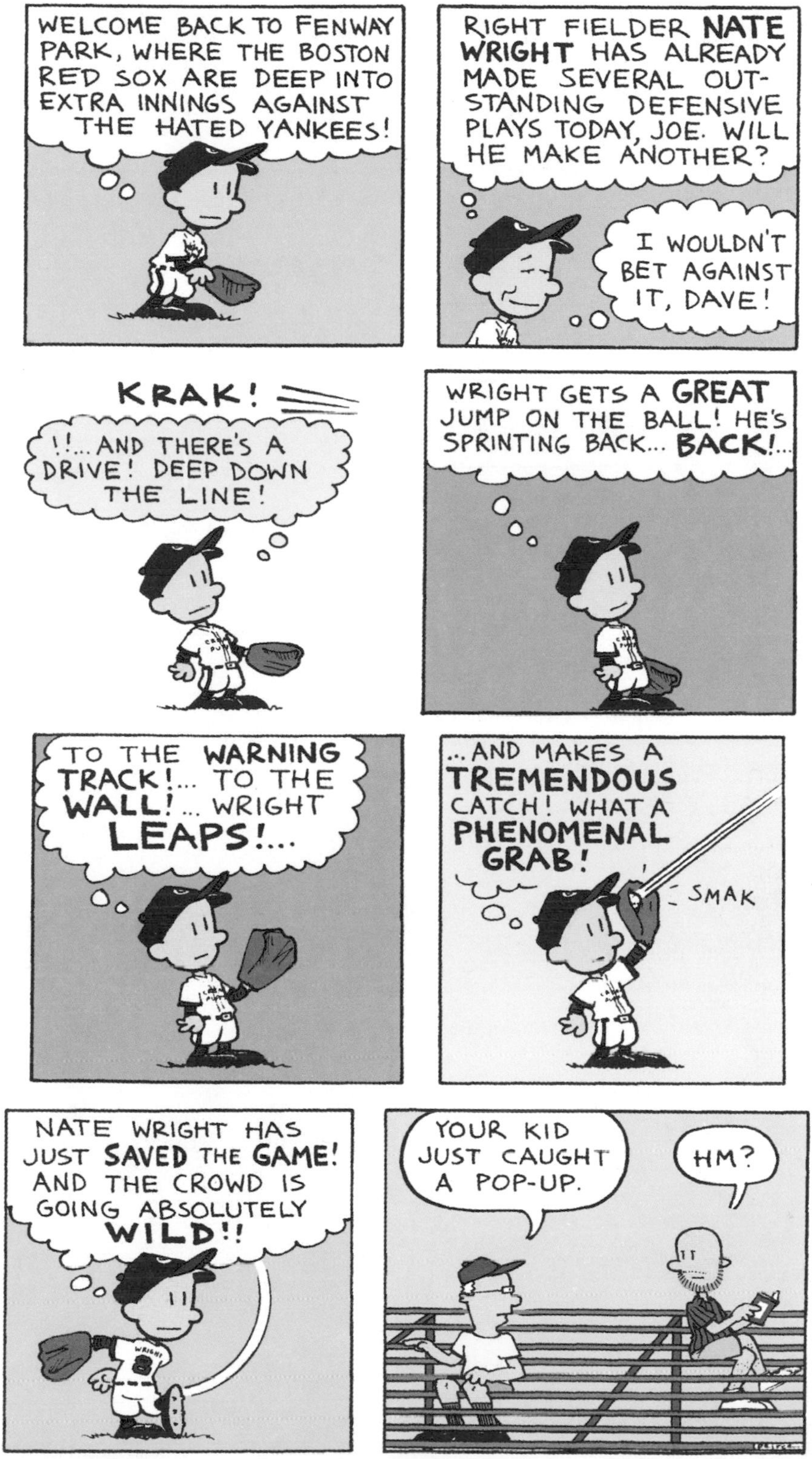

WELCOME BACK TO FENWAY PARK, WHERE THE BOSTON RED SOX ARE DEEP INTO EXTRA INNINGS AGAINST THE HATED YANKEES!
RIGHT FIELDER NATE WRIGHT HAS ALREADY MADE SEVERAL OUTSTANDING DEFENSIVE PLAYS TODAY, JOE. WILL HE MAKE ANOTHER?
I WOULDN'T BET AGAINST IT, DAVE!
KRAK!
!!... AND THERE'S A DRIVE! DEEP DOWN THE LINE!
WRIGHT GETS A GREAT JUMP ON THE BALL! HE'S SPRINTING BACK... BACK!...
TO THE WARNING TRACK!... TO THE WALL!... WRIGHT LEAPS!...
...AND MAKES A TREMENDOUS CATCH! WHAT A PHENOMENAL GRAB!
SMAK
NATE WRIGHT HAS JUST SAVED THE GAME! AND THE CROWD IS GOING ABSOLUTELY WILD!!
WRIGHT
YOUR KID JUST CAUGHT A POP-UP.
HM?

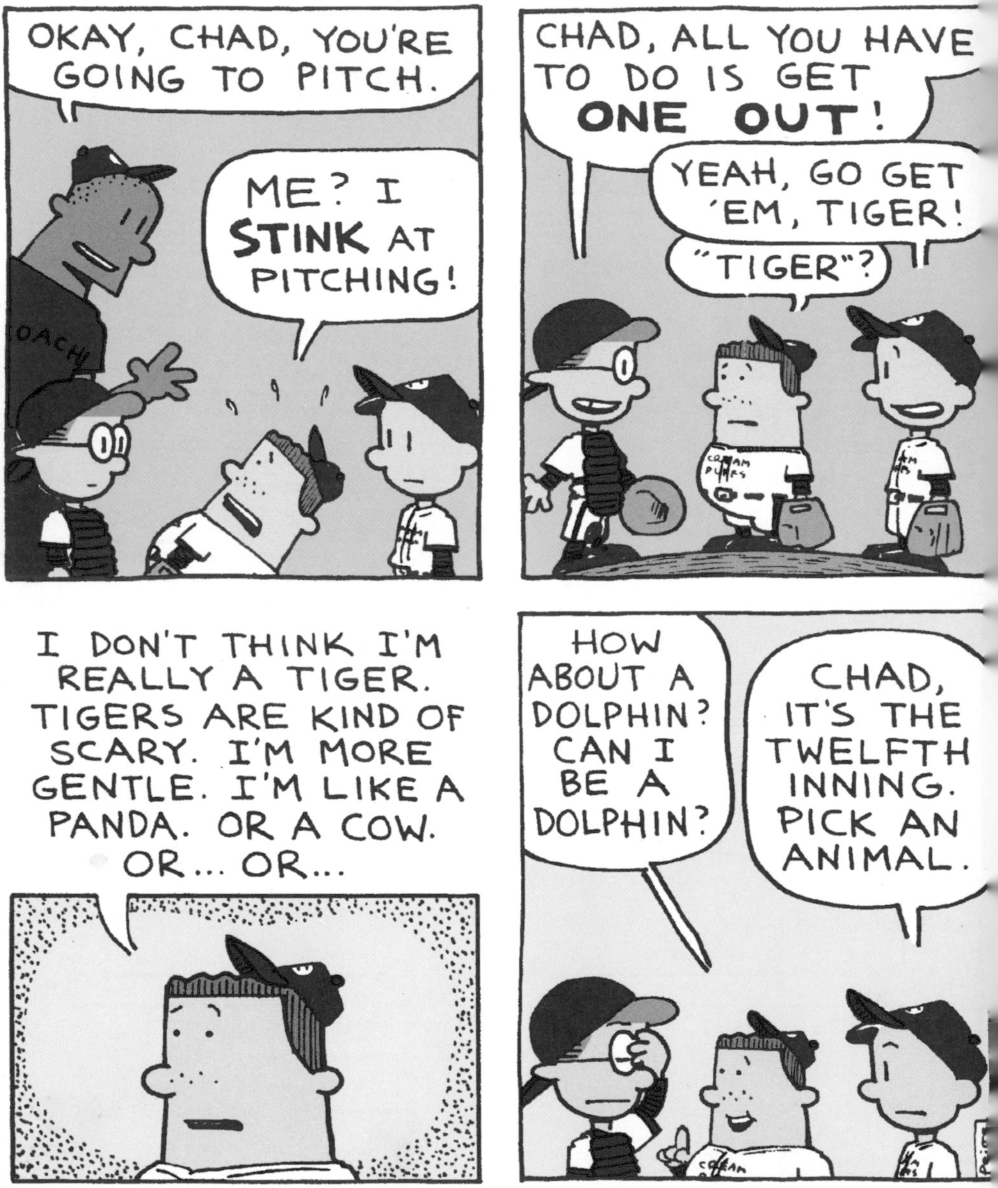
OKAY, CHAD, YOU'RE GOING TO PITCH.
ME? I **STINK** AT PITCHING!
CHAD, ALL YOU HAVE TO DO IS GET **ONE OUT**!
YEAH, GO GET 'EM, TIGER!
"TIGER"?
I DON'T THINK I'M REALLY A TIGER. TIGERS ARE KIND OF SCARY. I'M MORE GENTLE. I'M LIKE A PANDA. OR A COW. OR... OR...
HOW ABOUT A DOLPHIN? CAN I BE A DOLPHIN?
CHAD, IT'S THE TWELFTH INNING. PICK AN ANIMAL.

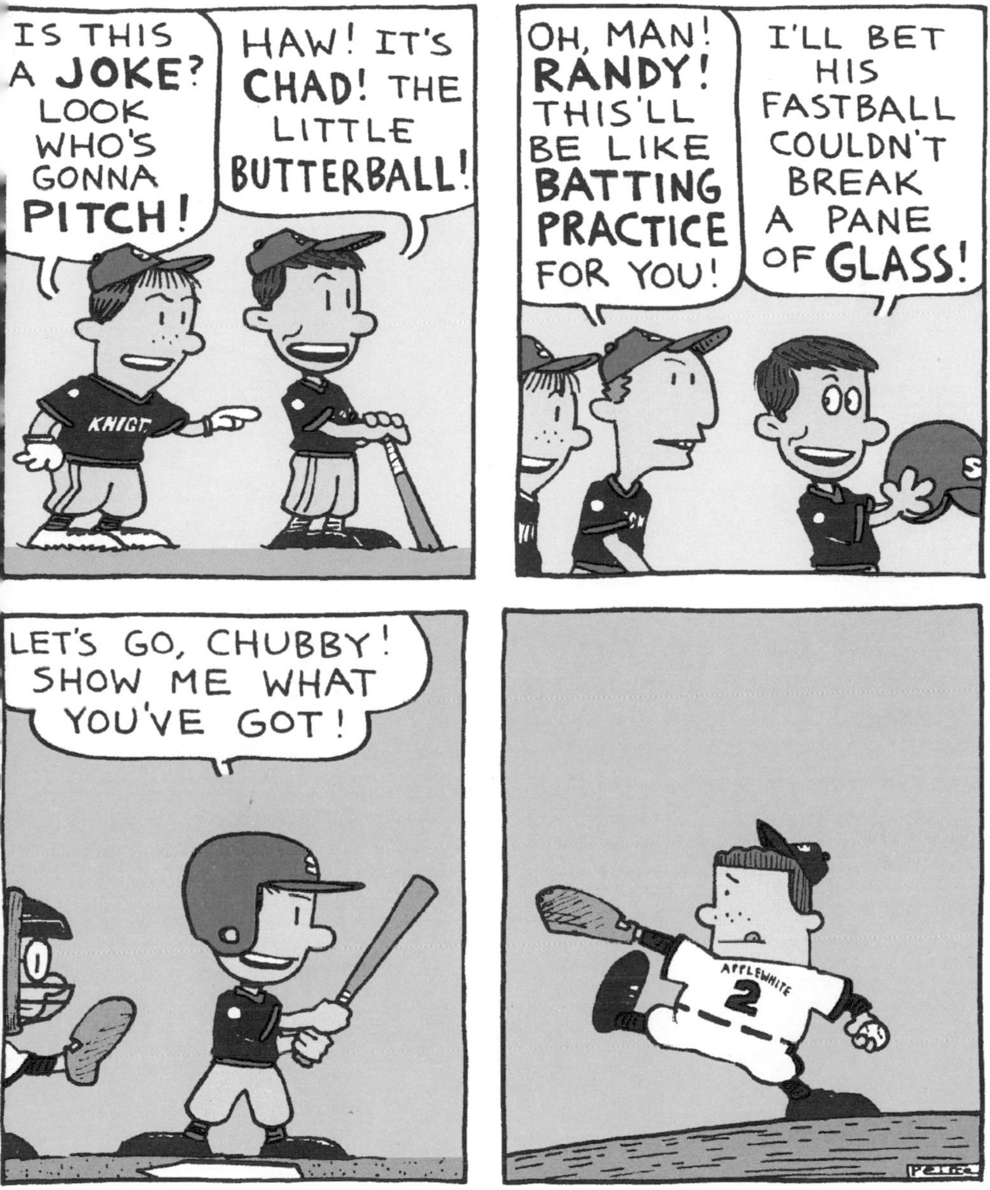
IS THIS A JOKE? LOOK WHO'S GONNA PITCH!
HAW! IT'S CHAD! THE LITTLE BUTTERBALL!
OH, MAN! RANDY! THIS'LL BE LIKE BATTING PRACTICE FOR YOU!
I'LL BET HIS FASTBALL COULDN'T BREAK A PANE OF GLASS!
LET'S GO, CHUBBY! SHOW ME WHAT YOU'VE GOT!
APPLEWHITE
2

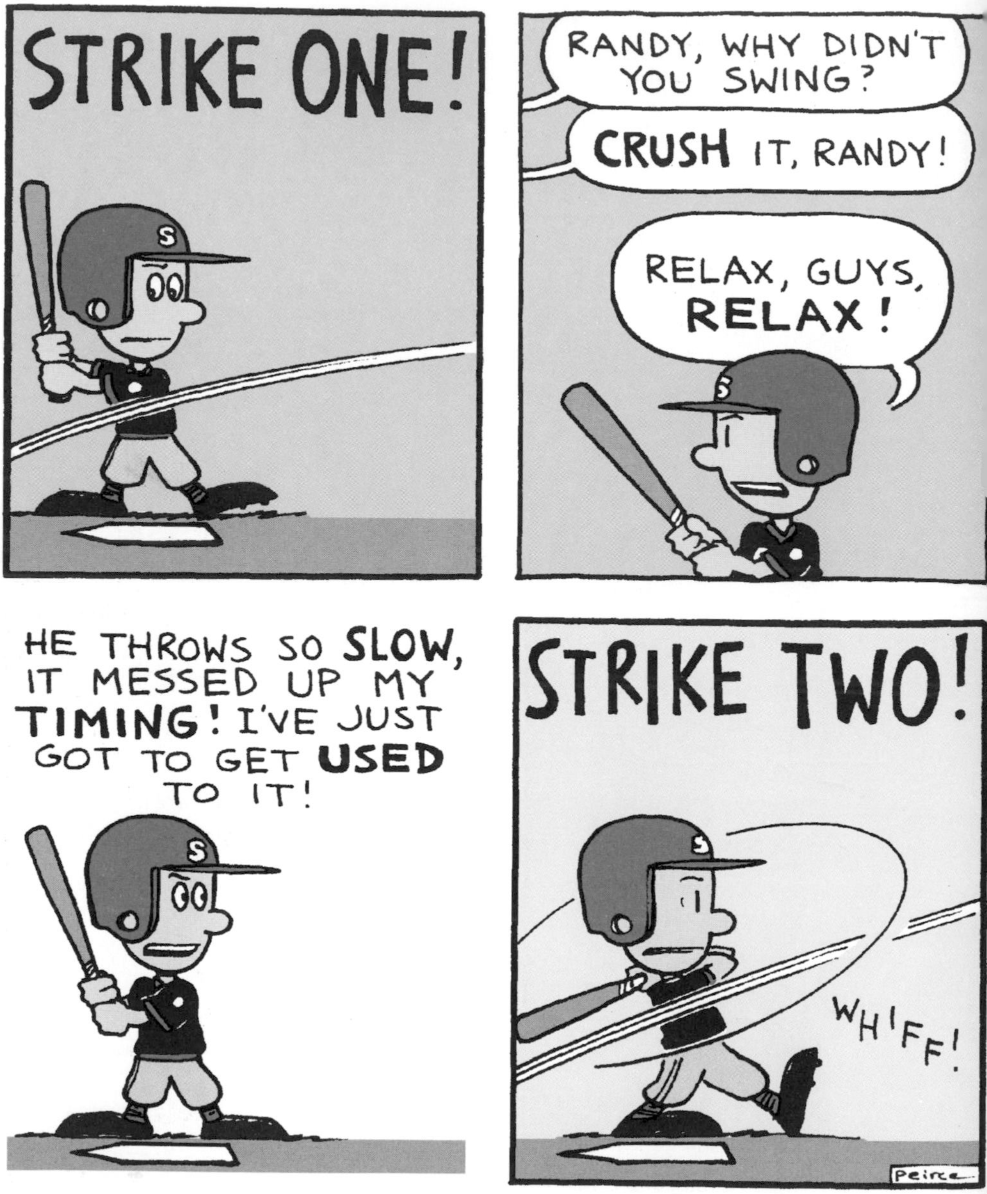
STRIKE ONE!
RANDY, WHY DIDN'T YOU SWING?
CRUSH IT, RANDY!
RELAX, GUYS, RELAX!
HE THROWS SO SLOW, IT MESSED UP MY TIMING! I'VE JUST GOT TO GET USED TO IT!
STRIKE TWO!
WHIFF!
Peirce

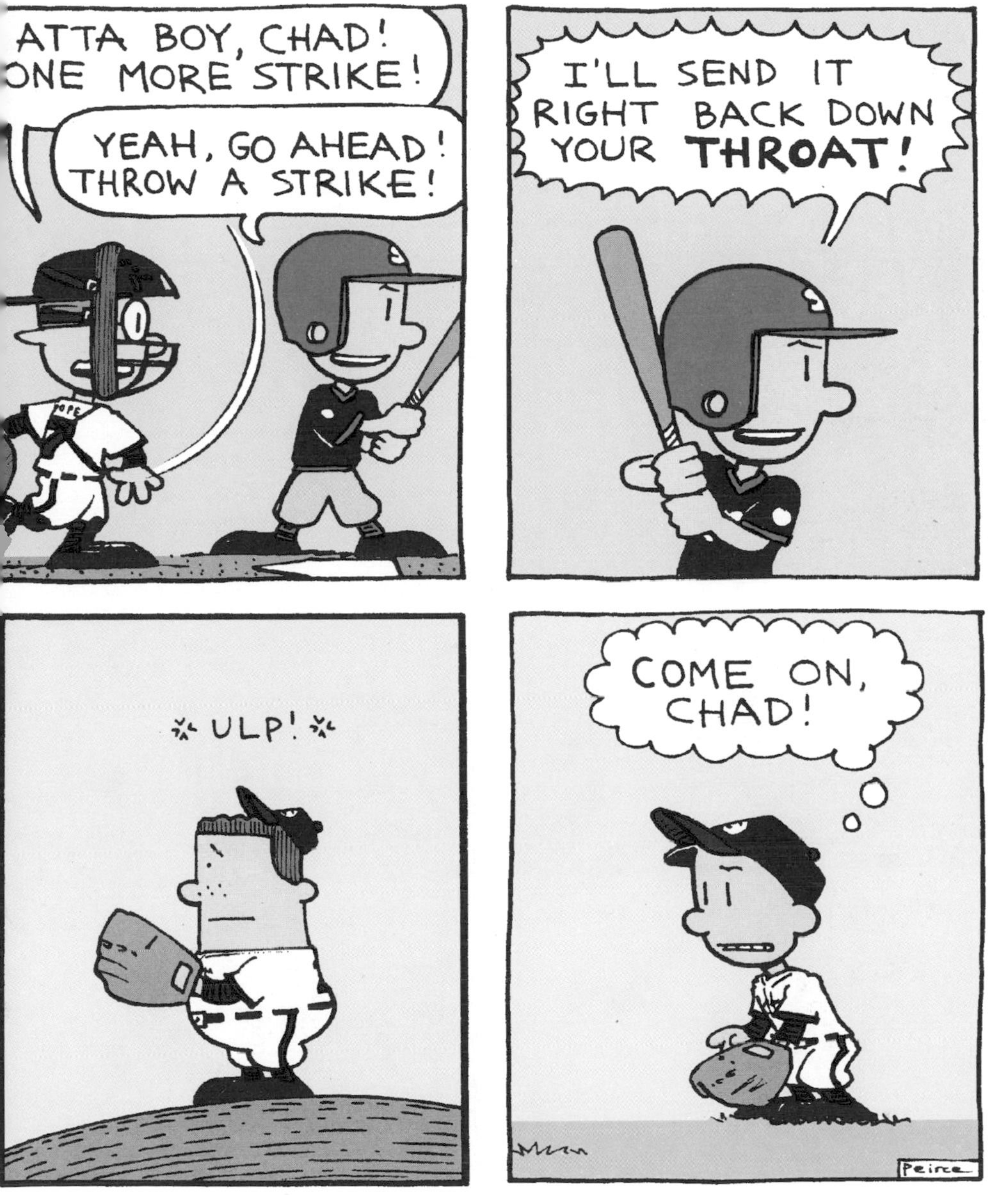
ATTA BOY, CHAD! ONE MORE STRIKE!
YEAH, GO AHEAD! THROW A STRIKE!
I'LL SEND IT RIGHT BACK DOWN YOUR **THROAT**!
ULP!
COME ON, CHAD!
Peirce

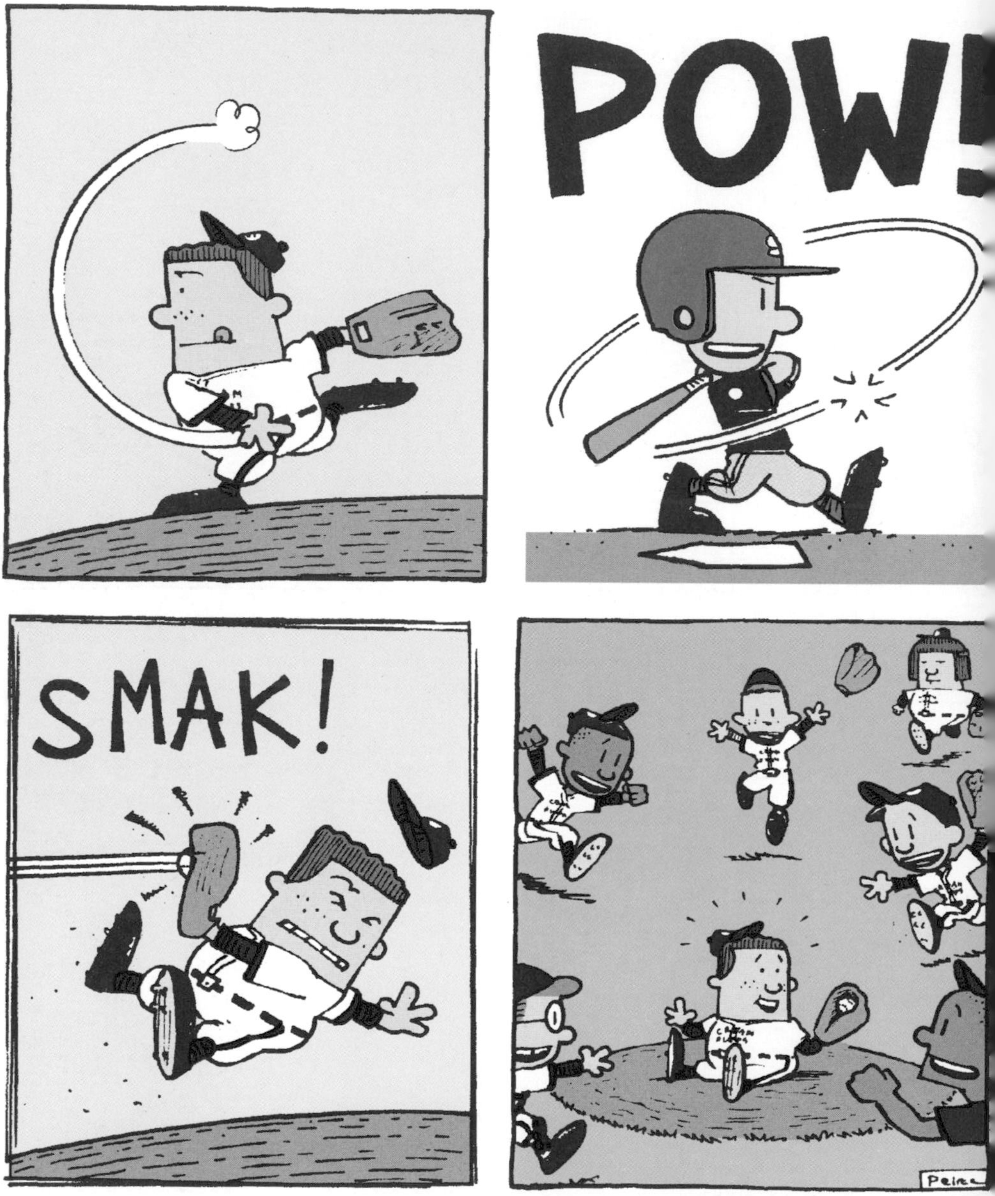
POW!
SMAK!

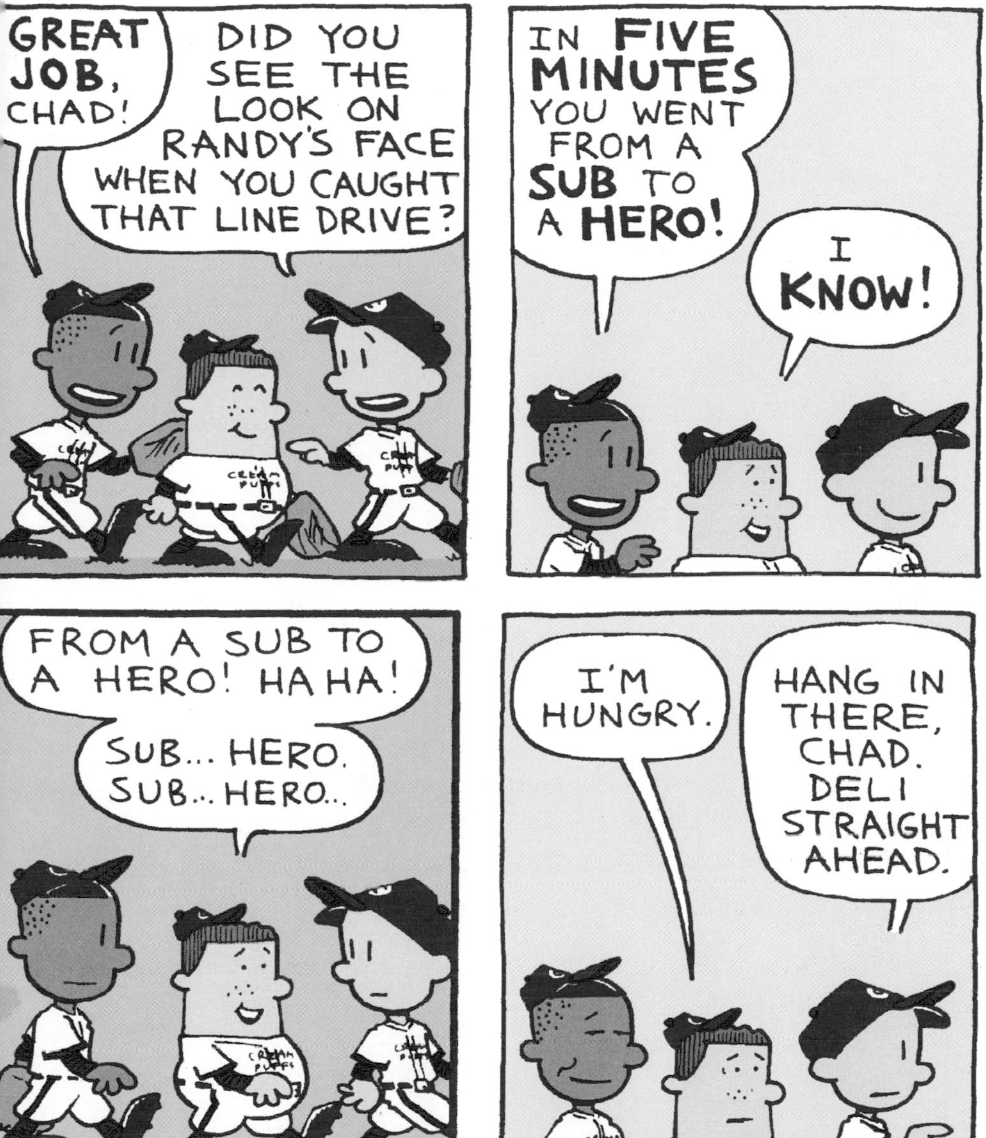
GREAT JOB, CHAD!
DID YOU SEE THE LOOK ON RANDY'S FACE WHEN YOU CAUGHT THAT LINE DRIVE?
IN FIVE MINUTES YOU WENT FROM A SUB TO A HERO!
I KNOW!
FROM A SUB TO A HERO! HAHA!
SUB... HERO. SUB... HERO...
I'M HUNGRY.
HANG IN THERE, CHAD. DELI STRAIGHT AHEAD.
Peirce

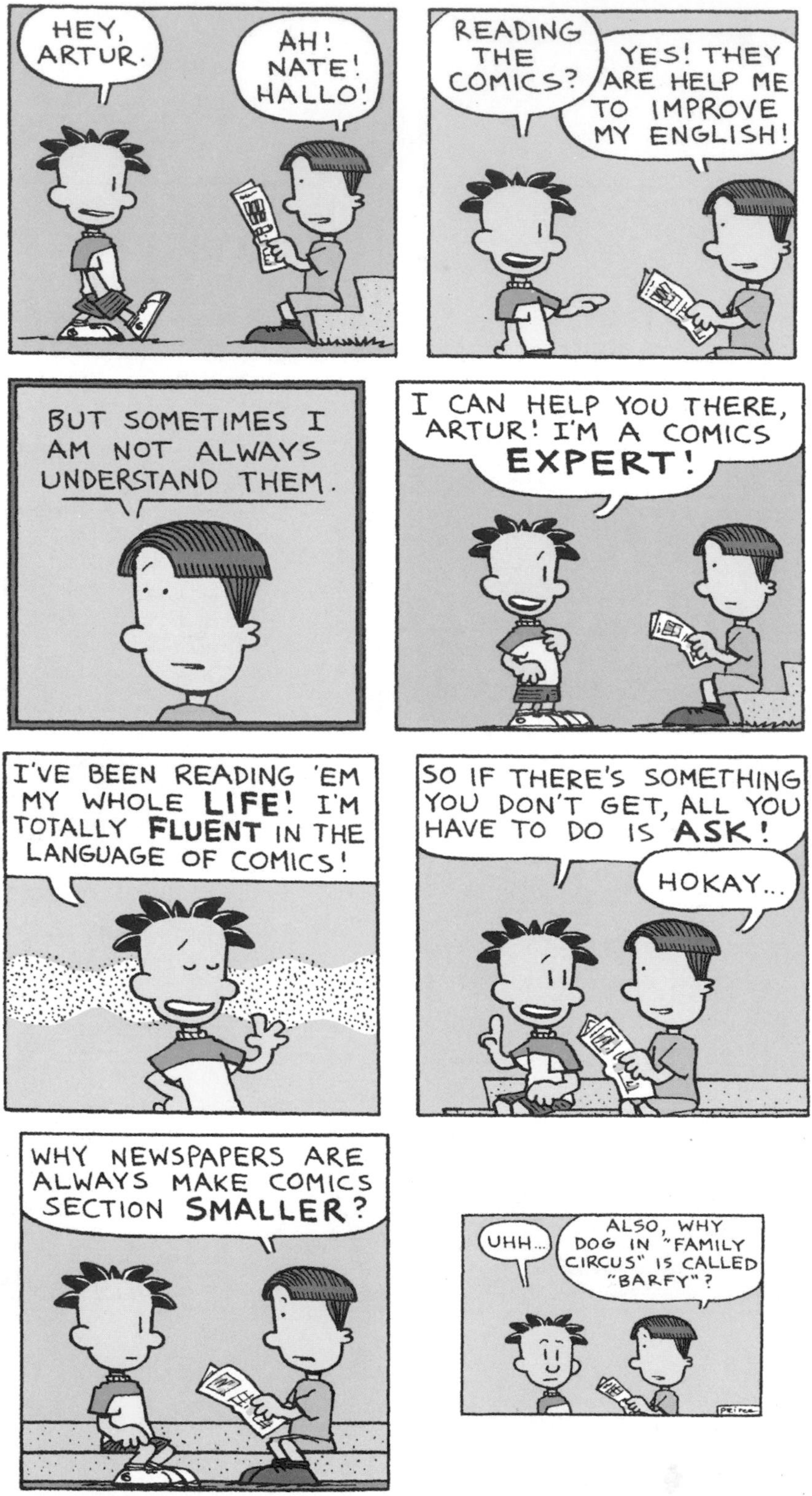
HEY, ARTUR.
AH! NATE! HALLO!
READING THE COMICS?
YES! THEY ARE HELP ME TO IMPROVE MY ENGLISH!
BUT SOMETIMES I AM NOT ALWAYS UNDERSTAND THEM.
I CAN HELP YOU THERE, ARTUR! I'M A COMICS EXPERT!
I'VE BEEN READING 'EM MY WHOLE LIFE! I'M TOTALLY FLUENT IN THE LANGUAGE OF COMICS!
SO IF THERE'S SOMETHING YOU DON'T GET, ALL YOU HAVE TO DO IS ASK!
HOKAY...
WHY NEWSPAPERS ARE ALWAYS MAKE COMICS SECTION SMALLER?
UHH...
ALSO, WHY DOG IN "FAMILY CIRCUS" IS CALLED "BARFY"?

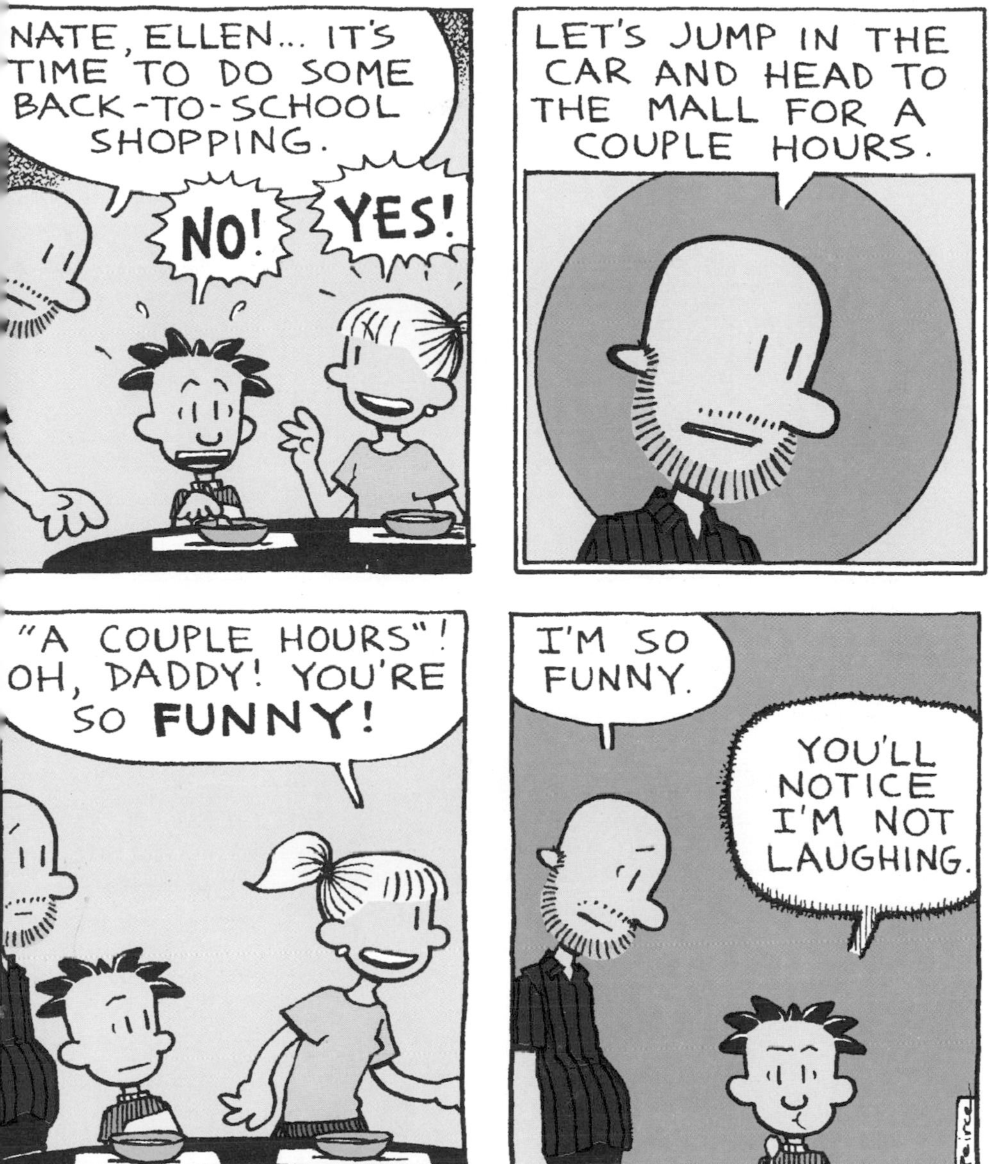
NATE, ELLEN... IT'S TIME TO DO SOME BACK-TO-SCHOOL SHOPPING.
NO!
YES!
LET'S JUMP IN THE CAR AND HEAD TO THE MALL FOR A COUPLE HOURS.
"A COUPLE HOURS"! OH, DADDY! YOU'RE SO FUNNY!
I'M SO FUNNY.
YOU'LL NOTICE I'M NOT LAUGHING.
Peirce

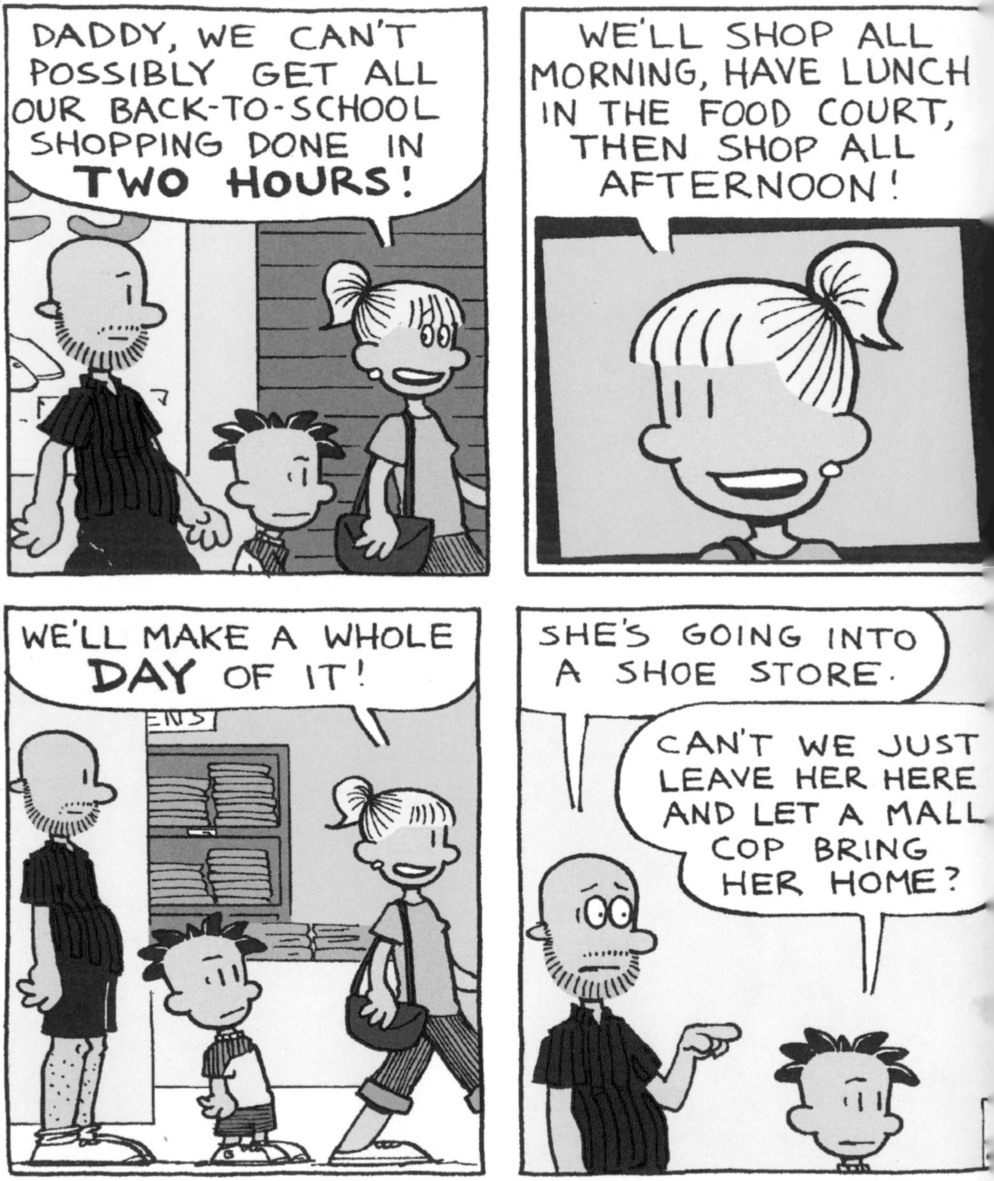
DADDY, WE CAN'T POSSIBLY GET ALL OUR BACK-TO-SCHOOL SHOPPING DONE IN **TWO HOURS**!
WE'LL SHOP ALL MORNING, HAVE LUNCH IN THE FOOD COURT, THEN SHOP ALL AFTERNOON!
WE'LL MAKE A WHOLE **DAY** OF IT!
SHE'S GOING INTO A SHOE STORE.
CAN'T WE JUST LEAVE HER HERE AND LET A MALL COP BRING HER HOME?

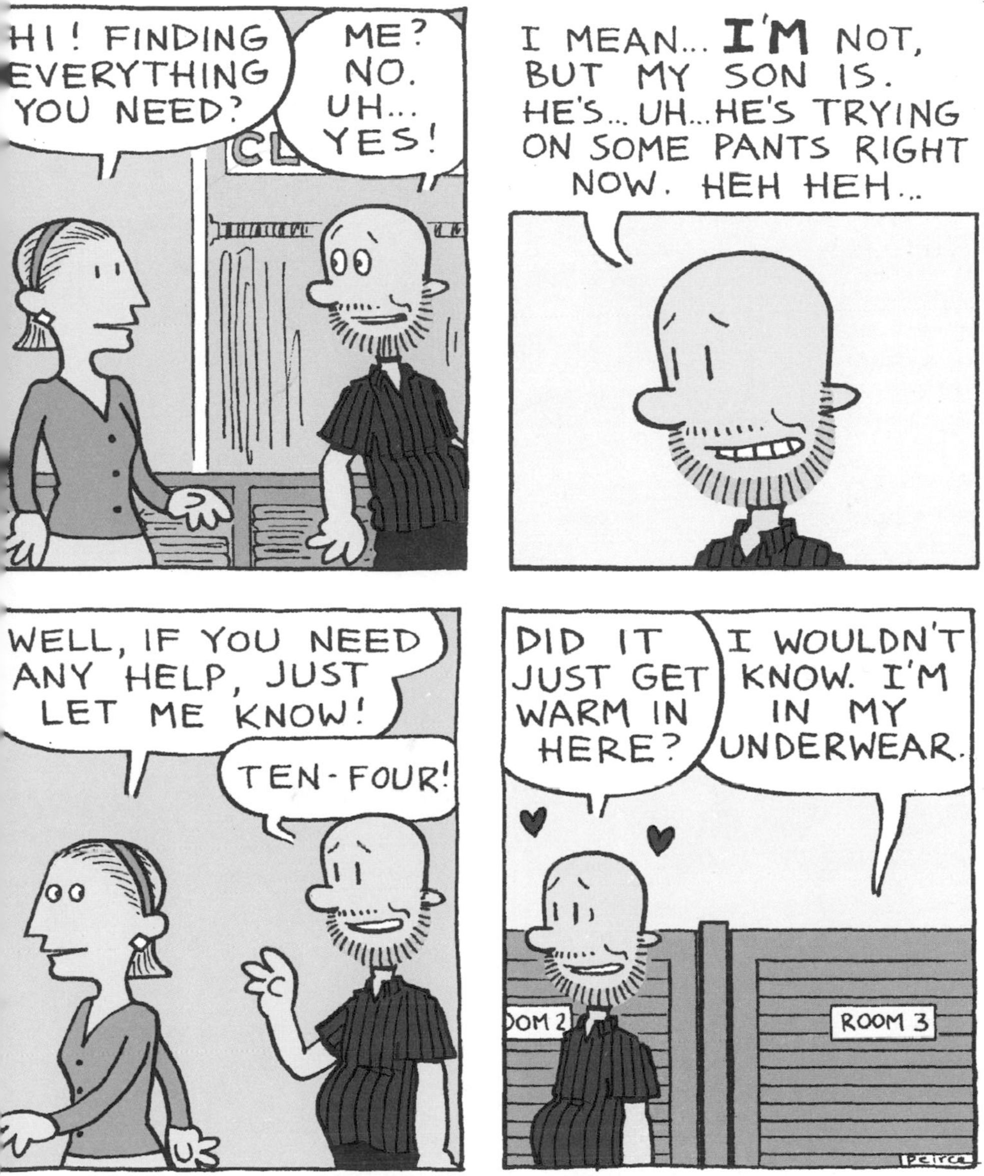
HI! FINDING EVERYTHING YOU NEED?
ME? NO. UH... YES!
I MEAN... I'M NOT, BUT MY SON IS. HE'S... UH...HE'S TRYING ON SOME PANTS RIGHT NOW. HEH HEH...
WELL, IF YOU NEED ANY HELP, JUST LET ME KNOW!
TEN-FOUR!
DID IT JUST GET WARM IN HERE?
I WOULDN'T KNOW. I'M IN MY UNDERWEAR.
OOM 2
ROOM 3
peirce

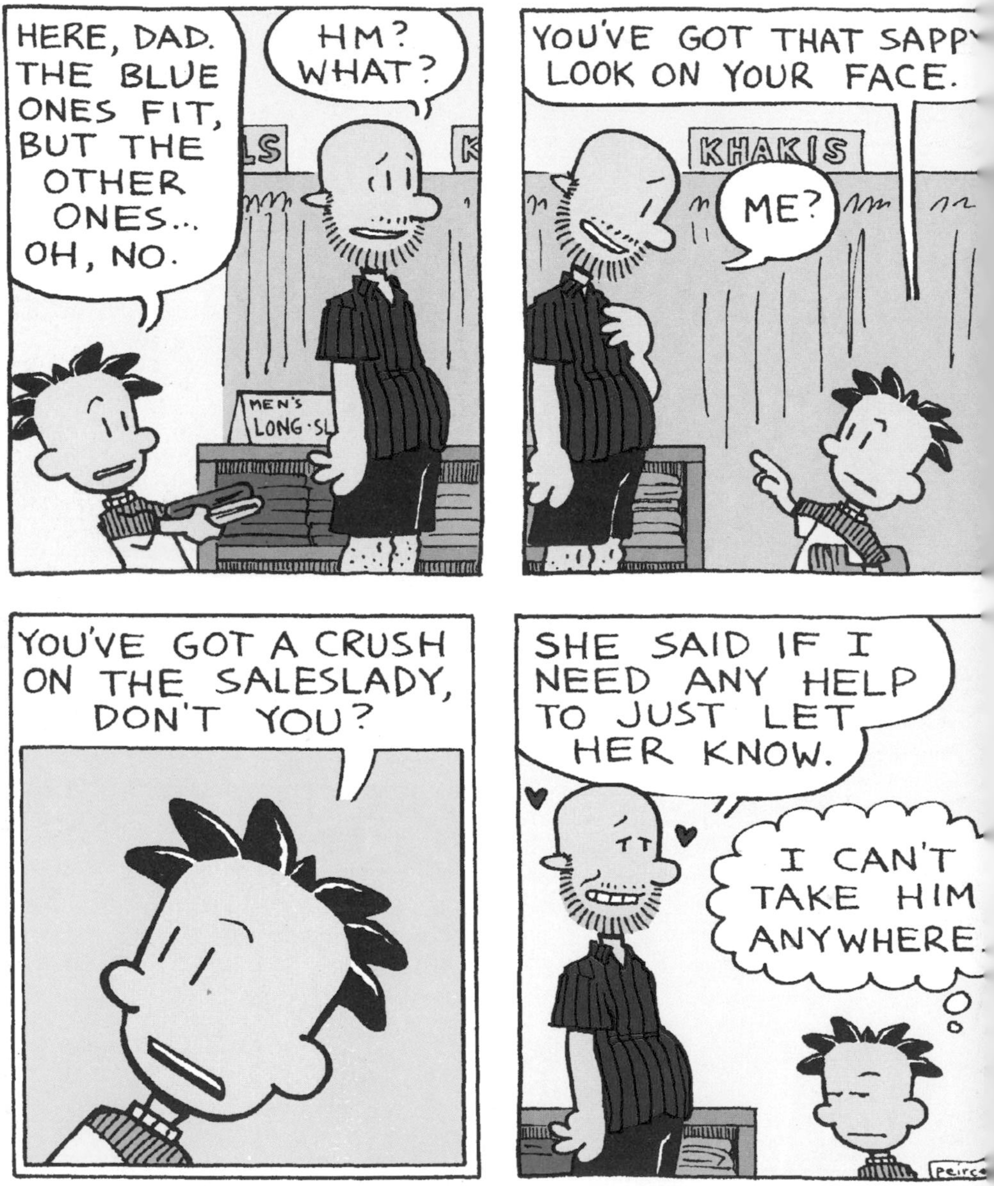
HERE, DAD. THE BLUE ONES FIT, BUT THE OTHER ONES... OH, NO.
HM? WHAT?
LS
MEN'S
LONG-SL
YOU'VE GOT THAT SAPP
LOOK ON YOUR FACE.
KHAKIS
ME?
YOU'VE GOT A CRUSH ON THE SALESLADY, DON'T YOU?
SHE SAID IF I NEED ANY HELP TO JUST LET HER KNOW.
I CAN'T TAKE HIM ANYWHERE

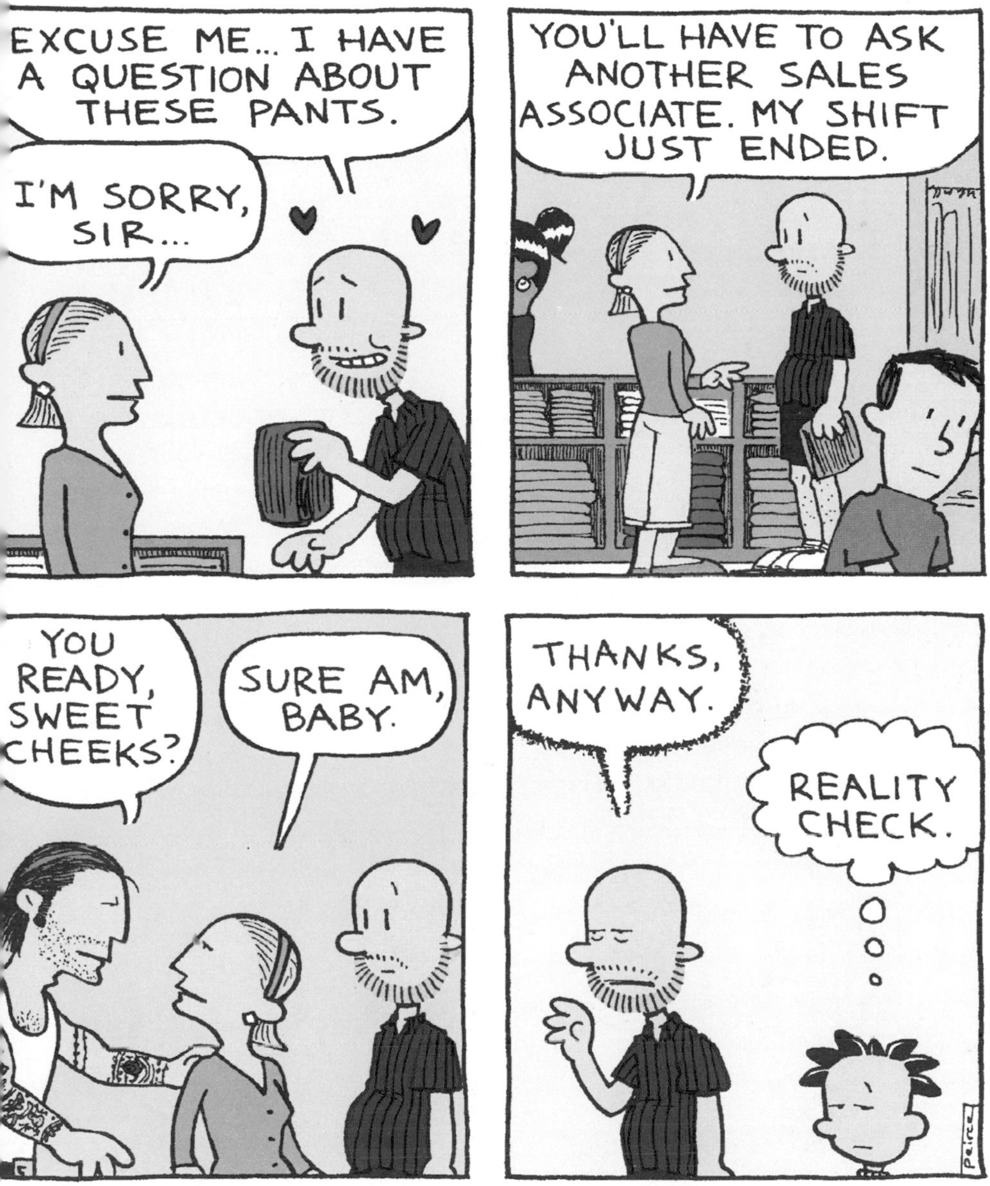
EXCUSE ME... I HAVE A QUESTION ABOUT THESE PANTS.
I'M SORRY, SIR...
YOU'LL HAVE TO ASK ANOTHER SALES ASSOCIATE. MY SHIFT JUST ENDED.
YOU READY, SWEET CHEEKS?
SURE AM, BABY.
THANKS, ANYWAY.
REALITY CHECK.
peirce

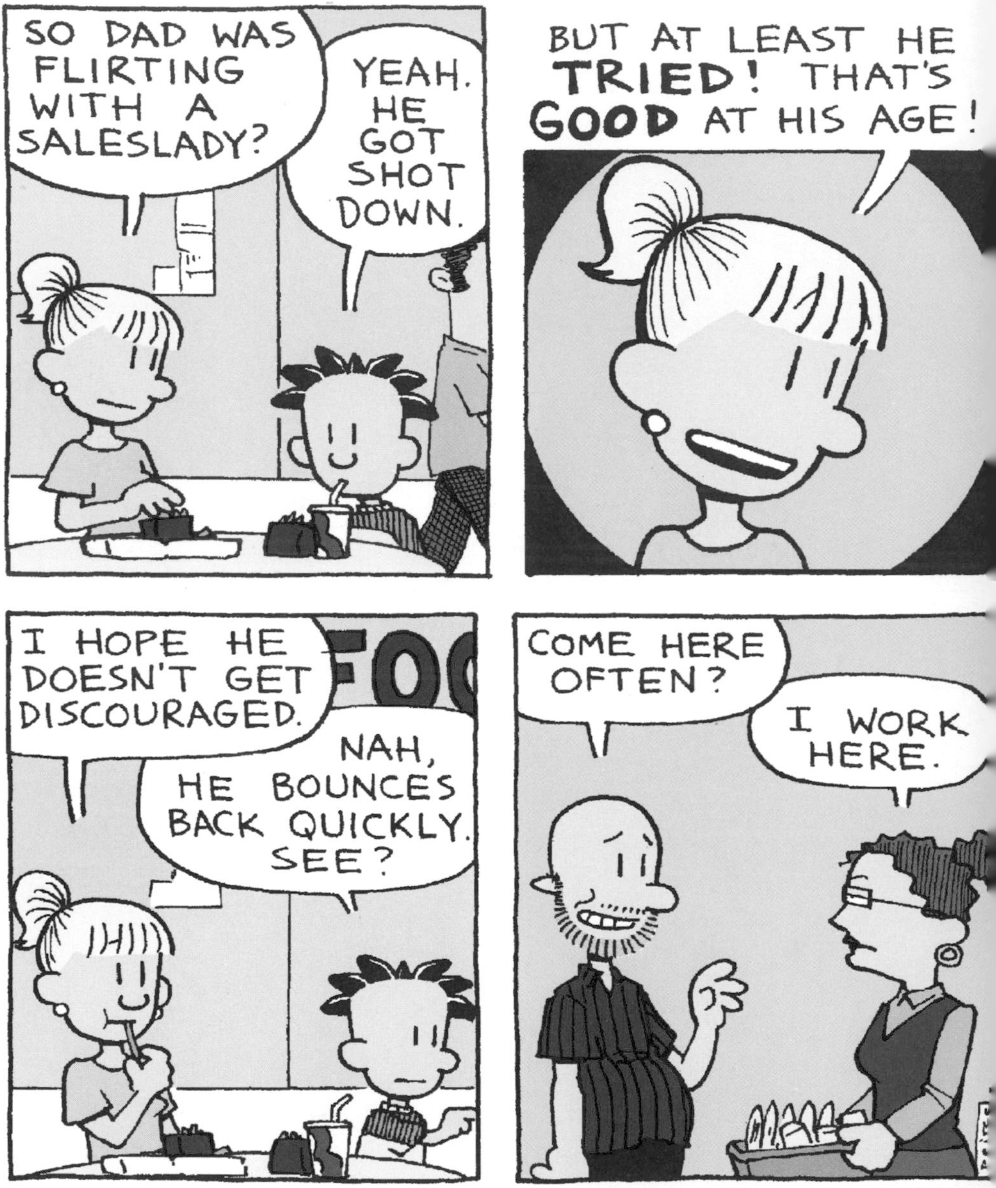
SO DAD WAS FLIRTING WITH A SALESLADY?
YEAH. HE GOT SHOT DOWN.
BUT AT LEAST HE **TRIED!** THAT'S **GOOD** AT HIS AGE!
I HOPE HE DOESN'T GET DISCOURAGED.
NAH, HE BOUNCES BACK QUICKLY. SEE?
COME HERE OFTEN?
I WORK HERE.

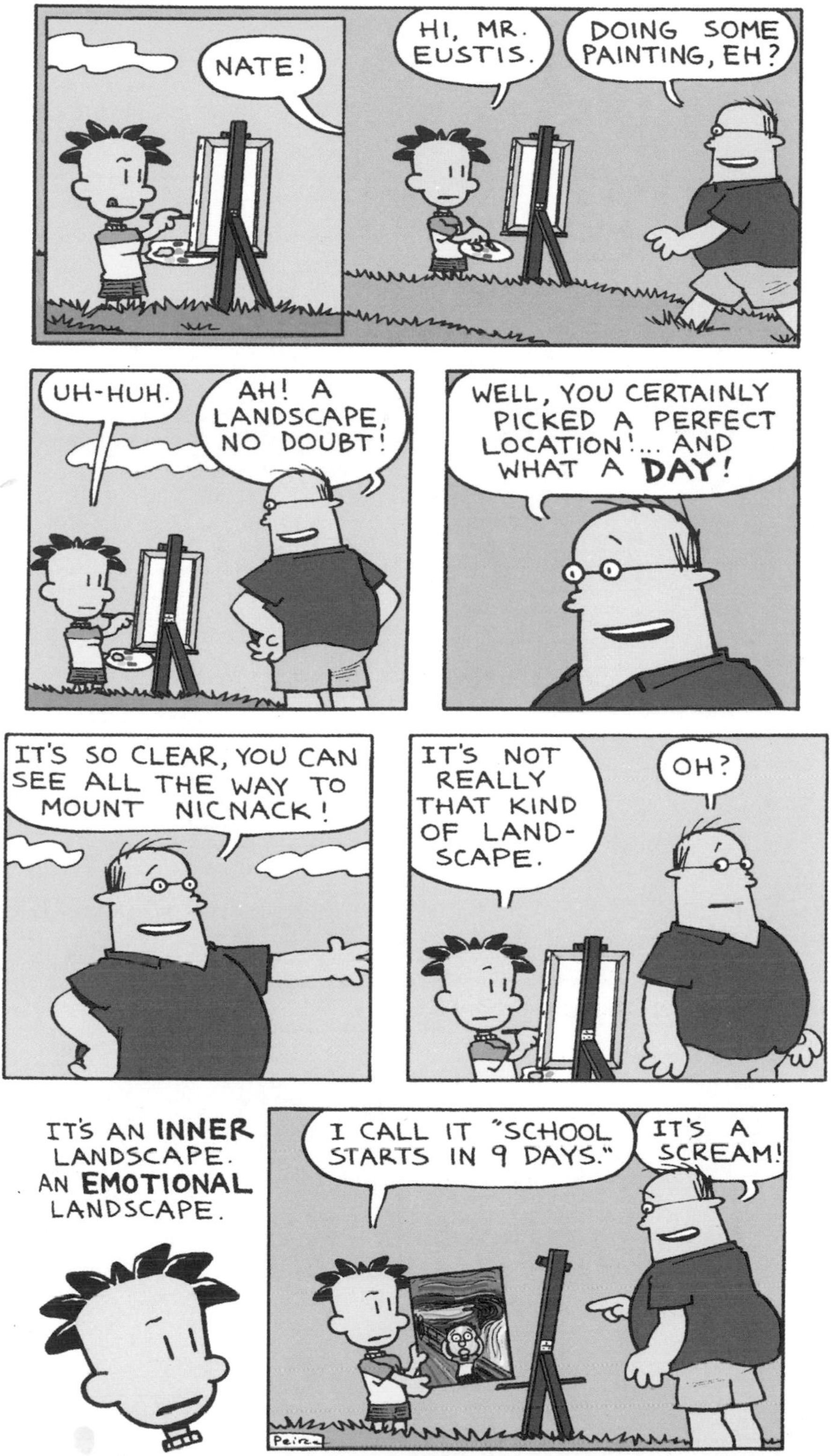
NATE!
HI, MR. EUSTIS.
DOING SOME PAINTING, EH?
UH-HUH.
AH! A LANDSCAPE, NO DOUBT!
WELL, YOU CERTAINLY PICKED A PERFECT LOCATION!... AND WHAT A **DAY**!
IT'S SO CLEAR, YOU CAN SEE ALL THE WAY TO MOUNT NICNACK!
IT'S NOT REALLY THAT KIND OF LAND-SCAPE.
OH?
IT'S AN **INNER** LANDSCAPE. AN **EMOTIONAL** LANDSCAPE.
I CALL IT "SCHOOL STARTS IN 9 DAYS."
IT'S A SCREAM!

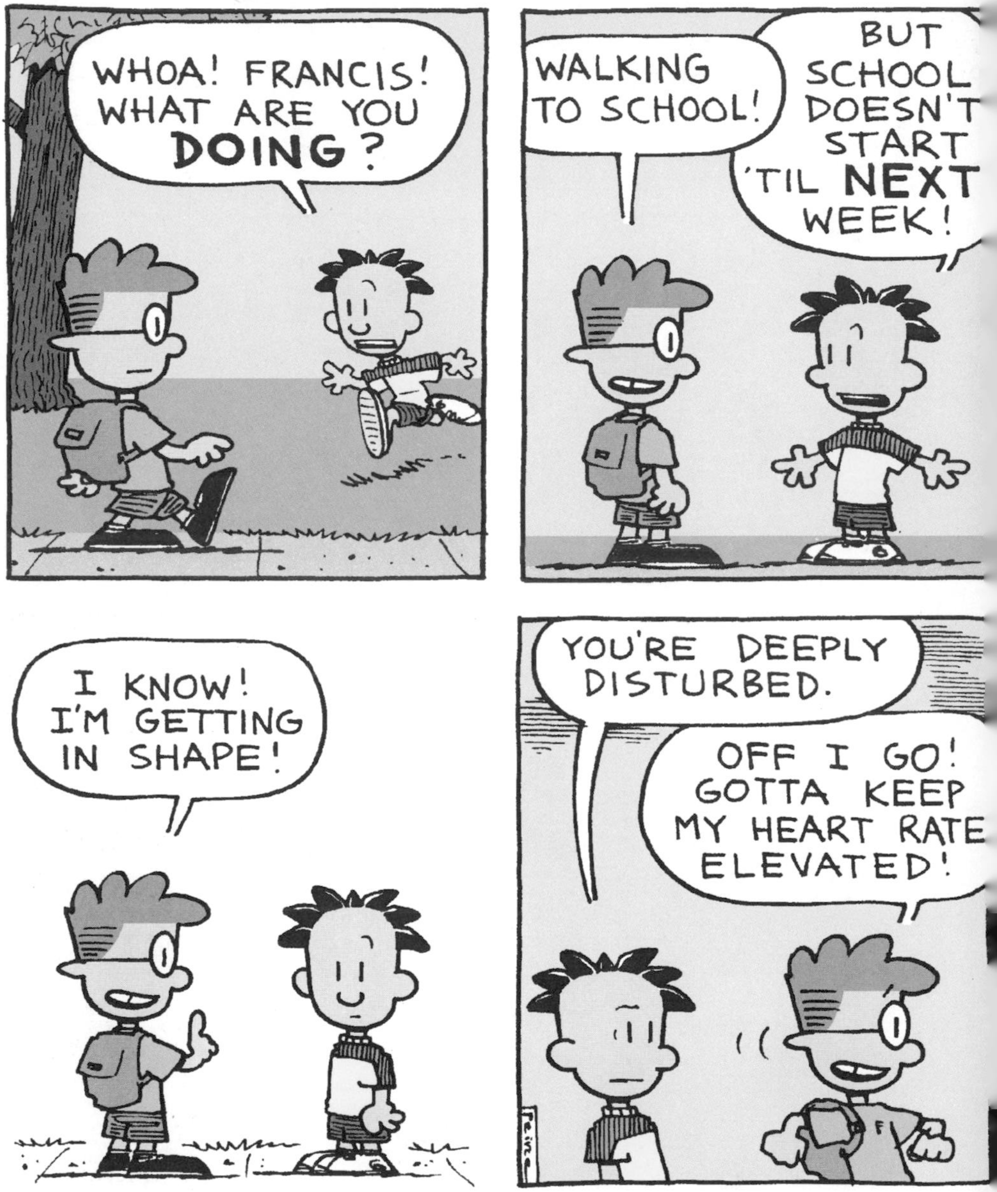
WHOA! FRANCIS! WHAT ARE YOU DOING?
WALKING TO SCHOOL!
BUT SCHOOL DOESN'T START 'TIL NEXT WEEK!
I KNOW! I'M GETTING IN SHAPE!
YOU'RE DEEPLY DISTURBED.
OFF I GO! GOTTA KEEP MY HEART RATE ELEVATED!

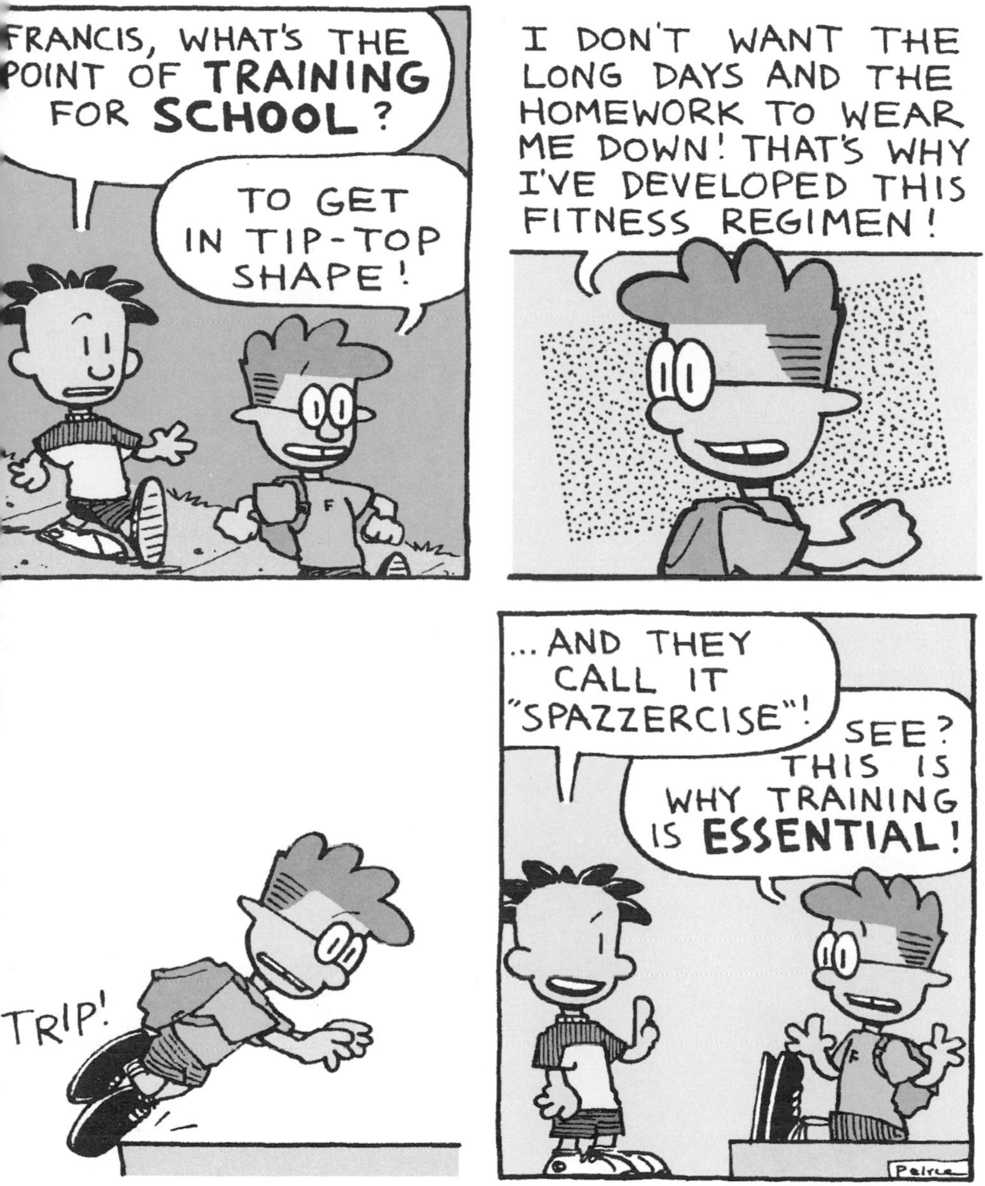
FRANCIS, WHAT'S THE POINT OF TRAINING FOR SCHOOL?
TO GET IN TIP-TOP SHAPE!
I DON'T WANT THE LONG DAYS AND THE HOMEWORK TO WEAR ME DOWN! THAT'S WHY I'VE DEVELOPED THIS FITNESS REGIMEN!
TRIP!
...AND THEY CALL IT "SPAZZERCISE"!
SEE? THIS IS WHY TRAINING IS ESSENTIAL!
Peirce

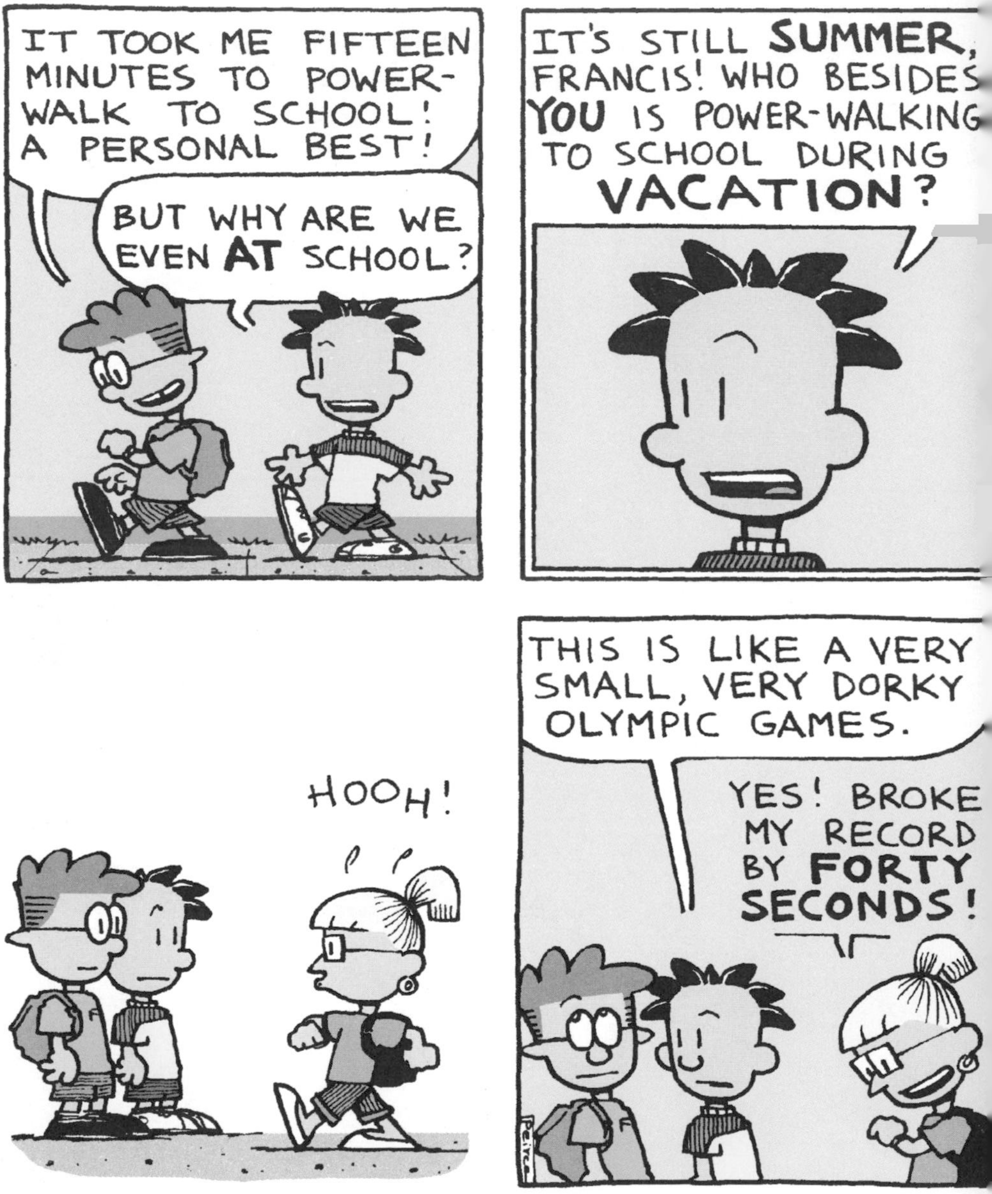
IT TOOK ME FIFTEEN MINUTES TO POWER-WALK TO SCHOOL! A PERSONAL BEST!
BUT WHY ARE WE EVEN **AT** SCHOOL?
IT'S STILL **SUMMER**, FRANCIS! WHO BESIDES **YOU** IS POWER-WALKING TO SCHOOL DURING **VACATION**?
HOOH!
THIS IS LIKE A VERY SMALL, VERY DORKY OLYMPIC GAMES.
YES! BROKE MY RECORD BY **FORTY SECONDS**!
Peirce

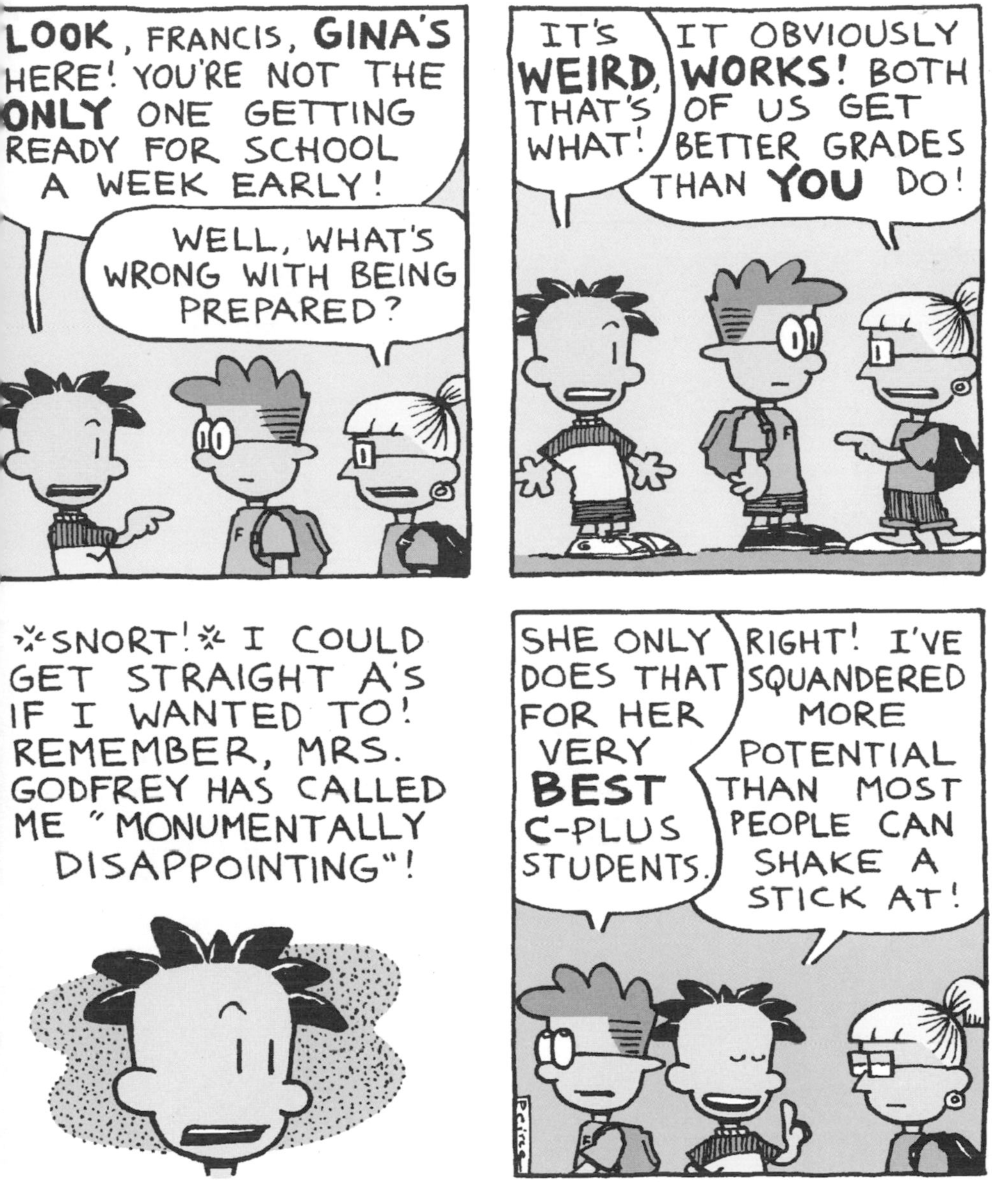
LOOK, FRANCIS, GINA'S HERE! YOU'RE NOT THE ONLY ONE GETTING READY FOR SCHOOL A WEEK EARLY!
WELL, WHAT'S WRONG WITH BEING PREPARED?
IT'S WEIRD, THAT'S WHAT!
IT OBVIOUSLY WORKS! BOTH OF US GET BETTER GRADES THAN YOU DO!
SNORT! I COULD GET STRAIGHT A'S IF I WANTED TO! REMEMBER, MRS. GODFREY HAS CALLED ME "MONUMENTALLY DISAPPOINTING"!
SHE ONLY DOES THAT FOR HER VERY BEST C-PLUS STUDENTS.
RIGHT! I'VE SQUANDERED MORE POTENTIAL THAN MOST PEOPLE CAN SHAKE A STICK AT!
Peirce

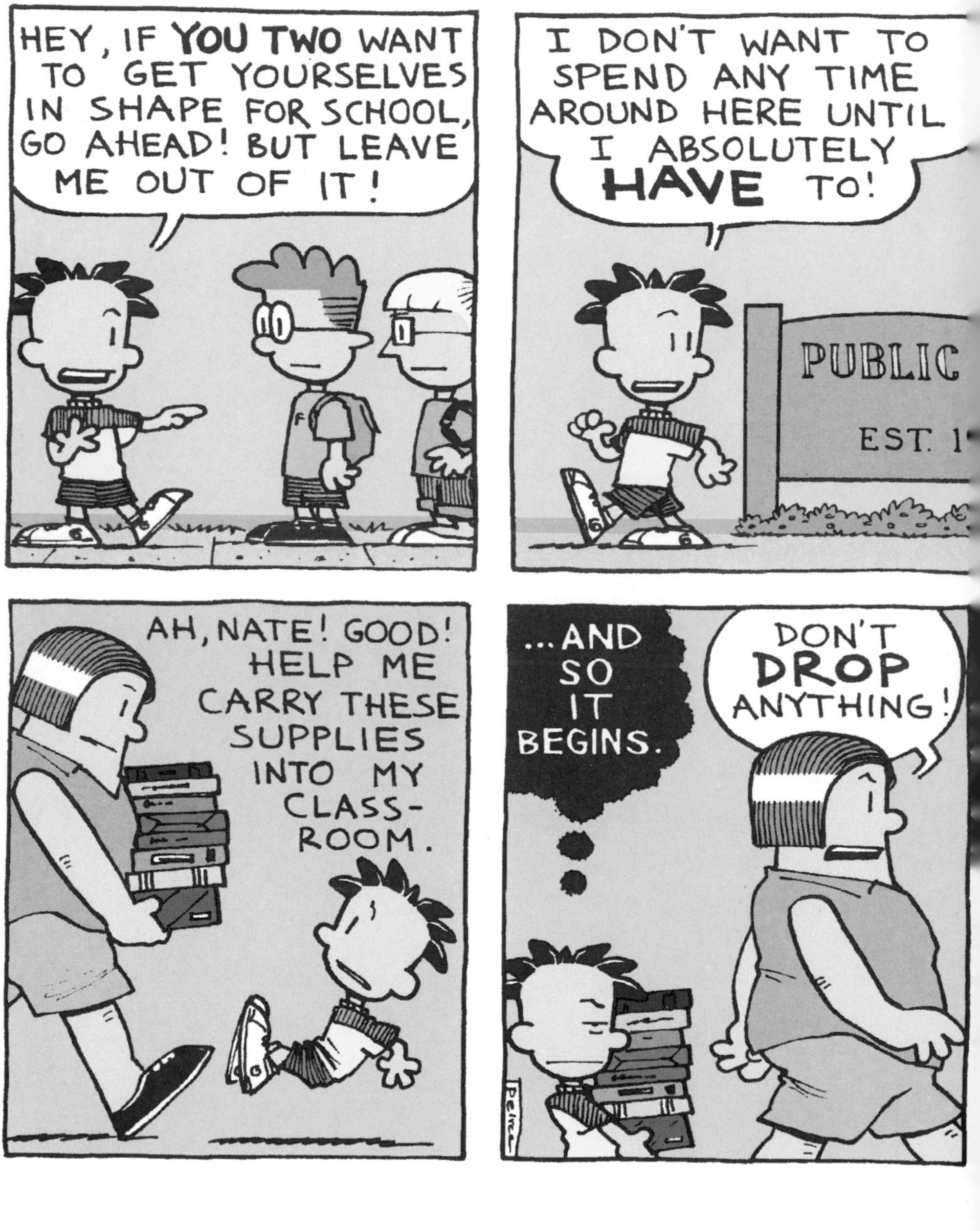
HEY, IF **YOU TWO** WANT TO GET YOURSELVES IN SHAPE FOR SCHOOL, GO AHEAD! BUT LEAVE ME OUT OF IT!
I DON'T WANT TO SPEND ANY TIME AROUND HERE UNTIL I ABSOLUTELY **HAVE** TO!
PUBLIC
AH, NATE! GOOD! HELP ME CARRY THESE SUPPLIES INTO MY CLASSROOM.
...AND SO IT BEGINS.
DON'T **DROP** ANYTHING!
PEIRCE

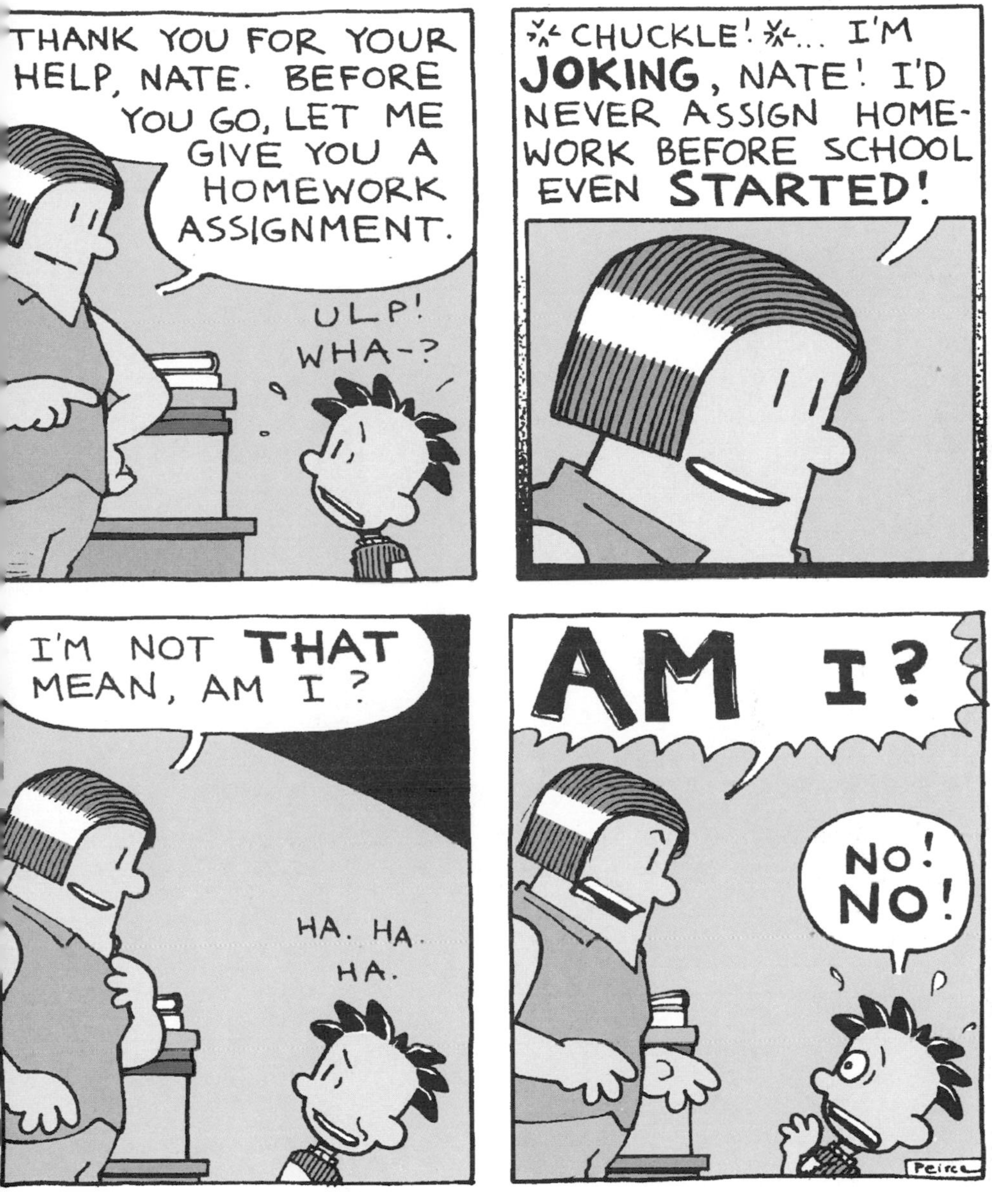
THANK YOU FOR YOUR HELP, NATE. BEFORE YOU GO, LET ME GIVE YOU A HOMEWORK ASSIGNMENT.
ULP! WHA-?
CHUCKLE! ... I'M JOKING, NATE! I'D NEVER ASSIGN HOME-WORK BEFORE SCHOOL EVEN STARTED!
I'M NOT THAT MEAN, AM I?
HA. HA. HA.
AM I?
NO! NO!
Peirce

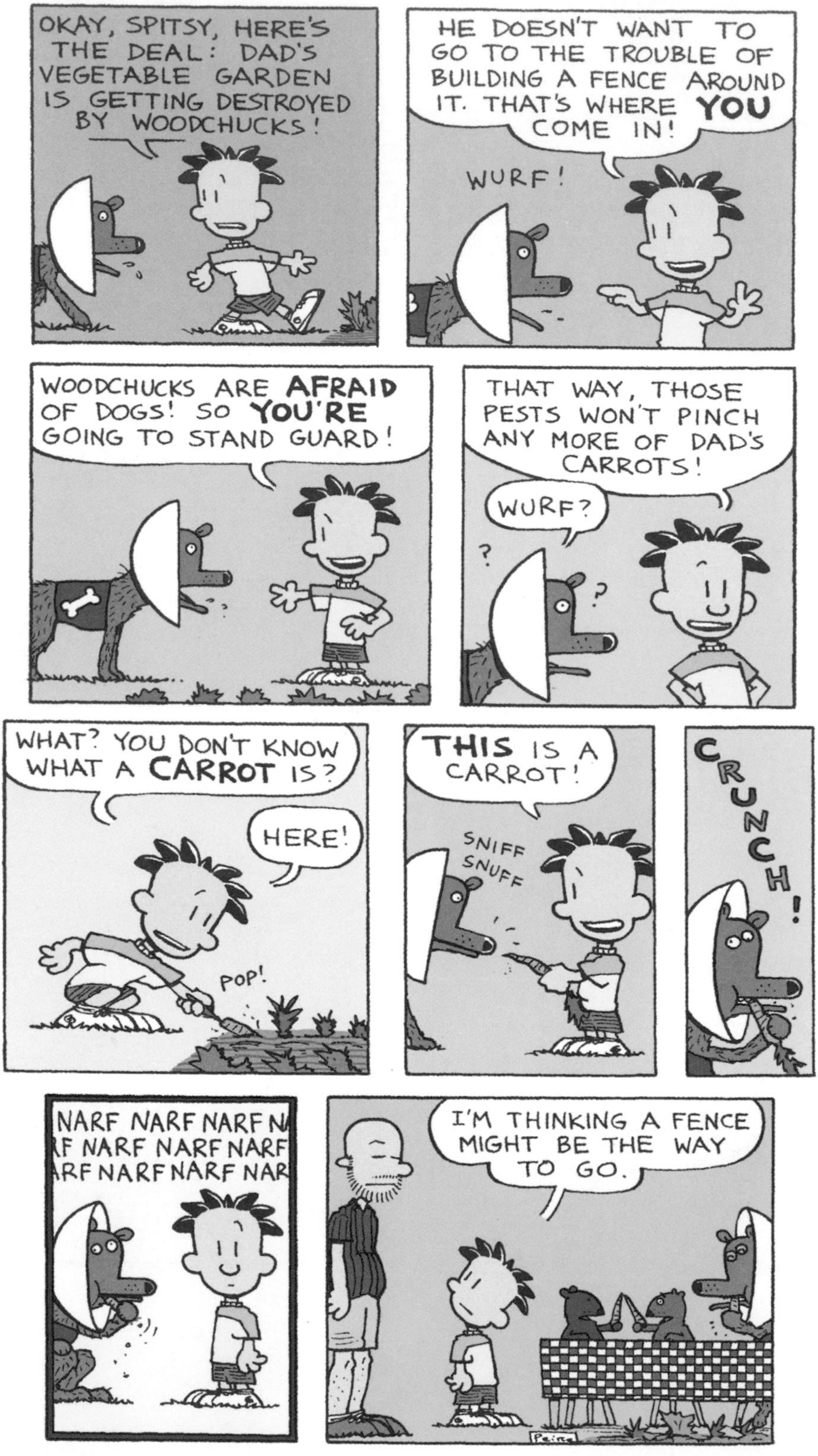

OKAY, SPITSY, HERE'S THE DEAL: DAD'S VEGETABLE GARDEN IS GETTING DESTROYED BY WOODCHUCKS!
HE DOESN'T WANT TO GO TO THE TROUBLE OF BUILDING A FENCE AROUND IT. THAT'S WHERE YOU COME IN!
WURF!
WOODCHUCKS ARE AFRAID OF DOGS! SO YOU'RE GOING TO STAND GUARD!
THAT WAY, THOSE PESTS WON'T PINCH ANY MORE OF DAD'S CARROTS!
WURF?
WHAT? YOU DON'T KNOW WHAT A CARROT IS?
HERE!
POP!
THIS IS A CARROT!
SNIFF SNUFF
CRUNCH!
NARF NARF NARF
I'M THINKING A FENCE MIGHT BE THE WAY TO GO.

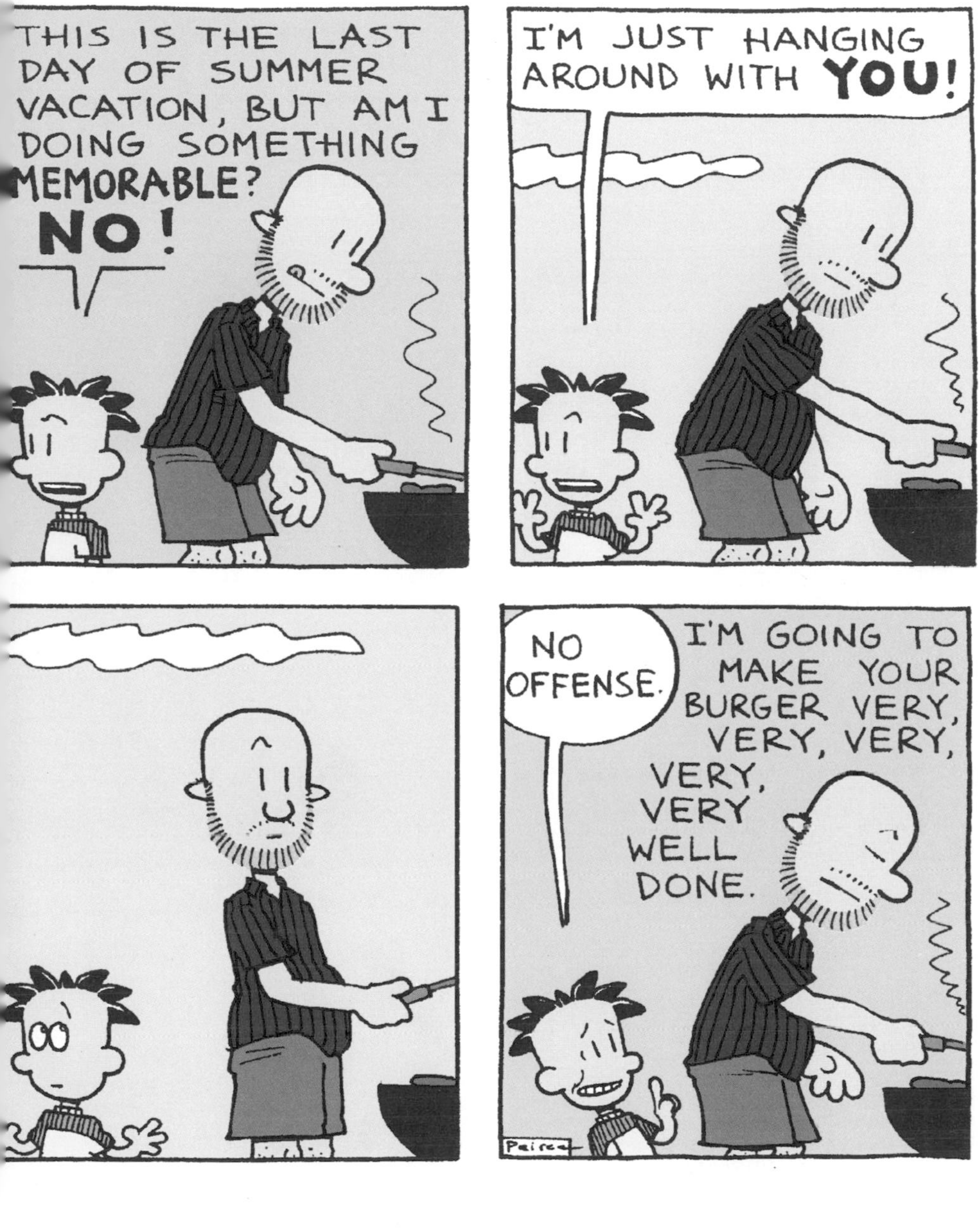
THIS IS THE LAST DAY OF SUMMER VACATION, BUT AM I DOING SOMETHING MEMORABLE? NO!
I'M JUST HANGING AROUND WITH YOU!
NO OFFENSE.
I'M GOING TO MAKE YOUR BURGER VERY, VERY, VERY, VERY, VERY WELL DONE.
Peirce

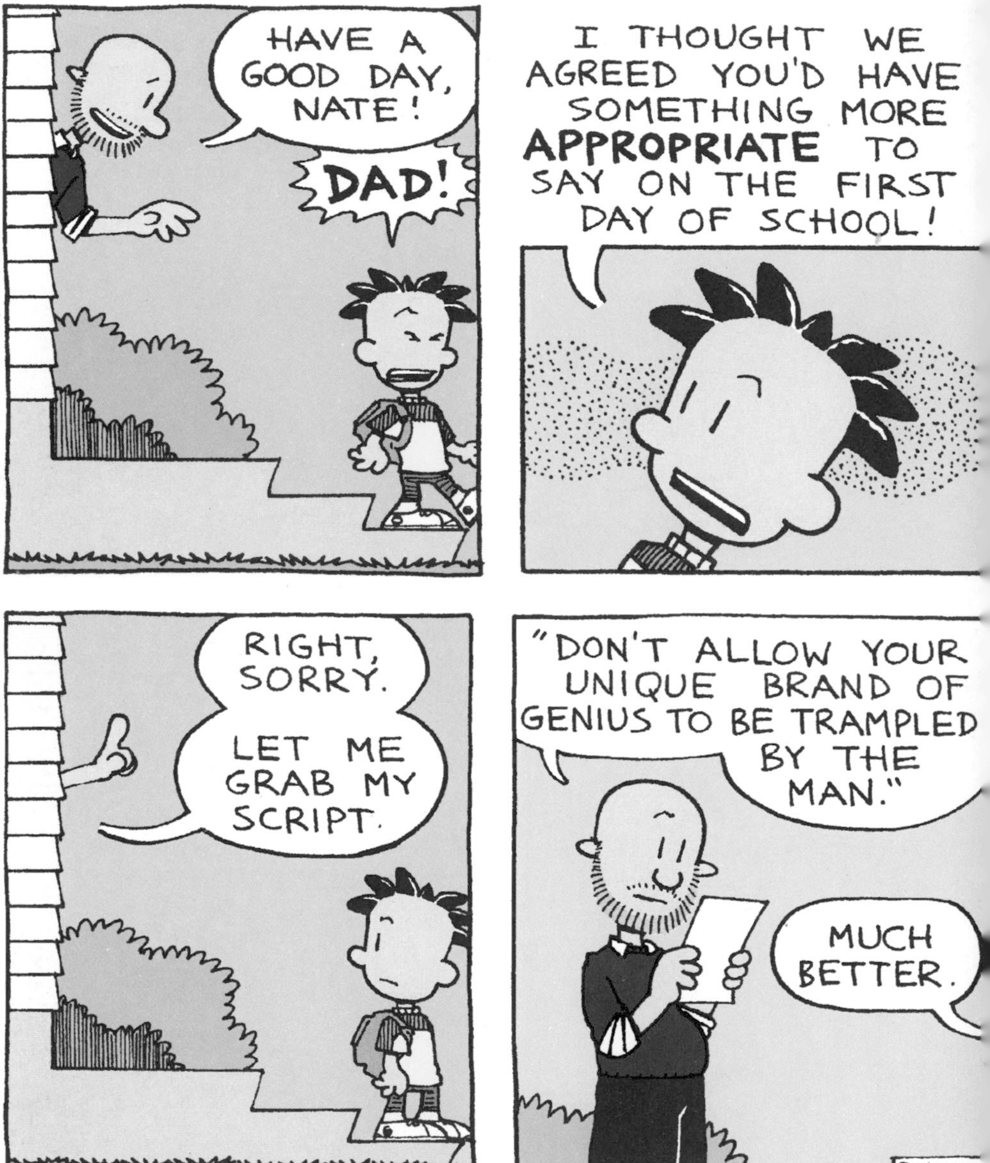
HAVE A GOOD DAY, NATE!
DAD!
I THOUGHT WE AGREED YOU'D HAVE SOMETHING MORE **APPROPRIATE** TO SAY ON THE FIRST DAY OF SCHOOL!
RIGHT, SORRY.
LET ME GRAB MY SCRIPT.
"DON'T ALLOW YOUR UNIQUE BRAND OF GENIUS TO BE TRAMPLED BY THE MAN."
MUCH BETTER.
Peirce

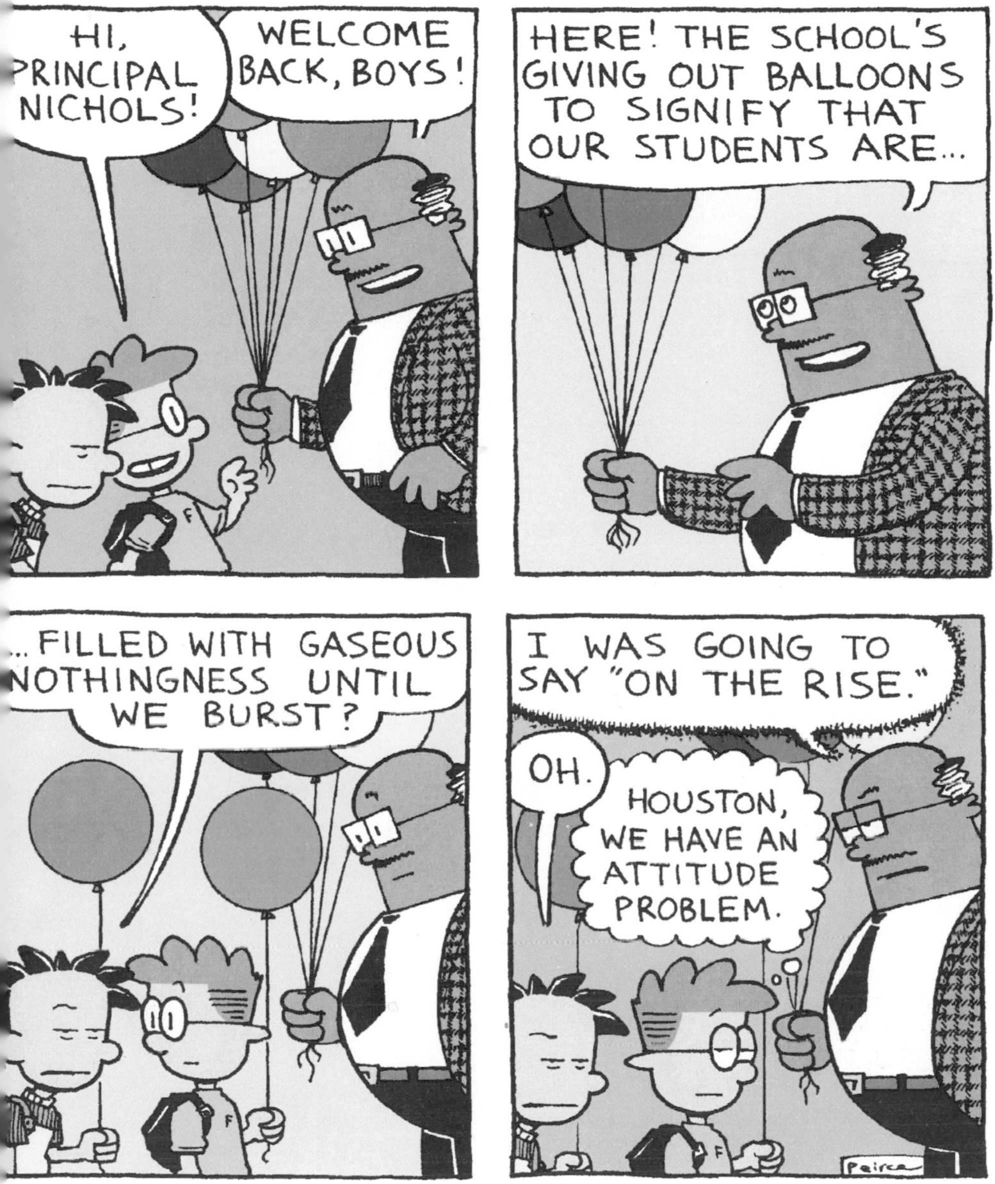
HI, PRINCIPAL NICHOLS!
WELCOME BACK, BOYS!
HERE! THE SCHOOL'S GIVING OUT BALLOONS TO SIGNIFY THAT OUR STUDENTS ARE...
...FILLED WITH GASEOUS NOTHINGNESS UNTIL WE BURST?
I WAS GOING TO SAY "ON THE RISE."
OH.
HOUSTON, WE HAVE AN ATTITUDE PROBLEM.
Peirce

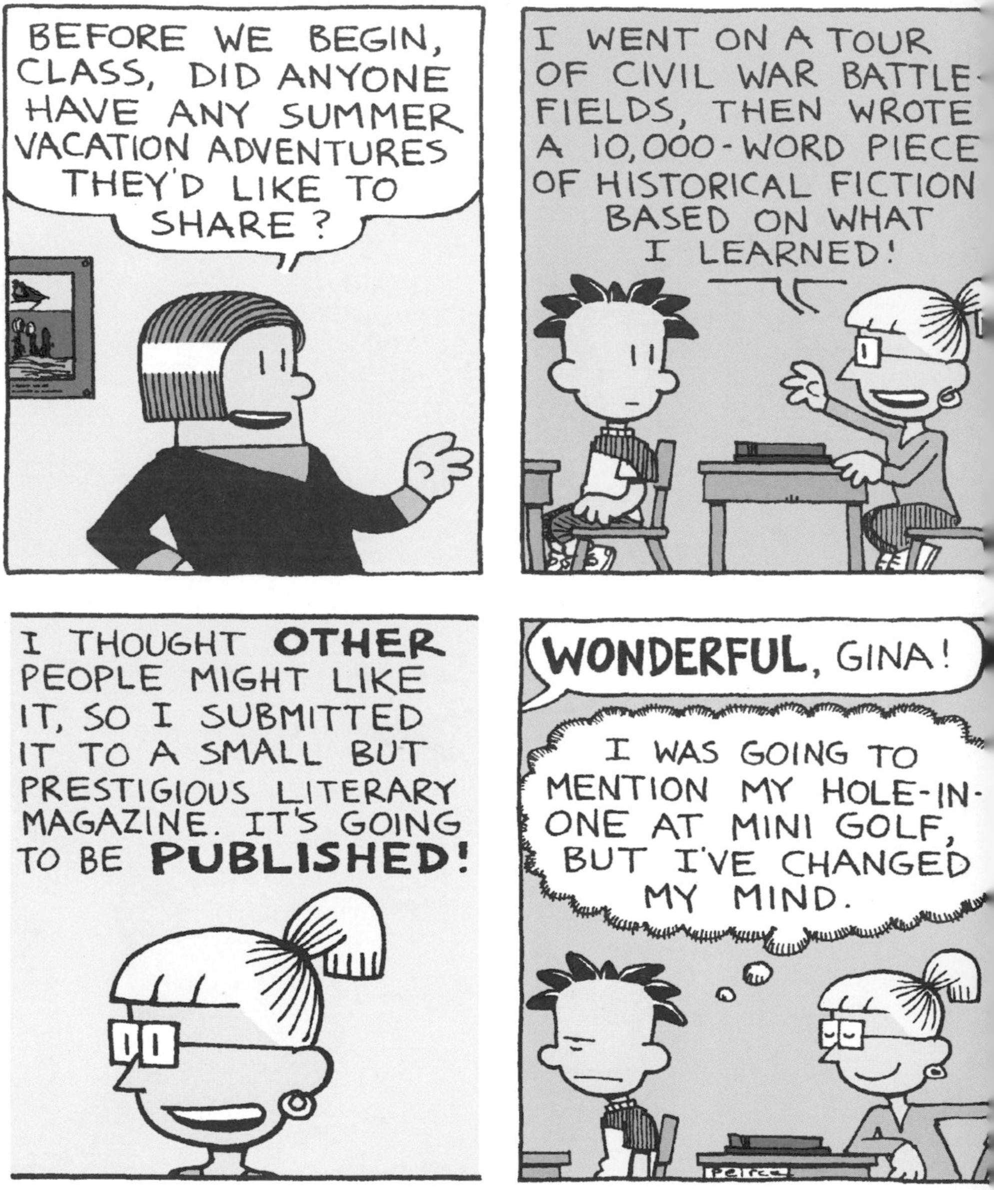
BEFORE WE BEGIN, CLASS, DID ANYONE HAVE ANY SUMMER VACATION ADVENTURES THEY'D LIKE TO SHARE?
I WENT ON A TOUR OF CIVIL WAR BATTLE-FIELDS, THEN WROTE A 10,000-WORD PIECE OF HISTORICAL FICTION BASED ON WHAT I LEARNED!
I THOUGHT **OTHER** PEOPLE MIGHT LIKE IT, SO I SUBMITTED IT TO A SMALL BUT PRESTIGIOUS LITERARY MAGAZINE. IT'S GOING TO BE **PUBLISHED!**
WONDERFUL, GINA!
I WAS GOING TO MENTION MY HOLE-IN-ONE AT MINI GOLF, BUT I'VE CHANGED MY MIND.

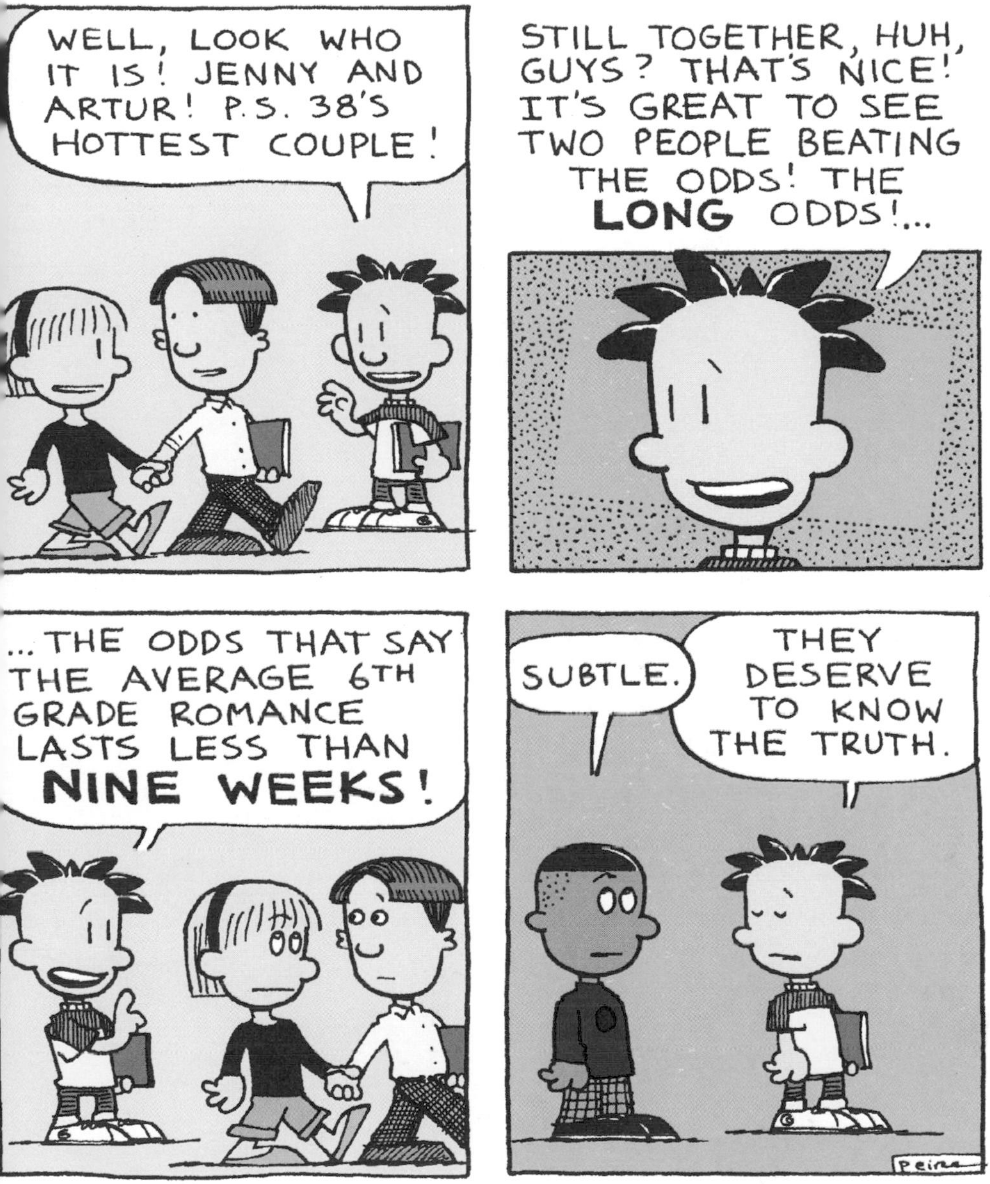
WELL, LOOK WHO IT IS! JENNY AND ARTUR! P.S. 38'S HOTTEST COUPLE!
STILL TOGETHER, HUH, GUYS? THAT'S NICE! IT'S GREAT TO SEE TWO PEOPLE BEATING THE ODDS! THE **LONG** ODDS!...
...THE ODDS THAT SAY THE AVERAGE 6TH GRADE ROMANCE LASTS LESS THAN **NINE WEEKS!**
SUBTLE.
THEY DESERVE TO KNOW THE TRUTH.
Peirce

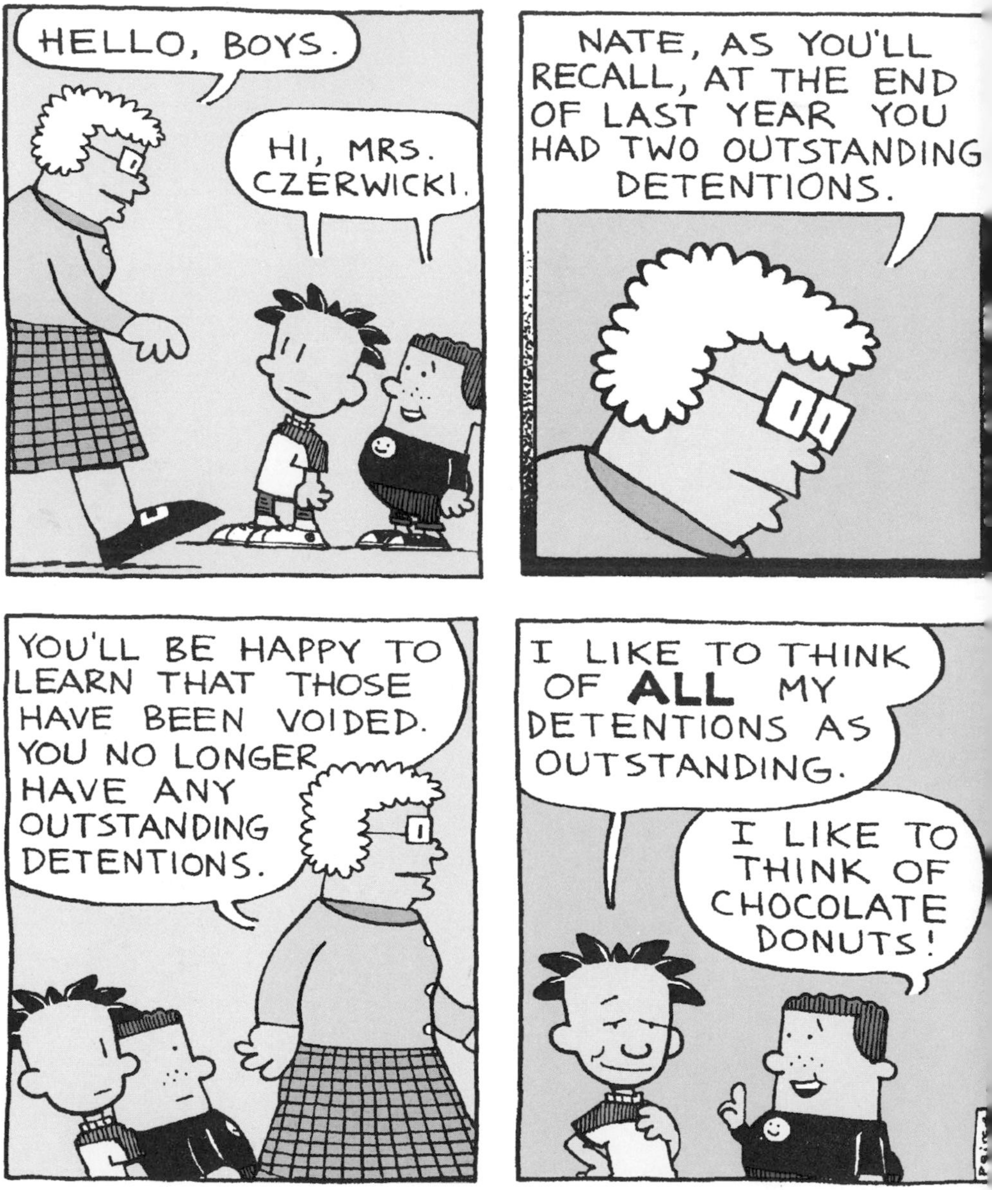
HELLO, BOYS.
HI, MRS. CZERWICKI.
NATE, AS YOU'LL RECALL, AT THE END OF LAST YEAR YOU HAD TWO OUTSTANDING DETENTIONS.
YOU'LL BE HAPPY TO LEARN THAT THOSE HAVE BEEN VOIDED. YOU NO LONGER HAVE ANY OUTSTANDING DETENTIONS.
I LIKE TO THINK OF **ALL** MY DETENTIONS AS OUTSTANDING.
I LIKE TO THINK OF CHOCOLATE DONUTS!

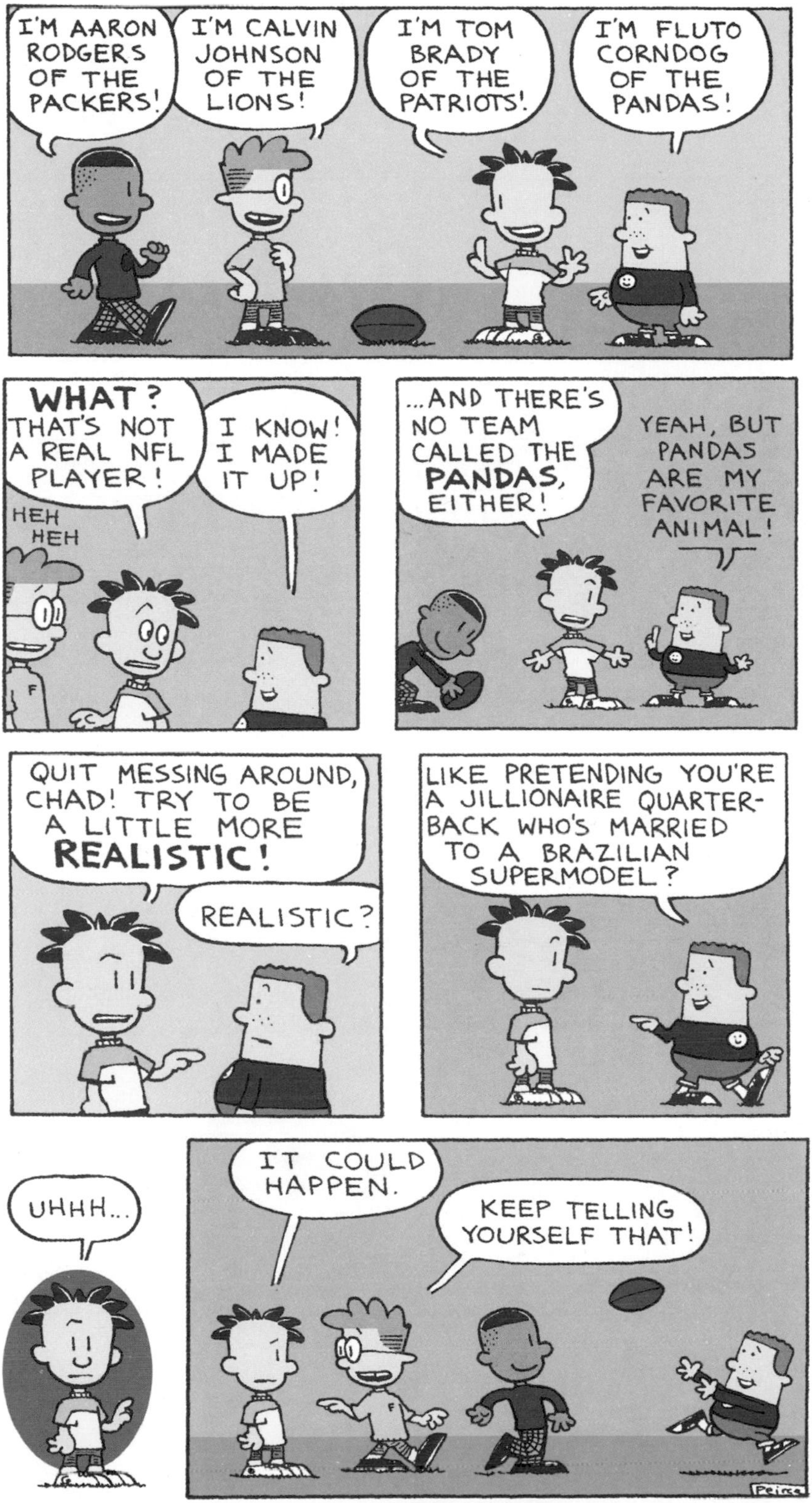
I'M AARON RODGERS OF THE PACKERS!
I'M CALVIN JOHNSON OF THE LIONS!
I'M TOM BRADY OF THE PATRIOTS!
I'M FLUTO CORNDOG OF THE PANDAS!
WHAT? THAT'S NOT A REAL NFL PLAYER!
I KNOW! I MADE IT UP!
HEH HEH
...AND THERE'S NO TEAM CALLED THE PANDAS, EITHER!
YEAH, BUT PANDAS ARE MY FAVORITE ANIMAL!
QUIT MESSING AROUND, CHAD! TRY TO BE A LITTLE MORE REALISTIC!
REALISTIC?
LIKE PRETENDING YOU'RE A JILLIONAIRE QUARTER-BACK WHO'S MARRIED TO A BRAZILIAN SUPERMODEL?
UHHH...
IT COULD HAPPEN.
KEEP TELLING YOURSELF THAT!
Peirce

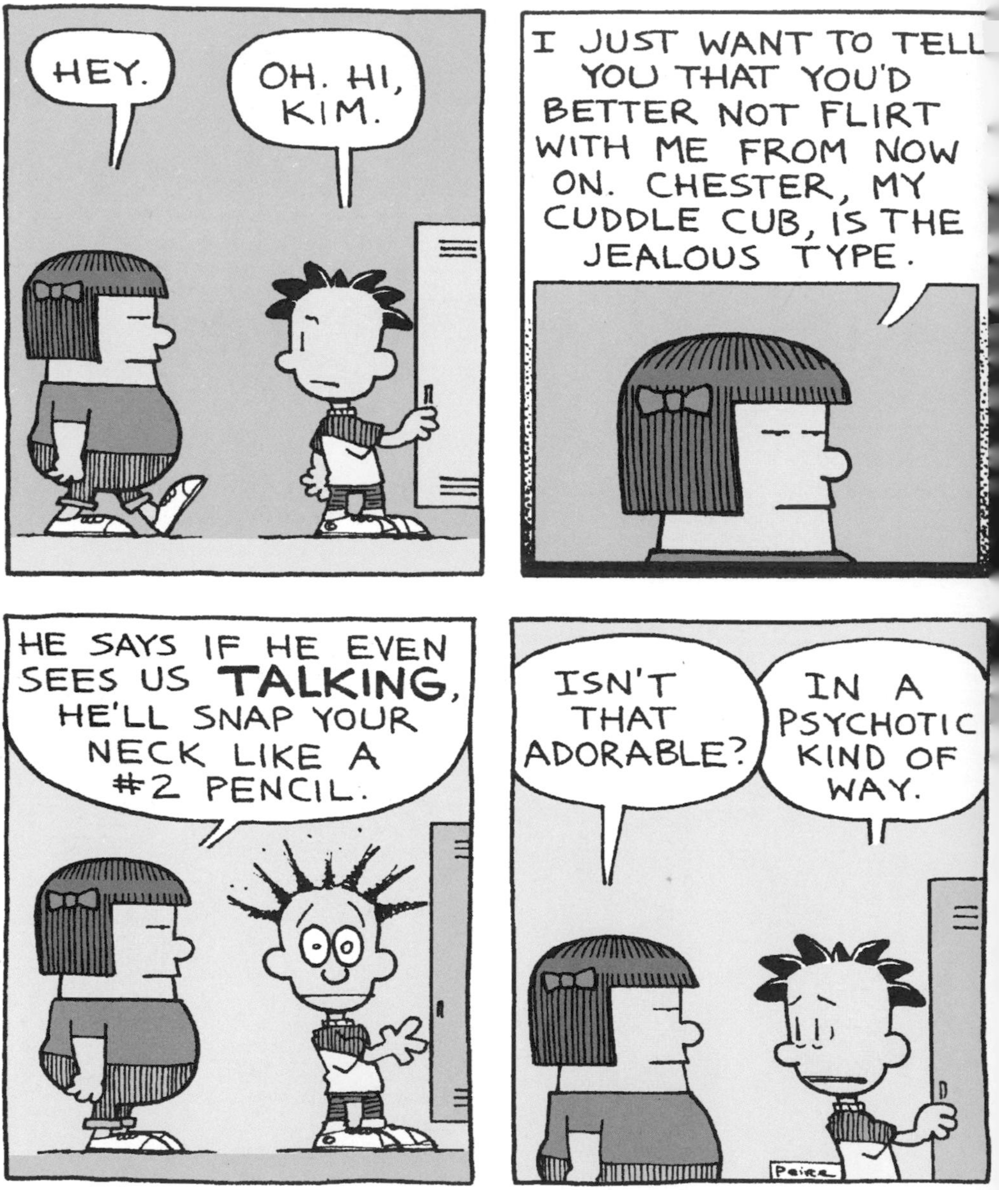
HEY.
OH. HI, KIM.
I JUST WANT TO TELL YOU THAT YOU'D BETTER NOT FLIRT WITH ME FROM NOW ON. CHESTER, MY CUDDLE CUB, IS THE JEALOUS TYPE.
HE SAYS IF HE EVEN SEES US **TALKING**, HE'LL SNAP YOUR NECK LIKE A #2 PENCIL.
ISN'T THAT ADORABLE?
IN A PSYCHOTIC KIND OF WAY.
Peirce

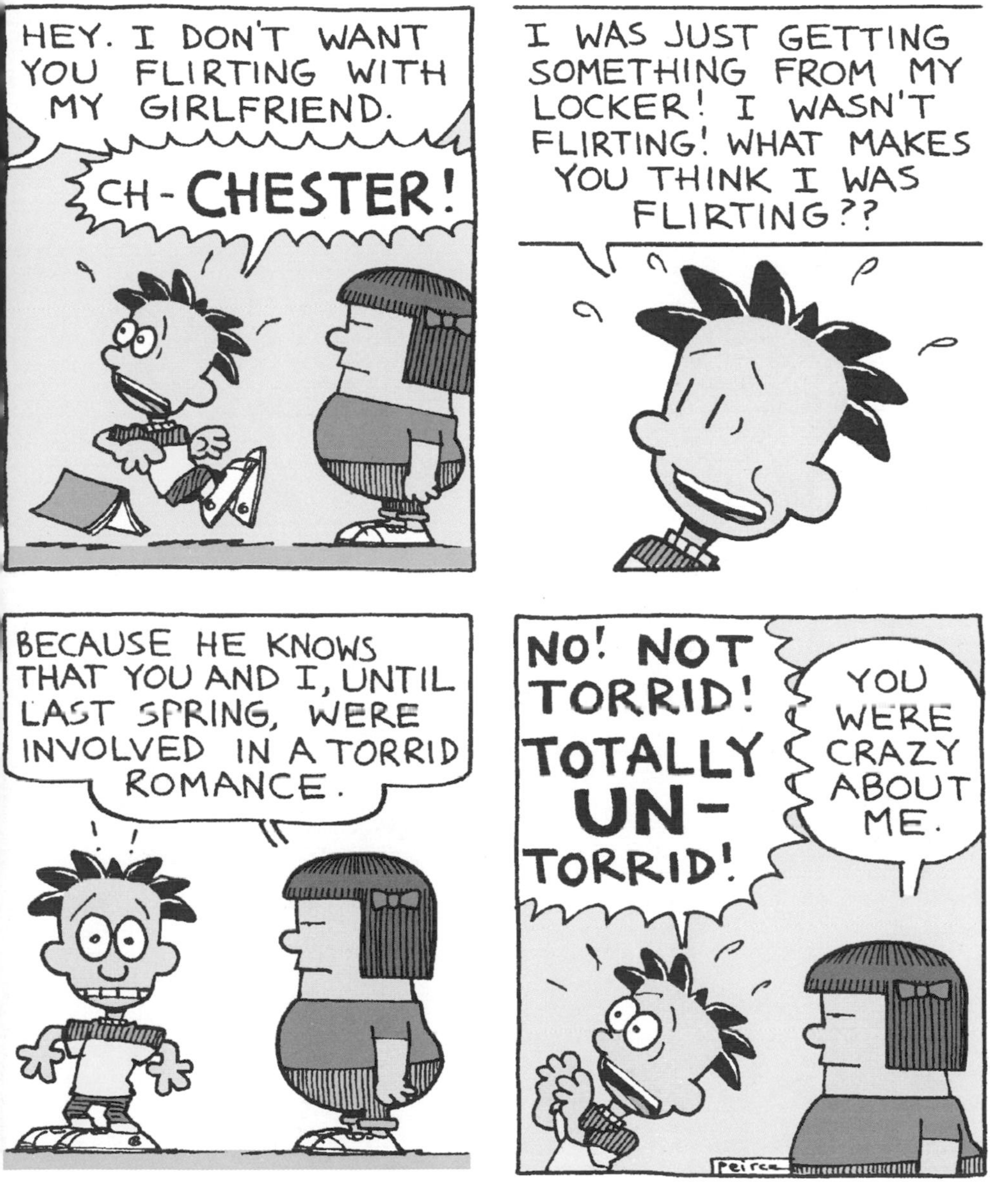
HEY. I DON'T WANT YOU FLIRTING WITH MY GIRLFRIEND.
CH-CHESTER!
I WAS JUST GETTING SOMETHING FROM MY LOCKER! I WASN'T FLIRTING! WHAT MAKES YOU THINK I WAS FLIRTING??
BECAUSE HE KNOWS THAT YOU AND I, UNTIL LAST SPRING, WERE INVOLVED IN A TORRID ROMANCE.
NO! NOT TORRID! TOTALLY UN-TORRID!
YOU WERE CRAZY ABOUT ME.
PEIRCE

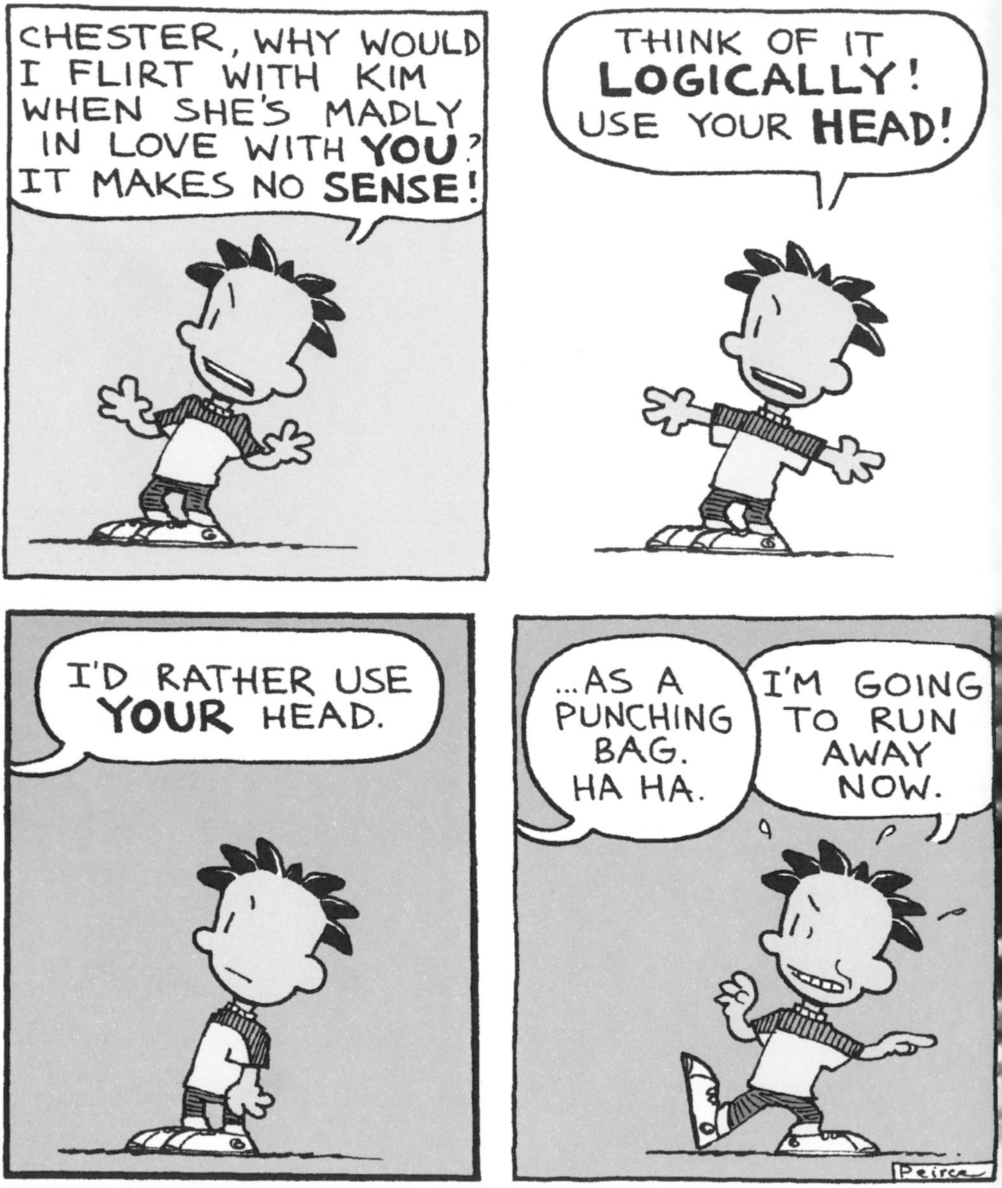
CHESTER, WHY WOULD I FLIRT WITH KIM WHEN SHE'S MADLY IN LOVE WITH YOU? IT MAKES NO SENSE!
THINK OF IT LOGICALLY! USE YOUR HEAD!
I'D RATHER USE YOUR HEAD.
...AS A PUNCHING BAG. HA HA.
I'M GOING TO RUN AWAY NOW.
Peirce

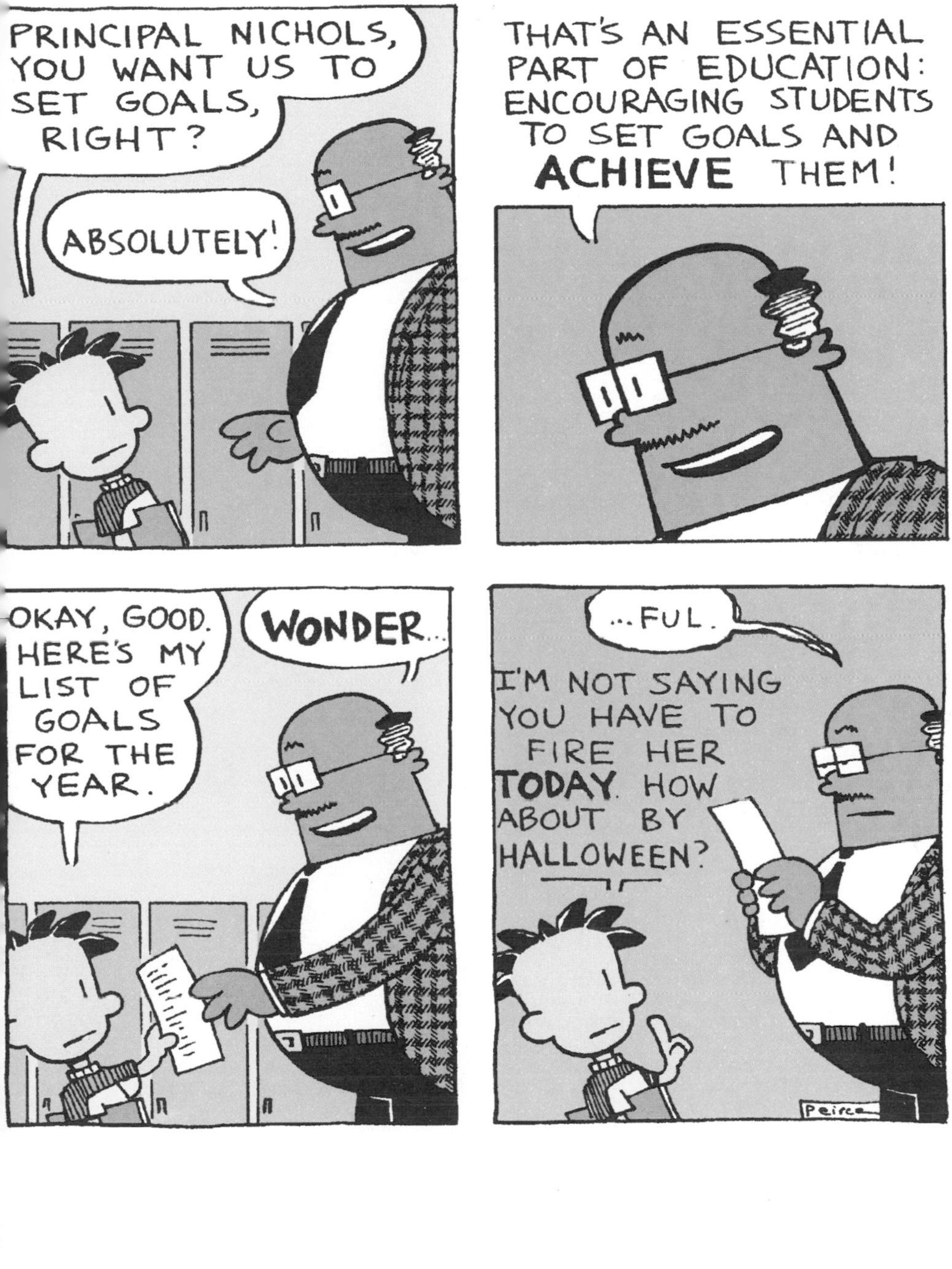
PRINCIPAL NICHOLS, YOU WANT US TO SET GOALS, RIGHT?
ABSOLUTELY!
THAT'S AN ESSENTIAL PART OF EDUCATION: ENCOURAGING STUDENTS TO SET GOALS AND **ACHIEVE** THEM!
OKAY, GOOD. HERE'S MY LIST OF GOALS FOR THE YEAR.
WONDER...
...FUL.
I'M NOT SAYING YOU HAVE TO FIRE HER **TODAY**. HOW ABOUT BY HALLOWEEN?
Peirce

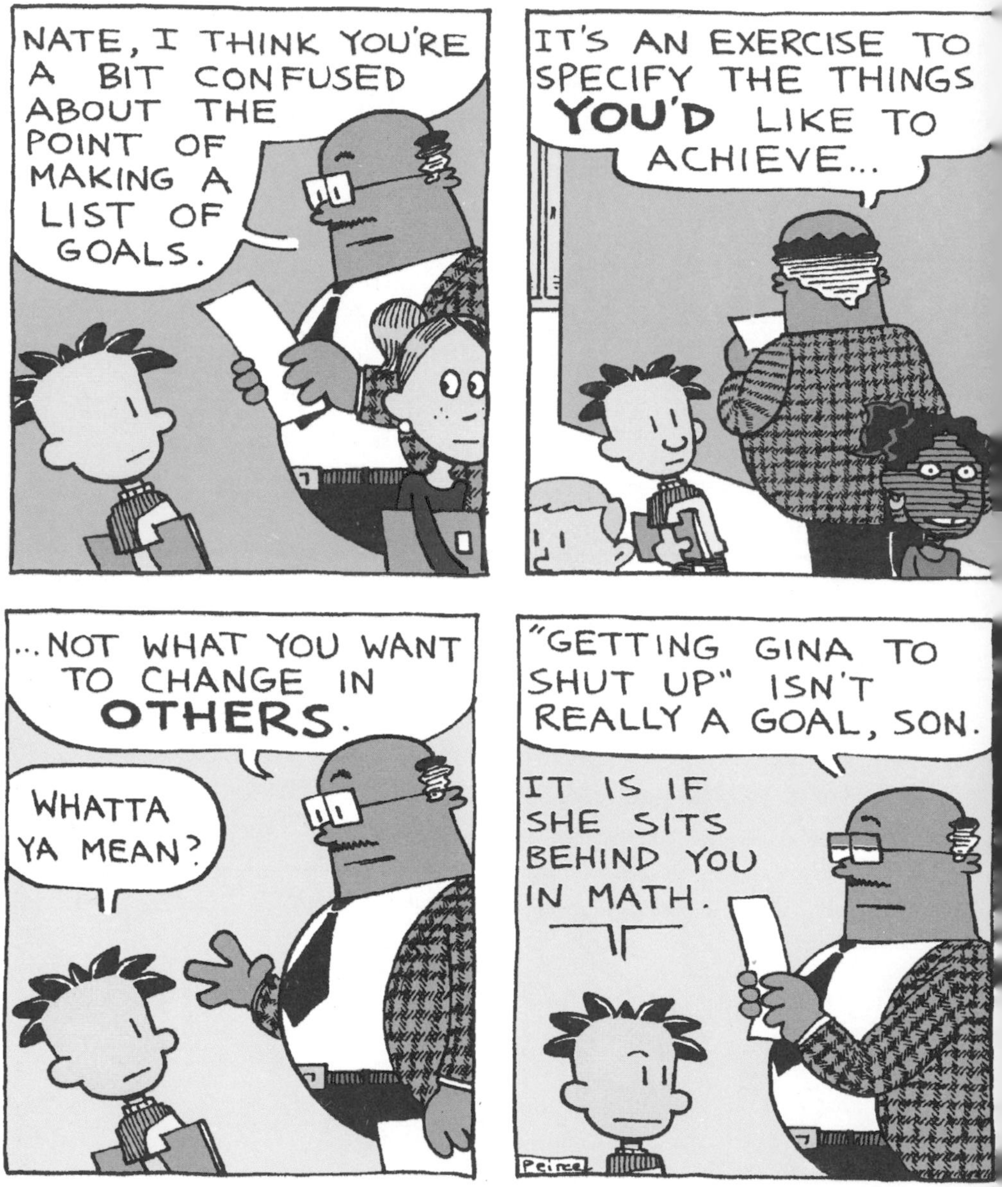
NATE, I THINK YOU'RE A BIT CONFUSED ABOUT THE POINT OF MAKING A LIST OF GOALS.
IT'S AN EXERCISE TO SPECIFY THE THINGS **YOU'D** LIKE TO ACHIEVE...
...NOT WHAT YOU WANT TO CHANGE IN **OTHERS**.
WHATTA YA MEAN?
"GETTING GINA TO SHUT UP" ISN'T REALLY A GOAL, SON.
IT IS IF SHE SITS BEHIND YOU IN MATH.
Peirce

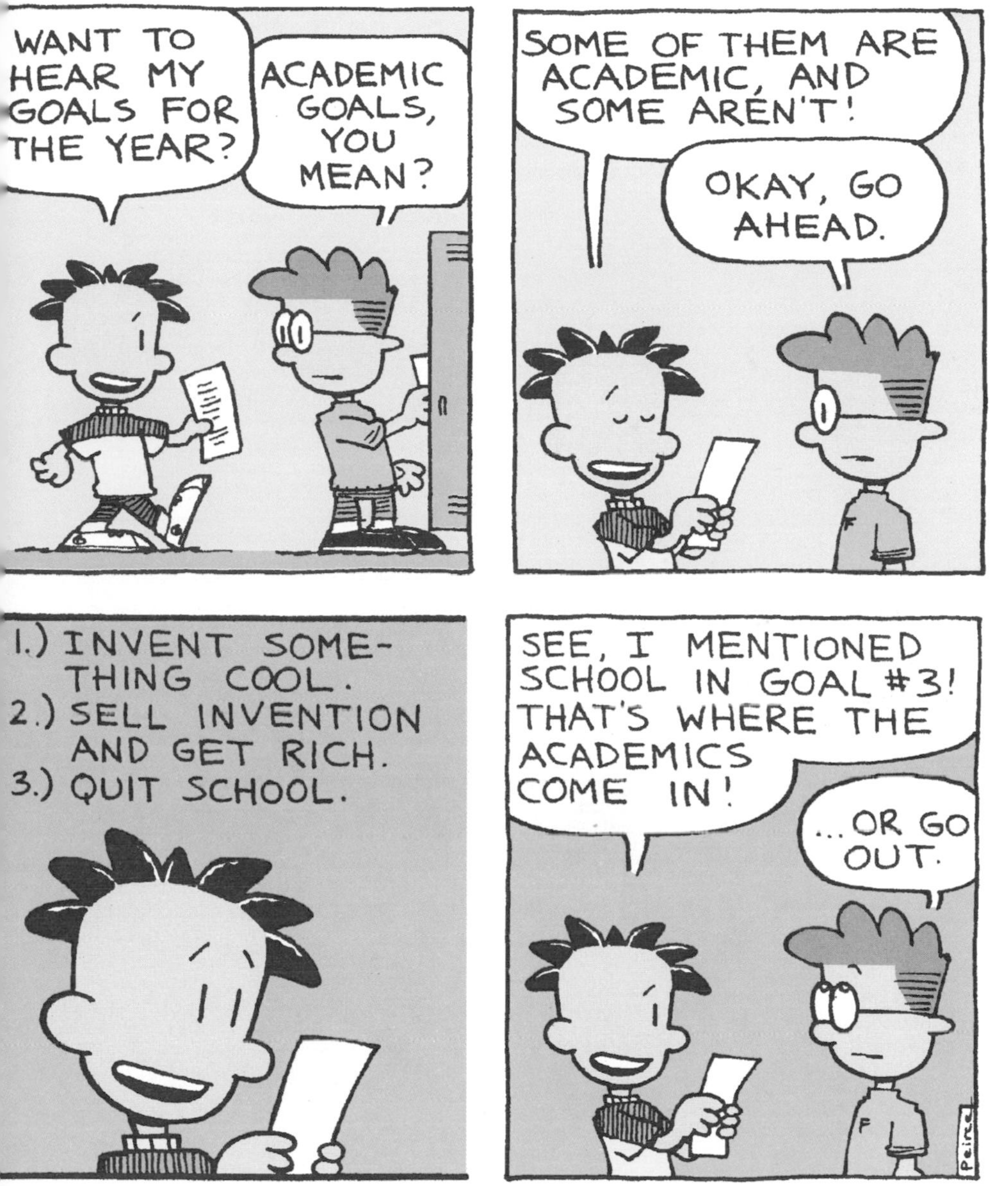
WANT TO HEAR MY GOALS FOR THE YEAR?
ACADEMIC GOALS, YOU MEAN?
SOME OF THEM ARE ACADEMIC, AND SOME AREN'T!
OKAY, GO AHEAD.
1.) INVENT SOMETHING COOL.
2.) SELL INVENTION AND GET RICH.
3.) QUIT SCHOOL.
SEE, I MENTIONED SCHOOL IN GOAL #3! THAT'S WHERE THE ACADEMICS COME IN!
...OR GO OUT.
Peirce

GEORGE WASHINGTON, FATHER OF OUR COUNTRY
By Nate Wright

People sometimes call George Washington the father of our country. I think those people are right, because indeed, George Washington truly WAS the father of our country, which as we all know is called the United States of America. But HOW did a shy young man from the humble little town of Wakefield, Virginia, grow up to become our first president? Well, allow me to give you some of the startling facts that will PROVE my point, which is that George Washington is the real father of our country. When young George was born, on February 22nd, 1732, he was just a baby. But soon, as so often happens, he grew up. Then George got smallpox, which was a disease back in the old days. As a result, George had bad skin.

Then his dad died. Oh, by the way, George's dad was named Augustine and his mother had the very simple name of Mary. Heartbroken, George chopped down a cherry tree and became a surveyor. After that he joined the army, which was in the middle of a war with France. George fought against the French in Ohio, which is kind of weird, and got them to surrender some forts. For example: one of those forts was called Fort Duquesne. George got out of the army and decided it was time to get married. He found a widow named Martha Custis who agreed to marry him even though he had wooden teeth. So they got married and went to live at George's mansion, which is called Mount Vernon. It is open 365 days a year and contains a museum, orientation center, and gift shop. Everything was going great until England came along and started raising taxes. George got so mad, he declared WAR ON ENGLAND!!

George was made commander of the Continental Army, and then he crossed the Delaware to fight the British at Valley Forge. There were many fierce battles, but thanks to George and his very, very good leadership, the British eventually gave up and went back to England. George wanted to retire to Mount Vernon, but the rest of the country was like: we don't THINK so. So they elected George as the first president.

George was inaugurated on April 30th, 1789, in New York City. Why New York City? Because George had not invented the city of Washington, DC yet. Pretty soon he did, though, and he made it the capital of the whole country. That was the first of many impressive accomplishments he accomplished as president. Most of them he did while he was alive, but some he achieved when he was dead, like getting his face carved into Mount Rushmore. On December 14th, 1799, tragedy struck. George went horseback riding in the snow, came down with acute laryngitis, and died. But what a very amazing life he led. As the first president and father of our country, George Washington definitely made history.

THE END

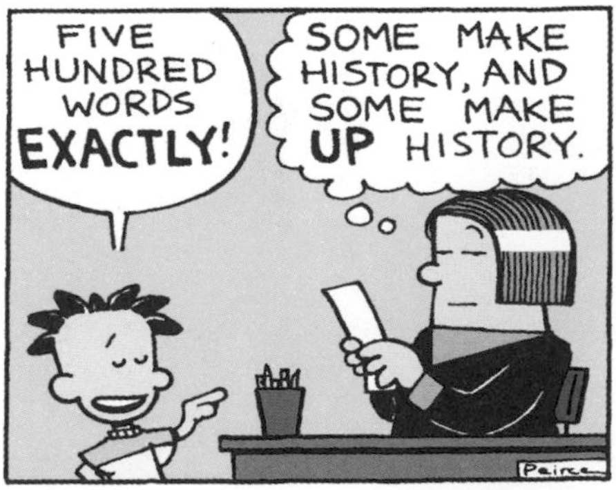
FIVE HUNDRED WORDS EXACTLY!
SOME MAKE HISTORY, AND SOME MAKE UP HISTORY.
Peirce

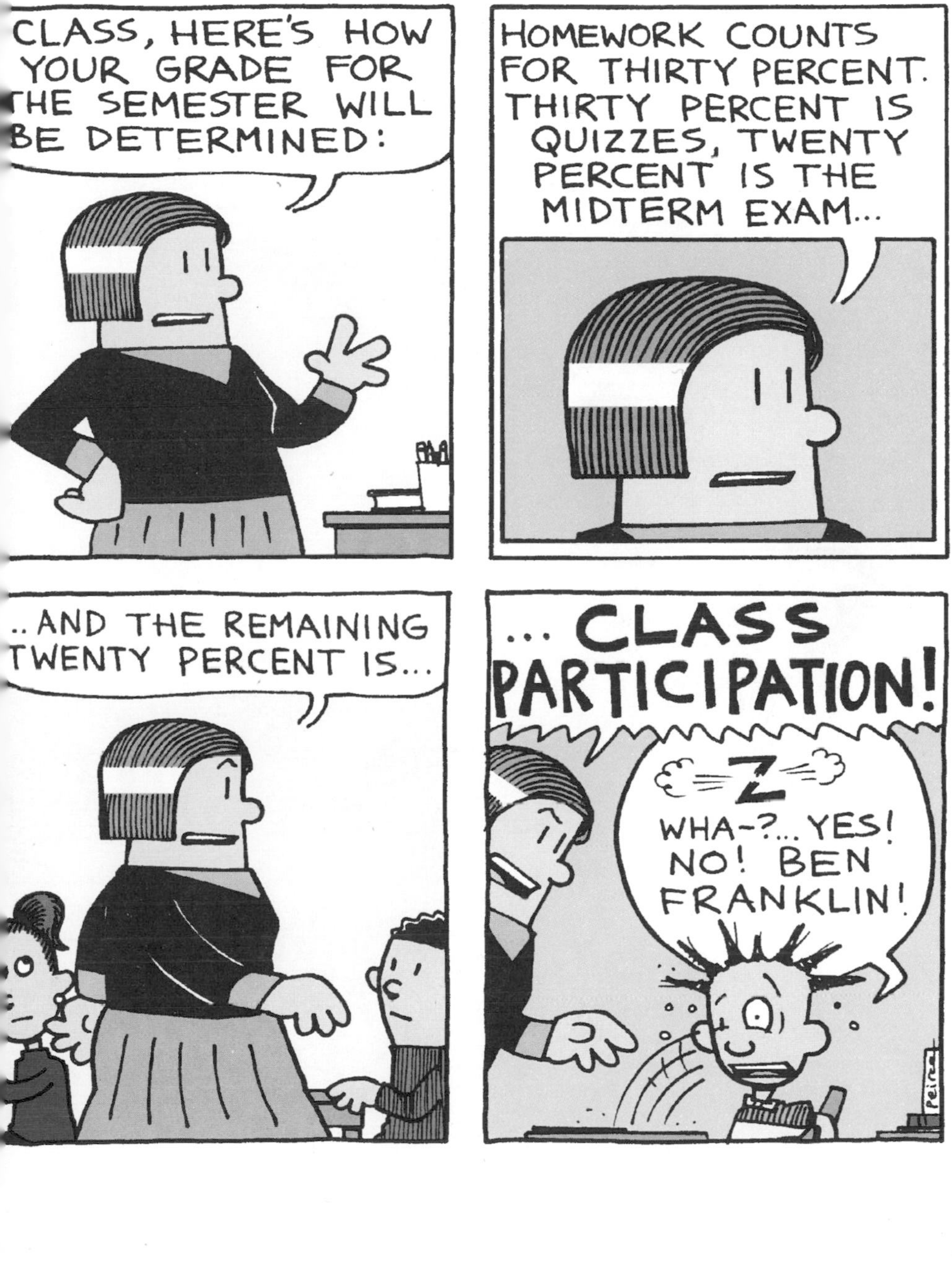

CLASS, HERE'S HOW YOUR GRADE FOR THE SEMESTER WILL BE DETERMINED:
HOMEWORK COUNTS FOR THIRTY PERCENT. THIRTY PERCENT IS QUIZZES, TWENTY PERCENT IS THE MIDTERM EXAM...
..AND THE REMAINING TWENTY PERCENT IS...
... CLASS PARTICIPATION!
Z
WHA-?... YES! NO! BEN FRANKLIN!
Peirce

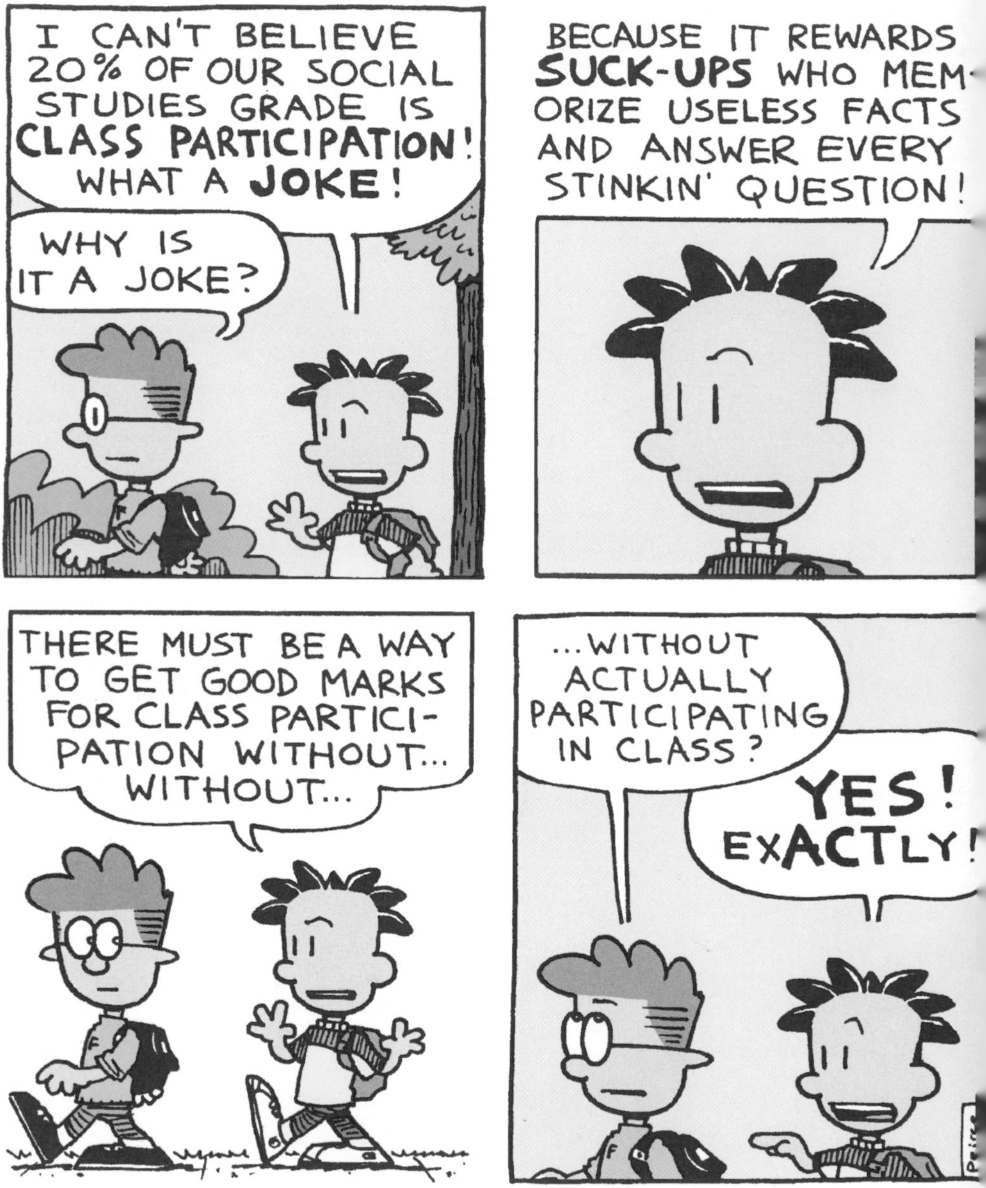
I CAN'T BELIEVE 20% OF OUR SOCIAL STUDIES GRADE IS CLASS PARTICIPATION! WHAT A JOKE!
WHY IS IT A JOKE?
BECAUSE IT REWARDS SUCK-UPS WHO MEMORIZE USELESS FACTS AND ANSWER EVERY STINKIN' QUESTION!
THERE MUST BE A WAY TO GET GOOD MARKS FOR CLASS PARTICIPATION WITHOUT... WITHOUT...
...WITHOUT ACTUALLY PARTICIPATING IN CLASS?
YES! EXACTLY!

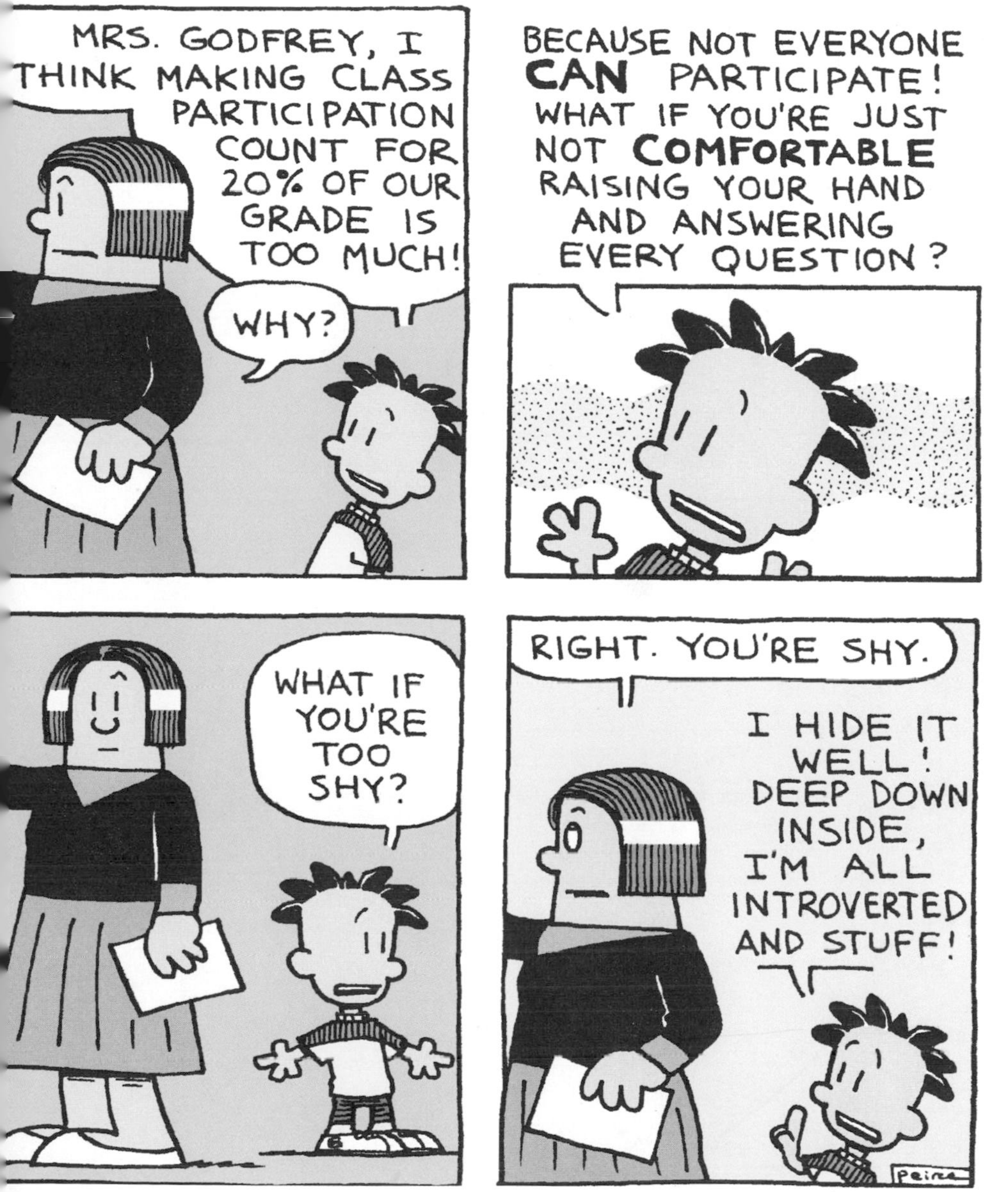
MRS. GODFREY, I THINK MAKING CLASS PARTICIPATION COUNT FOR 20% OF OUR GRADE IS TOO MUCH!
WHY?
BECAUSE NOT EVERYONE **CAN** PARTICIPATE! WHAT IF YOU'RE JUST NOT **COMFORTABLE** RAISING YOUR HAND AND ANSWERING EVERY QUESTION?
WHAT IF YOU'RE TOO SHY?
RIGHT. YOU'RE SHY.
I HIDE IT WELL! DEEP DOWN INSIDE, I'M ALL INTROVERTED AND STUFF!
Peirce

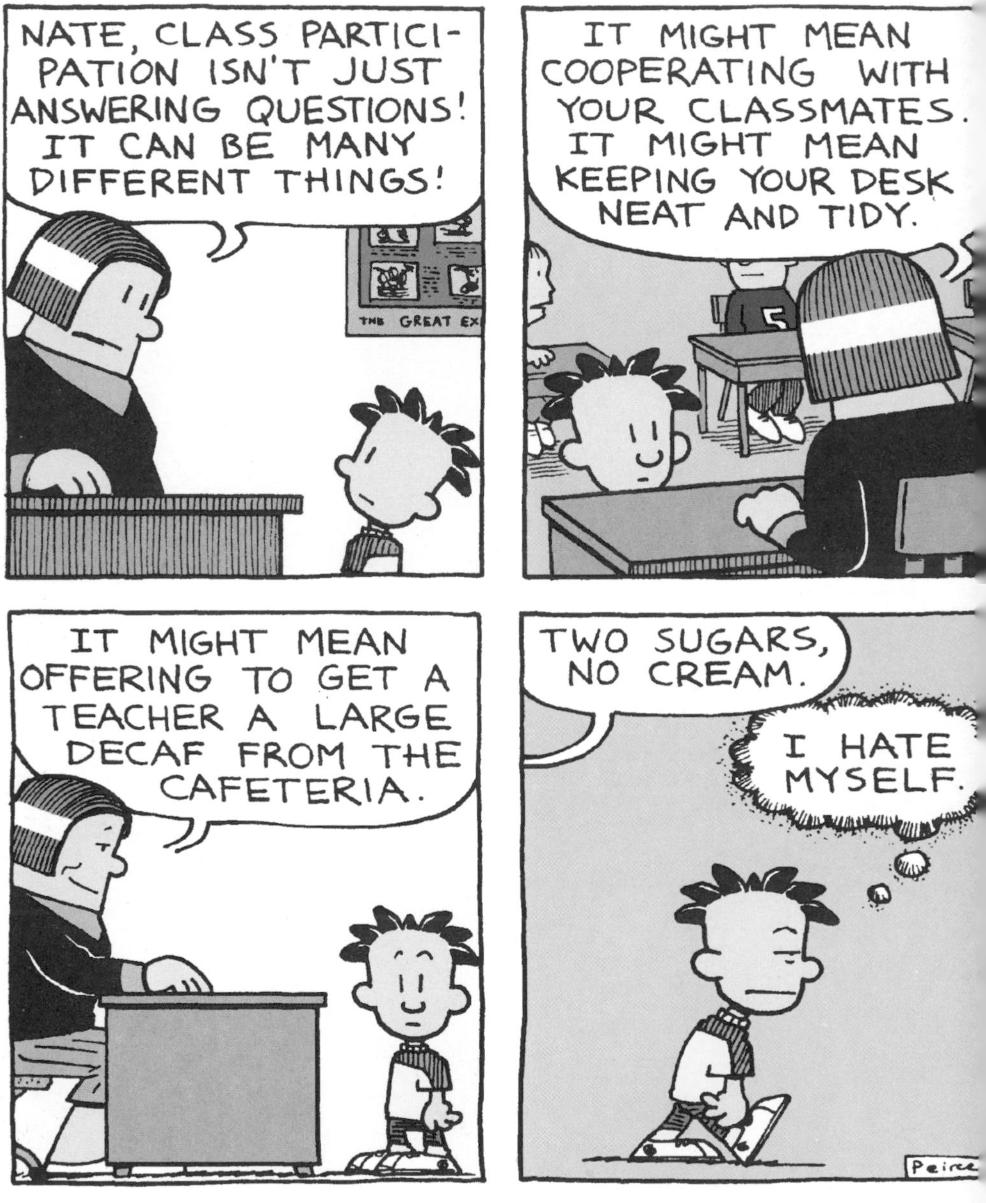
NATE, CLASS PARTICI-PATION ISN'T JUST ANSWERING QUESTIONS! IT CAN BE MANY DIFFERENT THINGS!
THE GREAT EX
IT MIGHT MEAN COOPERATING WITH YOUR CLASSMATES. IT MIGHT MEAN KEEPING YOUR DESK NEAT AND TIDY.
IT MIGHT MEAN OFFERING TO GET A TEACHER A LARGE DECAF FROM THE CAFETERIA.
TWO SUGARS, NO CREAM.
I HATE MYSELF.
Peirce

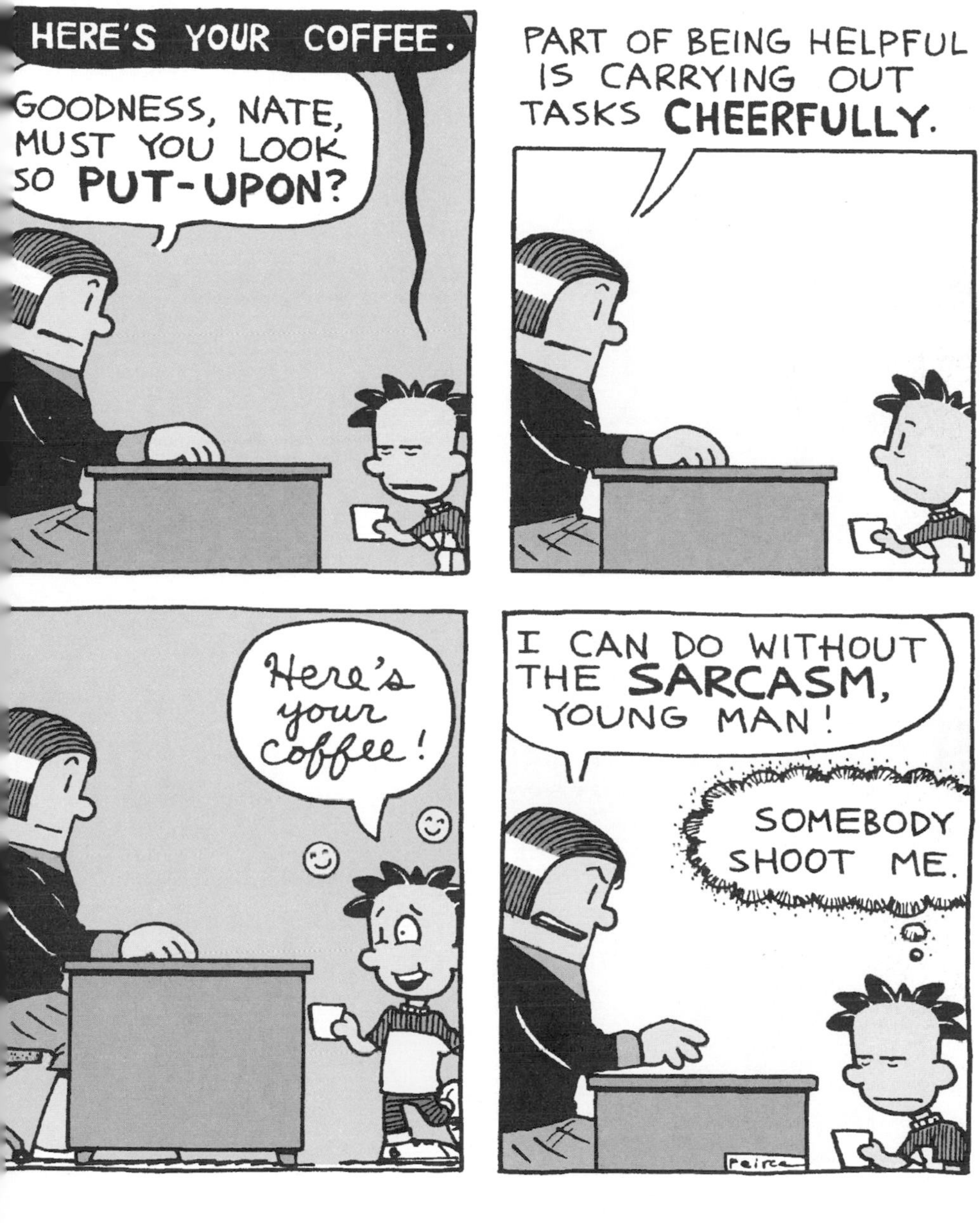
HERE'S YOUR COFFEE.
GOODNESS, NATE, MUST YOU LOOK SO PUT-UPON?
PART OF BEING HELPFUL IS CARRYING OUT TASKS CHEERFULLY.
Here's your coffee!
I CAN DO WITHOUT THE SARCASM, YOUNG MAN!
SOMEBODY SHOOT ME.
Peirce

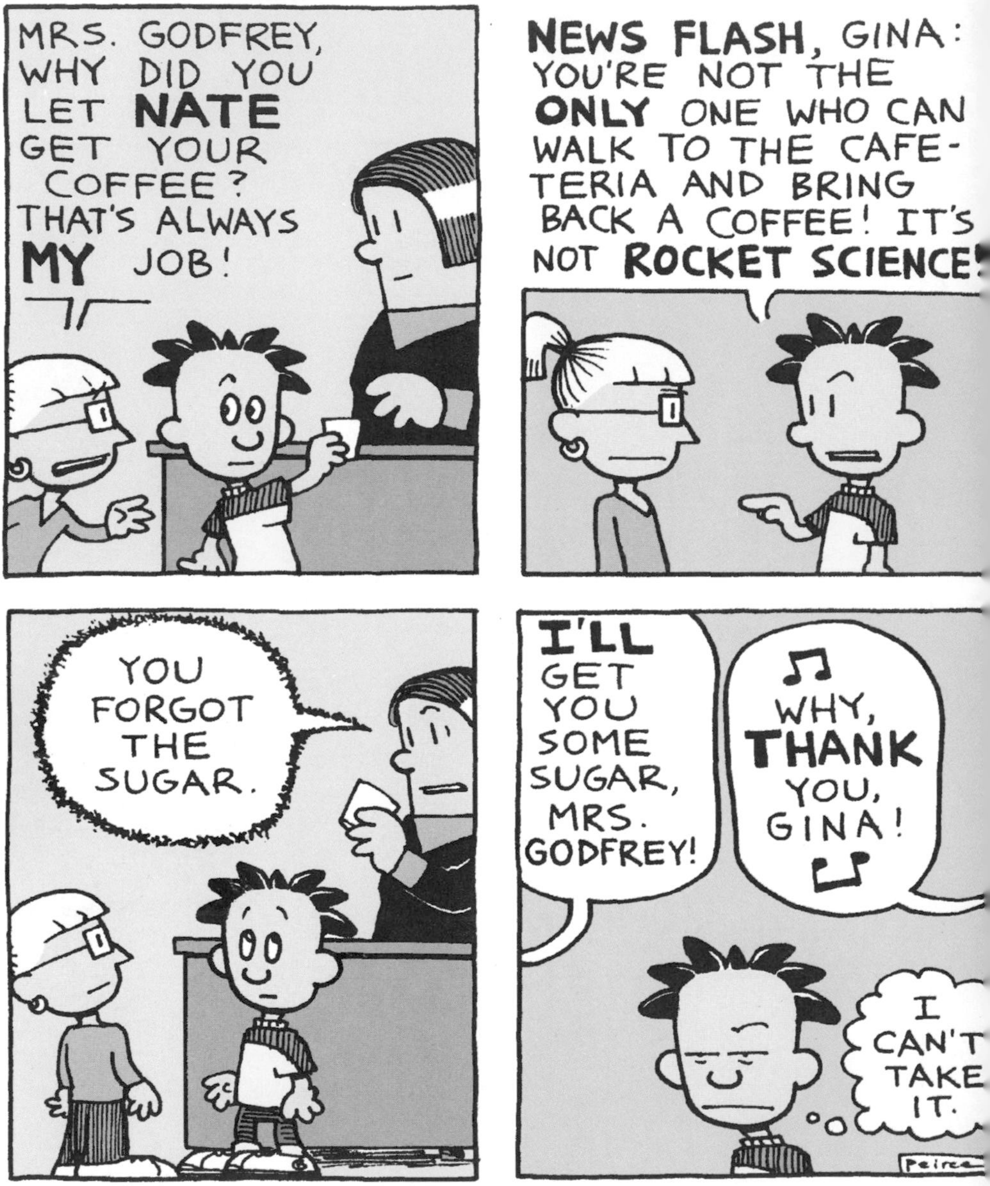
MRS. GODFREY, WHY DID YOU LET NATE GET YOUR COFFEE? THAT'S ALWAYS MY JOB!
NEWS FLASH, GINA: YOU'RE NOT THE ONLY ONE WHO CAN WALK TO THE CAFETERIA AND BRING BACK A COFFEE! IT'S NOT ROCKET SCIENCE!
YOU FORGOT THE SUGAR.
I'LL GET YOU SOME SUGAR, MRS. GODFREY!
WHY, THANK YOU, GINA!
I CAN'T TAKE IT.
Peirce

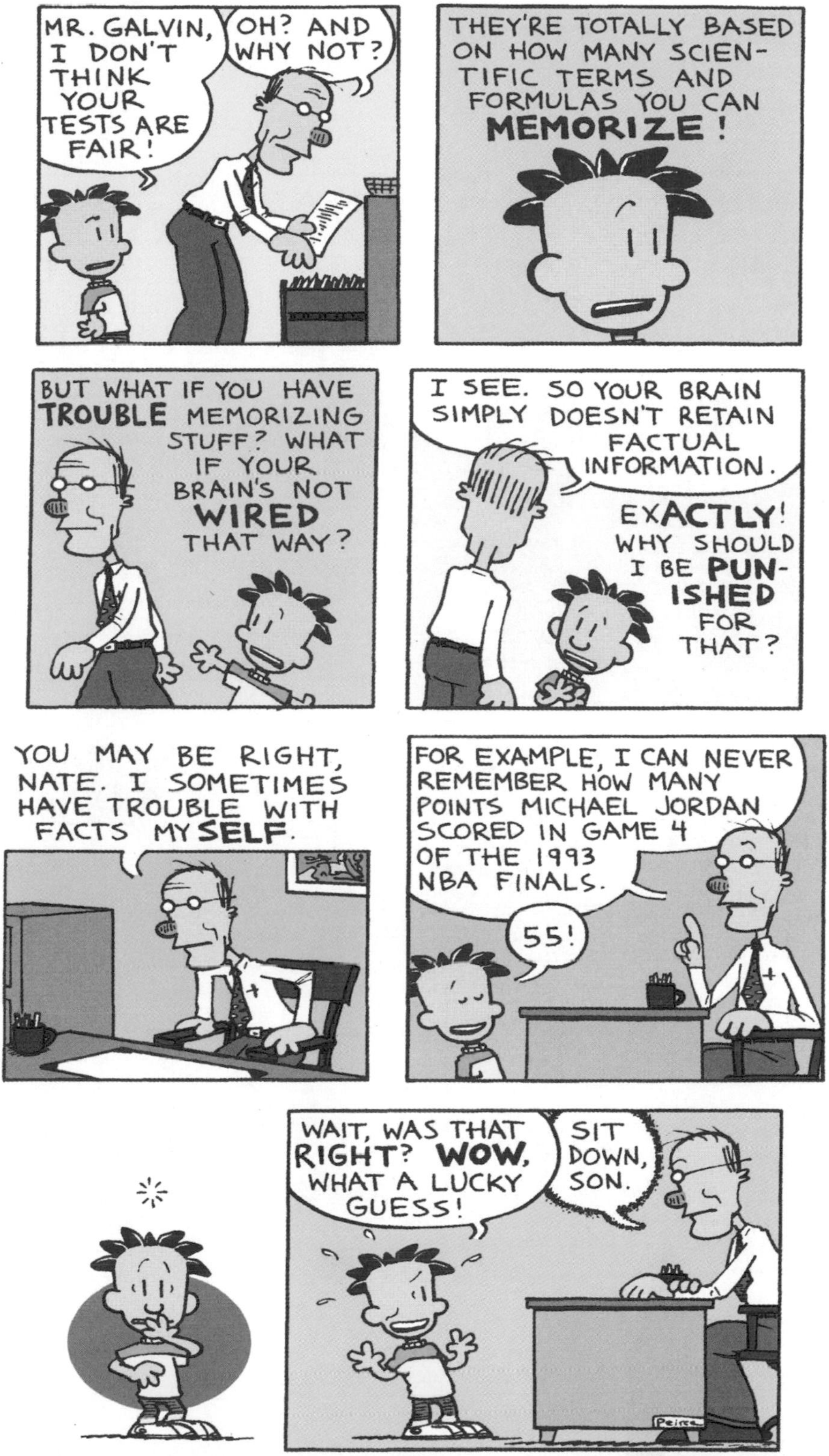
MR. GALVIN, I DON'T THINK YOUR TESTS ARE FAIR!
OH? AND WHY NOT?
THEY'RE TOTALLY BASED ON HOW MANY SCIEN-TIFIC TERMS AND FORMULAS YOU CAN MEMORIZE!
BUT WHAT IF YOU HAVE TROUBLE MEMORIZING STUFF? WHAT IF YOUR BRAIN'S NOT WIRED THAT WAY?
I SEE. SO YOUR BRAIN SIMPLY DOESN'T RETAIN FACTUAL INFORMATION.
EXACTLY! WHY SHOULD I BE PUN-ISHED FOR THAT?
YOU MAY BE RIGHT, NATE. I SOMETIMES HAVE TROUBLE WITH FACTS MYSELF.
FOR EXAMPLE, I CAN NEVER REMEMBER HOW MANY POINTS MICHAEL JORDAN SCORED IN GAME 4 OF THE 1993 NBA FINALS.
55!
WAIT, WAS THAT RIGHT? WOW, WHAT A LUCKY GUESS!
SIT DOWN, SON.
Peirce

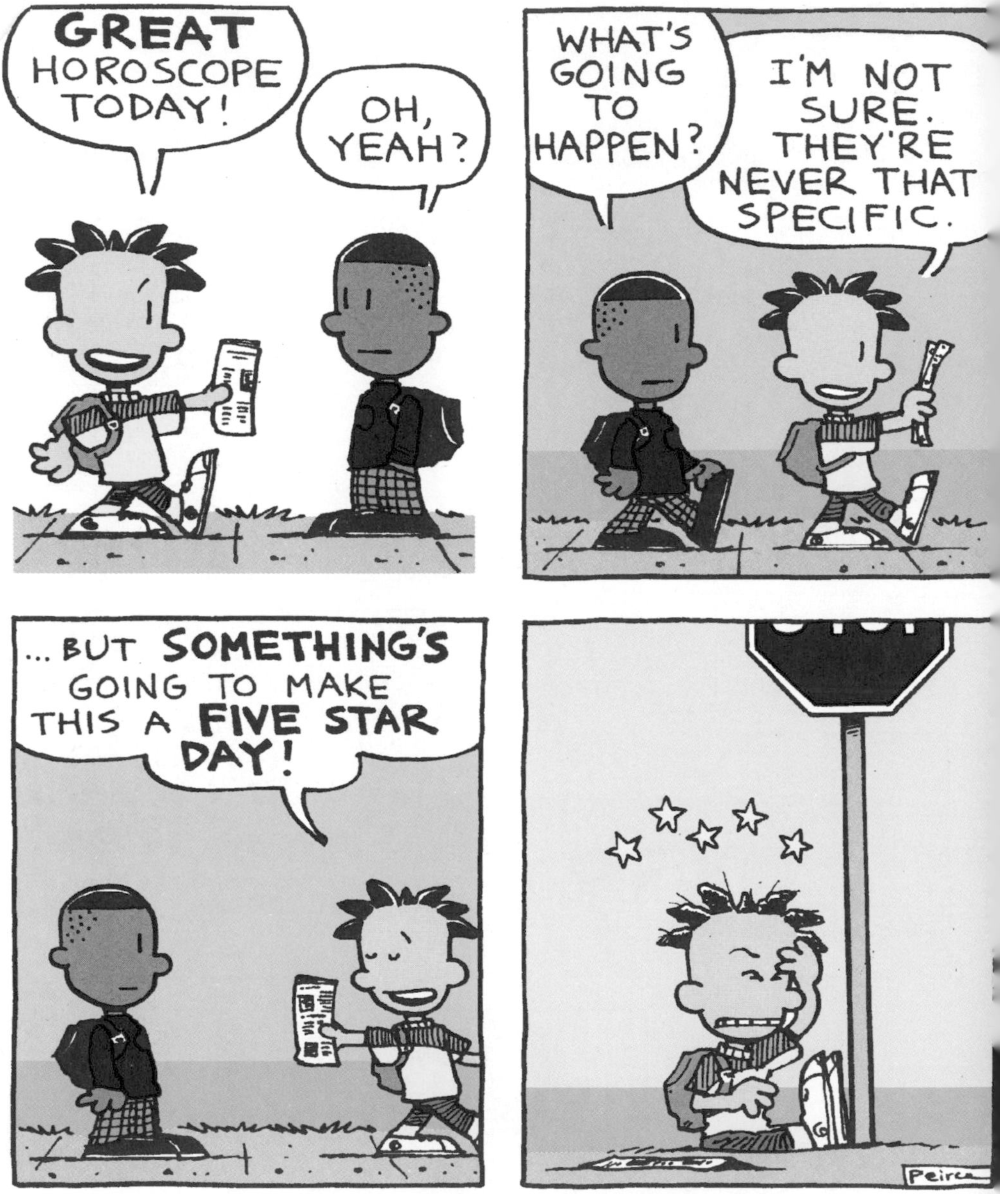
GREAT HOROSCOPE TODAY!
OH, YEAH?
WHAT'S GOING TO HAPPEN?
I'M NOT SURE. THEY'RE NEVER THAT SPECIFIC.
... BUT SOMETHING'S GOING TO MAKE THIS A FIVE STAR DAY!
Peirce

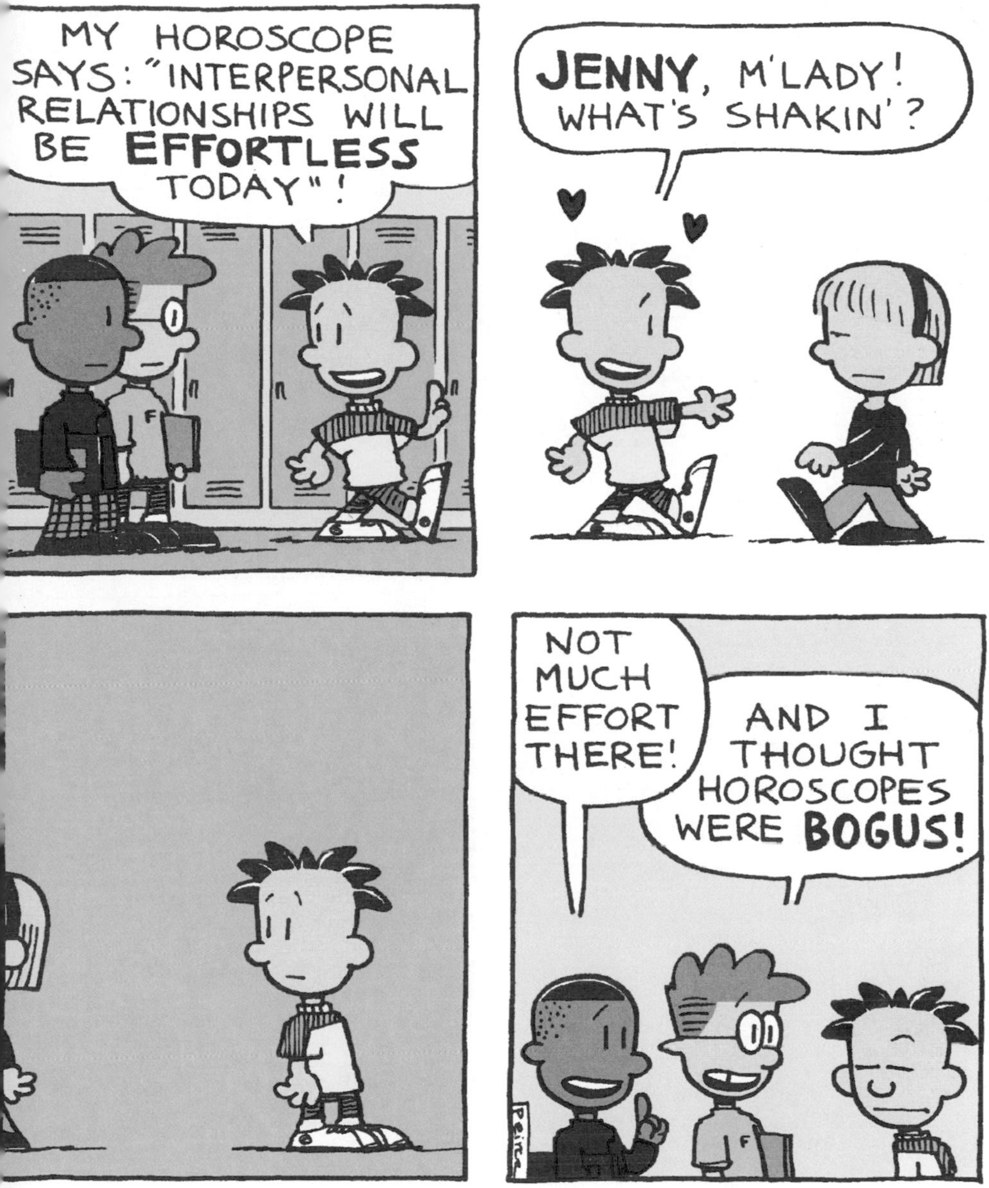
MY HOROSCOPE SAYS: "INTERPERSONAL RELATIONSHIPS WILL BE EFFORTLESS TODAY"!
JENNY, M'LADY! WHAT'S SHAKIN'?
NOT MUCH EFFORT THERE!
AND I THOUGHT HOROSCOPES WERE BOGUS!
Peirce

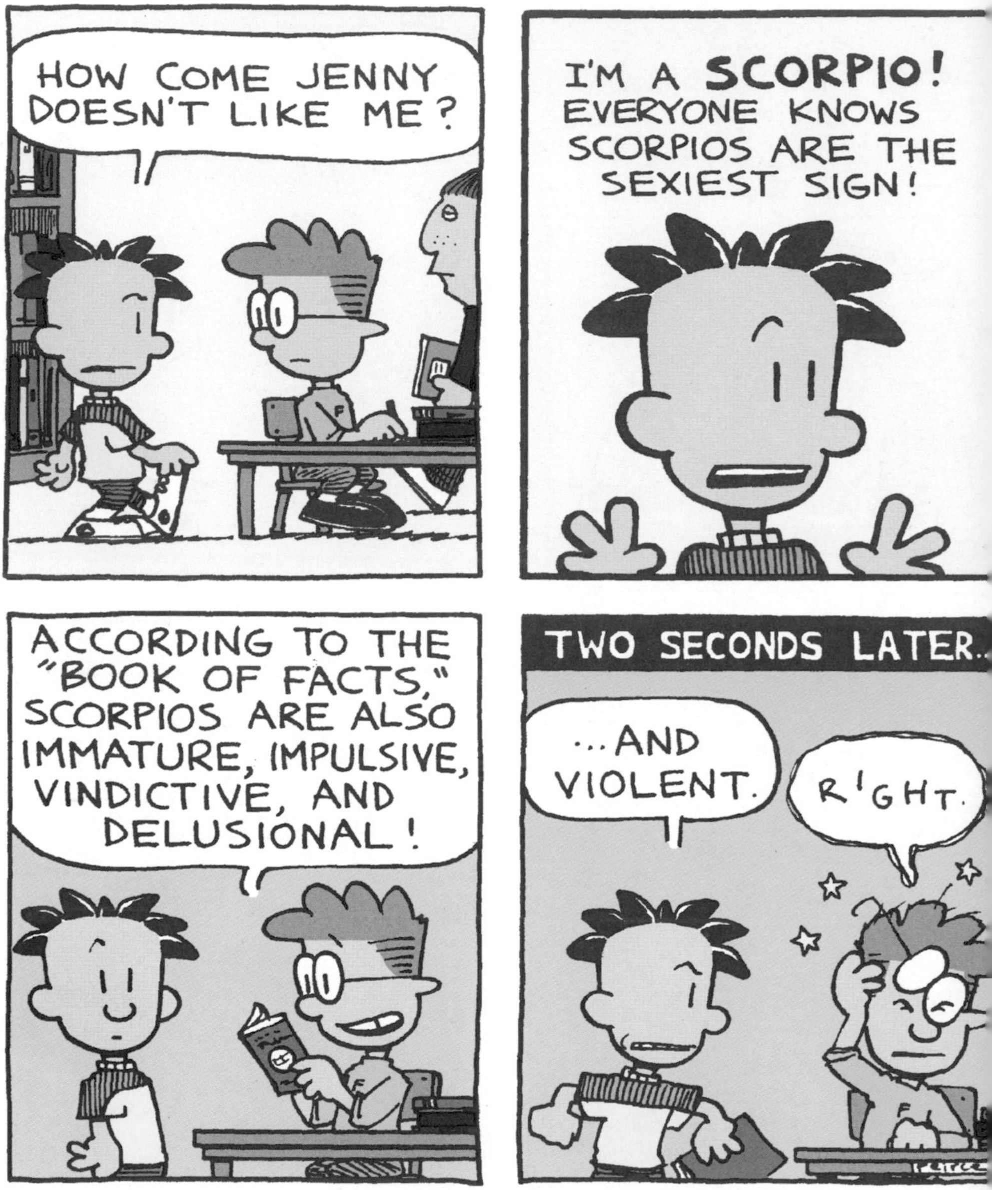
HOW COME JENNY DOESN'T LIKE ME?
I'M A SCORPIO! EVERYONE KNOWS SCORPIOS ARE THE SEXIEST SIGN!
ACCORDING TO THE "BOOK OF FACTS," SCORPIOS ARE ALSO IMMATURE, IMPULSIVE, VINDICTIVE, AND DELUSIONAL!
TWO SECONDS LATER...
...AND VIOLENT.
RIGHT.

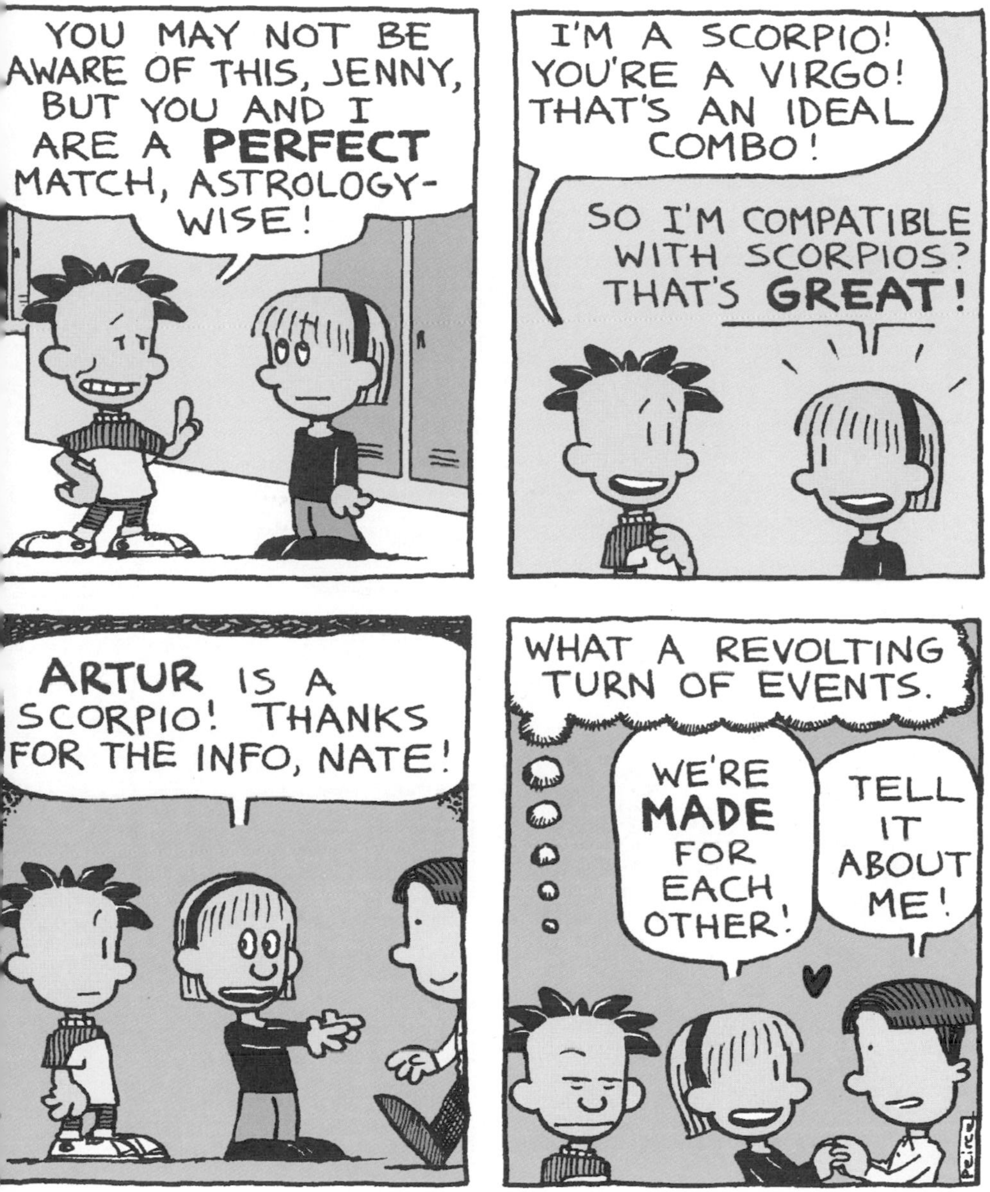
YOU MAY NOT BE AWARE OF THIS, JENNY, BUT YOU AND I ARE A PERFECT MATCH, ASTROLOGY-WISE!
I'M A SCORPIO! YOU'RE A VIRGO! THAT'S AN IDEAL COMBO!
SO I'M COMPATIBLE WITH SCORPIOS? THAT'S GREAT!
ARTUR IS A SCORPIO! THANKS FOR THE INFO, NATE!
WHAT A REVOLTING TURN OF EVENTS.
WE'RE MADE FOR EACH OTHER!
TELL IT ABOUT ME!
Peirce

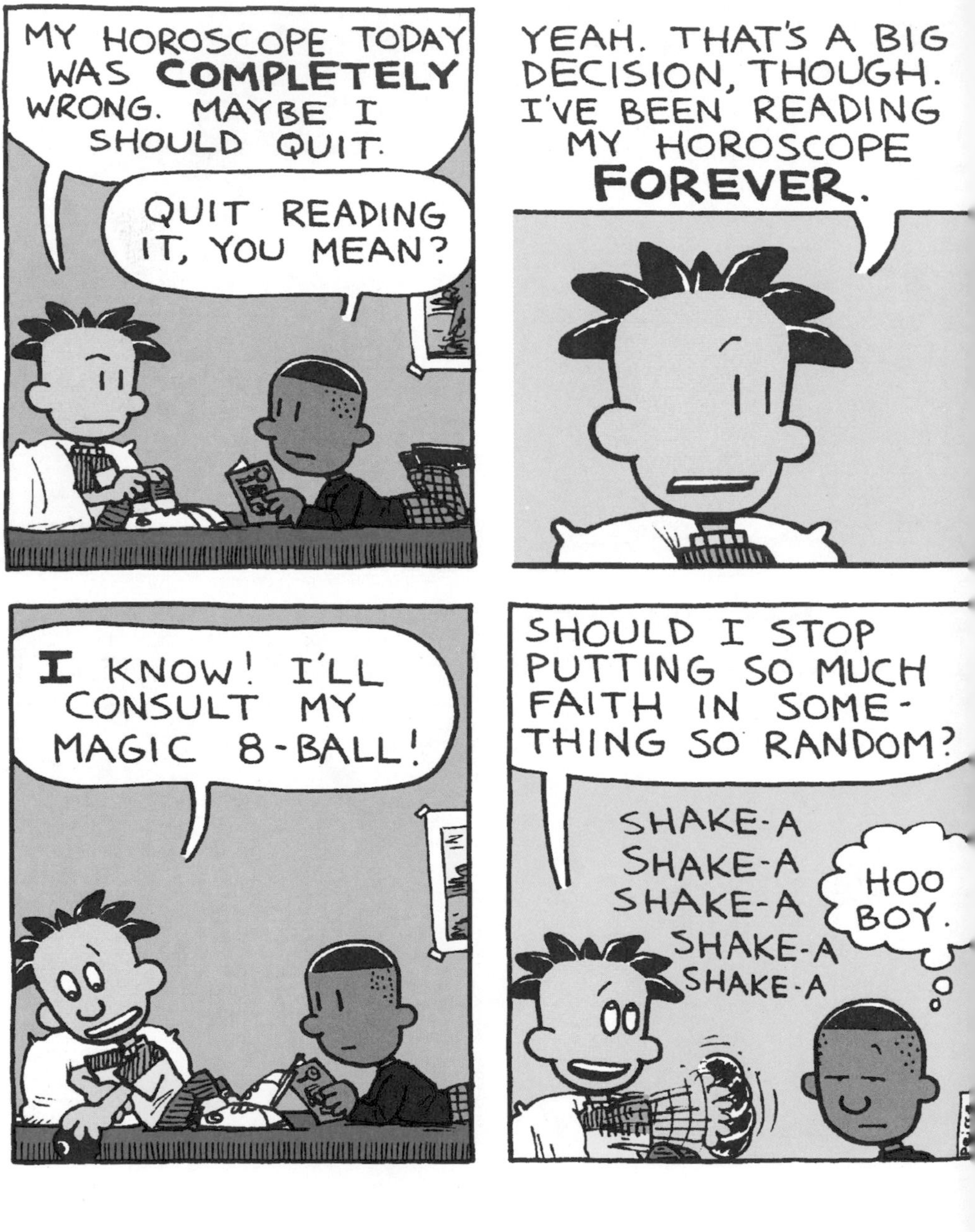
MY HOROSCOPE TODAY WAS **COMPLETELY** WRONG. MAYBE I SHOULD QUIT.
QUIT READING IT, YOU MEAN?
YEAH. THAT'S A BIG DECISION, THOUGH. I'VE BEEN READING MY HOROSCOPE **FOREVER**.
I KNOW! I'LL CONSULT MY MAGIC 8-BALL!
SHOULD I STOP PUTTING SO MUCH FAITH IN SOMETHING SO RANDOM?
SHAKE-A SHAKE-A SHAKE-A SHAKE-A SHAKE-A
HOO BOY.

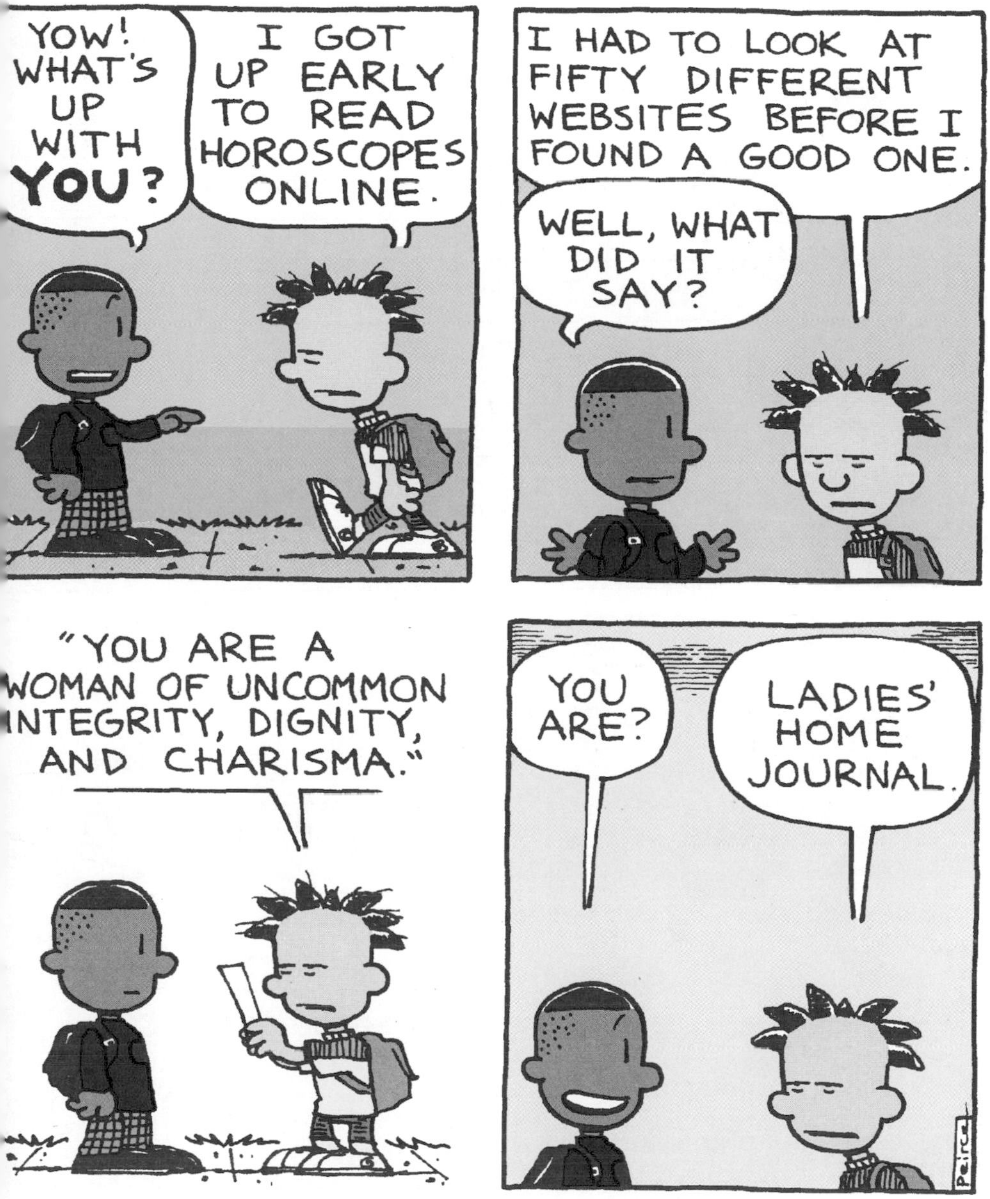
YOW! WHAT'S UP WITH **YOU**?
I GOT UP EARLY TO READ HOROSCOPES ONLINE.
I HAD TO LOOK AT FIFTY DIFFERENT WEBSITES BEFORE I FOUND A GOOD ONE.
WELL, WHAT DID IT SAY?
"YOU ARE A WOMAN OF UNCOMMON INTEGRITY, DIGNITY, AND CHARISMA."
YOU ARE?
LADIES' HOME JOURNAL.
Peirce

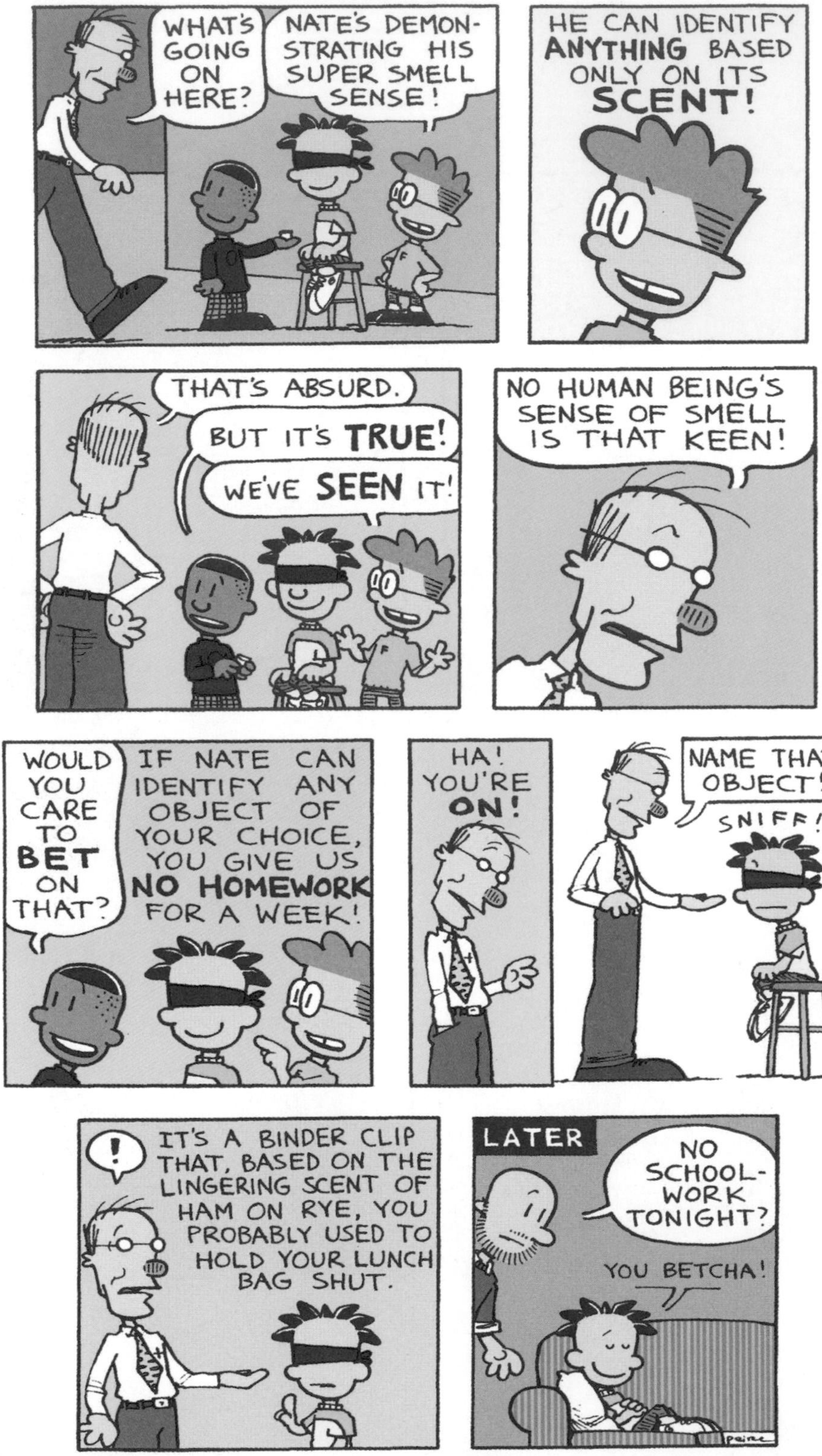
WHAT'S GOING ON HERE?
NATE'S DEMON-STRATING HIS SUPER SMELL SENSE!
HE CAN IDENTIFY ANYTHING BASED ONLY ON ITS SCENT!
THAT'S ABSURD.
BUT IT'S TRUE!
WE'VE SEEN IT!
NO HUMAN BEING'S SENSE OF SMELL IS THAT KEEN!
WOULD YOU CARE TO BET ON THAT?
IF NATE CAN IDENTIFY ANY OBJECT OF YOUR CHOICE, YOU GIVE US NO HOMEWORK FOR A WEEK!
HA! YOU'RE ON!
NAME THAT OBJECT!
SNIFF!
!
IT'S A BINDER CLIP THAT, BASED ON THE LINGERING SCENT OF HAM ON RYE, YOU PROBABLY USED TO HOLD YOUR LUNCH BAG SHUT.
LATER
NO SCHOOL-WORK TONIGHT?
YOU BETCHA!
peirce

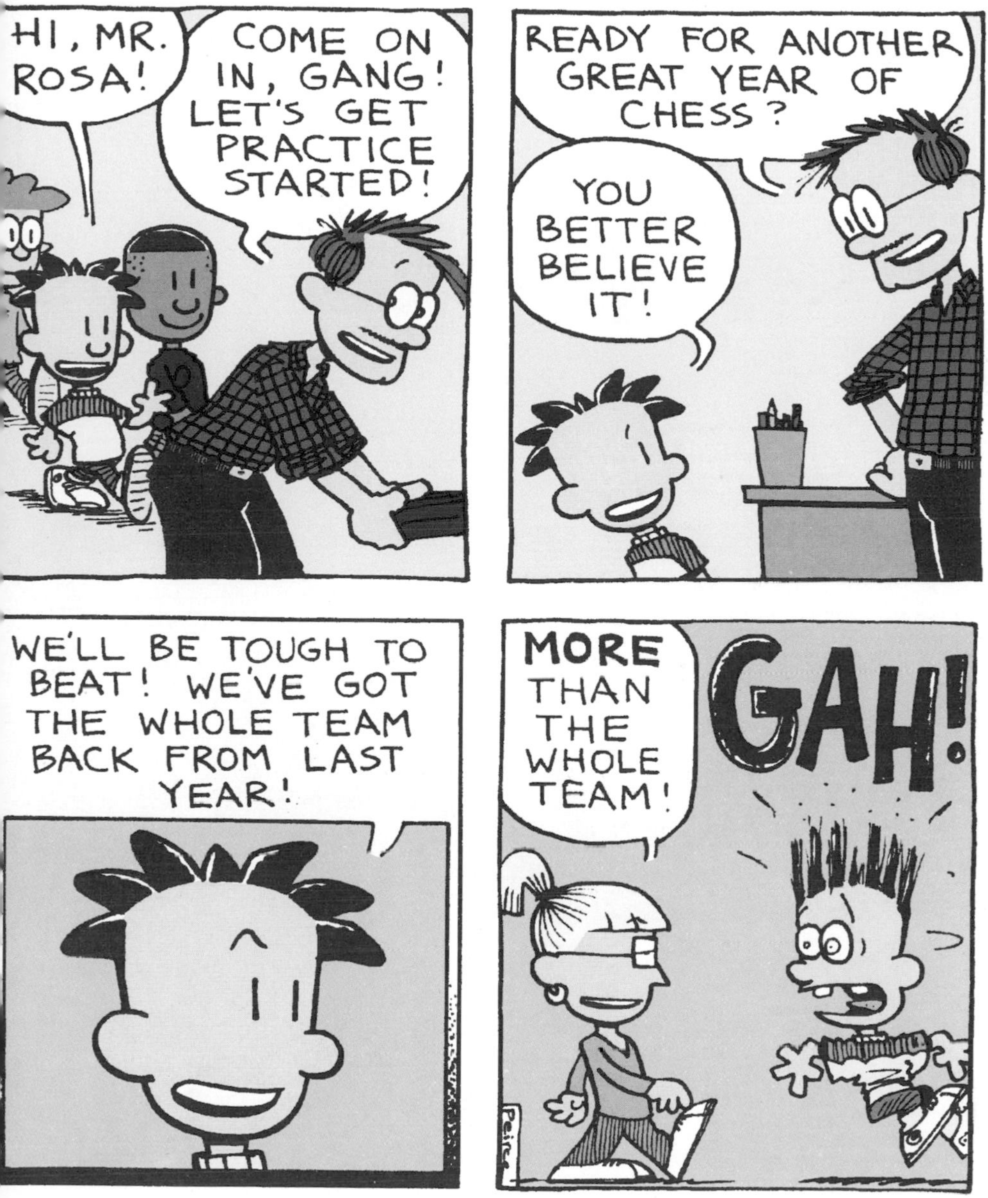
HI, MR. ROSA!
COME ON IN, GANG! LET'S GET PRACTICE STARTED!
READY FOR ANOTHER GREAT YEAR OF CHESS?
YOU BETTER BELIEVE IT!
WE'LL BE TOUGH TO BEAT! WE'VE GOT THE WHOLE TEAM BACK FROM LAST YEAR!
MORE THAN THE WHOLE TEAM!
GAH!
Peirce

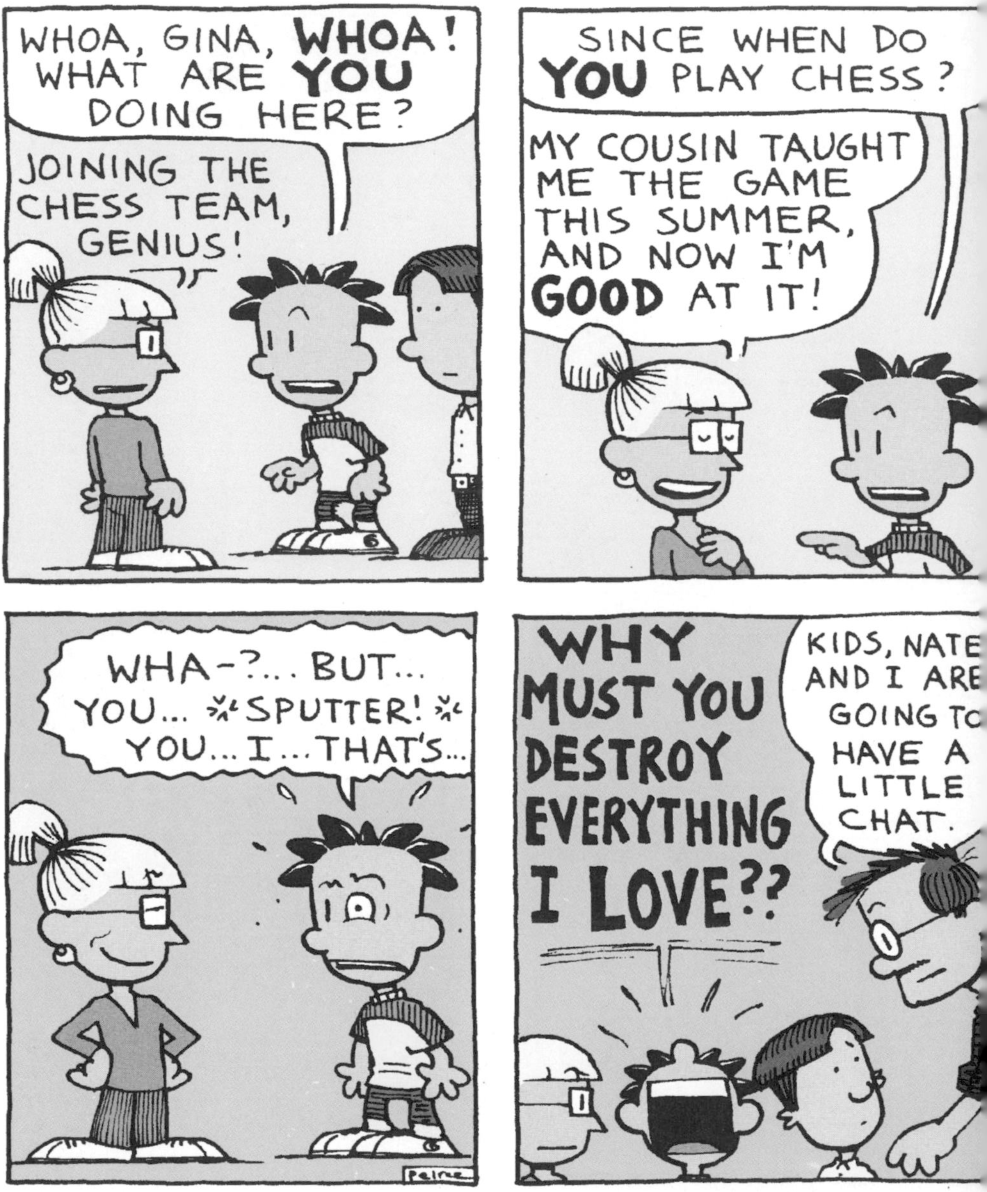
WHOA, GINA, WHOA! WHAT ARE YOU DOING HERE?
JOINING THE CHESS TEAM, GENIUS!
SINCE WHEN DO YOU PLAY CHESS?
MY COUSIN TAUGHT ME THE GAME THIS SUMMER, AND NOW I'M GOOD AT IT!
WHA-?... BUT... YOU... SPUTTER! YOU... I... THAT'S...
WHY MUST YOU DESTROY EVERYTHING I LOVE??
KIDS, NATE AND I ARE GOING TO HAVE A LITTLE CHAT.

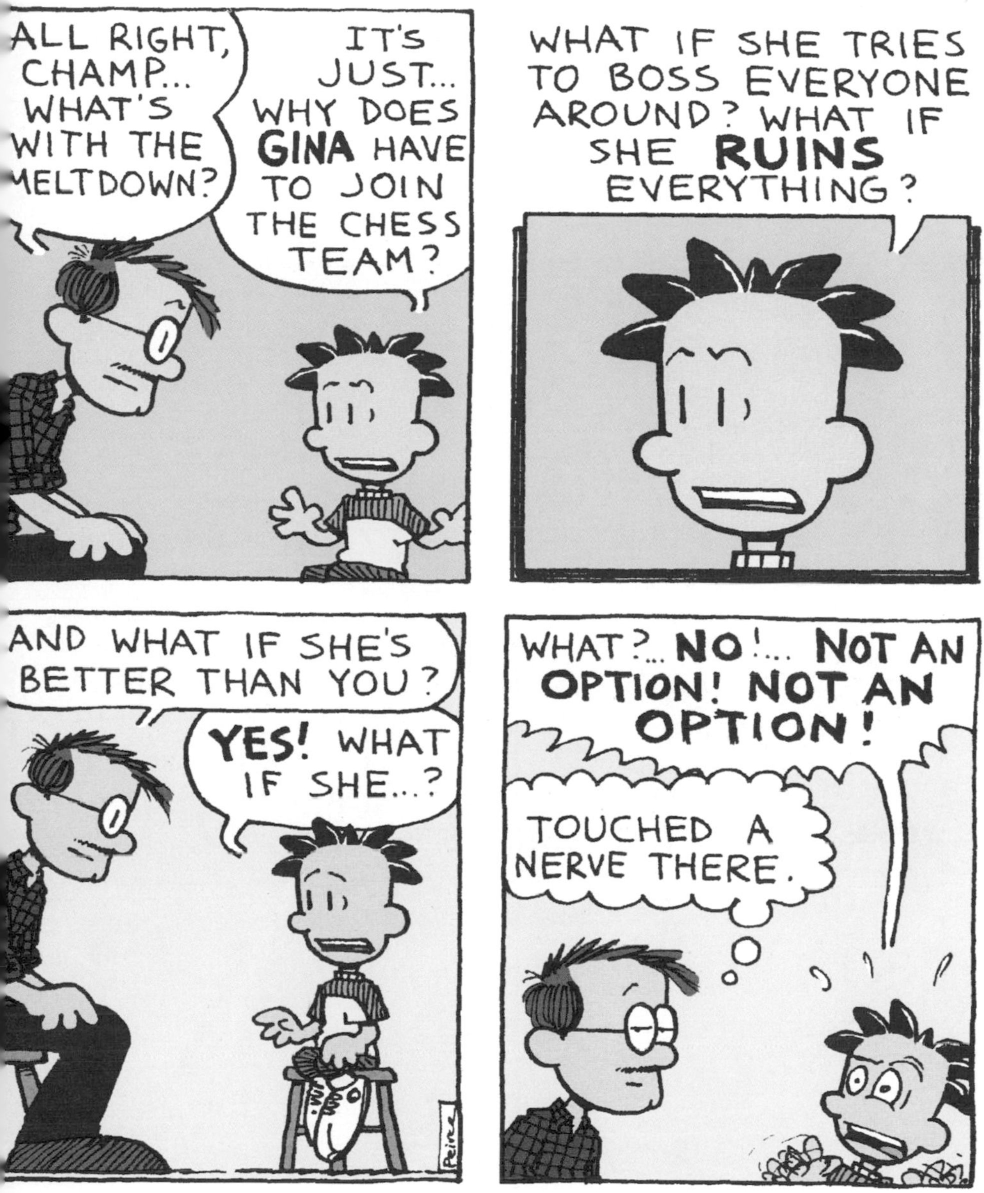
ALL RIGHT, CHAMP... WHAT'S WITH THE MELTDOWN?
IT'S JUST... WHY DOES GINA HAVE TO JOIN THE CHESS TEAM?
WHAT IF SHE TRIES TO BOSS EVERYONE AROUND? WHAT IF SHE RUINS EVERYTHING?
AND WHAT IF SHE'S BETTER THAN YOU?
YES! WHAT IF SHE...?
WHAT?... NO!... NOT AN OPTION! NOT AN OPTION!
TOUCHED A NERVE THERE.

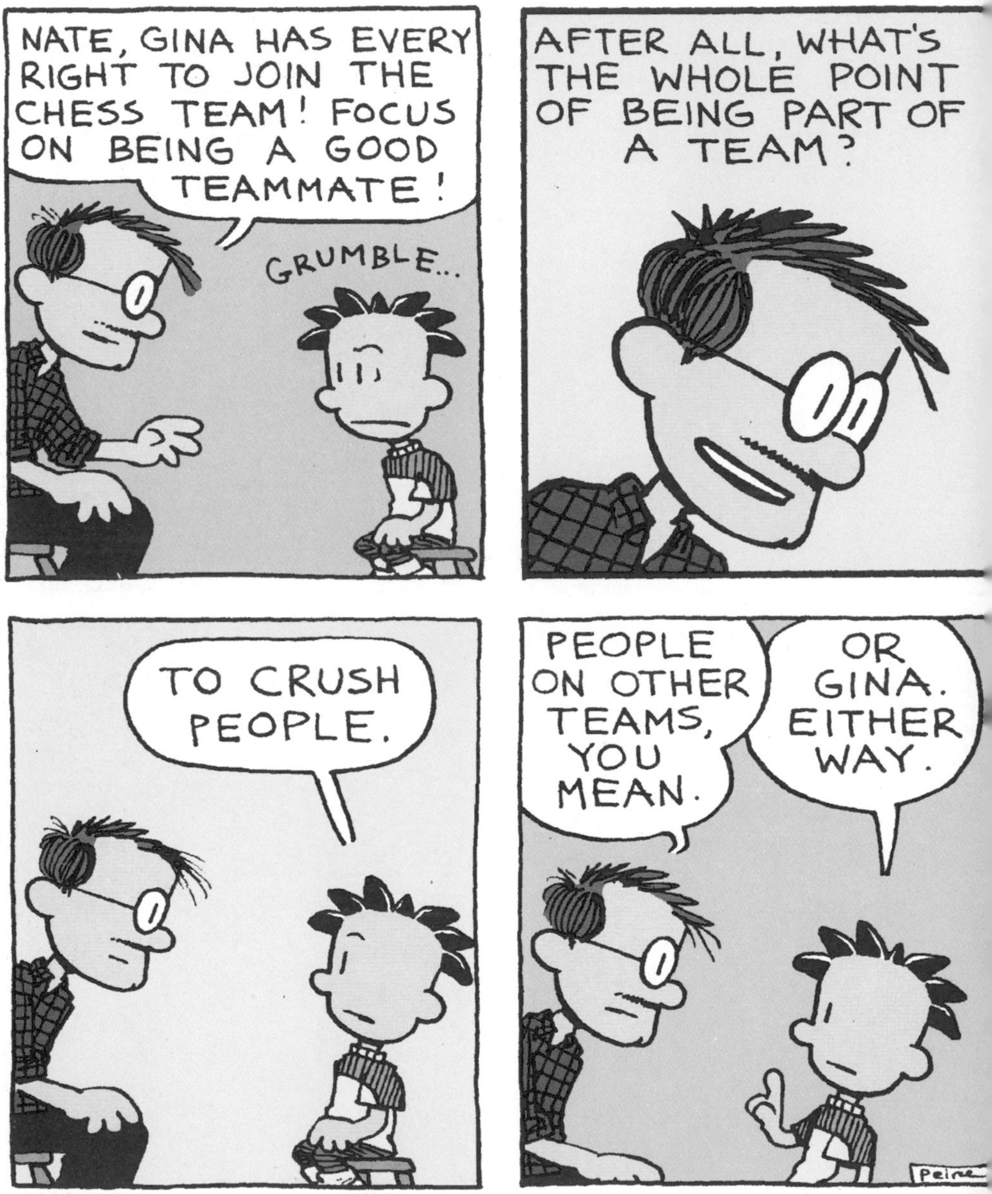
NATE, GINA HAS EVERY RIGHT TO JOIN THE CHESS TEAM! FOCUS ON BEING A GOOD TEAMMATE!
GRUMBLE...
AFTER ALL, WHAT'S THE WHOLE POINT OF BEING PART OF A TEAM?
TO CRUSH PEOPLE.
PEOPLE ON OTHER TEAMS, YOU MEAN.
OR GINA. EITHER WAY.
Peirce

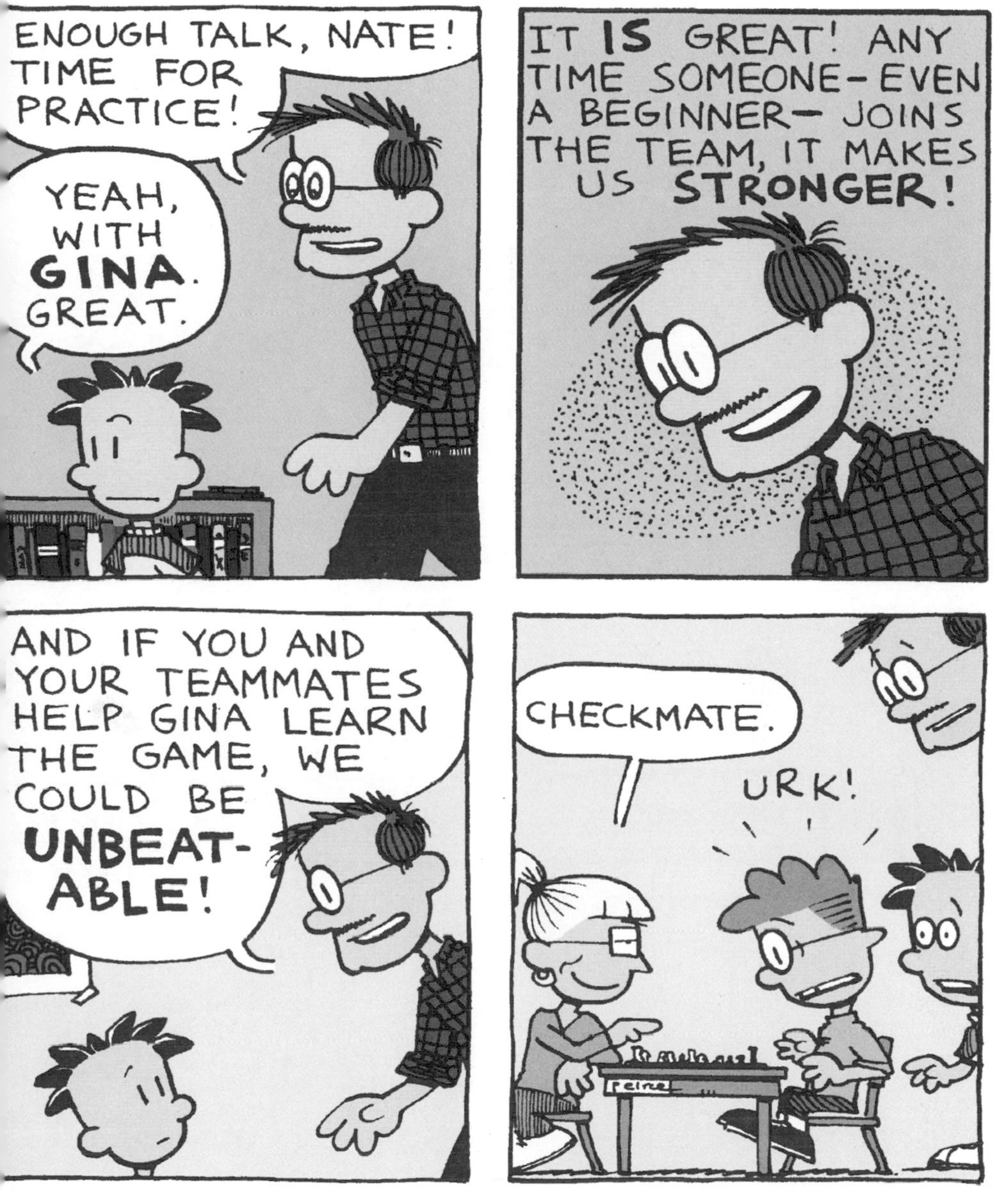
ENOUGH TALK, NATE! TIME FOR PRACTICE!
YEAH, WITH GINA. GREAT.
IT IS GREAT! ANY TIME SOMEONE—EVEN A BEGINNER—JOINS THE TEAM, IT MAKES US STRONGER!
AND IF YOU AND YOUR TEAMMATES HELP GINA LEARN THE GAME, WE COULD BE UNBEAT-ABLE!
CHECKMATE.
URK!

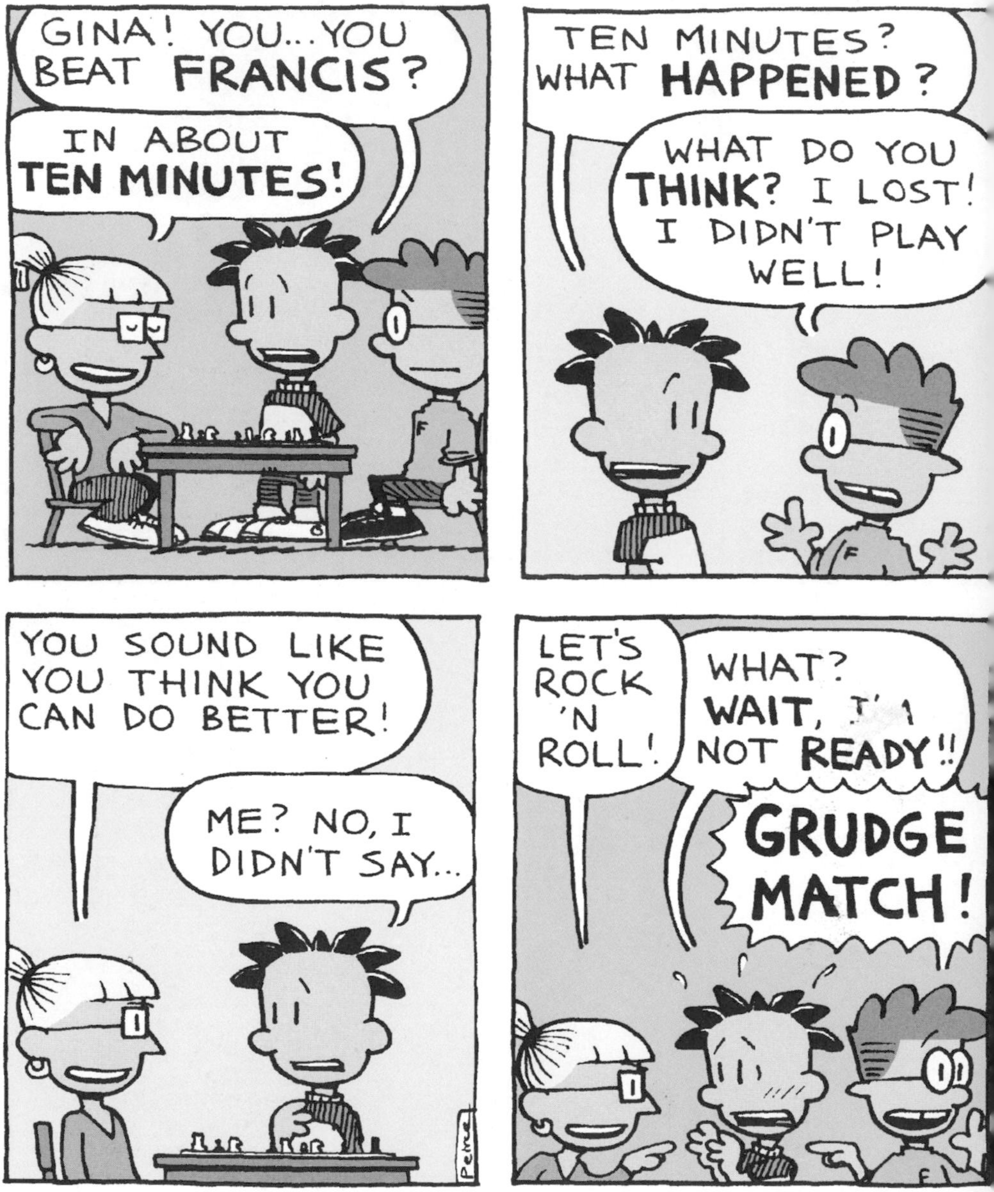
GINA! YOU...YOU BEAT FRANCIS?
IN ABOUT TEN MINUTES!
TEN MINUTES? WHAT HAPPENED?
WHAT DO YOU THINK? I LOST! I DIDN'T PLAY WELL!
YOU SOUND LIKE YOU THINK YOU CAN DO BETTER!
ME? NO, I DIDN'T SAY...
LET'S ROCK 'N ROLL!
WHAT? WAIT, NOT READY!!
GRUDGE MATCH!

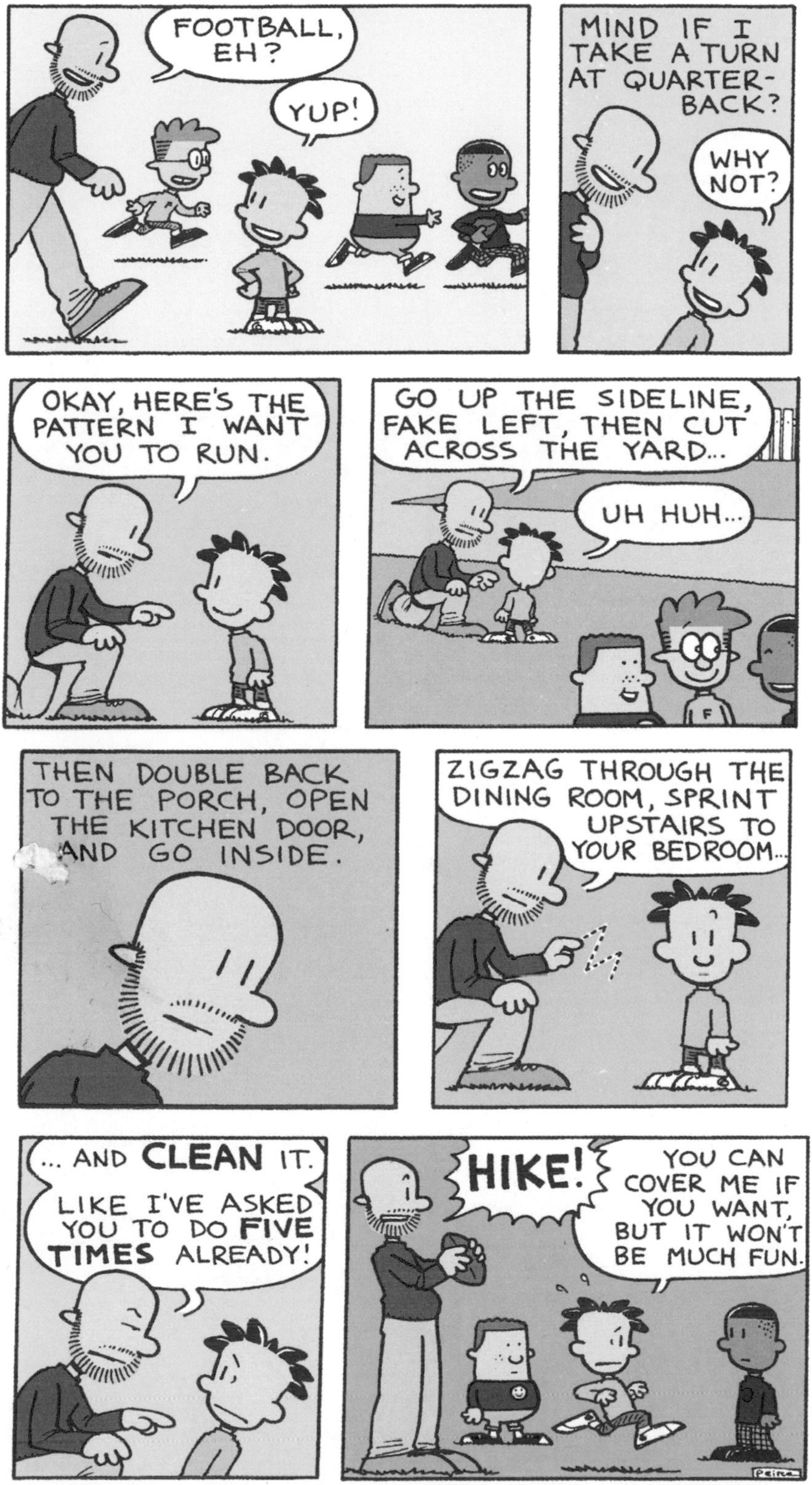

FOOTBALL, EH?
YUP!
MIND IF I TAKE A TURN AT QUARTER-BACK?
WHY NOT?
OKAY, HERE'S THE PATTERN I WANT YOU TO RUN.
GO UP THE SIDELINE, FAKE LEFT, THEN CUT ACROSS THE YARD...
UH HUH...
F
THEN DOUBLE BACK TO THE PORCH, OPEN THE KITCHEN DOOR, AND GO INSIDE.
ZIGZAG THROUGH THE DINING ROOM, SPRINT UPSTAIRS TO YOUR BEDROOM...
... AND CLEAN IT.
LIKE I'VE ASKED YOU TO DO FIVE TIMES ALREADY!
HIKE!
YOU CAN COVER ME IF YOU WANT, BUT IT WON'T BE MUCH FUN.
PEIRCE

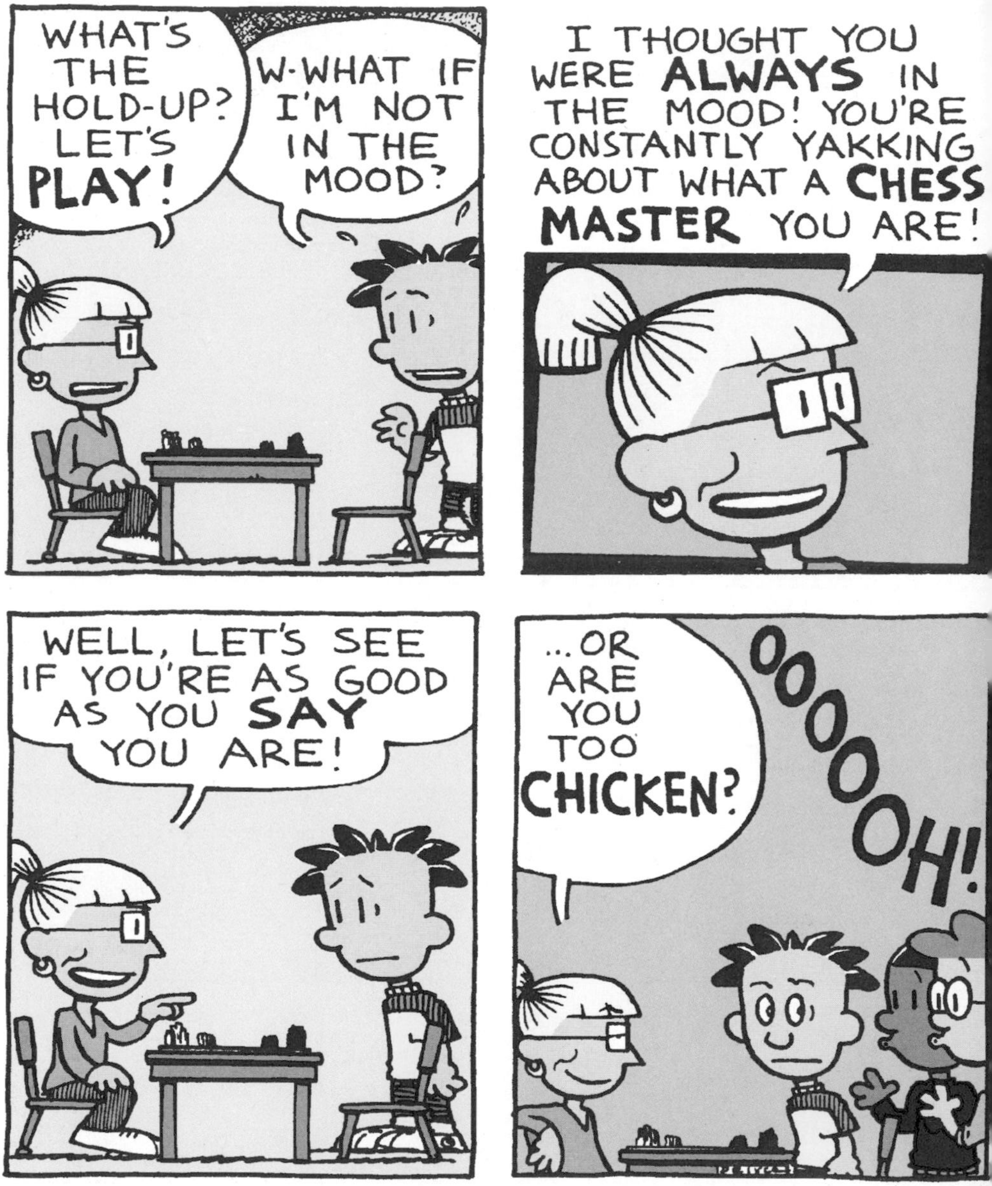
WHAT'S THE HOLD-UP? LET'S PLAY!
W-WHAT IF I'M NOT IN THE MOOD?
I THOUGHT YOU WERE ALWAYS IN THE MOOD! YOU'RE CONSTANTLY YAKKING ABOUT WHAT A CHESS MASTER YOU ARE!
WELL, LET'S SEE IF YOU'RE AS GOOD AS YOU SAY YOU ARE!
...OR ARE YOU TOO CHICKEN?
OOOOOOH!

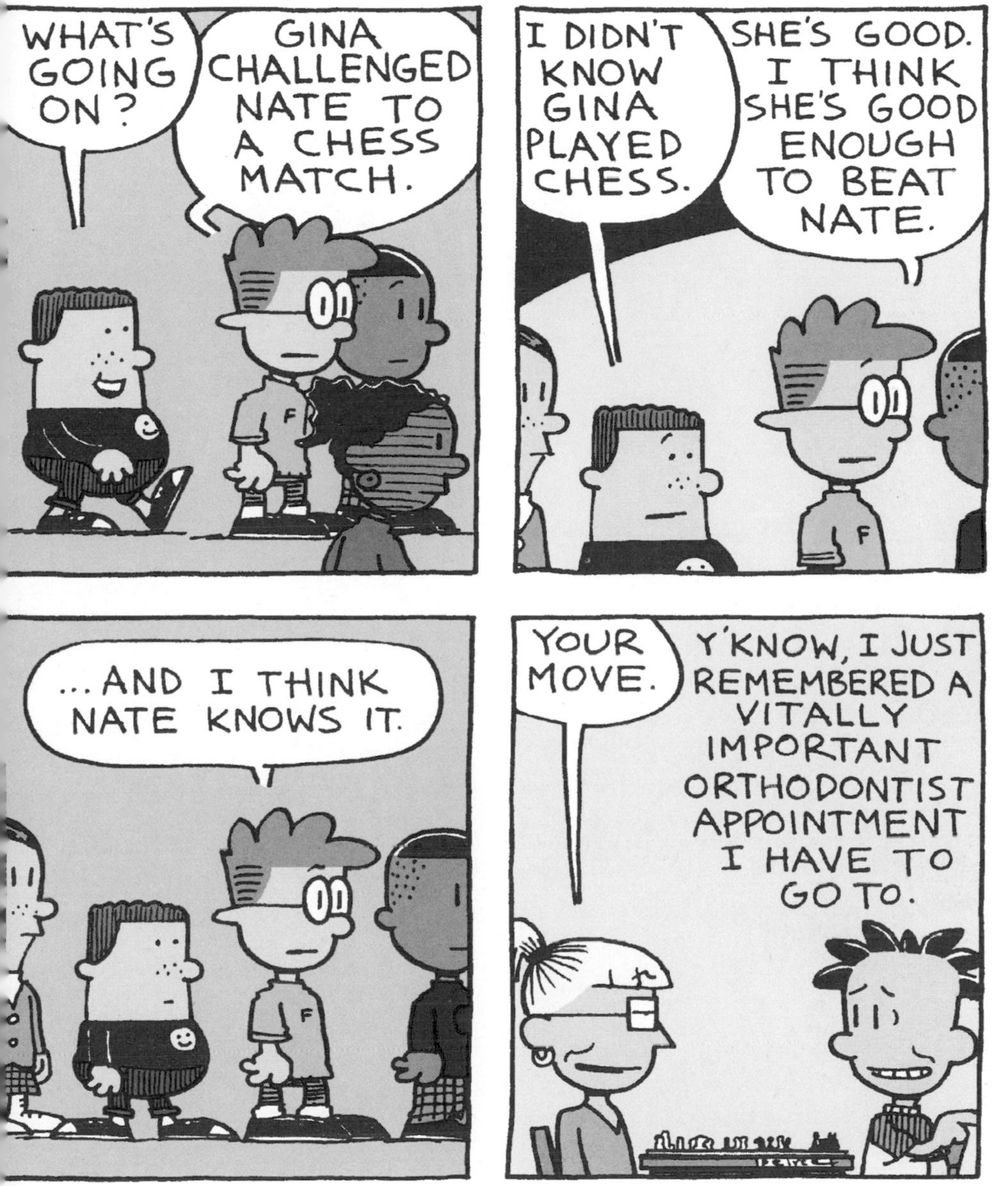
WHAT'S GOING ON?
GINA CHALLENGED NATE TO A CHESS MATCH.
I DIDN'T KNOW GINA PLAYED CHESS.
SHE'S GOOD. I THINK SHE'S GOOD ENOUGH TO BEAT NATE.
...AND I THINK NATE KNOWS IT.
YOUR MOVE.
Y'KNOW, I JUST REMEMBERED A VITALLY IMPORTANT ORTHODONTIST APPOINTMENT I HAVE TO GO TO.

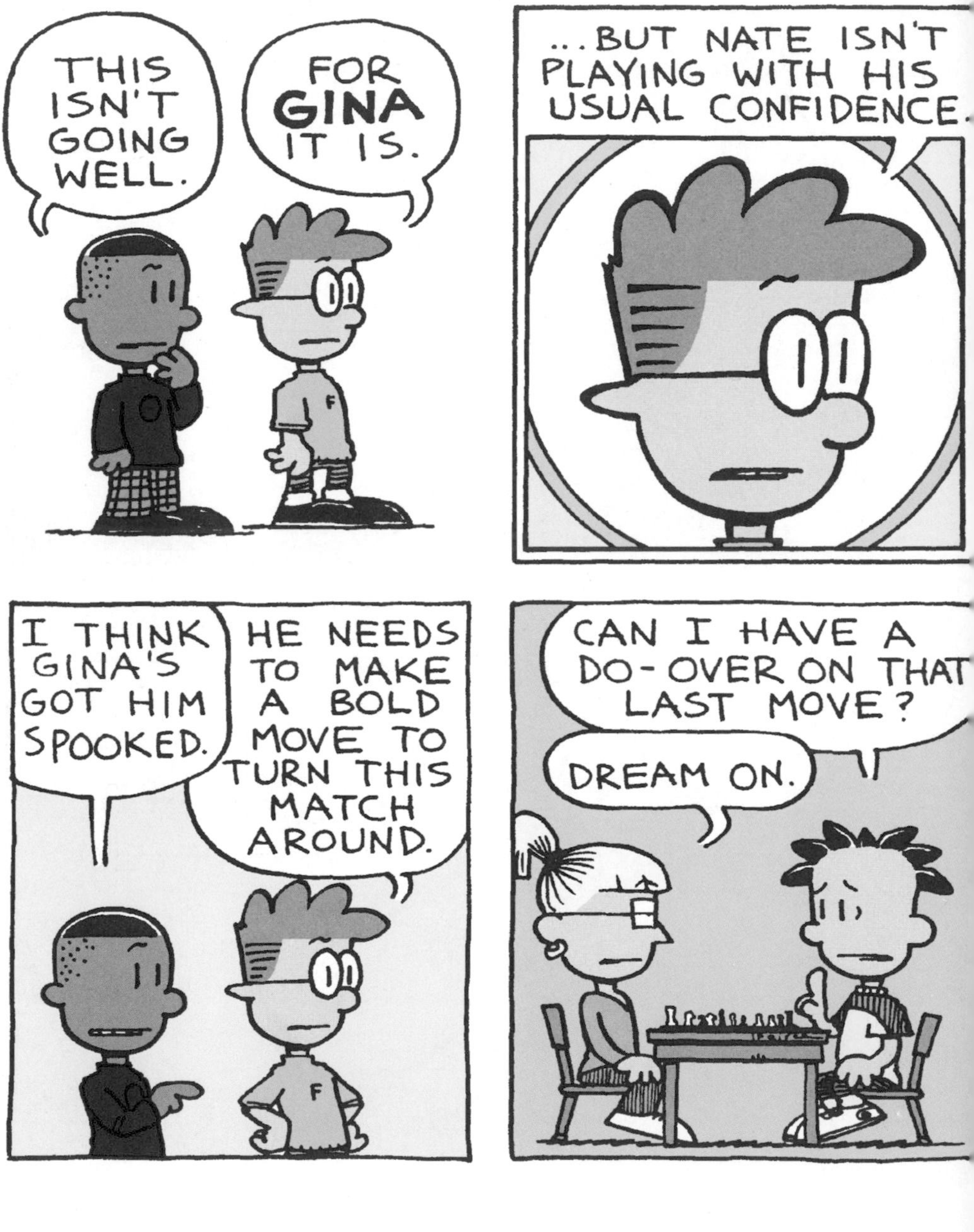
THIS ISN'T GOING WELL.
FOR **GINA** IT IS.
...BUT NATE ISN'T PLAYING WITH HIS USUAL CONFIDENCE.
I THINK GINA'S GOT HIM SPOOKED.
HE NEEDS TO MAKE A BOLD MOVE TO TURN THIS MATCH AROUND.
CAN I HAVE A DO-OVER ON THAT LAST MOVE?
DREAM ON.

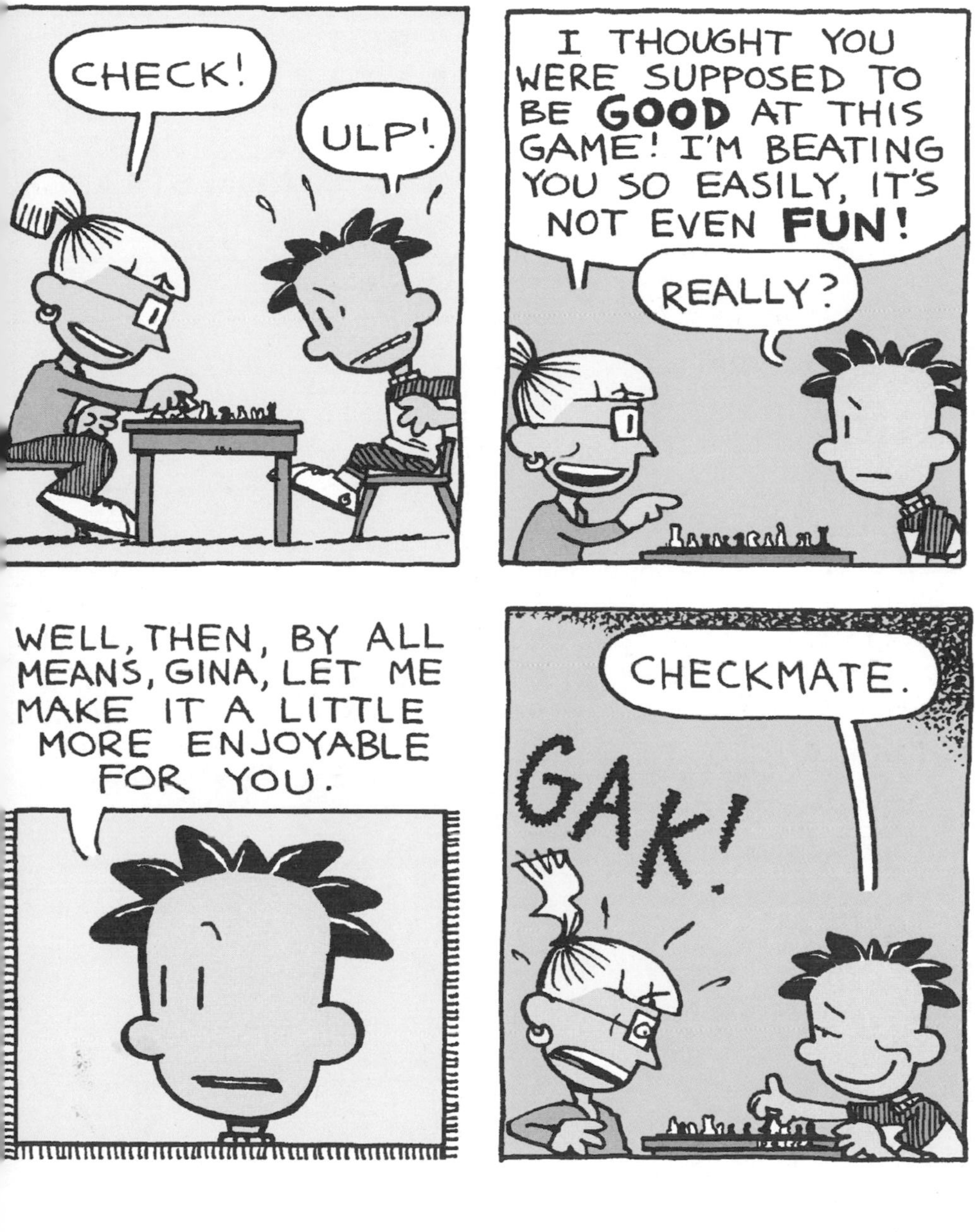
CHECK!
ULP!
I THOUGHT YOU WERE SUPPOSED TO BE **GOOD** AT THIS GAME! I'M BEATING YOU SO EASILY, IT'S NOT EVEN **FUN**!
REALLY?
WELL, THEN, BY ALL MEANS, GINA, LET ME MAKE IT A LITTLE MORE ENJOYABLE FOR YOU.
CHECKMATE.
GAK!

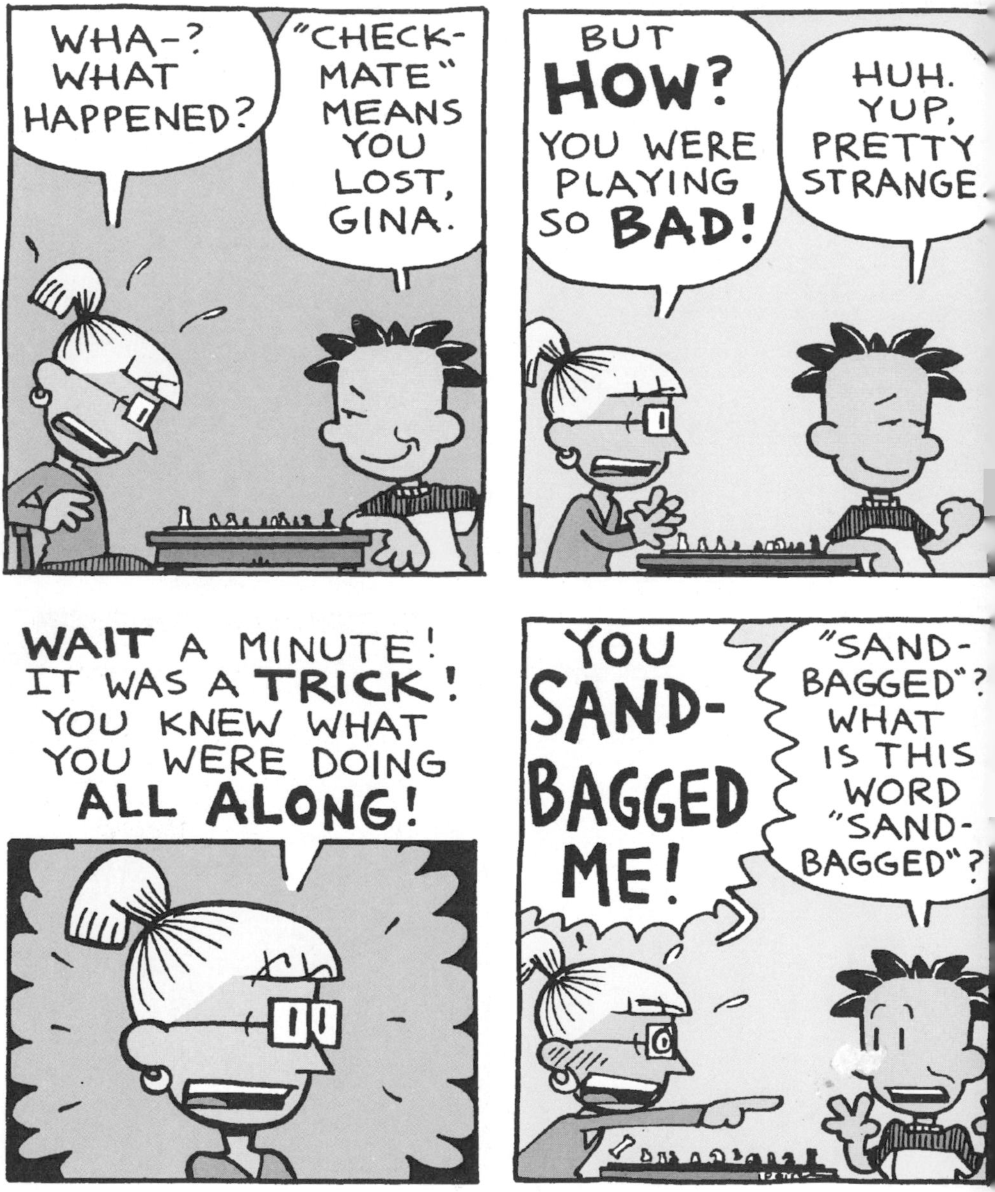
WHA-? WHAT HAPPENED?
"CHECK-MATE" MEANS YOU LOST, GINA.
BUT HOW? YOU WERE PLAYING SO BAD!
HUH. YUP, PRETTY STRANGE.
WAIT A MINUTE! IT WAS A TRICK! YOU KNEW WHAT YOU WERE DOING ALL ALONG!
YOU SANDBAGGED ME!
"SAND-BAGGED"? WHAT IS THIS WORD "SAND-BAGGED"?

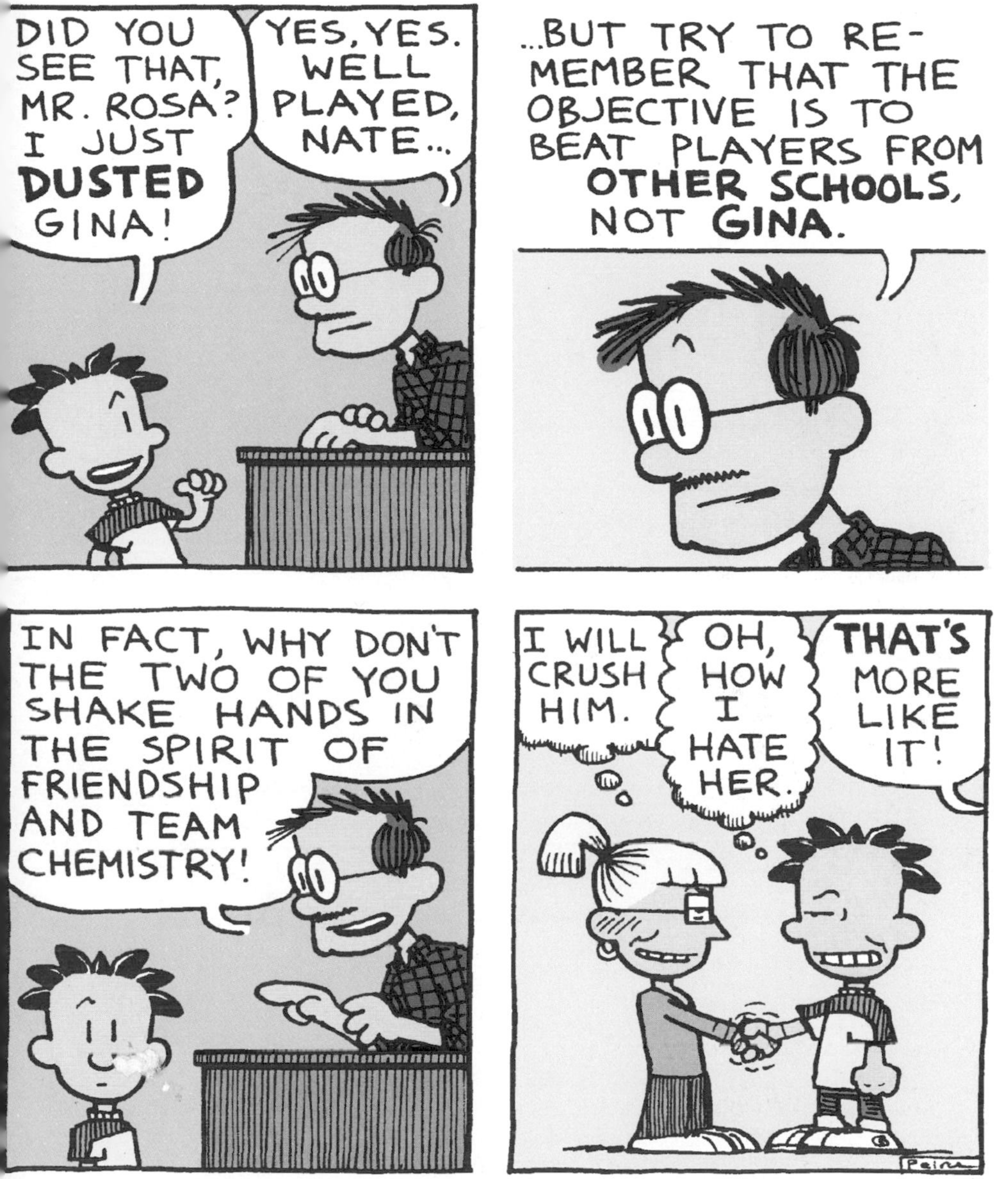
DID YOU SEE THAT, MR. ROSA? I JUST **DUSTED** GINA!
YES, YES. WELL PLAYED, NATE...
...BUT TRY TO RE-MEMBER THAT THE OBJECTIVE IS TO BEAT PLAYERS FROM **OTHER SCHOOLS**, NOT **GINA**.
IN FACT, WHY DON'T THE TWO OF YOU SHAKE HANDS IN THE SPIRIT OF FRIENDSHIP AND TEAM CHEMISTRY!
I WILL CRUSH HIM.
OH, HOW I HATE HER.
THAT'S MORE LIKE IT!

Big Nate is distributed internationally by Universal Uclick.

Big Nate: Revenge of the Cream Puffs copyright © 2016 by United Feature Syndicate, Inc. All rights reserved. Printed in China. No part of this book may be used or reproduced in any manner whatsoever without written permission except in the case of reprints in the context of reviews.

Andrews McMeel Publishing
a division of Andrews McMeel Universal
1130 Walnut Street, Kansas City, Missouri 64106

www.andrewsmcmeel.com

16 17 18 19 20 SDB 10 9 8 7 6 5 4 3 2

ISBN: 978-1-4494-6228-4

Library of Congress Control Number: 2016930933

Made by:
Shenzhen Donnelley Printing Company Ltd.
Address and location of manufacturer:
No. 47, Wuhe Nan Road, Bantian Ind. Zone,
Shenzhen China, 518129
2nd Printing—10/17/16

These strips appeared in newspapers from
April 22, 2012, through October 13, 2012.

Big Nate can be viewed on the Internet at
www.gocomics.com/big_nate

THE Epic Collection for Every *Big Nate* Fan

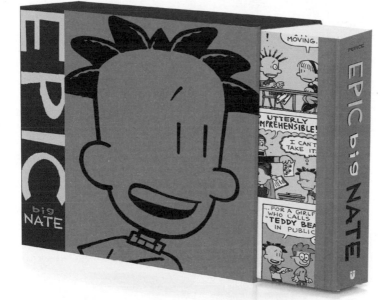

- How *Big Nate* got started

- *Diary of a Wimpy Kid* author Jeff Kinney's interview with Lincoln Peirce

- TONS of cartoons

AND MUCH, MUCH MORE!

Available Fall 2016 wherever books are sold.

amp! COMICS for kids

Check out these and other books at ampkids.com

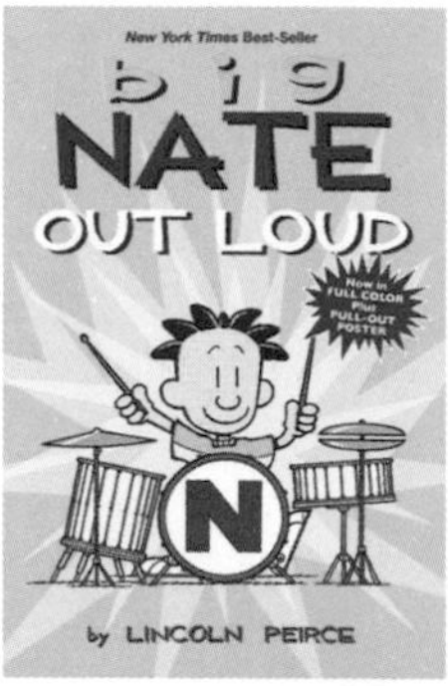
New York Times Best-Seller
big NATE
OUT LOUD
by LINCOLN PEIRCE

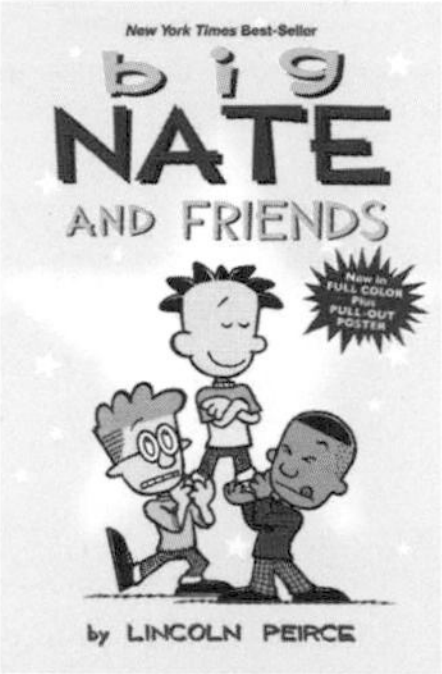
New York Times Best-Seller
big NATE
AND FRIENDS
by LINCOLN PEIRCE

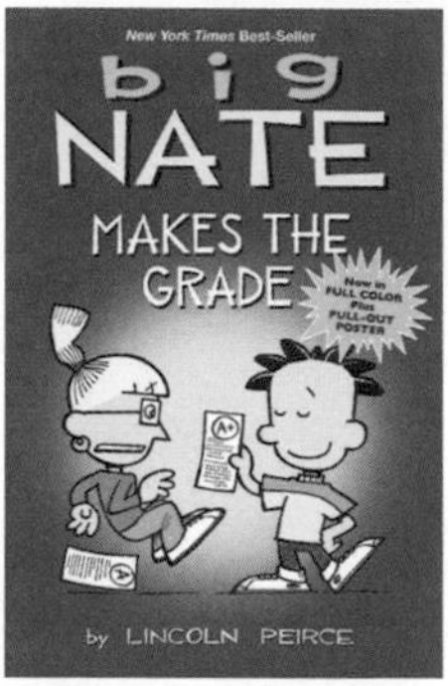
New York Times Best-Seller
big NATE
MAKES THE GRADE
by LINCOLN PEIRCE

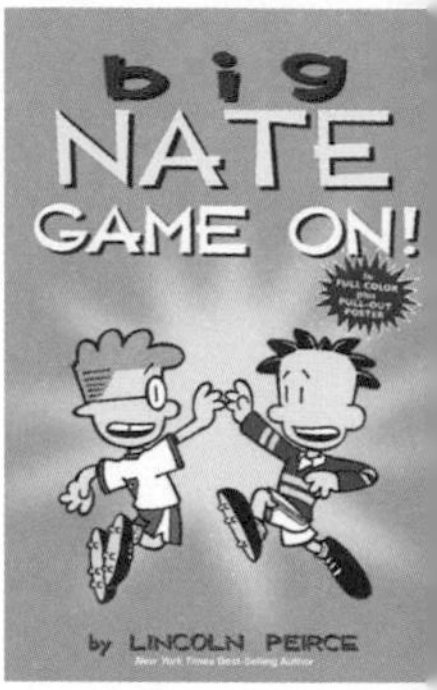
big NATE
GAME ON!
by LINCOLN PEIRCE

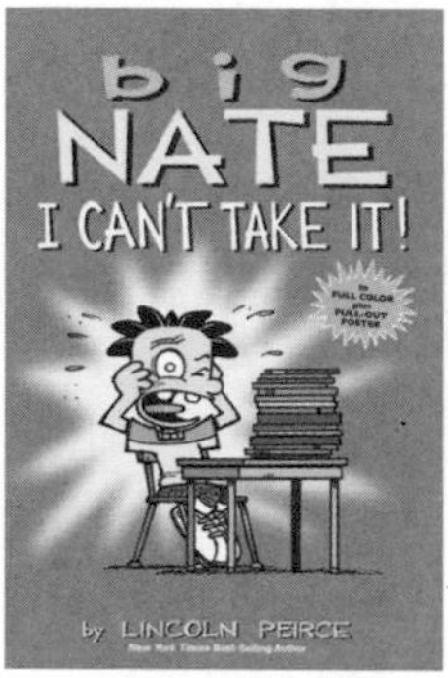
big NATE
I CAN'T TAKE IT!
by LINCOLN PEIRCE

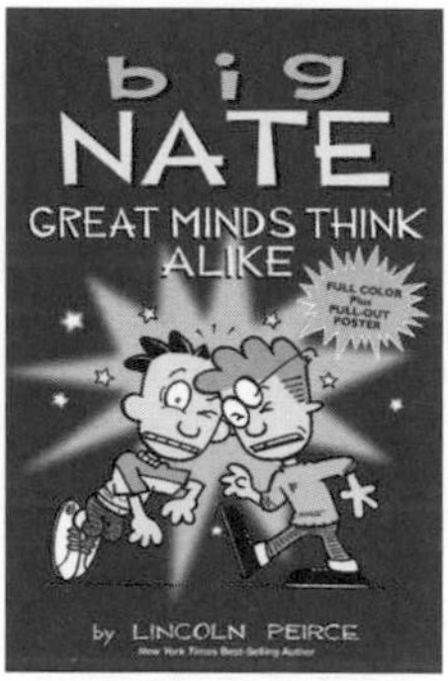
big NATE
GREAT MINDS THINK ALIKE
by LINCOLN PEIRCE

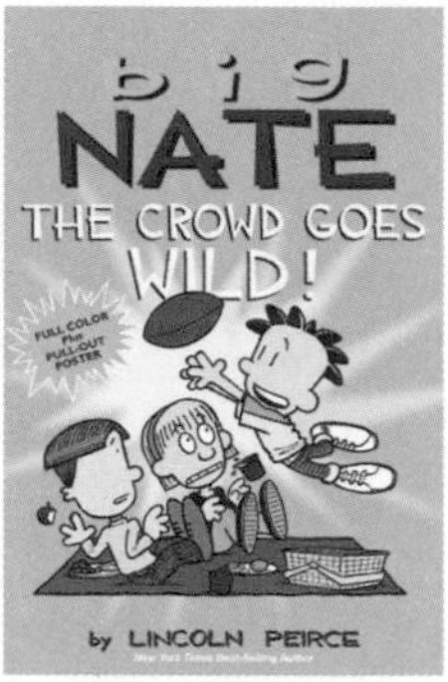
big NATE
THE CROWD GOES WILD!
by LINCOLN PEIRCE

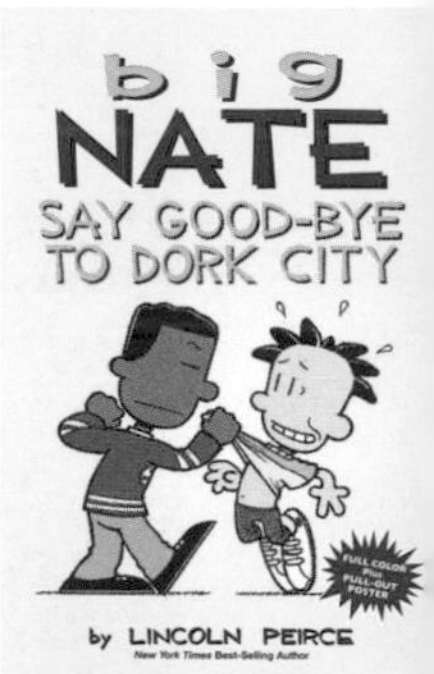
big NATE
SAY GOOD-BYE TO DORK CITY
by LINCOLN PEIRCE

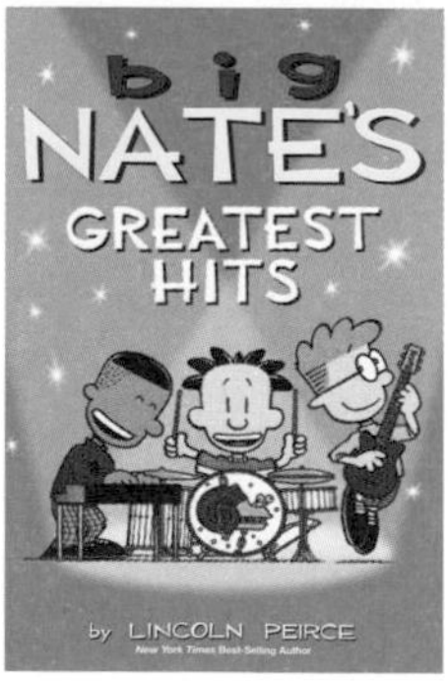
big NATE'S
GREATEST HITS
by LINCOLN PEIRCE

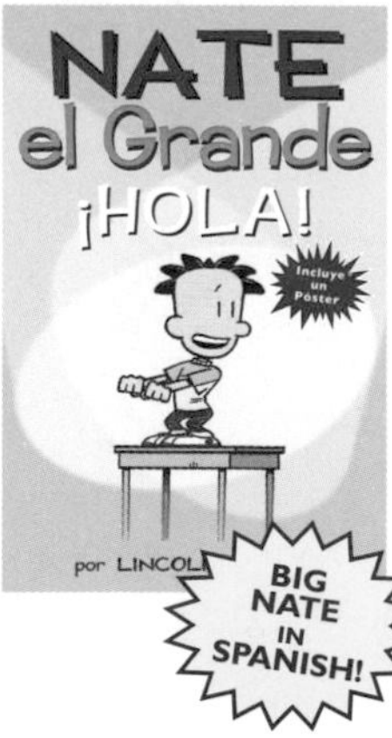
NATE el Grande
¡HOLA!
Incluye un Póster
por LINCOL

BIG NATE IN SPANISH!

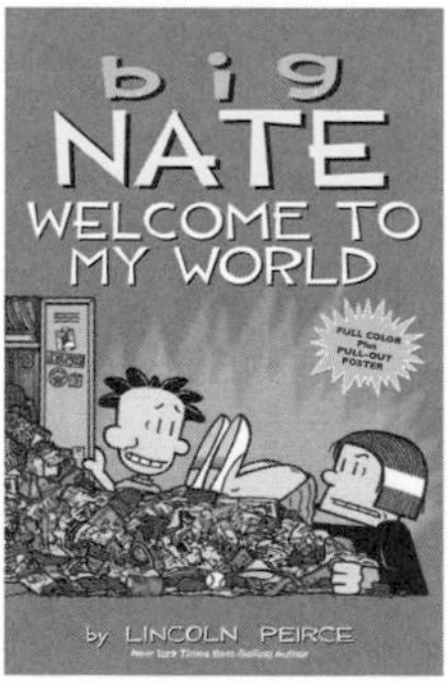
big NATE
WELCOME TO MY WORLD
by LINCOLN PEIRCE

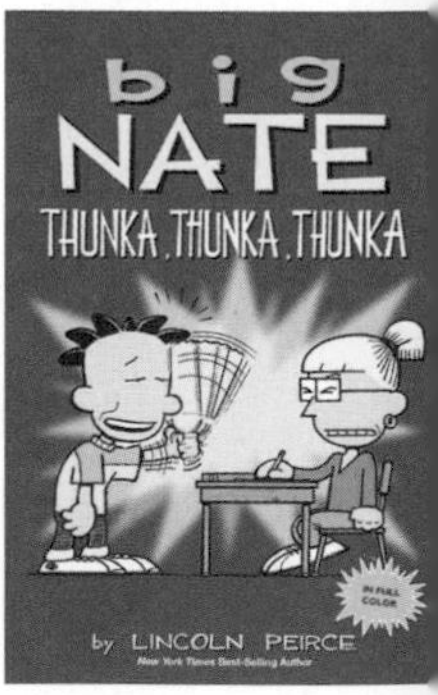
big NATE
THUNKA, THUNKA, THUNKA
by LINCOLN PEIRCE

Also available:
Teaching and activity guides for each title.
AMP! Comics for Kids books make reading FUN!

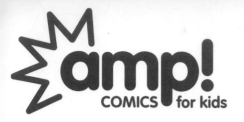